Olga Dies Dreaming

Olga Dies Dreaming

Xochitl Gonzalez

THORNDIKE PRESS
A part of Gale, a Cengage Company

Grateful acknowledgment is made for permission to reproduce from the following:

Pedro Pietri, excerpt from "Puerto Rican Obituary" from *Selected Poetry.* Copyright © 2015 by The Estate of Pedro Pietri. Reprinted with the permission of The Permissions Company, LLC, on behalf of City Lights Books.

Thorndike Press, a part of Gale, a Cengage Company.

Thorndike Press® Large Print Basic.

The text of this Large Print edition is unabridged.

Other aspects of the book may vary from the original edition.

Set in 16 pt. Plantin.

LIBRARY OF CONGRESS CIP DATA ON FILE.
CATALOGUING IN PUBLICATION FOR THIS BOOK
IS AVAILABLE FROM THE LIBRARY OF CONGRESS.

ISBN-13: 978-1-4328-9391-0 (hardcover alk. paper)

Published in 2022 by arrangement with Flatiron Books.

Printed in Mexico
Print Number: 01 Print Year: 2022

For Pop,
who taught me to be proud,
and
to all the South Brooklyn girls who
stare at the water, dreaming

I am myself, plus my surroundings, and if I do not preserve the latter, I do not preserve myself.

— José Ortega y Gasset

The price of Imperialism is lives.

— Juan González

■ ■ ■ ■

July 2017

■ ■ ■ ■

The Napkins

The telltale sign that you are at the wedding of a rich person is the napkins. At the not-rich person's wedding, should a waiter spill water or wine or a mixed drink of well liquor onto the napkin-covered lap of a guest, the beverage would bead up and roll off the cheap square of commercially laundered polyblend fabric, down the guest's legs, eventually pooling on the hideous, overly busy patterned carpet designed and chosen specifically to mask such stains. At the rich person's wedding, however, the napkins are made of a European linen fine enough for a Tom Wolfe suit, hand-pressed into smooth order and trimmed with a gracious hemstitch border. Should the waiter spill any of the luxury bottled water, vintage wine, or custom-crafted cocktails designed by a mixologist for the occasion, the napkin would, dutifully, absorb any moisture before the incident could irritate a couture-clad guest. Of course, at the rich person's wedding the waitstaff don't spill things; they have been separated and elevated from their more slovenly, less-coordinated brethren in a natural selection process of the service industry that judges on appearance, gait, and inherent knowledge of which side to serve from and which to clear. The rich person's wedding also never features hideous carpet. Not because the venue or locale might not have had one, but because they had the money to cover it over. And not necessarily just with another nicer, more tasteful carpet, but with hardwood flooring, black and white Havana-inspired tiles, or even actual, natural grass. These, though, were the more obvious markers of wealth at a milestone life celebration for the rich person, and while Olga Isabel Acevedo's job required her to worry about all of these elements and more, the present moment found her primarily concerned with the napkins. Mainly, how she could steal them when the party was over.

"Carlos!" she called out to the authoritative-looking waiter who was leading the caterer's setup team. "Carlos, let's talk about the napkins." He eagerly made his way over, followed by three of his other black-clad compatriots.

The rich person's wedding not only had better napkins, it had elaborate plans for them as well. They were manipulated into intricately folded shapes and wrapped around lavishly printed menus or adorned with anything ranging from single-stemmed flowers to braided ribbon to — on one occasion, of which Olga was particularly proud — a leather band burnished by a miniature branding iron. (The groom: a fourth-generation cattle rancher.) Olga demonstrated a complex pleating pattern, which was then placed on a diagonal across the display plate, with a place card then set atop that.

"Now Carlos, it's critical — critical — that the napkins be placed at exactly thirty-degree angles from what would be twelve o'clock on the plate, and even more critical that the place card be set parallel and not perpendicular to that angle. The mother of the bride said she might do some spot checking with her protractor, and after a year of working with this woman, I'd say odds are high that she actually does it."

Carlos nodded with understanding, almost as if he knew that the mother of the bride had an advanced degree in geometry that had been gathering dust for the past thirty years while she reared her brood and supported the career of her automobile CEO husband, and that she had chosen to channel her intellectual frustrations into the anal-retentive micromanagement of her eldest daughter's wedding. Of course, Carlos knew none of this, but, having been in the business for decades, he didn't need the specifics to understand the importance of executing the task at hand with precision. (The wedding of a rich person also had, at least for the workers involved, the looming possibility of litigation hovering in the near future. Not-rich people's events had forgettable glitches. Gaffes to the ultra-wealthy were unforgivable grievances that only the courts could remedy. A recent tale of a florist in fiscal ruin because she substituted an Ecuadorian rose for an English one after her shipment was stuck in customs had struck a nerve. Everyone, from the delivery guy to the wedding officiant, was on their toes.)

"Now listen," Olga continued, "these were custom made just for the wedding, and the bride wants to have them for her house —"

"What's she gonna do with three hundred napkins?" one of the waiters interjected. He was clearly new.

"Six hundred, actually," Olga offered.

"Always good to have extras, right?" The staff laughed. "She claims they'll be heirlooms. Point is, we need to be sure that we keep these separate from the rented linens at the end of the night; got it?"

The waiters collectively nodded and, like a colony of ants given orders from their queen, ran off to execute the said napkin plan. Olga did some mental math. It would take six pairs of hands another four hours to create an optic that the guests would undo in seconds with the flick of a wrist — 290 guests, to be exact. Barring a crazy incident — some overgrown frat boy spraying the bridesmaids with champagne, say, or a drunken guest knocking over the croquembouche display — they should end the night with between 150 and 175 brand-new beautiful linen hemstitch napkins that she could take for her cousin Mabel to use at her wedding that fall.

Olga hated her cousin Mabel.

Of course, it hadn't always been this way. Yes, Mabel had been a loudmouth girl who developed into a loudmouth, know-it-all woman, but despite this they had been, in their youth, quite close. Slowly, though, a rift had formed and expanded. Then, last year, at age thirty-nine, Mabel was concurrently promoted to mid-level management at Con Edison and proposed to by her long-term boyfriend. The combination rendered her insufferable. Olga was only a year or so older, and for the entirety of their lives Mabel had been in a one-sided competition with her where action of any sort in Olga's life was interpreted by Mabel as a sign of aggression and met with a "So, you think you're better than me, huh?" Truth be told, for most of their lives, using a traditional American metric for measuring success, Olga *was* better than Mabel. Olga had left Sunset Park, gone to a fancy college, started her business, had been featured in magazines and on TV, had traveled the world, and gone to dinners costlier than one of Mabel's paychecks. But now, with this engagement, Mabel was going to achieve something Olga never had: being a bride. Never mind that Olga bristled at the idea of third dates, let alone marriage. To Mabel, in this one arena, she had finally won, and she was not about to let her victory go unnoticed. On Christmas Eve, drunk on coquito, she waved her engagement ring in Olga's face repeatedly, saying, "Julio got it from Jared's, bitch, what did you get? That's right, nothing." At the bridal shower that her family pressured her to host because "she's the one with all the party hookups,"

Mabel gave a special toast to her "cousin Olga, who can help the brides, she just can't get a groom."

Olga had taken this in stride. Primarily because if finding someone like Julio to be tied to for all eternity was the one contest she would lose to Mabel, then she had chosen well. She was equally placated knowing that, when the time was right, she would think of the perfect fuck-you gesture to take just a bit of wind out of Mabel's sails on her wedding day. Just the right little something to be the pebble in her shoe when she reflected on the day. It was during her sixth meeting with Mrs. Henderson, the mother of today's bride, specifically about the topic of napkins, when the idea came to her and she was immediately filled with delight, knowing that she could strike two birds with one tiny stone.

From the beginning, Olga knew the napkins were going to be the "thing" with this event. At every first meeting with a client there was one comment casually uttered that Olga filed in her mental Rolodex, knowing that, in several months' time, she would spend hours or even collective days dealing with what had been a seemingly innocuous statement or question. So it was when Mrs. Henderson and her daughter came in the first time and, just as they were about to sign Olga's pricey contract, Mrs. Henderson exclaimed, "We didn't speak about one of the most important things! The napkins! I do hate when they leave lint on your gown." Olga agreed immediately and waxed on about that and a number of other nuanced considerations regarding table linens. Within moments, the paperwork was signed, and Mrs. Henderson was phoning their "money person" to deal with the matter of getting Olga her not-insignificant deposit payment. With her one comment about lint, Mrs. Henderson had revealed herself to be, at best, neurotic and, at worst, crazy. Olga had only quoted them her fee for normal rich people. Anxiety consumed her when she realized she had not charged them nearly enough.

She had not been wrong. Mrs. Henderson's daughter, the bride, was a forgettable girl marrying a forgettable guy. They both, wisely, allowed Mrs. Henderson to do whatever she wanted with the wedding, knowing that if she was satiated, Mr. Henderson was far more likely to give them the cash they needed to purchase their own place in Bridgehampton. Yet even with the bride and groom largely absent, Mrs. Henderson had kept Olga and her staff's hands full, mainly with the aforementioned napkins. What would they be made of? How wide would the hemstitch be? How would they be folded? What about the cocktail napkins? What about the hand towels in the bathroom? Was a white napkin rude? Did the same rules apply to napkins as to guests about wearing white at a wedding? Should they switch the order to ivory? Was that same quality of linen even available in ivory? Should they add in a pop of color? What would people say about a blue napkin? Would that be good luck? Would that leave lint?

In the end, she settled on a standard white linen hemstitch napkin, which she insisted be custom made for the occasion so that "the children can have them as heirlooms." Olga easily obliged, knowing that they would cost her $7 apiece to have made by a Dominican woman she knew in Washington Heights and that she could very easily charge the client $30 a napkin, attribute the cost to Mrs. Henderson's exquisite taste in fabrics, and pocket the difference. Of course, even a seasoned professional like Olga could never have predicted that Mrs. Henderson's neurosis about the napkins would escalate to the degree that it did. Fear that her guests would, at any point, be forced to use a soiled napkin gripped her. Gradually, she increased her original order of three hundred napkins until eventually she doubled it. Of course, Olga knew there was simply no fathomable way that her guests could possibly go through this many napkins. She also knew that telling Mrs. Henderson that her fear was irrational? Well, that was pointless. Instead, Olga assured her that such a degree of thoughtfulness was the sign of a truly considerate hostess, while silently delighting in the knowledge that she'd concurrently figured out the perfect touch for Mabel's big day while also earning a few extra thousand on this job.

Olga did not see this as a theft as much as an equalization of resources: Mrs. Henderson had aggressively accumulated too much of something while her family had acutely too little. At the Henderson wedding, despite all the time and energy spent discussing, procuring, pleating, and angling these napkins, they would go unnoticed. But at Mabel's, like a black Chanel suit in a sea of knockoff Hervé Léger bandage dresses, they would stop people in their tracks. "¡Qué elegante!" she could hear her Titi Lola saying. She could picture her Tío Richie holding two of them over his chest and saying, "Hey, how many do you think

I'd need to make a guayabera?" There would be countless cousins uttering, simply, "Classy," as they thumbed the fabric between their fingers. This was the least Olga could do, she felt. Why shouldn't her family get to know the feeling of imported Belgian flax against their laps? Because Mabel's father was a janitor? Because that was the job he could get after he dropped out of high school? Because he dropped out mainly because he was dyslexic? A disorder that the family only learned of, mind you, when one of his grandchildren was diagnosed with it at school and Tío JoJo, to comfort the child, said, "It's okay, mijo, I've seen the letters backwards my whole life, and I've been okay." Her family should have to wipe their mouths with $3 polyester rags because Tío JoJo's teachers were too fucking lazy to ask why he struggled with reading? Because no one blinked at another dumb Puerto Rican dropping out of a shitty public high school? Fuck that.

Also, it was doubtless that her family would attribute this elegant touch to Olga, and that would absolutely kill Mabel. Titi Lola, Tío Richie, Tío JoJo, all of them would immediately know that this was something only Olga would think to do. After the cousins said the word "classy," then they would say, “Olga.” That was just the way it was in her family. This was her role.

“Meegan,” Olga called out to her assistant, who was busy sorting through seating arrangements. “Meegan, at the end of the night, get the soiled napkins to the laundry service and have them messengered to Mrs. Henderson first thing Monday. Take the extras back to the office.”

“Wait. Aren’t we sending those, too?”

“Nope.” Olga knew what was coming next.

“But she paid for those.”

“She did.”

“So, if you take something that she paid for, isn’t that . . . ?”

“Isn’t it what, Meegan? Because what I know I’m doing is executing our clients’ wishes. Mrs. Henderson wants the napkins used at her daughter’s wedding to pass on to her someday grandchildren. We are sending those. We are not sending her the hundred or so napkins that will sit in a box in the back of the kitchen, unused, for the rest of the night. Not only is that not what she asked for, but ask yourself why, after she is delighted with the entire thing, we would advertise to her that we allowed her to wastefully indulge in such an irrational expenditure?”

Meegan was about to say something and then paused. The suspiciousness in her eyes faded and a smile came over her face.

"This is why you are the best. You are so right. I wouldn't have thought of it that way, but you're right. This is why I begged my mom to get me this job."

Meegan was the most effective assistant that Olga had had in a long time. She was also the most annoying, having come herself from linen napkin stock. Her mother, a client of Olga's, hadn't so much asked her to give Meegan a job as threatened to take her business elsewhere if Olga didn't. Yet, this was not what grated on Olga. No, what bugged Olga was Meegan's insistent application of kindergarten ethics to every situation and her genuine desire to be around weddings. Indeed, while the former quality had the greatest potential to cause trouble for Olga, it was the latter that incensed her the most. It would be easy to enjoy this profession, Olga felt, if turning a profit weren't of concern.

Eager to move on, Olga changed the subject. "When does Jan get here? I want to go through the timeline for tonight."

"He's not coming," Meegan said sheepishly. "They are sending Marco instead."

To handle the mental minutiae of her job

and mitigate risk of complaint, Olga, like many in her profession, had established a reliable stable of vendors — caterers, bakers, and the like — on whom she could rely to execute at the scale and level that her clientele demanded. From this roster, after more than a decade in business, she had a list of preferred staffers whom she would request. Jan, the best floor captain for one of the finest caterers in the city, was on her frequent rotation. He was, in many respects, her emotional security blanket for her toughest jobs. His elegant appearance, soothing demeanor, and unplaceable European accent pleased her clients in the front of the house. His first-generation American work ethic coupled with a robust supply of dirty Polish jokes pleased her team in the back of the house. She felt a panic at the thought of facing Mrs. Henderson's protractor without him.

"What? But I specifically asked for Jan. Marco is fine, but if I ask for Jan, I want Jan here. What reason did they give?"

Meegan cowered. "I actually didn't ask."

Olga needn't say anything, her silent turn on her heel enough to let Meegan know that that was not the right answer. She took out her phone and texted Jan to ask why he was abandoning her and then she dialed Carol, the owner of the catering company, to register her complaint.

"Carol," she spoke loudly into the phone, to set an example to all the other vendors readying the hotel ballroom for the festivities. "With all the business that I throw your way, I expect you to accommodate my fucking staff requests and at the very least give a bitch a call if you're going to make a change like this. I really —"

But she had been cut off by Carol's sobbing. It was all so sudden, she said. Olga dropped the phone. She couldn't deal with this now. Meegan, sensing something was wrong, was just standing in front of her, with her stupid, naïve, eager face.

"Jan isn't coming to work because Jan is dead."

A Polish Wake

Jan's wake had left Olga even more glum than she'd anticipated. The mourners, gathered at a funeral home in a stucco-faced storefront on a corner of Greenpoint, had revealed Jan's rigidly segmented double life. On one side of the room, beneath an oversized framed photograph of Pope John Paul II, sat his mother, surrounded by a gaggle of black-clad Polish women who Olga could only assume were his aunts. On the other side, below an oil painting of a Polish pastoral scene, sat Christian and his team of mourners — a group of once and future cater waiters, nearly all gay boys whom Jan and Christian knew from their two decades living together in their Chelsea walk-up.

Observing them, Olga was unsure whom to greet first. She'd never met Jan's mother before, wasn't even sure if she and Jan were close. But her own Catholic, outer-borough upbringing had ingrained in her an unspoken ethical code (an ethnical code?) that required deference to mothers, no matter how estranged. The inverse property of "yo mama" jokes. She walked towards the Polish contingent.

"Mrs. Wojcick?" Olga placed her hand on the grieving mother's shoulder. "My name is Olga; I was a friend of your son's. I'm so sorry for your loss."

Mrs. Wojcick took Olga's face in her hands, kissed her cheek, and whispered something in Polish that a younger woman next to her translated.

"She said thank you for coming. She always wanted to meet one of Jan's girlfriends."

"Oh no," Olga said gently. She turned directly to Jan's mother and, as one instinctively does when bridging a language gap, raised her voice. "Jan and I worked together. He catered some of my parties. I plan weddings. He was very hardworking."

The younger woman translated to the mother, but not before throwing Olga a miserable look. After a moment, the mother laughed out loud, looked at Olga, and said, "My Jan too handsome!"

Olga politely smiled and turned away, relieved that the awkward exchange had come to an end. She felt a tap on her arm.

It was the translator.

"Listen, I told my mother that Jan wouldn't commit to you because he wanted to play the field. If anybody else asks, can you just — I don't know — act the part?"

"She didn't know he was gay?"

The sister motioned to the photo of John Paul.

"It's bad enough he killed himself, she needs to know he was gay?"

"I'm sorry for your loss," Olga offered curtly, respecting the sister's grief enough to suppress her own vexation.

The room, she saw now, was more battlefield than funeral parlor. At stake was the way in which Jan would be memorialized: with fact or fiction. Lest she come across as sympathetic with the enemy, Olga crossed the room, where Christian greeted her warmly.

"Darling, thank you for coming."

"I'm so sorry for your loss."

Olga truly meant it. She'd had dinner with Jan and Christian a handful of times over the years and while she didn't know Christian well, she had a deep affection for him and had delighted in the playful aspects he brought out in a sometimes somber-seeming Jan. She leaned down to embrace him, inhaling him deeply. He smelled of Chanel

No. 5, cigarette smoke, and vintage clothes. His scent recalled that of her grandmother, a woman who, even in dire times, would never run low on either Chanel No. 5 or cigarettes. Christian, a cabaret singer who'd met Jan while working a club together, had draped a black cardigan over his shoulders, and paired it, tastefully, Olga thought, with a sleeveless cream silk blouse with a tie collar. In a nod to Jan's Catholic roots, Christian had accessorized this with several mother-of-pearl rosary strands. His face was weary, but his elegant demeanor did not appear smote.

"Girl," he said, stepping back, "there isn't anyone sorrier than that motherfucker. Wait until I catch up with him on the other side and give him a piece of my mind. Making me sit with his crazy-ass family like this."

They chuckled in spite of themselves.

"How is it possible that they didn't know he was gay?" Olga whispered.

"Olga, people always thought we had an open relationship because I was a ho, but really I just wanted to give him one place to have nothing to hide."

She wondered aloud, "Was it the secret keeping that killed him, do you think?"

"Fuck that," Christian said. "Jan was a sad motherfucker; he could get pretty . . .

dark. But, mainly, I think he was scared. A few months back he found out that he was sick. I could never convince that man to get on PrEP; he always had a reason he couldn't figure it out. He took some chances, tested positive, and I just watched him withdraw. A few weeks later, I found him in our closet."

Christian teared up at the thought but continued.

"If that isn't a metaphor and a half? He literally went back into the closet to die. It would be poetic if I didn't know that it was the only practical place in our apartment to do it."

"Fuck," Olga said.

"So, not only was I the one to find this bitch, now I have to think about him hanging there every time I get dressed. The only considerate thing he did was leave his note on the coffee table, so at least I wasn't surprised. I'm forty-four years old, I could have had a fucking heart attack."

"Are you going to stay in that apartment?" Olga asked.

"Girl," Christian replied, "do you have ten grand to move? Because that's what it takes to get into a new place these days. To rent. To fucking rent. Lord, I can't even talk about this right now. It will get me worked up."

He sighed and fanned himself and she leaned in to embrace him. Olga rubbed his shoulders gently. She could feel him shaking as he again began to cry. She hadn't factored in how the stress of money must be multiplying his sense of grief. Cater waitering wouldn't make anyone rich, but with his wealthy clientele, Jan's tip money had surely greased the wheels of their lives.

"You know what?" Olga muttered. "I should have brought it today, but I have a tip envelope for Jan that I'd never had a chance to give him. Probably at least five hundred."

"Really?"

Jan's gratuity for the Henderson wedding had, of course, gone to Marco, but the relief in Christian's voice felt worth $500. Maybe she would send a little more. They were interrupted by another mourner and Olga figured it was a good time to go pay her respects to the dead.

The casket's lacquered white wood and gilded handles gleamed under the soft lights that illuminated Jan. Olga approached, pausing for a moment to take in his physical form one last time. This aspect of Catholicism had always troubled her, the viewing of the dead. A really piss-poor placebo for the matter-of-fact status that is death. She had always felt the Jewish faith got mourning right; there's no pretending there, a quick burial and a time where you can be as grief stricken as you need to be, without the presence of mirrors, surrounded by family, friends, and comfort foods. The wake struck Olga as a disrespectful farce. It's absurd to think that kneeling before Jan's cold, chemically stuffed body and waxen face was anything like being in the presence of his living self. A self who, if alive, would surely be outside chain-smoking, sipping from his flask, and flirting — with man or woman. The only thing Jan and the body in this casket had in common, Olga thought, was the suit, which was impeccable.

She knelt down, with the intention of saying a prayer, but her mind wandered back to his mother, grieving a child she only sort of knew. It's a myth about motherhood, Olga felt, that the time in utero imbues mothers with a lifelong understanding of their children. Yes, they know their essences, this she didn't doubt, but mothers are still humans who eventually form their own ideas of both who their kids are and who they think they should be. Inevitably there were disparities. Some mothers, like Jan's, simply wished them away, no matter how glaring. Others, like Olga's own mother, focused on them with laser precision, feeling confident that with enough effort, the gap could be narrowed. Either way, in Olga's assessment, it was hard to not let that disparity turn into a feeling of deficiency. Olga knew firsthand how harrowing that could be. How weighty it must have been for Jan to don his mother's version of himself every time he rode the subway back to Brooklyn for a visit. To make sure he didn't let any of his other self slip, for fear of disappointing her. She reconsidered Jan's sister, her previous irritation replaced by empathy. She was only protecting the image Jan wanted his mother to have of him. Olga knew that for her brother she would do the same.

As she rose and turned away from the coffin, she ran into Carol, Jan's old boss. Carol had started her catering business out of her apartment thirty years ago and had grown it into a vast and lucrative operation, something that would be almost impossible to do now. She started out doing small weddings, then bigger and ever more prominent affairs, eventually securing the contract for the annual Met Gala, all the Fashion Week parties, and, well, just about every A-list happening in the New York City area. Now, on a given day, they were servicing anywhere from fifty to a hundred functions, and Carol seemingly knew the intimate details of each of them. Her business consumed her thoughts and life. All she could talk about were parties, and clients, and trends in catering and food, and which captains were good and which captains were overrated and, of course, her favorite topic, how to grow her margins. And while Olga long admired Carol's business acumen, Carol herself often rankled her, as she was, to Olga, a mirror to the vapid concerns of her own chosen profession.

So commerce focused was she that Olga had been surprised by how absolutely broken up Carol had sounded on the phone. She opened her arms to embrace her now.

"Olga!" Carol exclaimed as she broke from the hug. "Oh my God. Isn't it awful?"

"Carol, it really is."

"He was my best captain!"

"And a really great human being."

"Of course, goes without saying. And the best worker! They don't make workers like him anymore, Olga. What am I gonna do? We're about to get to the busy season, and you can't imagine how many events I had him on for."

"Grief can be very disorienting, Carol."

"No, Olga, this is devastating! We have a private dinner at Agnes Gund's next week and she won't let anyone but Jan even look in her wine refrigerator! Not even a peek! You can't imagine how particular she is."

Olga nodded. She felt her blood pressure rising.

"He was on all my biggest fall events," Carol lamented with a sigh. "He had so much to live for."

Olga said with a smile, "Yes, Carol. If only Jan had reached out before he took his life, you could have reminded him what an inconvenience his death would be for New York society. Surely that would have given him something to live for."

She excused herself without waiting for a response, beelined out the door and onto the street where she found a taxi, and directed it to her local dive bar.

The Hoarder

Noir was a satiating place to be sad, Olga thought as she sidled up to the bar and ordered her usual. Filled with regulars who seemed to have nowhere to be and no one who cared if they made it there, it lacked the sense of possibility that the newer spots in her rapidly gentrifying corner of Brooklyn conveyed. There were no reclaimed woods or cleverly reimagined industrial lamps with Edison bulbs lighting the place. Noir was more like a well-insulated garage, illuminated by mismatched lamps and filled with old kitchen stools, in a completely unironic way. The air-conditioning was weak, so on warm days like this one, you were never quite hot, but never quite cool, either. Its major draw, for Olga anyway, was its jukebox, filled with old funk and R & B from the '70s, '80s, and '90s. She paid for some songs she thought Jan might like and Syreeta's "Keep Him Like He Is" filled the small bar. When she made her way back to her seat, she felt a hovering presence behind her.

"Can I help you?" she turned to say.

Before her was a swarthy, unfamiliar fellow. A sad sack who, though she had never seen him before, had escaped her attention because he blended in so well with the other pouty faces.

"Hey, so . . . You know, I was just finishing up a meeting and I stopped in here and then you went and played one of my favorite songs. Did you know she was once married to Stevie Wonder?"

"Everyone knows that."

"Do they?" He tapped a woman named Janette on the shoulder. Janette, who practically lived at Noir, particularly in these summer months when she was on break from her job as a public school administrator. "Excuse me, ma'am, but do you know who this artist is?"

"Yeah. It's Syreeta Wright. She's one of Stevie Wonder's ex-wives."

Olga didn't know what to do. On the one hand, she was amused that this musically smug stranger had been so efficiently smacked down. On the other, she knew that once anyone said anything more than hello to Janette, they were in danger of having to listen to her oratory on the problems of the Department of Education for the next four hours. A speech that, no matter the variation on the details or grievances, always ended with Janette proclaiming, yet again, "The shit of the whole thing is we traded a corrupt democracy for an inept autocracy," delighted by her clever rhyming.

She picked her battle; before Janette could open her mouth again, she jumped in.

"See, common knowledge. Anyway, I appreciate your truly excellent taste in music, but I came in here to clear my head and have a drink, so if you don't mind . . ." And she turned away.

"Well, seems more like you want to cloud your mind."

"Excuse me?"

"Just that drinking isn't what anyone does for real clarity, is it?"

"Isn't it?" Olga answered. "I think there are about a million writers and artists who would beg to differ."

"Are you a writer or an artist?"

"I'm a wedding planner."

"I'm a Realtor."

"I didn't ask."

Yet something about that descriptor made her give the stranger another look. He was disheveled. His button-down shirt wrinkled, a rolled-up tie spilling out of his pocket. He carried under his arm an oversized ledger notebook with dog-eared pages and Post-its and business cards sticking out of the ends. He was wearing a massive JanSport book bag, stuffed like that of an overachieving eighth grader from an era before laptop computers.

"Wait, you're a Realtor?"

"Yeah. You looking for a place? Interested in exploring life in New Brooklyn?"

She was insulted. "Psssh. Fuck outta here! I bleed Old Brooklyn, thank you very much. My family's been in Sunset Park since the sixties. One of the first Puerto Rican families in the 'hood *and* we owned our house."

Now the stranger appraised her. "Really, now? Impressive given the redlining going on back in the day."

"My grandmother was gangster. Never involved a bank. Bought our house from her landlord, cash. He sold it to her for a song when the area got too Brown for his taste."

"Is that right? Well congratulations to your abuela for taking advantage of white flight."

Olga couldn't help but laugh. "¡Salud!" She raised her glass and drank the last of the wine in it.

"I'm from South Slope," the stranger offered. "In case you were wondering."

She hadn't been, but now paused. "Really? Born and raised?"

"Born and raised."

On the rare occasions that Olga met a fellow native, she was always surprised by how relaxed it made her feel. Like she could slip into a dying tongue and talk about the old country.

"So, listen, don't take this the wrong way or anything, but from one Brooklynite to another, I've got to ask you something."

He laughed. "Shoot. But I'm already gonna take this the wrong way because nobody starts with that if they're going to say something positive."

She smiled. "So, this neighborhood is hot right now. Luxury properties. New money coming in. The Realtors I know are all kind of slick and polished. . . ."

"And you want to know how I get away with looking like a crazy community college professor?"

"Yeah, I guess that's what I was getting at."

He took his backpack off, sidled up to the bar, and leaned in towards her.

"Well, I'm really talented, I'm very smart, I've got some swag, and frankly, I'm well connected. I went to the best schools — literally — Packer, Bennington, the works."

"That's interesting."

"You're wondering why I'm just a Realtor?"

Olga was in fact wondering exactly that, but before she spoke it aloud, she asked herself, *Well, why the fuck are you a wedding planner, Olga?* and decided to shut her mouth.

"No," she lied.

"My mother died and I never got over it and I got my real estate license to deal with her house and then one thing led to another and the next thing you know I'm doing this and I'm living in her house and I kind of became a hoarder."

"Excuse me?" Olga was sure that she had missed something.

"Yes, I have a lot of stuff. Mainly furniture."

"But you mean that metaphorically. Not like the TV show."

"Um, no. I mean exactly like the TV show. Technically, since I don't keep newspapers or food, I might not meet the clinical definition, but trust me, it's not normal. Like I said, my thing is really furniture. And electronics. And knickknacks. I have a Hummel room."

Olga laughed and the stranger laughed, and Olga forgot for a second that she wanted to be alone.

The stranger, who'd now sat down on the stool next to her, offered his hand.

"I'm Matteo."

"Olga."

Close up, Olga could see that Matteo was quite handsome underneath his scruffy semi-beard. He had a spattering of freckles and the kind of light brown eyes that Olga used to call Coca-Cola colored when she was a kid. His short curly hair was going more salt than pepper, but she could tell that he was five, maybe six years older than her, at the max. His rolled-up shirtsleeves revealed muscular forearms covered in hair that was quite sexy.

"So, Olga, let me get you another drink while you tell me what you were trying to clear your head about?"

As they downed two more glasses of wine, Olga told Matteo all about the funeral and Jan's suicide and, of course, his double life.

"I suppose though," Matteo offered, "most of us in New York live double lives, with a secret of some sort living behind closed doors."

"Really? What's your secret?"

"I already told you. I'm a hoarder."

She giggled.

"So, what's your secret?" Matteo asked.

"I'm a terrible person."

Outside Noir they stood kissing under a streetlight for an hour, their clothes growing damp from the humid summer night. His hands on the small of her back, on the nape of her neck. Olga could feel Matteo hard on her thigh through his khakis. It excited her, kissing on a corner. Something she was happy to discover she hadn't outgrown. The kisses tasted like memories and wine and salt and she lost herself in them.

"Come to my place?" she whispered in his ear.

He fucked with his socks on, yet it surprised Olga how little she cared.

November 1990

Nov. 11, 1990

Querida Olga,
I write to you on your thirteenth birthday, one I'm sad to miss. There is work in the world that I've been called to do, mija, and the time has come for me to do it. I believe, in my heart, that I've given you and your brother all the wisdom that I, as a mother, can impart. Because thirteen, Olga, is a magical age. Yes, you leave girlhood behind, but now you get to decide, day by day, what kind of woman you want to become. The big picture of the world becomes clearer. You begin to learn more for yourself than any parent or teacher could possibly tell you.

I know it was that way for me; nobody could tell me about nothing. Not my mother, not my brothers, certainly nobody at school. In those days, our whole universe was just a few blocks wide. We walked to and from school; Mami walked to work at the factory. Even so, by thirteen it was clear to me that our people — Black and Brown people — were treated worse by just about everybody. In class, the teachers favored the white kids. At home, as the whites left the neighborhood and the Puerto Ricans came, suddenly there were less cops in the streets, less garbage trucks cleaning up. I didn't need anybody to point this out to me, I saw these things for myself and knew it wasn't right.

For you, I expect this will be doubly true. When you were born, your Papi noticed your eyes, how they seemed to take in everything. They say babies can't see much, but I thought he was right. You looked wise. And unlike when I was growing up, when girls like me and Lola were put in dresses and told to be polite while we sat like dolls in a corner, you've always been able to run wild and free. Where we grew up having to use our "inside voice," to play our music low, you and Prieto grew up dancing and singing loud. Stomping up and down the stairs of a house your family owned, not getting policed by a landlord who wants your money but not the smells of your food or the sounds of your language.

Me and your Papi took great pains to ensure that you and your brother were raised with all the knowledge we'd had to seek for ourselves. To know that we came from kings and queens who lived off the land, from people who were raped and enslaved but stayed strong, kept their spirit. Things we were told to be ashamed of — my curly hair, your father's dark skin — you grew up knowing that these things were beautiful. So, when I think of you at thirteen, I know how prepared you are for the challenges of the world. You are no ordinary little girl, but a beautiful young Boricua.

And so, Olga, you must see yourself and my absence not as one little girl missing her mother, but as a brave young woman who knows that in a world of oppression, achieving liberation will require sacrifice. You can't stay in your room and cry. You can't keep Abuelita up at night with your tears. You have to keep your head held high, you have to be strong. Like the revolutionary we raised you to be.

Life, you will unfortunately learn, is

full of hard choices. For everyone, but especially for you, a Latina girl in America. Your options will be fewer and choices harder. The cost and value of your life decisions must be carefully weighed.

Nothing, Olga, is more valuable than people being free. Which is why, despite this being one of my own harder choices, I must leave you and your brother. I don't know when I will return.

I need you to be strong. To behave. Not to fuss like a child. You are made of powerful stuff. And I don't leave you alone, mijita. Your brother loves you and he has had three extra years with his parents to learn what's right. You have Abuelita, my sister, my brothers. Your father has his troubles, but his heart is still full of love and his mind still has wisdom that will benefit you. Above all, just because I'm not there doesn't mean I'm not watching. Just as the government watches our comings and goings, my Brothers and Sisters in this struggle will have their eyes on you. Your family is bigger and vaster than you can even imagine.

Querida, one day my work will make you proud. You will see our people take off the shackles of oppression and say, "Mami helped to do that." And you can take pride, knowing your sacrifice was a part of it. This is my word.

Pa'lante,
Mami

■ ■ ■ ■

July 2017

■ ■ ■ ■

Morning Routine

In the morning Olga opened her eyes and wondered how expediently she could get him out of the apartment. The coitus had been remarkably satisfying, the proper amount of fast and slow, rough and gentle, biting and caressing. He was a confident man. This complicated things. Olga frequently had male companions, but rarely allowed them to spend the night. On the odd occasions that she did, she usually triggered a swift morning exit by delivering an ego-bruising remark in an offhand manner. Usually, she was comfortably alone again before the coffee percolated. This tactic was doubly effective as it not only drove the offended party from her abode, it usually saved her the trouble of then having to ignore their texts seeking further mediocre conversation as preamble to even more mediocre intercourse. This morning felt a bit different. She had enjoyed Matteo —

both before and during — and wanted to keep her options open. That did not mean she didn't want him gone now. She cleared her throat, loudly, in an effort to wake him up. She slid out of bed and into her robe, climbing over her black funeral/wedding dress, his rumpled button-down shirt, and, inexplicably, his Teva sandals. She looked back for visual confirmation that she had, indeed, just fucked a guy who wore socks and sandals. In the summer.

Yes. There they were. Peeking out from under the comforter, attached to his muscular, hairy calves.

"Morning!" he said. "This is some mattress. I slept like a baby."

"Um, thanks?" she said, hearing the awkwardness of her own voice. She quickly scuttled into the kitchen, cut on the news, and started her coffee. She did this as loudly as possible, hoping the noise would send the message she seemed unable to verbally communicate. As the coffee filled the pot, her angst began to mount, his presence threatening to cross the invisible line into her morning routine. She opened the cabinet, contemplated pulling out two mugs, but instead took out just one. Her go-to, with the mascot of her own fancy New England college. Its presence at the start of her every morning both a comforting aide-mémoire of her own ambition and intelligence, and a disquieting reminder that she was likely squandering the two.

Even with his socked feet and the hum of the central A/C, she could hear him making his way to the bathroom, down the short corridor towards her. In her adult life Olga had only been in one real relationship, and that had ended nearly fifteen years before. This type of intimacy was unfamiliar, leaving her unsure how to act. Would he greet her like a husband? Like a lover? How should she react to that? A grimace? A sweet kiss? Pretend, for a moment, to be like a normal woman, eager for an instant of domestic bliss?

"Shit! This is some view!" Matteo exclaimed. It was. The apartment was located on the seventeenth floor of one of the older of the new high-rises that had come to dominate, and transform, one of the previously neglected enclaves of her hometown. The unit itself, decorated with sparse perfection, featured the best of HGTV and IG: stainless steel appliances, an open concept floor plan, a kitchen island with poured concrete countertops, and the showstopper — floor-to-ceiling windows that offered sweeping views of what Olga considered her little patch of Brooklyn. From her kitchen she could look down one of the bustling avenues and practically see the neighborhood she had grown up in.

"I mean, the construction of these buildings is garbage — I hope you're leasing and didn't buy — but wow, the view. Chef's kiss!"

Olga stared at him. He was naked, his flaccid penis dangling as he paced the room clocking each angle of the view.

"You're naked."

"I am," he said. "Is that weird, somehow? We were naked all night."

"Yes, but now it's daytime. So, I guess I was just a little surprised you were still —"

"Naked? This is interesting, I didn't take you for the Puritan type, but then again, I didn't know you'd spent formative years with the witch burners up north." She looked at him quizzically and he gestured towards her mug.

"Ah!" She chuckled. She was less uncomfortable than she thought she would be, the realization of which made her uncomfortable. For a moment there was a silence between them, the meteorologist on the TV lamenting about climate change. A clip of her brother on the news brought her back to her senses. "So, yeah. Listen. It's just that normally —"

"God," Matteo exclaimed to the TV, "is there a day when this homie *isn't* on the news?"

She put her mug down. "Not a fan, I take it?"

Matteo laughed. "Of what? His schmaltz or his unbridled ambition? I was half expecting him to announce his bid for president the day after the last election!"

Olga didn't really want to engage him; after all, chances were she would never see him again. But she was proud of her brother. "We should be so lucky. My brother'd be an amazing president. He'll never run though. So, for now, I guess the people of Sunset Park have to be content with having their own personal Pedro Albizu Campos."

Matteo looked from Olga to the TV and back to Olga again.

"Hold up. Please don't tell me that you're related to Congressman Pedro Acevedo?"

"Okay, I won't tell you." She smiled, a bit smugly.

"Damn."

"Damn." She laughed.

"No hard feelings?"

"None. You know what they say about opinions and all . . ."

"Funny girl!" He smiled. "Listen, ma,

since there's no hard feelings, let me ask you what's a dude's got to do to get a cup of coffee? Where's that Brooklyn hospitality?"

She was embarrassed. She knew better and he'd called her on it.

"How do you take it?" she asked as she reached for a second mug.

"Light and slightly bitter?" He was suddenly up close behind her, his erection brushing the back of her robe. He reached around her for the mug. "Don't you worry about me; I can fix my own coffee. Go do your thing. Just going to drink my java and charge up my phone and I'll be on my way. You're not the only one with shit to do."

This last part he said playfully and pinched her cheek for good measure. She stared at him. Who was this naked hoarder?

Olga could feel him looking at her things while she showered. Her color-sorted bookcase filled with tomes that had whispered to her soul. She imagined him staring at art on her walls: the Barron Claiborne print of Biggie Smalls, the framed Puerto Rican flag she paid too much for on eBay despite her doubts about its authentic role in the failed '50 revolution, a framed *Beats, Rhymes and Life* album cover. She felt a shiver down her back at the thought of him gazing at the photos on her desk. Her at her college graduation, looking fraught with anticipation. The portrait of her grandmother she had taken back in high school. Her brother getting sworn into Congress; how she beamed with pride. The black-and-white shot of her parents on the subway, the one that was burned indelibly into her eyeballs, of them leaning on each other, exhausted after a day of protesting. The signs that had rested on their laps are cropped out of the shot, but she didn't need to see them to know what they said. *Viva Puerto Rico Libre* and *Tengo Puerto Rico en mi Corazón.* Her mother, beautiful and young, her face, as always, makeup free, a scarf stylishly wrapped around her head. Her father with his smooth brown skin and mustached face, his beret and army jacket covered in protest buttons. Her heart raced imagining Matteo staring at these photos, his mind forming questions that his mouth would soon bring into the air. She could not imagine discussing her parents with this stranger, especially not this morning.

Though still covered in soap and mid-leg-shave, she shut the water off. She put her robe on as she ran from the shower, leaving a trail of water behind her. "You need to get out of here!" she shouted as she entered the living area. "You can't be touching my things."

Matteo was not, as she had imagined, thumbing through her books or staring at her photos. He was fully dressed, overstuffed knapsack already on his back, standing at the sink rinsing the two coffee mugs. He shut off the water and dried his hands with the dish towel.

"Whatever's clever, girl. Wash your own dishes!"

He walked past her dripping-wet self and patted the arm of her damp robe.

"Ciao," he called to her as he walked out the door.

THE PRICE OF MANGOS

Prieto Acevedo woke up before dawn resolving to have a good day. He ran a few laps around Sunset Park, got his daughter Lourdes up, fed, and ready for the ridiculously bougie Art & Talent Day Camp his sister had paid for, and then, despite the heat, donned his suit jacket. This morning's agenda included what he considered the best part of his job: greeting his constituents on their way to work.

When he first ran for public office — City Council nearly seventeen years ago — he did this every single morning from the day he announced until the election, working all the N and R stations along Fourth Avenue within his district. The party leaders would tease him: "Acevedo, you realize you're a Democrat in Brooklyn running for an uncontested seat, right? Just keep breathing till election day and you'll win." But Prieto didn't want to just win. He wanted people to feel good about voting for him. These were his neighbors, after all. People whom, if he didn't know personally, he'd seen around the neighborhood his whole life. His whole friggin' life. People his grandma used to know, who would come to their house so she could do alterations on their party dresses. He wanted them to know that he wasn't just a guy collecting a paycheck; he was one of them. They could come to him with their problems. He wore the suit not because he wanted to look like a politician, but because he wanted them to see that he took them seriously.

Of course, running for office and being in office were very different things. After he got elected to City Council, he tried to work the stations once a month. Once he got elected to Congress (again uncontested, the seat virtually grandfathered to him by a mentor) his chances to do these meet-and-greets were even fewer and farther between. The stress of going back and forth to D.C., of maintaining two households. To say nothing of the sheer bullshit and internal politics of the job, of donors, of people who weren't donors but tried, with great pressure, to wield influence. There were days when he felt so jaded and down. Pushed into a corner so tight he could hardly breathe. But today was not going to be one of those days. No, the days when he got to do this, to shake hands and hear about people's lives and needs, these were the days when he remembered why he got into this game in the first place.

It was a hazy day as he made his way out of his house — his grandmother's house, the home he'd grown up in — and over to the Thirty-sixth Street train station, his favorite to work. It had a local and an express, so it attracted more people, but mainly he liked it for sentimental reasons. This was the station his parents would post up at when they were selling *Palante* papers for the Young Lords. Unlike in the Latino enclaves of Manhattan, the Lords' footprint in South Brooklyn was relatively small, so his parents stuck out. They were sort of local folk heroes. Or crazy Puerto Rican hippies, depending on who you asked. Either way, Prieto enjoyed imagining them out there, a generation before, connecting with the people of their community, and him, a generation later, carrying the mantle now. Or so he saw it on his good days.

The first forty-five minutes passed more or less as usual. Lots of handshakes. Some daps. A heated rap battle with one of his favorite younger voters. Prieto carrying several strollers down the staircase. (It's really ridiculous, he thought, that we don't have more accessible stations.) Then, an older lady with a grocery cart was struggling to get her things up the station steps, but when Prieto went to help her, she took one look at him and swatted him away.

"Thank you, pero, no thank you. With you helping me, I'm likely to end up with all my groceries in the street, starving to death."

God bless the viejitas and their flair for the dramatic.

"Señora, let me just help you, and then you can tell me why I stink, okay?"

She acquiesced and allowed him to take the cart but did not wait for him to get to the top of the stairs before she began running through her litany of offenses.

"First of all, you let them build that . . . mall, pero where are the jobs? Why does my grandson still have no job? Next, mis vecinos. Nice people. From El Salvador. One day I see them, the next they are gone. I find out that the ICE came and took them away —"

"Yes, I've heard about this family and my office is —"

"Then! Then, I see they put a new, nice-looking grocery store on Third Avenue. I think, oh, good, no more taking this train to

Atlantic with this pinche cart just to save a few dollars. Pero no. This place! No coupons. No nothing. The prices are sky-high! Three dollars. For a mango! How is a senior citizen supposed to survive here? This is a neighborhood for working people! I live off of retirement!"

"Señora," he said, mildly out of breath, which disturbed him because it was only a flight of stairs, "I assure you; I understand. I was raised by my abuela, she was a retiree —"

"Save your story for the cameras, okay? I know you. You've been around forever. I even remember your grandma. Nice lady. Did the rosary society. But that doesn't make you good at your job. You are no good at your job!"

But before Prieto could say anything, she took her cart and pushed off. He took out his handkerchief and wiped his brow. He called out to her.

"Tell your grandson to come by my offices and I'll see what I can do about a job!"

But she just dismissed him with her hands and kept on walking.

"Whaddup, team! Has my sister been on yet?" Prieto called out as he walked into his district office.

The TVs, normally tuned into CNN or NY1, were all showing *Good Morning, Later,* the show where, occasionally, his sister did segments on weddings and etiquette.

"Not yet," Alex, his chief of staff, called out, "but I'm hoping it's soon because I'm losing brain cells by the second watching this nonsense."

"Tsk, tsk." Prieto sucked his teeth. "It's not nonsense if it involves my sister."

"My bad. I didn't mean that as a diss, sir, I just don't get it," Alex continued. "I've hung out with Olga. I mean, the work she did on your last campaign. She's smarter than ninety percent of the people I know working in Washington —"

"And Olga would say that's why she's not one of them."

"Touché."

"That's a direct quote, by the way. She's literally said that shit to me before. Listen, Alex, my sister built this business from the ground up, all by herself. She makes a nice living. She's very generous to my kid, our family. If this wedding shit makes her happy, what kind of East Coast elites are we to question it?"

Prieto was protective of his sister. When their mother had left, Olga was still in middle school, just a year or so older than his daughter was now. He'd been charged with watching out for her, and he took that charge seriously. Over the years, though, at times the roles felt reversed. Alex was right, his sister was smarter than most people he knew, and not just in D.C. Prieto always had to work hard at school, but Olga barely had to crack a book. And she'd been a good artist, too. Beautiful photographer. But the thing that his sister had that most impressed him was her street smarts. That, he knew, she got from their grandmother. Prieto could make people feel good when he was talking to them, but nobody could anticipate a problem or solve it faster than Olga. Indeed, he sometimes resented her ability to wriggle out of trouble just by dialing up the charm at precisely the right moment in exactly the right way. But it was this same skill that had also made her Prieto's most trusted consigliere. She was only a college student when he ran for his first office, but she had helped write every press release and campaign speech. When he and Lourdes's mother split, it was his sister who helped him rebuild his life. Once he got to Congress, it was Olga who coached him on speaking to donors. On how to say yes to things without really committing to much. Whenever he got into a bind — personal, professional, political — his sister was always his first call. Almost always.

For these reasons, Prieto was both befuddled by and defensive of his sister's career. To Prieto, his sister could be or do anything: fix the MTA, run the Met Museum, replace snarky fucking Alex as his chief of staff. He was unclear why, therefore, she chose to tie her life and fortune to the minutiae of other people's personal lives. It felt too small an arena for her talents and, invariably, their lives encroached upon hers. Her clients called her any day of the week, any hour of the day. And he knew these people. They were the same kinds of people he had to spend time with when reelection season rolled around, courting donations. They were nice people, generally, but their litany of problems, real or imagined, never waned. Nor did their sense of urgency around getting these problems resolved, their allergy to even a moment's discomfort quite severe. Still, Prieto made certain to keep these opinions to himself. His mother, in her letters to him, had made clear her disappointments with Olga's career. A betrayal of their family "legacy." He knew she had made this clear to Olga as well. Prieto felt no need to pile on. Instead, he tried, both publicly and privately, to champion her successes as a business owner and encourage her, in any way, to broaden her options. To ask for more.

The segment today was short. Etiquette in the digital age. Very helpful stuff, actually. He was proud of her. Of them both. Not bad for two kids from Sunset Park.

"She's great, isn't she?" Prieto said to no one in particular. "Honestly, she's better than these hosts. They could replace Tammy or Toni with her today and I bet their ratings would go through the roof, having a Latina anchoring a show like this!"

He picked up his phone to text Olga, and he could feel Alex staring at him.

"Congressman, can I put the real news back on?"

"Psssh," he said, "you've got to lighten up, Alex. But yeah. And before I forget, what's going on with that Salvadorean couple from Fortieth Street that ICE picked up?"

"We're working on it. Not a lot of info. The pressing thing this morning is down in P.R."

"Shoot."

"There's been more protests at University of Puerto Rico. They've been tear-gassing the students and —"

"What? Why hasn't this been in the news?"

"It was in *El Diario;* you know that national media isn't interested in P.R. Anyway, it all has to do with —"

"I know. PROMESA. Fuck."

"Well, they finally got a new university president in place, but the PROMESA board is digging their heels in on those budget cuts, and the school can't operate on their allocation."

He'd rather be getting yelled at by the viejita at the train station. After a slate of federal tax breaks expired, corporations slowly fled Puerto Rico, causing the colony's income to fall, debt to rise, and infrastructure to fall apart. Recently, the seemingly abstract issue of Puerto Rico's fiscal crisis had turned into a professional and personal nightmare for Prieto. Professionally, because his vote for PROMESA — which put in place a politically appointed control board to restructure the island's debt — had completely backfired. In the year since Obama made it law, the austerity imposed had sunk the colony into worse shape than ever. Personally, because everyone from his mother to the lady who did his dry cleaning was pissed off at him about it. The former more seriously than the latter. This PROMESA vote haunted him.

"Look, Alex, I get it. We've got that hearing coming up. Let's fly some UPR students up here, get them on TV, let people see these are just kids, like theirs, trying to get an education. Maybe we can make someone care about this?"

"Sounds good," Alex offered, hovering. "Anything else?"

"Yes, Arthur Selby's office called to invite you to a dinner party next week."

His pulse quickened. "Tell him that I'm previously engaged."

"His secretary said he wouldn't take no for an answer."

"Is Arthur Selby my constituent, Alex? The last time I checked he wasn't even one of my fucking donors."

"So, that's a definitive no then, sir?"

But Prieto knew that it was not a no.

"Mark the info on my calendar and if I can make it, I'll make it."

Reality TV

Becoming a post-recession, slightly better-than-'hood-rich wedding planner had required a significant amount of cunning on Olga's part, but becoming a famous one had been surprisingly easy. Yes, there had been lots of grunt work, but like a '70s game show, behind each door there had been opportunity. She'd started her business in the nascent era of reality TV and social media and discovered quickly that, if leveraged properly, something of a facsimile to real fame could result. She'd left the fancy college with not quite the right connections to secure one of those lucrative management consulting gigs, but certainly a good enough network to score her a one-off appearance on a Real Housewives franchise as wedding coordinator for Countess von Vonsberg's third marriage. A decently written press release led to coverage in a magazine, which, when pitched correctly, led to an in-store appearance in the coveted registry department at Macy's, which in turn got her booked as a regular on a Style Network wedding show. Along the way, she adopted each new social media platform as it was invented, humble-bragging every magazine feature, speaking engagement, and five-second clip in which she opined about wedding trends in advance of celebrity nuptials. For nine years, she did this with exhaustive frequency, until one day a call came with an offer of what was, to wannabe service industry celebrities, the holy grail. A widely watched cable network wanted to shoot her very own TV pilot.

It was an epic disaster.

The initial pitch had been "Sophisticated New York City planner goes cross-country fixing up people's wacky weddings." A cross between *My Fair Lady, Queer Eye for the Straight Guy,* and *Bridezillas.* To Olga, it sounded like a hit, but from the first day of taping things seemed off. Reality TV is nothing if not completely fabricated, and Olga had done enough of it to know to act shocked at the cost of something that the network had already negotiated to get for free, or how to feign surprise when seeing a locale for the first time, even after you'd already done ten takes. It all helped the story in the end, and a good story was good for Olga. Yet, from the beginning of this shoot the producer kept giving directions that seemed both overly abstract and inappropriate for the situation. "Be more fiery!" he suggested when she entered a room. During a scene in a bakery they asked if she could have "more passion" when she tasted the cake. The requests irked Olga in a way she could not put her finger on. The shoot lasted several days and by the end, sensing her own irritability, she willed herself into a cooperative temper. When, in a reaction shot, she was meant to be pleased about something or another, the producer asked a question posing as direction.

"Do you think you might dance if you heard news like this?"

Olga pointed to herself, incredulously. "Me? Do I think I would dance when I heard that we found a string quartet to play Coldplay's 'Yellow' for their wedding ceremony?"

"Yes," the producer said. "You've wanted to find something to make this wedding more elegant and now you've succeeded. It's a moment of professional fulfillment. You know how excited it's going to make your bride. Maybe you'd dance a little bit? It will be cute, really."

Olga was skeptical but wanted to be a team player. She began to dance to the song that played in her head anytime she needed to be inspired to move: Teena Marie's "Square Biz." After a few seconds the producer chimed in again.

"Yeah, Olga, that's great, but what about something a little more rhythmic?"

"I have rhythm," she said, her jaw tight.

"Of course. But how about a little salsa! Huh? Channel your inner Marc Anthony!"

For a moment she stood completely still as the full picture crystallized before her. A voice, her father's, whispered in her head: *Is this what it's come to? Dancing on command?* Then, she reflected on the near decade-long slog, which had all been intended to build to this moment: her own show. The wedding business had been a hustle. On the surface, if one were counting social media followers or press mentions, few were more successful. But by conventional measures of a business's health, she barely had her head above water. On her way to tape the pilot she'd stopped at a newsstand to buy a magazine one of her weddings was featured in. Her credit card was declined. The first time she had appeared on TV, she had redone her website and gotten a second phone line to handle all the calls. They came, but few of the leads were real. And though her clients' budgets grew progressively larger, the workload scaled in turn. That meant more staff and more expenses. If she could get past this moment, this ridiculous request, ahead of her lay true financial opportunity: a party product line at Target, a spokesperson gig with Sandals Resorts, a coffee table book! She imagined herself, for a moment, the Puerto Rican Martha Stewart.

She took a deep breath, stepped out to the left, out to the right, stepped together, held a beat, repeated. Once. Twice. A third time. It was maybe ten seconds, but she felt herself red with shame.

"Enough!" she screamed.

"Aw! That was so cute, Olga! Just a little bit more."

"I said enough!"

The producer, the camera crew, and even the couple from rural Pennsylvania who had signed up to tape this pilot in the hopes of free wedding stuff all laughed.

"I think that's the fiery he was looking for!" one of the cameramen quipped.

A few weeks later, Sabine, the network executive who brokered Olga's pilot deal, asked her to lunch. They met at a trendy Mexican place in Midtown whose kitchen was helmed by a white guy who claimed that while on an ayahuasca trip, Quetzalcoatl, the Aztec serpent-god, had spoken to him, directing him to abandon classic French cooking and dedicate his life to elevating Mexican cuisine. The restaurant and the story had gotten wall-to-wall, A-list media coverage. Though Olga distinctly remembered reading the glossy Sunday Styles piece about him and thinking, "Who says Mexican cuisine needs elevation?" She nevertheless began uploading photos of her dining experience to social media the second she and Sabine sat down.

"Marshal, the chef, is a friend of mine from Dalton," Sabine offered. "It's the only way I was able to get us a reservation! Even at lunch, it's just impossible. But I thought this was the perfect place to tell you that you are about to be the biggest thing to happen to Latino people on TV since *Ugly Betty*!"

"Really? That big?" Olga replied, flatly. "Not to split hairs, Sabine, but I thought this was meant to be more of a city slicker/country mouse thing?"

"It is! It is. It is all of that. It's *also* got unique appeal to a growing demographic that we have just not been able to crack. But you know what? I don't even want to talk. I just want to show you the trailer we cut for the pilot."

She pulled an iPad from her bag, placed it on the table, offered Olga headphones, and pressed play with a giant smile on her face. Olga heard the sound of a trombone and her stomach dropped. A vibrant salsa began to play as the camera cut to shots of Olga walking around Manhattan in fitted business attire, with close-ups of her red-lipsticked lips, gold bangles, and — in a shot Olga found a bit risqué for a lifestyle show — her butt while she walked. Then, a voice-over Olga could have sworn was the same woman from *House Hunters International* began as the camera rapidly cut between shots of the Great Plains, a small-town main street, Mount Rushmore, and a seemingly endless array of stock shots of happy white couples.

A Latino invasion is coming to your hometown this fall. . . .

A quick succession of shots: Olga walking in different primary color outfits. . . . When did we even film this? she wondered.

A STYLE invasion!

The promo then cut to a series of wedding images of various portly white people getting married in church basements,

Knights of Columbus halls, and affordable hotels.

Olga Acevedo is here to take your bland, American wedding . . .

That seems offensive to those families, Olga thought to herself.

And SPICE IT UP!

As the music swelled to full Willie-Colón-at-the-Palladium levels, there was a quick montage of a Mexican mariachi band, a Salvadoran Pupusa vendor, and the final shot, Olga, dancing her salsa on a seemingly endless loop. A graphic of big, bold, hot pink sans-serif words appeared on the screen, timed exactly to the final beats of the music:

Spice
It
Up!

There was a moment of silence while Sabine, grinning ear to ear, waited for Olga to join in her ebullient excitement that they, together, had just set Latinx identity in America back to pre–Ricky Ricardo levels. Again, Olga heard her father's voice.

Pendeja.

Luckily for Olga, white America was nearly

as upset over *Spice It Up* as she had been, albeit for different reasons. When the network tested the pilot, they discovered that white audiences were, in varying degrees, afraid of Olga. In the heartland, people were not bothered by the fact that Olga was Latina; there had been growing pockets of Latin migrants in these areas for years and their service work and tasty snacks had been generally well received. No, they were bothered that she was going to come in and tell them what to do. The reversal-of-power dynamic was too disconcerting. Focus group participants who reported enjoying the show during the screening were calling back hours, even days later to say that they had been haunted — "haunted" was the word — by the prospect of "someone like Olga" coming in and bossing their family around. In coastal suburban enclaves, the show fared even worse. One focus group participant said Olga represented a new "threat" to "normal women." "It's bad enough," this woman was quoted as saying, "that we need to fear au pairs and yoga instructors. Now we need to worry about 'spicy' wedding planners?"

Olga was so relieved when Sabine told her that the network would not be picking the show up that she could barely feign disappointment. She had been quietly calling lawyer friends to review her contract to see if there was any way to block the pilot and, barring that, plotting a public relations offensive to mitigate the humiliation this would inflict on her. Of course, Sabine was clueless and Olga could hear the worry in her voice. The good news, she told Olga, was that it wasn't completely in vain — the pilot would see the light of day! Contractually they were obliged to air it at least once, so she — Olga — could DVR it, or gather her family for a little viewing party, or whatever else Olga thought would be a "fun way to celebrate this experience!"

The onetime public broadcast of *Spice It Up* was on a Saturday morning at 5 A.M. Olga spoke of it to no one but set an alarm for herself at 5 A.M. and again at 6 A.M., just so she would know when the horrible humiliation was finally a worry of the past. She had no idea how her mother found out about it, but a few days later she got a note in the mail — her mother's sole communication method — that simply said, *Saw you on TV the other day. You dress nice for a maid. Love, Mami.* She'd enclosed a portion of Pedro Pietri's *Puerto Rican Obituary,* careful to underline key words and phrases, in case her point wasn't clear enough:

These empty dreams
~~from the make-believe bedrooms~~
~~their parents left them~~
~~are the after-effects~~
of television programs
about the ideal
white american family
with ~~black~~ maids
and latino janitors
who are well train —
to make everyone
and their bill collectors
laugh at them
and the people they represent

By way of a consolation prize, Tammy offered Olga a less "narrative-driven" opportunity with their sister network on their hit morning news program, *Good Morning*'s fourth hour: *Good Morning, Later.* It was a confection of a show. Their only attempts at news coverage were occasionally reading presidential tweets on air and then quickly moving on to celebrity gossip and how to artfully dress a backyard table for an Instagram-worthy Fourth of July blowout. It was, therefore, the most popular program on morning television.

Five or six times a year, Olga would head to the studio for an entertainment segment in which she would offer banal bits of advice on how to keep your guacamole from going brown or what kind of waistline a petite bride should choose to elongate her torso in wedding photos. Today, after kicking Matteo out, she'd headed over to the studio where they readied her naturally curly hair into sleek, blown-out waves and glossed her lips to a perfect rose pink. She then taped a segment called "Digital Etiquette: Are Manners a Thing of the Past?" Predictably, the snarky text from her brother, who found her public identity as a mistress of upper-class etiquette amusing, arrived shortly after she walked off set. *When does the segment on "sucia chic" air, hermana? 'Cuz that's where your expertise will really come in handy!* She texted him back a middle finger emoji, which she knew he'd receive with good humor since he, of all people, understood leveraging a public persona. Her brother: the charismatic politician, the darling of the local news networks, and a favorite foil for the city's more conservative tabloids. While the man Prieto presented to the cameras and his constituents was not a total fabrication, it hung more firmly on a few carefully chosen facts while diligently avoiding others. They were good secret keepers for each other. And though she felt that he, like herself, couldn't quite understand how she ended up in this profession, she knew that he was proud of her. "A bright, beautiful Latina on the national stage," he would say, "is a role model to young Latinas everywhere, no matter what she's doing." (She never told him about *Spice It Up,* though who knows what her mother wrote to him in her missives.)

Typically, following one of these segments, her phone blew up with messages, and today was no different. Besides her brother, cousins, tíos, and tías, they were mainly past or current clients, excited to see her on a staple of morning television. This gig would never make Olga a household name, but it had enabled her to raise her fees. The women of the Upper East Side, Dallas, Palm Beach, and even Silicon Valley all felt just a bit better about their choice in party planner knowing that they could tell the ladies at SoulCycle or Pilates that yes, the wedding is overwhelming, but at least they have that fabulous girl from *Good Morning, Later* helping them out, so things are under control. Those kinds of bragging rights carried a premium. In the aftermath of the *Spice It Up* debacle, Olga realized that she'd allowed herself to become distracted from the true American dream — accumulating money — by its phantom cousin, accumulating fame. She would never make that mistake again.

Mixed among the texts was a message from Meegan and another message from a number she did not recognize. Meegan reached out to say that Mr. Eikenborn had called; he had something that she'd been looking for and he hoped she would drop by his offices around lunchtime. The unknown number simply said: *Got your number off one of the cards on your desk. Had I known I'd fucked a D-list celebrity last night, I would have asked for an autograph before you chased me out. Drinks this week?*

She knew he'd been looking through her things.

A Man Named Dick

Dick Eikenborn had biked eighteen miles that morning, shaving two minutes off his personal best, and rewarded himself by posting a series of shirtless selfies, including one almost dick pic, to his secret online dating profile. He didn't actually use the profile to meet anyone but enjoyed seeing the reactions the photos elicited and reading the more provocative messages that some of the women sent. If they were, in fact, real women. That germ of possibility had never entered his mind until Olga placed it there, where it festered and grew, quietly diminishing the pleasure of every digital wink. Indeed, while he knew Olga was a woman able to eviscerate an ego with a pointedly chosen turn of phrase, in this particular case she had cut down his fantasy in such a casual manner, he knew her observation wasn't intended for injury, and was simply offered as matter-of-fact. Which made its claws all the more tenacious. The irony, which had not escaped him, was that posting to the app, and even the taking of the selfies, had all developed out of his frustration with Olga herself. Olga and her inability to show passion anyplace other than the bedroom.

He was traveling at the time and had woken up thinking of her, with an erection. Normally had this happened, he would have simply tried to see her, to physically touch her and hold his hands on her ample hips. But on this day, the day of the first selfie, they were apart. They were apart and he wanted her badly, a longing that made him feel so young again that he'd come to think of Olga as his own personal fountain of youth. His need for her left him feeling vulnerable, exposed. He needed her to want him in that moment as badly as he wanted her. He took the photo of himself, naked on the hotel terrace, his body reflected in the suite's large mirror, and sent it to her, then waited, eagerly. For nothing. He went about the business of the morning — a conference call with their factory manager in China, getting an in-room massage — and as he was coming out of the shower, he caught a glimpse of himself again. Not bad for fifty-four, he remembered thinking. He massaged himself to hardness and, grabbing his phone, snapped another photo and sent it Olga's way before heading to whatever meeting it was that he had. Hours later a reply: *Be mindful. This is my business line. Thank you.*

He took her at her word and, given that at the time (a) he was still married and (b) she was planning his daughter's wedding, saw some wisdom in her words. This was careless behavior, for both him the sender and her, the receiver. Which was why he had his assistant go out and buy them each new phones. Hers, he promptly messengered to her office with a handwritten note that had simply said, *Our private line,* to which he added a wink and his new number. An hour or so later, the new line rang. He had saved her new number in his phone, but she called from her old one.

"Dick, that was cute. The phones thing. But seriously, I don't have the patience to be one of these two-phone types."

"Oh, but Cherry!" (Cherry was his pet name for her. He loved everything about her, except for her name: Olga sounded far too serious for such a sexual creature.) "Now we can send each other the kind of messages you don't think are appropriate for a work phone."

"Or maybe we just don't need to send each other those kinds of messages."

Dick was not dissuaded. He kept his phone. She never used hers. The dick pics persisted. Eventually, she addressed it with him, explaining that while she enjoyed seeing his naked person in real life, no one needed mounting photo evidence of their affair. He conceded her point. Particularly since by then he had done the unthinkable and asked Sheila for a divorce, a move that felt liberating, exhilarating, and expensive all at once. Olga wisely pointed out that if it felt expensive now, imagine how much costlier it would be should Sheila find out that he'd been fucking the wedding planner this whole time. So, he let up for a while. A time when he was lonelier and sadder than he had imagined himself being.

That had nothing to do with the pics, of course. Not really. His sense of loneliness was caused by the vast disparity between the realities of his newfound bachelordom and his predivorce imaginings of it. For starters, at the advice of his lawyers, in an effort to not lose or sell the estate on the Vineyard — the one that had been in his family for generations — he had camped out there to establish it as his primary residence. A lonely place to be in the early spring. Then, there were the kids: Victoria, at the time twenty-four and newly married, Richard, twenty, and Sam, seventeen. He had not factored in the defensive and, frankly, accusatory stance that his daughter would take. He had also not calculated how much of his time with his sons, as they danced on the periphery of adulthood, had been casually accrued around their penthouse in Manhattan, moments gathered in their comings and goings. As busy as his own work kept him, it was equally hard to get on their schedule, the allure and excitement of their own nascent adult lives proving more seductive than time with Dad. A sentiment he himself remembered and understood, but still, he missed them. Their absence and growth made him aware of his own mortality in a way that he hadn't felt before, and cast a dark shadow on his generally optimistic worldview.

His greatest miscalculation, though, was with Olga.

While Dick had not technically left Sheila for Olga — their marriage had long been strained — it had simply never occurred to him that when he moved out, Olga might not move in. His assumption of this outcome had been so total, so complete, it was only after his departure, during his early days on the Vineyard, that he found himself blindsided by reality. He had tired of his wife's company but had no desire to be alone. He FaceTimed Olga, offering to send movers to pack up her place, and she looked at him quizzically. He realized he had never even told her he was calling it quits with Sheila, never spoken his other assumptions out loud. He felt a bit foolish; he couldn't expect her to be a mind reader (something Sheila had repeatedly chided him over year after year). Yet, when he did finally ask her, back in New York, over a room service dinner at his suite at the Carlyle, he was shocked by her reply. He'd said that he wanted them to be together, officially, and for her to come and live with him and she had laughed and said, "No, Dick, you don't." But he assured her that he did. He didn't just want it, he needed it. He needed her.

"You only think that you need that, Dick. Right now. In time, you'll be happy that it's like this."

"But don't you want to live with me?" he asked. Then, and he revisited this sometimes on his runs, she didn't hesitate for a second before saying that she liked things exactly as they were. Enjoying each other when they could because they wanted to at that time.

Without the pressure of commitment.

Later, when he would confide in Charmaine, his assistant who had been his father's assistant before Dick inherited her and in whom Dick entrusted all of his secrets and fears, that his offer had been rebuffed, he found himself nearly whining with disbelief. "Isn't this what every woman wants? To be the person that the rich guy actually leaves his wife for? Don't all women want that, Charmaine?" But that was later. In the moment, when Olga rejected his offer to cohabitate, before he could become pouty or offended, she had come over from her side of the little dining table where they were eating and straddled his lap, opening her robe as she did so, reminding him of how much more fun everything is when it's spontaneous, and didn't he agree with that? And he had said, enthusiastically, yes.

Charmaine reminded him that the city was full of women who would want to be that girl, that he didn't need to chase after Olga. The problem was that he *wanted* to chase after Olga. He didn't simply want to catch her, he wanted to pin her down, and make her love him as much as he loved her. (The irony of this did not escape him. The challenge throughout his entire marriage had been his deep-seated resentment of having himself felt caught by the former Mrs. Eikenborn.) The unevenness of their relationship both vexed him and moored him, rendering him unable to fix his mind on anyone else. In an effort to open his eyes to another woman, any other woman, he signed up for one of those dating apps, anonymously, of course. He wasn't famous, but his face and name were in the financial papers — and his divorce on Page Six — enough that he knew better than to show his recognizable self. So instead he showed the parts of him that were less frequently seen, carefully cropping out his head. He wrote his self-description cautiously: his aim to be truthful, but not too revealing. "Five-foot-ten Caucasian businessman and entrepreneur, athletic build, passionate about travel, cycling, flying planes, and wine collecting. Enjoys a good joke and live concerts." He could be anyone, he thought to himself.

The "likes" started immediately. He was overwhelmed and flattered. He never responded to the messages with anything more than, maybe, a wink. He never gave out his number. Yet, rather than take his mind off Olga, these other women only made him more resolved to wrestle commitment, of some sort, from her. To make her see what even strangers on the internet saw: Richard Eikenborn III was a catch.

"Why don't you like my photos?" he asked her one evening in bed.

"The Dick dick pics?" she asked.

"All of them. The body shots, the dick pics. Yes. Why don't you like them?"

"No women like photos like that. We're just told that we're supposed to by a lazy patriarchal culture that assumes that women must like the inverse of what men like. Men like topless boob pics, ergo, women must love bare chest shots . . . it's just lazy."

He felt himself getting defensive. "If I were to post these photos on a dating app, Cherry, women would love them, I bet you anything."

She laughed.

"Are you on a dating app, Dick?"

"Of course not! Why would I be on an app when I have you here with me?" He pressed himself closer to her back as he spooned her in bed.

She giggled again and rolled away from his embrace.

"If you posted pics like that on a dating app, I have a feeling that the 'women' " — and here she put her fingers in the air to emphasize the point with air quotes — "who like them might not turn out to be women at all. Or at least not the kind who don't expect a monetary exchange at the end of the evening."

Dick was both grazed and perplexed.

"What are you trying to say? That people on these apps aren't real people? Why would someone do that?"

"I'm not saying that they aren't real people, I'm just saying that they might not be the people they are presenting themselves as. Grifters. Married guys too afraid to download Grindr. Online hookers. A whole assortment of explanations. My cousin Mabel went on a date with a guy and when he showed up, he was only five feet tall. In one of his photos he was towering over Jon Hamm — she showed me!"

"Did she bring it up?"

"Hell yeah! She showed him the photo and he admitted he was standing on something."

"But why would he do that?" Dick had said, genuinely confused.

"Richard," she said — she always used his full name when she was being serious — "I know that no one has given you any reason to worry that you are anything less than perfect, but some people don't like themselves the way they are."

"This doesn't make any sense to me," he

said sincerely.

She turned to him and smiled, her face right near his face. "Your inability to see people's dark sides never fails to awe me."

He didn't, in fact, agree with that assessment; he sometimes felt Olga underestimated him. When it came to business at least, Dick always saw the dark sides of things, but his gift, he felt, was for sensing the opportunities that often lie in wait. Certainly, this had saved him — and their national chain of hardware stores — when his father, still CEO at the time, had been diagnosed with Alzheimer's. Business had already been contracting and Dick knew their investors would pressure them to sell as soon as word got out. So, he got ahead of it, calling an emergency meeting of their board of directors, in which he laid out a plan for expansion into Puerto Rico, Mexico, and Canada that would triple business valuation within two years, making everyone in the room far richer than unloading the business would. A decade later, when the housing market crumbled, people around him panicked; construction and contractors were a huge part of their customer base. But Dick sensed opportunity: if people couldn't afford new homes, they would likely fix up their old ones. He invented Eikenborn DIY Reno Schools. He cut out the middleman, invested in developing their own line of paints, tools, and toolboxes. He licensed their name to a DIY show on HGTV. By the time the recession was over, Dick had grown Eikenborn and Sons into one of the most profitable retail operations in America. Similarly, while his friends and colleagues lamented the seemingly endless environmental rules and regulations of the Obama era, Dick saw a burgeoning market. He was the first hardware retailer in the country to carry LEED lighting fixtures. They began retailing home solar systems, then launched their own solar panel production operation. From Dick's point of view, climate change — be it efforts made to mitigate it, or efforts to repair the havoc it caused — would be his greatest boon. Eikenborn Green Solutions would keep the business thriving into its sixth generation, when he imagined, and hoped, that Richard or Sam, or maybe even Victoria, might take the reins from him one day.

These successes had left Dick feeling confident about his place in the world. He had architected a business and a life far greater than the one that his father had mapped out for him. In his mind, having a woman like Olga by his side was the missing piece. Getting her to commit was simply a matter of finding the right approach. His money, he'd come to realize, was not enough. Finally, though, he felt he'd landed on exactly the right tack.

Flying Private

Olga had fucked Richard Eikenborn III before she even met him, having siphoned anywhere from $20,000 to $30,000 from his bank accounts and credit cards in the form of administrative fees, product markups, and a new clause in her contract that she realized was a true stroke of brilliance: a late fee that automatically kicked in every day that her clients' payments were past due, which was almost always.

This idea came to her one Sunday at dinner at Tío Richie's house out on Long Island. One of her cousins was complaining about his exorbitant credit card bill, largely composed of late fees, which then were compounded with interest. Richie started to lecture on the importance of fiscal responsibility and keeping track of his payment due dates and her cousin whined that the credit card company could have at least called him to remind him about the payment *before* it was too late, not to mention that he didn't always have the money exactly when the due date came up. Olga started to explain how that might mean he was charging more than he could afford, but then it hit her. Her clients *did* have the money to pay her when the due dates came, yet they never did so. Though they never failed to pay her, the only checks sent promptly were the first and the last. The "motivation" payments, as she thought of them. The ones they sent when they were excited for her to start and terrified that she wouldn't finish. Beyond that, she would always need to call to remind them, and it never achieved anything, except annoy them. "Are you implying that I'm trying to stiff you?" one father of the groom once asked. Subsequently, she ended up being tardy with her own bills, which almost always cost her money, none of which she ever passed on to the clients, because, she had long felt, wasn't the onus on her to manage her cash flow better? She was certain that these families, with their administrative assistants and money people, never sent a late payment to Amex or Visa. Yet with her, just a small shop, barely a company, they never cared when she got paid. As point of fact, they almost seemed to resent having to send the check.

But what if she acted like a credit card company? What if she stopped calling when the bill was due? What if, in very fine print in her very long contract, she said she would bill them $750 for every day that they were past due and after 15 days she would automatically charge their credit card on file? Only she didn't write out the $750. Instead, she calculated it down to a percentage of their total fee, which seemed such a minuscule amount. Less than 1 percent, really. So that even when people did bother to read the clause, they usually shrugged, the amount seeming so nominal.

She thought the idea so bold when she implemented it, she was certain she would lose clients or have wild fights about it when her invoices went out. Instead, she discovered something else about the ultra-rich. The only thing they enjoyed less than parting with their money was talking about it. It seemed to physically pain them. She had one person ask what the fee was and as soon as she explained that they could refer to item 26a in their contract they apologized, said they would FedEx a check, and hung up the phone.

The Eikenborns were particularly reticent to talk about bills or budgets or anything of that sort, yet maniacally uninclined to spend a penny, Olga noticed, on other human beings. Mrs. Eikenborn delightfully coughed up cash for luxury bathroom trailers, fine wine, freshly shucked oysters, Kobe beef steaks, and custom tuxedos for Victoria's two dogs. Yet, she balked at the cost of feeding the staff who installed the tents and lighting, proclaimed outrage at the photographer's need for breaks, and once booked Olga on a double layover to save $200 on a $750,000 event.

The flight to the Vineyard was a quick shot from LaGuardia, Olga knew. Yet she and Meegan somehow found themselves with not one, but two layovers. A two-hour flight turned into a six-hour ordeal. They had insisted there was no need for Olga to book a hotel, as the estate had a large guest cottage. Upon arrival, however, they discovered the cottage was under repair, as was a guest bedroom, and so she and Meegan found themselves sharing a drafty, twin-bedded spare room next to the bride's suite. In the dark, they whispered their complaints about the awkwardness of the situation to each other, terrified that they would be heard through the walls. For her next visit, the food tasting, Olga refused to allow them to book her travel, instead suggesting she bill them back. The bride insisted that if Olga "really needed" to fly direct, she should fly up with her father, Mr. Eikenborn, who would be coming up on his private jet. This, the bride felt, would "save money" and "reduce the carbon footprint" of the wedding.

By this time, Olga had come to detest the bride. She had a shorter fuse for younger brides, whose senses of taste and style were so loosely formed, they clung to their mothers' opinions in a way that Olga found pathetic. Victoria was no different in this regard, but her beigeness was coupled with a hypocritical sense of social justice. Victoria's day job was at a global human rights foundation, and during the many lunches, dinners, and car rides together that planning events of this scale required, she often filled the empty space with impassioned monologues regarding inequity of women in Ecuador or Yemen, always buttressed by her mother's proclamation that "Victoria is out to change the world!"

Olga ruminated on this as she willed herself into a meditative state while riding to Teterboro to fly with Richard Eikenborn III up to the tasting. Rather than be irritated, she thought, she should focus on the infallible hilarity of the ultra-wealthy to be penny-wise when it came to compensating human sweat, and dollar-foolish when it came to everything else. She shouldn't be irritated at all, she counseled herself, and instead laugh her way to the bank.

She boarded the jet, a newish-seeming Legacy, promptly. Despite having charged his credit cards and cashed his checks, Olga had never met Richard Eikenborn III. Though she had Googled his image before, as she waited — at first for minutes, then an hour, and then a second hour — she began to picture him as an old fifty-four. Pot-bellied and balding. As time went on, she grew first hungry, then eventually desperate to use the bathroom, but refused, lest he board the plane while she relieved herself. He should, she felt, see that he had kept her — a person whose time was also valuable — waiting. With each passing moment, he grew increasingly homely in her mind's eye. When he did finally arrive, she had her legs crossed tightly, her face buried in an out-of-date magazine.

"What," she barked, "is the point of flying private if you still have to wait on the tarmac for two hours?" She rose, not to greet him, but to rush to the bathroom. As she peed, she thought to herself: That is one fine white man.

Within fifteen minutes of takeoff their

physical desire for each other was mutually understood. Forty-five minutes in and Olga had already rationalized the dubious morality of this lust as the perfect counterbalance for the despicable behavior of Dick's wife and child. By the time they landed, they had made a plan for him to join her for a nightcap at her hotel once the others had gone to bed.

Afterwards she wondered, would she have made the same decision had they booked her direct?

Access

Her freshman year in college, Olga had taken a part-time job at a preppy clothing store near campus, where she worked in the menswear department. Day after day they would come, her classmates, in their cargo shorts and T-shirts. Casually trying on a $300 sports coat or slipping into a $500 pair of loafers. Sometimes they would pull out a credit card, sometimes they would buy nothing — the indifference always striking her. She studied them, noticing that the wrinkled dress shirts they wore over their college tees, the ones fraying at the cuffs, were also monogrammed. Their watches, and they all seemed to wear watches, were thick banded and heavy. Rolexes and, more often, brands she'd never even heard of before. Sometimes they would come in with girlfriends — always sun-kissed, waifish girls — to look for a shirt or a tie for a formal or fraternity banquet. Weekends brought the moms and dads. Older, starched versions of the sons and girlfriends. Occasionally, one of the women would be wearing a pricier version of Olga's own work uniform: a button-down, man-tailored shirtdress, which Olga would bind herself into with safety-pins to prevent from gaping where her bust and hips swelled. Olga noted how differently the garment communicated on their lithe, flat bodies. How it bathed them in effortless elegance. She noted how much she felt herself in a costume for a life she could never have.

Olga worked at that store for one full year and none of the boys who came in ever recognized her from class or the dorms or the library. If they did, they never said hello. No one ever asked if she was also a student at the college, and surely no one assumed so. She was, in that environment, to those boys, like a hanger, or a price tag, or the machine that swiped the black American Express cards. Not an object to be desired, but a tool to facilitate the acquisition of desirable things.

But Dick — who if never a customer in that exact store, had certainly bought his Nantucket Reds in a similar establishment — saw her. That, she knew immediately. When she fucked him, she felt that she was fucking every son and father who had made it through an entire transaction without ever once making eye contact. Not even when she handed them the bag of their carefully tissue-wrapped purchases. After she fucked him — and this would last for days, sometimes — she felt as if she had taken her middle finger and poked it in the eye of every flat-chested, narrow-hipped girlfriend, wife, and mother who never even registered her existence as they flicked through the racks of clothes and held up ties questioning aloud if this blue would match the blue in their Lilly Pulitzer dress. When she ignored him — his texts or calls or invitations for weekends away — the knowledge that she was both an object that he desired and the gatekeeper preventing him from having it filled her with delight. The pleasure of being lusted for was amplified by the consciousness that she might be the only thing he'd ever coveted that couldn't be his.

For nearly a year Olga rode this high, but now, finally, it had begun to wane. When it was just sex, she delighted in the affair, but lately Dick had been pressing for a real relationship, a circumstance that interested her not at all. Dick was tedious and needy in a way that she was repulsed by, yet felt compelled to indulge. He was sweet, but she found him simple: he'd married his college sweetheart, they had kids, he inherited his father's hardware store empire. He was competent enough to grow the business, but he was hardly an innovator. Even his divorce was boring. Because no one knew about their affair, the financial matters were settled quickly and quietly. And what, after twenty-six years of marriage to one person — five of which were completely sexless — did Dick then want to do? Just repeat the whole thing, but with another woman. No sooner did Dick move out than he was pressing Olga to move in. Had she been a different type of girl, one who valued her sanity less and inherited wealth more, perhaps Olga would have seen this as an opportunity. Instead, she could imagine nothing more boring than a life filled with the minutiae of Dick's personal wellness routine or intermittent fasting rituals designed to keep him "young." She couldn't imagine the horror of suffering a holiday with Victoria and her dough-faced husband, no matter how exotic the locale they were in. She also could not bear the thought of letting Dick get one more thing that he wanted.

After she rejected his offer to cohabitate, rather than cooling things off, his demands for her time and desire to go public as a couple only became more urgent. No one needs to know that we got together before I left Sheila, he would say, I can just tell people I couldn't get you out of my mind. If you think people would buy that, she'd reply, I've got a bridge to sell you. He was relentless. To provide them cover for getting reacquainted he went so far as to have the Historical Society, his pet charity, hire her to plan their annual gala honoring his generous support of their recent exhibit, "Free Markets and Freedom: Commerce in New York City." Dick had made good use of the time, luring her to his office under the guise of gala planning. And while Olga resented this move, she was not so resentful as to turn away the business. Instead, she began to sleep with other people, in a passive attempt to assert her independence and a reminder to herself that Dick Eikenborn did not own her. She had only the faintest qualms about her behavior, feeling justified that she had never made a commitment to Dick, but uneasy about why, then, she didn't just cut things off.

As she walked through the sleek lobby, past the security guard who waved her in, it occurred to her that this "thing" Dick had for her might be another of his juvenile euphemisms for sex. Dick had a millennial-like obsession with dirty texting. It was, after his oblivious sense of his own privilege, the thing she found the most annoying about him. There was seemingly no rhyme or reason to when he might send his missives, meaning Olga could be in the midst of a meeting, a wedding, or visiting her twelve-year-old niece, when suddenly a giant pic of Dick would pop up on her screen. This notion that his sex needs, thoughts, or desires were so pressing that they should be allowed to rupture her day was galling to her. She rode the elevator to the upper floors of the building where his suite of offices was, all the while becoming more convinced that this was a ploy for a midday tryst. She was not amused.

"Richard," she said, as she entered his office, "if this 'thing that I need' has anything to do with your penis, I'm walking out and I think we just might need to take a break from each other for a while."

He looked up from his computer and meal supplement shake.

"What's happening, Richard?" came a male voice from his speakerphone. It was only then that Olga realized that this was not a sex ploy.

"Background noise, Nick," Richard said

into the phone, shooting her a biting look. "I've got to go, but listen, our San Juan stores are doing well, so if you say there's more opportunity down there, I'm all ears. Charmaine will set some time with your office."

He hung up the phone, his face sour. "You were saying?"

"Oh." She grimaced. "Sorry? I guess I couldn't imagine what was so urgent that I needed to rush over here and thought maybe this was some kind of a ruse."

"Do I need a ruse?" Dick said, pouting.

Although life had rarely wounded Richard, Olga discovered that he bruised easily. In dramatic fashion. Like a baby's wail, it elicited a knee-jerk rush to comfort him. She stepped towards him, took his face between her hands, and pressed herself up against him.

"No, of course not. It's just been a hectic day."

He put his arms around her waist.

"I know, I know, busy woman! And I wouldn't have bothered you if it weren't for something I know will tickle you." With that he reached over to his desk and presented her with a neatly calligraphed envelope.

Mr. Richard Eikenborn III & Ms. Olga Acevedo

She knew what it was before she opened it. An invitation to the Blumenthal annual end-of-summer party in Easthampton. An event she had been angling to get invited to for years, and which, for several critical reasons, had taken on new urgency this season. Recently, Carl Blumenthal, the long-divorced host, had married Laurel, an actress of some acclaim who had reached an age too old to actually be cast in films, but just right for being the second or third wife of an aging billionaire. With her came a fresh, more glamorous guest list than this event — long a high point of the summer for the finance set — had known in previous years. Additionally, Laurel brought to the table her twenty-seven-year-old adopted daughter, herself an aspiring actress, and, more important to Olga, recently engaged. To a YouTube cooking celebrity, whatever that meant. Olga knew that if she had the chance to work that room, she would walk out with two or three new clients, and possibly the big fish themselves. Looming over all of this, though, was her knowledge that Meegan, her assistant, would be there. Meegan's boyfriend had been newly hired at Blumenthal's hedge fund and each year the top earners and first years were invited. A world where Meegan, by simply swiping right on an app, could be at a party Olga had unsuccessfully climbed her whole adult life to be invited to was an unjust one. Olga had been texting, calling, and setting up drink dates with anyone and everyone who might be able to correct the situation for weeks, but to no avail.

Now, here in her hands, was her golden ticket. How had Dick even known she wanted to go?

"So? What do you think? Is it a date?" he asked. "It should be a good party, right? I hear that Oprah is going to be there. So, if Oprah is there, everyone will be worrying about where they are in relation to Oprah and no one will be paying any attention to us, don't you think?"

Years before, Olga had worked with a genuinely lovely couple with quirky taste and gentle hearts. Together they conceived an untraditional, soulful wedding. A dawn ceremony in a forest; a dance party around a bonfire. But the parents — who were footing the bills — deemed it all "too weird" and insisted they undo all their plans. The bride pleaded with Olga to advocate for them, and she tried, but ultimately, she explained, with the purse come the strings. She thought of that as she looked at the envelope, their names written there, together.

As if he could read her mind, he suddenly said, "Carl's assistant plans his parties, you know. It was fine when they were sort of call the caterer, clambake, bachelor-pad kind of affairs, but now, with his new wife and all, they are putting him through it and he's at his wit's end — at least that's what he was telling Charmaine. Anyway, seems like it could be a nice piece of business up for grabs. Certainly, I'll put in a good word for you. . . ."

He took the invitation out of her hand, placing it back on his desk as he drew her near.

"I'll think about it."

"That's almost a yes, Cherry, and that makes me very happy."

She felt herself stiffen in his arms, knowing that she was trapped by his offer. She was too weak-willed to refuse this kind of access, and the fact of that repulsed her. She felt smothered already, knowing what accepting the invitation would mean.

"And God knows," Dick whispered in her ear, "won't the old Exeter guys be wide-eyed when I walk in with the sexiest woman on the planet."

March 1995

March 30, 1995

Querida Olga,
Though your Papi hated what he was made to do in Vietnam, he always felt grateful for the opportunity it gave him to see the larger world. To see that oppression existed beyond the borders of the barrio he grew up in. For someone your age, fresh perspective can be invaluable. It's why I was happy when Prieto decided to go upstate for college, and upset when he decided to move back home. Leaving home, getting space, it can be very helpful in teaching us who we are. It's an experience I wish I'd had at your age. I say all this to make clear: my issue is not with you moving away.

No, nena, my issue is with this school. This kind of school. These bourgeois institutions that do nothing but reaffirm that in a capitalist society there are those who are anointed to rule and those born to serve. Do not confuse admission for a chance at power. This kind of college has no place for you, even if they offered you one of their precious "affirmative action" spots. They do not want to teach your people's history; they don't want to read your people's books. They see no value in our culture, or the culture of any minority people. Your classmates won't be the children of factory workers or housekeepers or even teachers. They will be the children of bankers and politicians. Children of a ruling class waiting for their turn at bat.

What will you do there? It's dangerous at your young age to be surrounded by people who don't value who you are. Who don't understand you. A child can become lost.

I am sure that this opinion is unpopular. I bet you are being fawned over at school for the rare "achievement" of being admitted to an Ivy League college. That mi familia is so proud, so bowled over by the famous white names and faces that have gone there before you. So pleased that a place built on the back of slaves, funded by the sheep-like descendants of slave owners, run via nepotism towards advancing more of those descendants, took in someone like you. As if, somehow, you breaking into that system, your intelligence being affirmed by this institution, means that they, too, have accomplished something. I can imagine how my brother Richie is crowing! That somehow this means our family is an "exception" to every worst belief about our people.

Olga, don't delude yourself. This means none of these things. Yes, you are bright. But you are also pretty and fair skinned and speak in a way that doesn't rub white skin the wrong way. Your admittance to this place is nothing more than a minuscule gesture to reaffirm the myth of an American meritocracy, one that makes this school feel benevolent without damaging their elitist system. A system in which the only thing you're certain to lose is your sense of self.

And, of course, your money. I won't even waste my time discussing the ridiculous debt you will take on to do this. You will barely get your start in the world and be shackled already: your choices hampered, your options reduced. Debt is one of The Man's great tools for keeping people of color oppressed. But, of course, you know that.

I must tell you, I resent you involving your Auntie Karen in all of this, asking her to write you that letter of recommendation. You put her in a terrible position, as even she, who is aware of my feelings about this, seems enchanted about this "opportunity" for you. For your photography. For your mind. That was what she called it. An opportunity. To this, I ask, for what? An opportunity to forget the values with which you were raised? To be surrounded by people who don't understand you or where you are from or what you were born to fight for?

At the end of the day, though, this is your life. One that will be defined by choices that you make. All I can do, as your mother, is express myself.

Pa'lante,
Mami

■ ■ ■ ■

August 2017

■ ■ ■ ■

Sylvia's Social Club

It was the golden hour when Olga found herself on what she imagined was one of the last undeveloped corners of Williamsburg, navigating the broken concrete sidewalks in her heels. The sun's last light so strong, it gilded the weeds that had popped up between the cracks. She passed an empty lot filled with old cars and a swing set, fenced in with chain link. The three-story, brick-front apartment building that cradled its left side was emblazoned with a spray-painted mural that paid homage, with improbable success, to the Puerto Rican flag, the coquí, Lolita Lebrón, Héctor Lavoe, and Big Pun, all at once. Underneath it said #respecttheanscestors and, as she read it, Olga reflexively made the sign of the cross, lowering her eyes as she did so. When she looked up, she noticed Matteo, seated at a card table outside the building, deeply invested in a game of dominos with three older, wrinkled men. They all four wore guayaberas and their bare forearms grasping at the dominos formed a melanin-rich ombré that Olga found beautiful.

"Hi," she said, finding herself a bit shy.

"Hey, hey!" he said, jumping up and breaking the rainbow right in the middle. "Caballeros, you'll excuse me, but, frankly, something better has come my way."

The viejitos surveyed her quickly.

"Bendición," one of them said to her.

She winked at him in response and he laughed. It had been a while since she'd been blessed by a man, of any age, in the streets, this pleasurable spark of Brooklyn life largely extinguished by gentrification. It delighted her and made her homesick for Sunset Park all at once. How could one be homesick for a place just a few miles away? She made a mental note to go back to the neighborhood and see her niece that weekend.

Olga realized now that they were outside a bar, of sorts, though she'd only discovered that by looking inside the door, which was propped open with a Bustelo coffee can filled with pennies and screws. The interior was dark, the space paneled with wood that absorbed what little light came through the small windows on either side of the door.

The bar itself was clearly handmade, the top nothing more than a Formica kitchen counter, the stools a shiny gold glitter vinyl, the back bar festooned with blinking Christmas lights despite it being August. There was a pool table in the back and a disco ball over the center of the room, card tables and folding chairs scattered around the edges of the place. Faded covers from the *Post* and the *Daily News* sports pages featuring Bobby Bonilla and Jorge Posada were taped onto the walls, flanking both sides of an oil painting of Roberto Clemente, done, it seemed to Olga, by the same artist as the mural outside. She spotted the jukebox — the old-fashioned kind, no debit cards welcome here — tucked in the corner. Cheo Feliciano played in the background. The only thing up-to-date in the whole place was a small flat-screen TV mounted on a wall, which Olga instinctively knew was for baseball and baseball only. She was surprised it wasn't on now.

"What is this place?" she asked, slightly incredulous.

"Sylvia's Social Club. The last of the Puerto Rican social clubs. There used to be a ton of them, but you know rules, regulations, that kind of thing, most of them closed. I got the sense that you were into a good dive bar, so I thought you might dig this spot."

"I mean," she said, beaming, "this is real-deal Brooklyn. I can't believe no one has torn it down and erected a high-rise. Is this place even legal?"

Matteo chuckled. "Why? You too upright a citizen to patronize an unpermitted establishment?"

She laughed, too, as they sat on a couple of the barstools. A woman came out of the restroom, uttering apologies in Spanish, rushing to her place behind the bar and immediately pouring out a rum, neat, for Matteo and a small foam bowl of peanuts for them to share.

"To answer your first question, believe me, they have been trying for years to get Sylvia to sell, and she won't budge. Isn't that right, Sylvia?"

Sylvia winked at him. "Oye, Matteo, it isn't mine to sell. This place is for the community, isn't that what you always say?" She turned to Olga. "And what can I get you, mami?"

"Same for me is good."

She poured her a glass, and Olga took a sip.

"Wow!" she said. The rum was smooth and rich with spice.

"Sí, ¿verdad?" Sylvia's raised her eyebrows. "This is the good stuff. They don't even sell this here; you can only get it on the island. I always keep a bottle here, just for him." She patted Matteo's hand.

"To answer your second question," Matteo continued, "Sylvia's all aboveboard, aren't you, señora? It was too risky with all those developers lurking around."

"Ay, Matteo." Sylvia swatted her dish towel at him playfully. "You're making an honest woman out of me! I'll be in the back, but holler if you need me, honey."

She was in her late sixties, Olga figured. The skin around her ample décolletage — the same golden brown as the rum they sipped — had begun to crepe and was adorned with several gold necklaces and religious medallions. She wore shorts a bit too short for her age and wedge sandals that elongated her very shapely legs. Her hair, a shade of dark blond that matched her jewelry, was pulled up into a soft bouffant, large gold hoops showing off her long neck. She was, Olga thought, beautiful.

"Is she flirting with you?" Olga whispered when she was sure Sylvia had sauntered away.

"Is that jealousy in your voice?"

"Jealous? Please! Not every Latina is the

jealous type, you know."

"And certainly not you, ye with the New England ice in her veins."

She laughed. "What do you have against New England? If I'm not mistaken, you went to school there, too."

"Exactly, and that's why I know of what I speak. They have a very specific way of letting you know what they think, without exactly saying it, if you know what I mean."

"Well that's definitely true, but how is that not just tact?" Olga asked.

"Because tact is, by definition, meant to spare people's feelings and New England is designed to make you feel like an outsider. I mean, didn't you?"

"Feel like an outsider? Hmm. There's this myth that white Americans don't have a culture, but they absolutely do, and New England is the cradle of it. So, I felt a bit like an anthropologist."

"So, that said . . ." Matteo took another sip of his drink. "I have to ask. How did your parents feel about your . . . anthropological studies of the white elite?"

She felt her cheeks redden with anxiety at the direction this conversation was taking. As if he knew what she was thinking, Matteo continued.

"Don't worry, I wasn't going through your

drawers or anything." He put his hand on her knee and gave it a squeeze. "All I did was look at the stuff that was out in the open. You can't be mad at a brother for being observant. Well, maybe *you* could be, but generally, it's not socially acceptable grounds for anger."

She exhaled and took another sip of her drink.

"Okay. Fine. Hit me. Ask what you really want to ask."

"Well, I guess I did. But I can get more specific. It appears, based on that photo you keep out on top of your desk, that your parents were members of the Young Lords Party — one of, if not the singular, large-scale paramilitary pro-socialist Puerto Rican political protest organizations in American history. The Puerto Rican equivalent of Black Panthers. They were dedicated to toppling a capitalist, racist society, bringing social and environmental justice to inner-city minorities, and, of course, liberating Puerto Rico. And now, you, their daughter, seem to have found a way to make a living — a living that, despite the shoddy construction of your apartment building, seems pretty lucrative, if I may be so observant, but, if I may further observe, is a living reliant upon embracing the very people and values that your parents were trying to topple less than a generation before. So, my question is, how do your parents feel about that?"

A moment of thick silence passed between them. Olga stared at Matteo, her face blank. La Lupe was coming from the jukebox, and in the distance the sound of a motorcycle crew out for a summer night ride. Olga slapped the bar top and hopped off her barstool.

"You know what, fuck you." Her hard-suppressed South Brooklyn accent jumped off her tongue as her chest and neck grew hot with anger. "Fuck. You. I really don't know who the fuck you think you are, judging me, or what kind of fucking wack idea of a date you have in your head that you text a bitch nonstop for a week trying to get together, drag me out to bumblefuck Williamsburg just to take up my time by insulting me and how I make my fucking —"

Matteo grabbed her waist with one arm and, with his other hand, took hold of her hand, which seconds before had been shaking in his face, and kissed her. Intellectually, Olga knew that this was a cheap ploy to calm her righteous anger, but physically, she felt a surge that made the walls of her vagina contract, sending a charge up her spine, relaxing her shoulders, loosening her neck until her head dipped back in full surrender. Her intellectual resistance melting in recognition that this was why she had shown up to bumblefuck in the first place.

"Listen," Matteo said, when they finally broke apart. He took hold of her hands in his and caressed them as he looked into her eyes. "I'm going to ask you to try and suspend disbelief for a moment and hear me out here: I'm not trying to diss you. I'm really not. My time at college was wasted. I did not learn the ways of the people of New England. I have no tact. I'm just genuinely curious about you. It's not every day I get to meet a smart, sexy Brooklyn girl. That's why I've been blowing up your phone and trying to drag you out to dive bars since we met. I just want to get to know you. I'm not good with small talk. I ask bad questions. I'm a bit of an asshole. And who the fuck would I ever be to judge you and the values of your profession? I'm a native Brooklynite earning my living as a fucking Realtor in gentrified Brooklyn. So, please, sit and let's just get to know each other a little bit, okay?"

Olga looked at him and sat back down. She could hear kids outside squealing in play and wondered if it was possible that somewhere in the borough of Kings adults still opened fire hydrants for children to dance in on hot summer days.

"Let's change the topic," he said. "Why don't you ask me a question? Anything you want to know."

She looked around for a second and back at him, trying to glean something she couldn't articulate. She felt a bit out of her element.

"Yeah," she finally said. "You play dominos, you know the salsa classics, and you certainly seem to be a regular here. But, I don't think you're actually even Puerto Rican. Am I right?"

Matteo put his hands on his heart, his face grimaced.

"Ah! You've called me out! You really do know how to poke a man where it hurts. I didn't pass the smell test. Damn. What gave me away?"

"Honestly? You know too much of our history. Dead giveaway. This begets another question, though. We're a wonderful people and all, but why do you want to be one of us so bad in the first place?"

"That's a longer answer that requires more rum and some better music, but let's get ourselves sorted and then I'm more than happy to tell you."

They spent the next forty-five minutes taking turns picking songs that the other simply "had to hear" and nursing another glass of rum, telling stories of Old Brooklyn, discovering common ground they had shared while never quite crossing paths: the *Kids* days of Washington Square Park, hanging out at Fat Beats, Sundays at the Tunnel. People that they inevitably knew in common.

Eventually, Matteo told her the story of his Jewish mother and Black father and their divorce, after which his father faded into his native Los Angeles, leaving his biracial son with his white mother in South Slope, Brooklyn. When he would play in the street with the other kids on the block, people always assumed that little Matteo, with his lightly freckled café-con-leche skin and tight head of curls, belonged to the Puerto Rican family who lived next door, and after a while, Matteo kind of felt the same way. He would be at all their family gatherings, sometimes dragging his mother, sometimes alone. He learned to dance, he learned to play dominos, he even learned how to cook.

After high school he got a partial scholarship to Bennington College, where he planned to study music composition, but soon discovered he would leave with more debt than he had talent. He switched his major to political economy, wrote a letter to one of the few other Bennington alumni interested in making money, and landed himself a job at an investment bank. The annual bonuses made it easy to forget he was the only Black guy he saw all day who didn't work in the mail room. He bought a loft in SoHo, DJ'd parties downtown to keep life interesting, and did a ton of coke, so it all ran smoothly.

Then his mother was diagnosed with stage 4 ovarian cancer. She had always wanted to go to Hawaii, to see the sunrise on Haleakalā, so he took time off to take her. They woke in the middle of the night to drive up the winding road to the top of the volcano where it was as dark and cold as outer space, so high up that clouds embraced them with their cold mist. When the sun rose, revealing the planet around them to be a terrifyingly vast and beautiful space, he looked over and saw his mother was crying. They drove down the volcano in silence, against the bright of the morning. When Matteo saw a pay phone, he pulled over, called his office, and told them that he quit. He moved out of the loft, stopped DJ'ing the parties, and cared for his mother until she died. And then, knowing no other family other than the people on his block, decided to stay.

Olga was touched. And enchanted. As a kid, she'd been embarrassed by the complexity of her family story. The nuance required to understand it escaped most people. By the time she hit high school she felt exhausted of explaining it, and simply resigned herself to not revisiting the past with strangers. But Matteo's life trajectory, and his openness about it, made her feel a glimmer of possibility that this time she might be understood.

Open Your Eyes

It was her turn.

"By the time I left for college," Olga started, "Papi was already dead, so he had no opinion, and my mom was gone, so she didn't have too much say in the matter, but no, she wasn't happy about me going to that school. Far too bougie for her tastes."

Sylvia had just poured them their third round of rum. Outside, the sky had turned to twilight and the domino players had moved their game to a back table. Matteo had very carefully avoided asking her any more direct questions, but she felt relaxed and strangely eager to talk about an aspect of her life that rarely saw the light of day.

"I was twelve, almost thirteen when she left us. Or maybe it's more accurate to say when she didn't come back, because the truth is, my mom was in and out for as long as I could remember. They joined the Young Lords together, my parents. They had already been together for a minute by then, already activists. My Papi was one of the dudes who took over Brooklyn College. So, joining the Lords was an extension of what they were both already committed to. But my dad was older. He'd already gone to Vietnam. I think by the time the Lords collapsed, he was just tired. Depleted. They had my brother and then me, and he was into being a dad. Wanted to have a normal life. Or normal-ish.

"My mom though? I think she got this early taste of being part of change and couldn't shake it. She tried teaching, tried to 'settle down,' but she was always getting called somewhere — Latin America, South Africa. Always off to a fight; always on the road. They grew apart, he moved out. And then one day she just didn't come back."

"Where'd she go? Your mom, I mean," Matteo asked.

Olga shrugged. "We don't really know. . . . Actually, you seem to know your Puerto Rican history. Have you heard of Los Macheteros?"

"I can't say that I have."

"Let's just say that they were a group very committed to a free Puerto Rico. More pre-Mecca Malcolm than Martin, if you get my drift?"

"Ahhh," Matteo said.

"Well, it seems for a time she was in P.R. with them. Then, we'd heard she was in Cuba. My brother, he's got a friend at the FBI who let him see her file a few years back. The last time someone had seen her she was in Mexico with the fucking Zapatistas. But that was years ago. The only person who probably knows her location with certainty is her best friend Karen, but she'd go to the grave before she shared that information."

"Hold up," Matteo now whispered, "are you saying your mother's a fugitive?"

Olga laughed. "Damn, my mom has even got you whispering! ¡Bienvenido a mi vida! She brings out the paranoia in all of us. I swear me and my brother literally have code names for her and shit." She laughed again. "But seriously, is she a fugitive? I suspect my brother knows more, but honestly? I try not to ask too many questions."

"Plausible deniability, and all."

"Exactly!" Olga laughed.

"But you hear from her? You've talked to her?" Matteo asked.

"Hear from her? Hell yes. Talk to her? Not quite. She sends these letters. She's always managed to keep tabs on us, somehow always knows what we're up to, but we know nothing about her. It's creepy, frankly. And frustrating. There are 'Brothers and Sisters in the movement' that we either don't or barely know, who know how to reach her. Who pass her letters along. Who've probably even seen her, but me and my brother haven't. Not in over twenty-five years. Isn't that fucking crazy?" She laughed even though it wasn't funny.

Matteo put his hand over hers.

"My mom has been gone for ten years and it's been the hardest ten years of my life, so yes, that is fucking crazy. I can't even imagine how hard that was."

Olga sighed. This topic always made her irritable and defensive. When her mother was first gone, young Olga was despondent for months. One day she overheard two teachers talking about her at school. Poor Olga. How sad. Her father a junkie. Her mother ran off. Poor little girl. The pity dripping from their voices. Being the subject of such sentiment disgusted her, made her feel small. She vowed to fix her face, to don a mask impenetrable to ruth. That instinct — to put the mask on — rose again now. She tried to shrug it off. To try something different this time. To tell the whole truth.

"Yeah. Actually. I don't talk about this much but yes, it was really fucking hard.

Especially at night. In my dreams she would disappear. Vanish right in front of me. And I would wake up crying. But you know. Eventually I bucked up. I mean, I'd get angry and stuff. At her and my dad, for leaving us. But, you know, revolution requires sacrifice, as my parents would say."

"But," Matteo interrupted, "you were just a kid. You didn't choose to join a fucking revolution!"

Olga laughed, a genuine belly laugh now.

"Matteo. You're a Black man in America. You were drafted into a revolution the day you were born, like it or not."

Matteo chuckled and raised his glass. "Well, damn."

"I'm kidding, but I'm not, right? See, my parents raised us, me and my brother, on an 'all power to the people' doctrine. 'Liberation' was the highest calling. So, what my mother did was, to some degree, noble. Or at least I knew I was supposed to see it that way. And at the end of the day, she didn't leave us on a street corner. We were with her mother — who I was always closer to, anyway. My father was still alive when she left. And of course, I had my brother. When my dad got sick, he moved home from college and everything. Just to be near me. So, I never felt abandoned, per se. I just started to feel like she was a soldier we'd lost to a war. Which, we kind of did."

"So." Matteo proceeded with caution. "Since you brought up your brother, I gotta ask —"

Olga laughed. "Hmm. I hope you're smart enough not to talk shit about my brother."

"Nope. Not me. I learned my lesson. But . . . you've got to see why people find him a bit schmaltzy, right? That whole schtick when he was being held 'political prisoner' for, like, five minutes, and then got released and was paraded home? And this part I remember from the New York 1 loop like it was yesterday! My man was paraded home, draped in the Puerto Rican flag while sitting in the back of a convertible, like his own one-man Puerto Rican Day parade float. I mean, come on, how is that not political theater?"

"Damn," Olga said, giggling while she tried to sound serious. "You're really testing me! First of all, my brother was a legitimate political prisoner. He went down to Vieques with Reverend Al and was arrested protesting military bombings there, okay? Second of all, it was pure coincidence that they placed him in a jail — for thirty fucking days, mind you — that happened to be in his district. Third of all, that was my Tío

Richie's convertible and we can't help it if he's flashy. Nor could we have planned that they would have released him on the eve of the actual P.R. parade."

Her argument fell apart because by now she was laughing too hard. "Okay! I can see how, combined, it may have come across as a little gimmicky."

Matteo laughed with her. "Was just trying to make a point about how someone not related to him might see things from the outside is all."

She sighed. "Truth be told, I have no use for politicians. Especially Puerto Rican ones. When I was little, my father would have these little history classes for us. Every Wednesday night — that was his day. We'd learn all the Puerto Rican history and American history nobody was teaching in schools. My takeaway? Politicians were always the sellouts, pushing our people down a river. Sometimes not even for money, just for approval by the Yanqui, as my parents would say.

"Prieto? My brother got all those same lessons and came out believing he could be different.

"My mother thinks what I'm doing is stupid and I'm not sure I disagree. I'm absolutely 'a slave to the capitalist needs of the White Man.' Worst of all, I really enjoy money. My brother though? He doesn't give a shit about any of that. All these City Council guys, these guys in Congress, pocketing this or that kickback so they can buy a house or send their kids to private school? My brother still lives in my grandmother's house.

"My mother'd like to topple the system, but my brother? He genuinely wants to fix it. For people like us. And he's not perfect — he's a little naïve, he's a people pleaser — but I also know we're better off that it's him in office versus some other crooked motherfucker."

"Olga, you think you're so cynical, but you could break into 'The Greatest Love of All' right about now."

"My brother just brings that out in me!" Olga sang. "But, I am cynical. Because I understand all the problems, I just fundamentally don't believe we can fix them. However, I fully support those on the bottom taking as much advantage of the top as humanly possible."

Matteo began to sing.

How gratifying for once to know,
that those above will serve those down
below!

Olga stared at him, quizzically. "I dig the sentiment, but don't think I know that one."

"Sondheim. Yeah . . ." He grew bashful. "Musical theater was big in my high school. I was on stage crew. Anyway . . ."

"You have a good voice," she answered awkwardly.

"I'll tell you what, though, girl." He raised his eyebrows mischievously. "I'm an okay singer, but I'm a hell of a dancer."

The bar was more crowded now, mostly old guys playing pool and dominos, a couple dancing a bachata on the dance floor. He called out to Sylvia to turn on the disco ball, and he headed to the jukebox. Bobby Caldwell started singing about opening your eyes to the possibilities that love could bring and Olga slammed down her rum so she could join him on the dance floor, as dizzy and bright as the electric disco ball that illuminated them.

June 2001

June 15, 2001

Mijo,
My heart is swollen with pride as I write this. The world now knows what I've known since you were a little boy: my son is a natural-born revolutionary. A fighter for the people of Borikén.

I was skeptical when I heard you were running for public office. More than a few Brothers from the Lords went in this direction and I found that participating within the system forced them to compromise their values. Watered down their sense of right and wrong. But when I saw you being taken off of Vieques — our stolen land — with the news cameras following you, I realized I'd been wrong. Suddenly the media — and the world — had their eyes on Puerto Rico and its struggles. I recognized what you, bendito, had already figured out: your platform as an elected official will enable you to do more for the liberation of the Puerto Rican people than working as a community activist ever could.

Prieto, any time in prison can change someone. Can bring on a certain darkness. When the public adulation ends, these next few weeks and even months may feel hard for you. We'd see Brothers from the Lords go away and come back totally different men. Even your Papi, when they sent him to Rikers for the CUNY protests, was changed. It was only two weeks, but when people treat you as less than human for even a day, it can haunt you. So, you have to do your best to just keep going. Pa'lante. With your eyes on the next fight.

But also, when I think about it, one thing your Papi had, that my Brothers in the Lords had too, was somebody to come home to. Someone to be soft with when they took off the armor they needed to survive in the White Man's world. While generally I worry that romance can be a distraction for activists, I think in your case, with the right person, it could be an advantage. It was easy to win your first election as a young bachelor, but as you age, un muchacho tan guapo como tú still out there in the field? Well, it makes people less excited and more skeptical.

For what my opinion is worth, mijo, it might be a good thing for you to take a wife. To have a good, strong woman by your side. Think of all you could do in the world if you didn't have to do it all by yourself?

Pa'lante,
Mami

P.S. Speaking of relationships, please talk to your sister. This man will hobble her. She'll listen to you.

August 2017

The Whip

The summer air was hot and thick, but Prieto rolled the windows down anyway, knowing that soon enough, he'd be driving fast, the velocity forcing the air to hit him in the face, again and again. The only thing that, after these meetings, he felt could cleanse his sense of shame. He removed his tie, unbuttoned his collar, and rolled up his monogrammed shirtsleeves. As he started the engine, he turned on the stereo, steadily raising the volume. By the time he pulled out of the parking garage, the car vibrated from the bass line of his soundtrack, the aggressive hip-hop beat piercing the late-night quiet of the Upper East Side and numbing his mind. He cut a left north onto Park Avenue, heading further uptown, hoping to extend his thirty-minute drive into one of necessary length for him to compartmentalize and rationalize his latest act of cowardice. Hoping that by tomorrow he could get up and attempt, in small ways, to atone for the sins he had set into motion so many years before. Sometimes, when he needed to settle his nerves this way, he would drive around the entirety of Manhattan, finding himself grounded by the water and the flickering lights of the outer-borough landscape. Tonight, he worried the island might not be big enough to do the job.

Prieto ran nearly every morning, lifted weights, even took the occasional yoga class, but nothing calmed him quite the way a drive did, his whip his fortress of solitude. Always with the music blasting, always with the windows open, even in the winter when the air bit, unless it was raining or snowing. It had been this way since he was first able to drive, and Abuelita got a call that his father needed to be bailed out of Rikers for some fucking crackhead shit that he was always getting into then. It was spring of Prieto's senior year, a Friday, and he was watching TV with one of his homeboys when the phone rang and then, a minute or so later, Abuelita called him into the kitchen. "Bendito, your Papi got into a little trouble and we need to get him some help." Prieto remembered the lump that formed in his throat when she told him what kind of help he needed, the feeling of heat that came with shame. *Yo, son, I gotta bounce and go get my sister* was the lie he told his friend. Lying, a survival tactic he mastered quickly. He remembered thinking the ground would swallow him up before he let anyone know where he was going and why.

Olga was out somewhere, likely being scandalous; she was never home in those days. So, he told his abuela he could go by himself, so the house wouldn't be empty if she came back. She gave him the keys to the hooptie she used, and he drove. The very first drive he'd ever taken alone. The car had a cassette player and before he left, he ran to his room to grab a tape — a Wu-Tang mix he'd gotten at the Fulton Mall after school. He blasted it and by the time he was crossing the bridge and could see the prison in the distance, he felt placid. Far from happy, but calm. Able to manage the process of going through security, showing his newly minted driver's license as a form of ID, extracting the exact bail from the envelope of cash — in mostly $10s, $5s, and $1s — that his grandmother had given him for this purpose. He was able to breathe as he sat in the plastic bucket seat in the waiting area behind the thick glass, waiting for them to bring his father out, gaunt, legs and hands cuffed together like he had done more than try to steal a TV. When the officer said, "I don't know much, but I know we'll be seeing you back here, son," Prieto wasn't sure if he meant to bail out his pops or as a criminal himself, but he was able to say, with calm and certainty, "No, I don't think that you will."

His father kissed his cheek as he'd always done when he greeted his son. Papi was tired. Prieto didn't know if that was him coming off a crack high or having doped up in jail. It was hard to tell with his father sometimes, but he had hunted him down enough to know that, up or down, when Papi wanted to get high, he would find a way. Prieto let him lie across the back seat. He changed the tape in the car to Joe Bataan, knowing it would please his father and it did; he sang along before he drifted into sleep. In this way, they drove home. Prieto pulled up to the little house on Thirty-seventh Street between Second and Third, where his Tío JoJo's friend rented Papi a basement apartment on the condition that he didn't smoke crack there. The rent was only $200 a month, but Prieto knew that JoJo, Lola, and Richie had been taking turns covering it the past few months. (They didn't complain, but you hear things.) His father was out like a light, so

Prieto climbed into the back to shake him awake, and that was when he saw it, on his father's neck — the KS lesion. He didn't even know that's what it was called, but he knew what it was — the mark of the beast, really. The mark of death. His heart raced. He carried his father out of the back seat and into the tiny apartment, wondering to himself how the fuck this homie had ever even been able to carry a TV when he didn't weigh more than a TV himself.

The room: a portrait of a tragedy. A Puerto Rican flag hung on the wall, and next to it Papi's Lords beret. A record player lay on the ground flanked on either side by what must have been a hundred records. The mattress was on the floor, a crate as a nightstand next to it, on top of which was a bare-bulbed lamp, a copy of *The General in His Labyrinth,* and, to Prieto's quiet horror, Papi's works, the needle in a cup of water, pink with blood. He set his father out on the bed and thought to himself: He'll be high again before the sun comes up. Prieto got back into the car, drove into Bay Ridge, east onto the Belt Parkway, before he ultimately did what he had long wanted and turned the beat-up sedan around to make his way over to the piers off Christopher Street by the West Side Highway.

If the needle was Papi's release, this was his.

Prieto had thought himself street smart, but he'd been a simpleton when he arrived on the political scene nearly seventeen years ago. A Pollyanna was what the City Council speaker had called Prieto when he first assumed office and was asked what his side business was going to be.

"Side business?" Prieto asked, genuinely confused. "I think my job representing Sunset Park isn't going to leave me much room for a side business."

The speaker had laughed, clapped his hand on his back, and said, "Turns out our political dynamo is a real Pollyanna." The nickname stuck, at least his first term, as he was genuinely shocked each time he discovered a new act of corruption or self-dealing going on with his colleagues.

They almost all had side businesses based in their districts. From pizzerias to laundromats to small accounting shops. Always storefronts that looked, to their constituents, like investments in their communities, but in reality were vehicles to clean the money that passed into their hands to secure votes for policies and measures favorable to a class of people living far from the neighborhoods they were representing. So much of this was happening in the open, or the near open, that, when discussing upcoming votes or meetings people were taking with developers and financiers, they would sometimes look Prieto's way and say, "Pollyanna doesn't have a problem with this, right?" This was their way of reminding him that if he wanted to play by the rules, no problem, as long as he didn't fuck stuff up for the rest of them. It was his sister who pointed out to him that he could work this to his advantage, parlaying his silence into leverage over his colleagues for votes on matters that would benefit his small idyll of South Brooklyn, an area that, in those days, commanded very little attention in the city.

Sometimes, when he contemplated the direction of his life, he felt his wounds were self-inflicted. He ran for office because everyone ignored his neighborhood — the board of education and their overcrowded schools, the cops (except when they shot kids in the street with impunity), the sanitation department, elected officials. These days, all eyes were on Sunset Park, and it was he, Prieto, who had put them there. For better and for worse.

Before his mom bounced, Prieto had planned on applying to colleges outside of

New York. He was desperate for some distance from what had heretofore been his life. His aunt took him to D.C. to see American and Georgetown; he sat in on classes at Howard. But when his senior year rolled around, his mom was gone, and his dad was in a bad way, and Prieto's brain hurt just thinking about filling out those financial aid forms. Whose income tax return did he use? The Radical or the Junkie? So, he applied to a bunch of SUNYs and wound up at Buffalo.

He joined a Latino Greek figuring that, with his own family in shambles, having some brothers might not be a bad thing. It turned into his lifeline. Pledging, living with his line brothers, the public vow of silence, wearing the uniform for nearly eight weeks. It provided him with structure and closeness at a time when he'd felt alone and flailing. His brothers held him up when no one in his own family could.

He'd started college wanting to become Brooklyn's Johnny Cochran: using law to fight police brutality. But an environmental justice class he took made him realize that the cops were just one small thread of a tightly woven system of discrimination. He was shaken to discover how systemically government and industry had imperiled the health of minority communities for convenience and profit. The course opened his eyes and invigorated him in a way his parents' Brown Power rhetoric never had. By the middle of his sophomore year, his father was in full-blown crisis. No one asked Prieto to come back, but he wanted to be there for his family. With Tía Lola's help he proved he was "legally emancipated" and transferred to NYU with a full ride, commuting to class from Abuelita's. It was right around this time that the city was trying to erect a waste-processing plant in Sunset Park, just a few blocks from their home. He emailed his line brothers saying, "I'm not religious, but God brought me home to fight this." He linked up with the Latino Youth League and the Community Board and made arguments so eloquent, he wanted to tape them and mail them to his professor up at Buffalo, just to let him know he'd been listening. The *Daily News, The New York Times,* even the *Post* covered their fight and the city buckled under the pressure. He'd found his calling.

Then, just a year later, despite public outcry, outside the light of day in a not-quite-legal move, the waste-processing plant seemed to have arisen overnight. By this time, Prieto was in law school. He was livid and scrappy — filing motions as a private citizen against the city, doing presentations on community health impact for the City Council. He was handsome and eloquent. The news cameras loved him; he was the perfect salve for White Guilt. He had been practicing law and running a campaign to block a prison expansion when the local Democrats came to suggest he might run for the City Council seat that was opening up. Prieto couldn't think of a better way to protect his 'hood.

He'd just started his second term on the Council when an envelope came through the mail slot of his office. It was hand printed, the card inside engraved, inviting him to dinner at a private residence on the Upper East Side. It had no return address or contact information and Prieto's assistant was about to throw it in the trash when the phone rang. The caller was confirming that the invitation was received and hoped that Councilman Acevedo would not be skipping their dinner. The timing freaked the secretary the fuck out and she ran into his office saying that she had canceled everything on his calendar before and after this dinner. He called one of his frat brothers who worked in real estate to see what he knew about the building.

"That address is nothing but money. I think they print it in the basement. The Selbys have two units in there. Both the brothers."

In a city of real estate dynasties, the Selbys were one of New York's most prominent. The father had spearheaded the redevelopment of Bryant Park a generation before, and the sons had sunk a fortune into redeveloping the Lower East Side, to mixed results. But, in the aftermath of September 11, they found opportunity. With downtown desolate of people, filled with dust, and backlogged by slow insurance payouts, and with landlords unable to collect rent, the brothers headed to Ground Zero with literal carloads of cash. Betting that the desire for immediate relief from misery would obscure any misgivings. The people — the small business tenants, condo owners, the landlords — certain that nothing could be built on top of all this tragedy, that nothing would ever be possible on this square of misery — thought them fools. In a highly public news conference, the Selby brothers unveiled a broad plan for the area, where, on a windy day, trapped ashes from the fallen buildings might still unwedge themselves and flurry the air with death.

The city, for its part, thought the Selbys Heroes of Hope — that's what the mayor called them — and Prieto's colleagues moved to reward them as such with tax breaks upon tax breaks. Who, in the wake of such disaster, wouldn't support such entrepreneurial vision? For his part, Prieto was unsettled by any one family scooping up such concentrated plots of land, tax free, but sensed that public morale was too low for such cynicism. Besides, as his sister pointed out to him, with all of his colleagues from the Manhattan districts on Selby payroll of some form or another, why squander the political capital by raising the issue? Just quietly vote against it. No need to poke an urban bear.

Which is why, when he realized that it was this very bear summoning him to their ultra-luxurious, doorman-and-private-elevator-entry-actual-motherfucking-Picasso-in-the-foyer-and-a-maid-in-an-actual-motherfucking-maid-outfit lair, he knew it could be nothing good. Prieto had never given much thought to The Man. The notion of one mythical, monolithic, rich, powerful White Man puppeteering the lives of people of color to keep them dancing in service of his larger plan seemed far too simplistic to serve the complex issue of systemic oppression very well. But, on that spring night in 2003, after the maid took his briefcase and the butler escorted him to a dining room half a city block away, passing a museum's worth of fine art en route, Prieto found himself thinking, if The Man existed, this would certainly be his apartment. He had made it a point to arrive fifteen minutes early — no person of color serious about being taken seriously was ever late to meet white people — but the two Selby brothers were already seated, napkins on their laps and wine poured. In that moment Prieto knew he'd already lost whatever battle he was about to fight. No matter what he had mentally prepared for, they were already a step ahead. It was a setup.

A place was laid for him, but where a plate would have been was an envelope. He sat and opened it, looking to their faces for a tell and finding none. He pulled out the photos and inhaled deeply; the first showed him fellating a man in what was clearly his own apartment, the next featured his face visible during intercourse, his partner clad in leather. He exhaled and stood up.

"I have to be honest, gentlemen. What have you got here? Some photos? Of me with a man? New York's a very liberal city; this is hardly leverage."

"New York is quite liberal, Councilman," the elder brother, Arthur, said, "but you're not the councilman for Chelsea or the West Village. You represent, as you so proudly say whenever a camera is near, Sunset Park. And I'm not so sure the Catholics and the macho Hispanic community you speak for would be quite as happy to be represented by — what's the slang your people use?"

Nick, the younger, chimed in: "Maricón, Arthur." He seemed pleased with his Spanish.

"We don't think your district would want to be represented by a maricón, Councilman, and we're prepared to put a lot of resources into making sure that they aren't."

When looking back on that night — the beginning of the collapse of who he had thought he was — Prieto often wondered how things might have played out had he been just a bit more courageous. Would anyone have cared who he slept with? How might he have responded if he'd found himself in that dining room a year, or even two, later? Once Ellen's talk show got its footing, or after Jim McGreevey came out? After his grandmother had died? What might his whole life have looked like? But at that moment, the idea of his most private life becoming public paralyzed him with fear.

"What is it that you need?" Prieto had asked.

"When the vote comes up," the younger brother replied, "you'll know."

They were right. As soon as the proposal was put forward to clear the path for the Bush Terminal Warehouses to be redeveloped by the Selby brothers, he knew what he was expected to do. For more than a generation, Bush Terminal had housed the industrial and garment factories that put food on many a table in the neighborhood. Abuelita had worked as a seamstress there, and of course Papi worked there until he wasn't able to work. Then, little by little, they all closed. Moved to Jersey or, more commonly, offshore, to places where people worked for even less money than the poor of Sunset Park. On its face, there was nothing wrong with encouraging some development in this dormant area, whose most robust commercial activity was a brisk drug and sex trade. Yet, Prieto knew this would do nothing for the area but quicken the ascent of rents, offering little by way of job opportunities, tax revenue, or even amenities for the working poor who made up his electorate. Prieto, the local hero, the straight man, would have fought for more. But, Prieto, the compromised, the closeted homosexual — which he wasn't even sure that he would call himself, it was just that when fucking men, he felt his most unbound — that guy folded like a fucking shirt. He voted to move the project forward. He gave a press conference about how this would attract new people from all over Brooklyn for cuchifritos and the wonders of Eighth Avenue's Chinatown, knowing full well that this would never happen. No one who went to the Selby brothers' waterfront supermall would ever venture into the real neighborhood.

Prior to this, he'd resigned himself to a compartmentalized life. One where his sexual desires were placed inside an iron box locked so tight, they'd be unable to burgeon into emotional attachments. He'd contented himself with his career, his friends, his family, and made peace with the fact that he would simply not have, nor pretend to have, a meaningful romantic relationship. But after the Selbys approached him, he felt desperate for a cover. Desperate to put some distance between their secrets and his public life. He married a neighborhood girl, Sarita, who he knew would be a devoted political wife. Who he knew would want kids, something he pined for and had assumed was beyond his grasp. He was eager to share the kind of love his father had given them with children of his own. They had a child, a girl, and for a while, he almost felt grateful to the Selbys for forcing him down this path. He'd asked that they name her Lourdes, in a nod to both his parents and the place of redemption he hoped she would be for him. She was not enough. Not Lourdes, and not Sarita. Not enough to keep him from what he longed for.

There were more votes. Yes to a basketball stadium downtown whose rezoning enabled them to move forward with dozens of luxury condo projects. No on a ferry project that would have saved his constituents hours of commuting time into Manhattan. And on and on. Yet, he was still able to eke through enough pieces of good for his neighborhood and for Brooklyn to feel his compromises worth it. For this reason, when one of his mentors, his local congressperson, announced his retirement, Prieto foolishly pursued it, naïvely believing the Selby brothers' interests too local to have any use for his one little vote in the House of Representatives. He won the election easily, and his strategy worked well. For a term or two he found some breathing room. By now divorced from Sarita, he wondered if there might even be a way to be free, to step into who he fully was. Then Hurricane Sandy hit, ravaging the waterfront of not just his district, but all of New York City.

The call came through his office; his chief of staff had Arthur Selby on the line. Terrible damage, they both agreed, awful for the people of New York, the businesses lost, the homes flooded. Wonderful that they had him as a champion in Washington. Just as Prieto relaxed into the conversation, talking the elder Selby through the environmental policy proposals he was planning to make, Arthur interrupted. This was all terrific, really, but he hoped that Prieto could see the wisdom in providing a tax incentive or, better yet, find some federal matching funds for anyone entrepreneurial enough to undertake redevelopment along the flood zones. The dollars for disaster relief, Prieto reminded him, are very competitive, with their priority being recovery and shelter for families displaced by the storm. Of course, Arthur agreed. Prieto hung up, confident.

Days passed before someone named Derek came to his D.C. office to see him. Thinking it a constituent, Prieto gladly said to show him in, but when he recognized

Derek as a john he used to see several years before, he threw him out, canceled his next slate of meetings, and sat at his desk and sobbed. He felt he would never be free.

Now, Prieto found himself heading southbound on the West Side of Manhattan, pulling off the highway near the Highline, and meandering his way down to the Village. It all had changed. Everything was shiny or under construction. Gone were the street urchins and young hustlers who populated the pier that night when his teenage self found the courage to see what this world was really about. Of course, he wasn't dumb enough to cruise, even if the opportunity was still there. But he liked to come down here, look at the water, and remember the nights when he was allowed to be completely whole, nights before anyone knew who he was. He tried to calculate if his total good done was greater than the sum of harm facilitated during his time in public office, and he wasn't sure of the equation's sum.

Tonight, when he arrived at Arthur Selby's apartment, he'd been surprised to find they were not alone, as was custom. Around the table sat a bevy of men, some he recognized from the financial news, others he did not.

Curiously, their agenda had nothing to do with upcoming legislation, his district, or even New York. Instead, they were "deeply invested" in the PROMESA oversight hearing he'd called for, as head of the Hispanic Caucus and member of the House Committee on Natural Resources. Deeply invested in it not happening. Though he couldn't pinpoint why blocking such a banal procedural hearing could be of such import to this group, he sadly knew that this many white men so laser focused on Puerto Rico could mean nothing good. His Papi had always told him that the United States made Puerto Rico's handcuffs, but it was other Puerto Ricans who helped put them on. He didn't quite get what Papi meant until now.

Five Stops

It was the tail end of summer, but the crisp of fall was already in the air when Olga walked out of her posh lobby — soulless, Matteo had called it — and onto the street. This was her favorite time of year. One of the perks of working with the wealthy was that they had better things to do in the heart of summer than to get married. So, while they holidayed in Nantucket or Maine or Europe, she could usually string together three or four weekends in a row for herself.

Her greatest occupational hazard was that her daily priorities were, first and foremost, the priorities of the families who paid her. As such, she often neglected her own. She cringed thinking of how many weeks it had been since she'd seen her niece Lourdes, her waking hours chock full of other people's lives.

As she made her way to the Atlantic Terminal, she couldn't help but marvel at the neighborhood transformation that had happened literally under her nose, while she was flying here and there, getting home drunk, leaving for the office early. Even as a younger woman, Olga never had a desire to live in Manhattan, put off by its nonstop pace and posturing. No one could ever just "be" there. It required trying, at all times, to be something else. Richer, thinner, more famous, more popular, more powerful, more in the know. For all of her ambition, at the end of the day, Olga wanted to shut it all off. Yet she'd recognized, as a practical matter, that being closer to "the city," as Brooklynites referred to it, would be an asset as she launched a business catering expressly to those trying to be more. So, she moved out of her grandma's house on Fifty-third Street and into a floor-through of a brownstone on a tree-lined street just a stone's throw from Fort Greene Park, one quick subway ride to Manhattan. Here, a utopia of creatives, mostly Black and Latino, all strivers by day, surrounded her, eager to let their hair down at night, to drink, laugh, and dance off the weight of a day spent trying to live up to a notion of White Success in this impossible city.

But eventually Manhattan's architecture and its sensibilities had begun to encroach on this corner of the world. First slowly and then fast. It started with the stadium, of course. Then, the first high-rise went up. It seemed so novel that Olga and several of her neighbors took leases there, tickled by the idea of a doorman and a roof deck just steps from their usual stomping grounds. Then, there was a second, double the height of the first. Now, there were so many tall gleaming towers, they had altered the wind patterns and created shadowy canyons on streets once flooded with light. The residents of these towers were different. They didn't run home to Brooklyn to escape, they ran back to continue their efforts of trying to be cool, edgy, artisanal, "low-key." Like milk in coffee, the potency of the neighborhood was diluted with each shining new edifice. As with all forms of white conquest, Olga knew that by the time acquisition was complete, the soul of whatever they were after would have already been destroyed.

The beige stones of the Clocktower Building gleamed white in the bright morning sun, the haze of summer already burned off the sky, leaving behind a rich blue backdrop for it all. For generations of Brooklynites, the Clocktower was a landmark — the tallest building in Brooklyn, by design. Now it was dwarfed in the cluttered downtown skyline. For decades it had been a bank where Olga's grandmother kept her accounts. Until recently, when the conversion to condos was complete, Olga had used its grand bones as the backdrop for lavish parties, guests dancing on the beautifully mosaicked floors, the teller windows serving as bars. The parties had bothered the residents though, and now, like much of the retail space downtown, the former bank sat empty, luxury apartments stacked on top of it. A precarious Jenga game. In fact, the only reason anyone noticed the bank at all was because it contained an entrance to the subway, where Olga now ducked belowground.

Only five stops separated Olga from her neighborhood of origin. As a teenager sneaking off to clubs, or as a recent college grad commuting to her first couple of jobs, she never gave them any thought, that extra distance that separated her from the buzz of Manhattan. Yet now, from as close as downtown Brooklyn, the old neighborhood felt far. Remote. The process of getting there something that required preparation. Time blocked off. A calendar invite, even.

It was such a beautiful day, she decided to walk a bit, so she hopped off the train at Thirty-sixth Street, noticing the hipsters exiting at the same stop. (Were they hipsters, even? Olga thought. Weren't these just yuppies by another name? For surely, with such ubiquity of style, they were no longer technically hip.) As she suspected, at the top of the subway stairs the group broke right, heading west to the waterfront mall that had sprung up there, eager for a day of poking through vintage clothes and eating poké bowls. She shook her head. How had Prieto ever thought this development would be good for the neighborhood? Olga broke left, heading uphill, east towards Fifth Avenue.

Sunset Park had two main strips of retail, each of which ran from the park, at the corner of Forty-first Street, south to Sixtieth or Sixty-fifth Street, depending on who you asked. What no one debated, though, was which belonged to whom. Fifth Avenue was the bustling Latino strip, while Eighth Avenue offered one of the best Chinatown experiences New York had to offer. Olga had grown up just off Fifth, and while some of the stores had changed and the restaurants had become more Mexican than Puerto Rican, she was comforted by how little, in the way of energy and spirit, was different. There were, inevitably, children's clothing stores, furniture shops still offering bedroom sets by layaway, and dollar stores whose awnings teemed with suspended inflatable dolls, beach chairs, laundry carts, and other impulse purchases a mom might make on a Saturday afternoon, exhausted by errand running with her kids. There was the sneaker store where Olga used to buy her cute kicks, the fruit store Prieto had worked at in high school, the little storefront that sold the kind of old-lady bras Abuelita used to wear. On the sidewalks, the Mexican women began to set up their snack stands. Mango with lime and chili on this corner, tamales on that. Until the Mexicans had come to Sunset Park, Olga had never tried any of this food, and now she always tried to leave a little room to grab a snack on her way home. Despite the relatively early hour, most of the shops were open, music blasting into the streets, granting the avenue the aura of a party. In a few more hours, cars with their stereos pumping, teens with boom boxes en route to the neighborhood's public pool, and laughing children darting in front of their mothers would add to the cacophony that Olga had grown to think of as the sound of a Saturday. In the distance, the pale green arch of the Verrazano Bridge, its arms gracefully splaying outward in embrace, presided over it all.

She walked a block past her own to Más Que Pan, her favorite bakery in the neighborhood, its windows full of lavish buttercream cakes the likes of which her clients had surely never seen: multitiered wedding cakes with a dozen plastic bridesmaid and groomsman figurines descending spiral staircases; a Ken-like doll wearing nothing but a Speedo lying in repose atop a cake intended for a bachelorette; a Barbie doll torso wearing a bridal veil popped out of a cake, her gown fashioned from mounds of cream. This one, Olga imagined, was for a bridal shower. She ordered a coffee and a buttered roll knowing that the coffee would come with frothed hot milk, the butter whipped and sweet, and that the two things would cost her $3, the price having risen a dollar in the past decade. There was no need for this snack — the idea that there wouldn't be food at the house was utterly ridiculous — but this was comfort food. Ritual eating she needed to do to know that she was back home.

Home. Olga hadn't lived here in over fifteen years, but time did not matter. It was bigger than its physical size, this house. It housed all her grandmother's hopes and fears for her young family on the mainland, all of her children's dreams and sorrows, and those of her grandchildren, too. Had her grandmother laid the stones and mortar herself, this place could not embody her more. When they first came from Arecibo — Abuelita, Abuelo, and their brood — they lived in a tenement in Spanish Harlem with another family. Abuelita saved her pennies, little by little, to buy their own house, but when her husband left — fed up with this mainland experiment — she had to adjust her plans. She found the rental apartment upstairs through a woman at the garment factory where she worked. How nice it would be to have a big apartment so close to her job, all to themselves. The neighborhood was Scandinavian and Irish back then and the landlord, Mr. Olson, did not want to rent to a Puerto Rican family. That he made plain. But her grandmother charmed him: she was high-heeled and lipsticked, and she had left her four young children at home. They rented there for years, living in the unit upstairs. Little by little, buying furniture, saving more money, warming Mr. Olson to their family. When he finally decided he'd had enough of Brooklyn, enough of the Puerto Rican wave flooding Sunset Park for the factory jobs nearby, he didn't just want to sell. He wanted Olga's grandmother to buy it. To give her a taste of the American dream. And somehow, she did it. Little by little, she used to say, everything impossible can come to pass. So, the family moved from the rental upstairs to the owner's unit downstairs. The first thing her grandmother did, or so everyone said, was to sit her children down and tell them that no one in their family would ever have to worry about having a roof over their head again. And no one ever did. The next thing she did, according to lore, was put on her music nice and loud so that they all could dance.

Olga turned off the main avenue onto her block, a line of attached limestones glimmering in the summer sun. Each just like her own: garden level and two short stories. A tiny wrought iron gate out front, bounding in the smallest patch of concrete front yard, large stone steps with a black iron banister leading up to the parlor floor. Like hers, most of the houses were owner-inhabited, landlords presiding over the bottom two floors, a rental unit up top. Like hers, the renters were almost always relations, someone in need of a reasonable place to lay their head while they finished school or got on their feet after a divorce or simply tried to make their way in a difficult world. As such, the block took on the nature of a long-running telenovela, with series regulars and guest stars, multigenerational feuds and intricate plot points. Already ladies were sweeping stoops and setting out their lawn chairs for a day filled with the busywork of neighborhood bochinche: watching the comings and goings of the street to see what this week's episode would bring. Her phone rang. It was Matteo.

"Whatcha doing, girl?" he asked.

She smiled. "I'm in my old neighborhood, hanging with my niece today."

"Aw, have I found myself a Tender Roni girl?" he asked.

She laughed. "I guess! What are you doing?"

"I'm . . ." He hesitated. "I'm picking up a sofa. . . ."

As they had only hung out a couple times, and always ended up at her place, Olga had managed to forget about Matteo's hoarding, and in fact, could not wrap her head around it. She despised clutter of any sort and had shocked herself by pushing past his confession. Yet, it was likely his openness about this defect drew her to him in the first place, her fear of her own imperfections softened by his acceptance of his own.

Before she could figure out the appropriate response, he jumped in.

"But look, ma, the reason I called is because I've got a hundred dollars of yours, and I wanted to let you know."

"What?"

"Apparently you left Sylvia a hundred-dollar bill on the bar the other night and she's not gonna take your money like that."

For some reason, Olga felt embarrassed. No money had exchanged hands between Matteo and Sylvia, despite numerous drinks consumed and tons of time on her barstools. While she was certain they had some kind of arrangement — clearly Matteo was a regular — she felt strange about not compensating the woman for her time and hospitality. Yet she also felt strange that Matteo knew she had done it.

"I wanted her to have it," she said. "She was so lovely to us."

Matteo sighed. "That's sweet, but Sylvia is stubborn, and believe me, she will check to make sure I gave you your Benjamin back. In other news, it's nice to know I have a crush on a chick who's such a generous tipper."

She felt herself blush, but luckily was, by now, in front of her house, where her niece was sitting on the stoop, surrounded by two dozen splits of champagne and a Michael's bag bursting open with turquoise tulle.

"Matteo, let me call you later."

Favors

"¡Ay, querida! What have you gotten into over here?" Olga asked.

"Olga!" Her niece bounded down the steps, and the turquoise fabric, somehow stuck on her shorts, transformed into a tail. She threw her skinny arms around Olga's waist and hugged her tight. "Papi said you were coming this weekend." She released her embrace, as if she'd just remembered something. "Where've you been all summer?"

"Working, mija," Olga replied, ready to own her crime. Lourdes had grown so much that summer, the sight of her made Olga melancholy for all she'd missed. "But, you're right, I let the whole summer go without us doing anything fun. I'm sorry. Tell me, what's all this?"

"Lourdes!" Mabel had popped her head out the window of the top floor. "I hope you're making those bows even!" She looked at Olga. "Oh, hey."

Olga looked up. "Hey, prima!" Mabel had been living in the rental apartment ever since she met Julio, her fiancé. She claimed she wanted the apartment to help Prieto with Lourdes, but all the cousins knew that what she needed was a fuck-pad, since up until then, despite being in their thirties, both she and Julio had lived at their respective parents' homes. As soon as Olga saw her cousin, she realized that her niece, along with the rest of her family, had likely been enlisted in Mabel's crafting army and that the house would be ground zero for preparing tacky takeaways for her upcoming nuptials. Celebrations in her family were more than a day of gathering. The planning, preparation, and postmortem chisme sessions were both how and why Olga's family marked any major occasion. She hadn't factored wedding prep into her visit, but should she dare to seem less than enthusiastic about helping, the whole day would devolve into war with Mabel, and Olga didn't want to sour everyone's mood.

"Oye," she said, "I just figured you could use some extra hands!"

"Oh yeah?" Mabel called down, suspiciously. "Well, I guess better late than never. Come in. I'll show you what to do."

Lourdes poked her and mimed a secret, which Olga bent down to hear. "I was gonna play with Camille today, but Mabel says no one plays until all the favors are done."

The favors, Olga soon discovered, were quite the production, involving at least five aisles of the crafting store. The garden level of the house was a sizable space, with a front sitting room that opened into the dining room, and the kitchen in the back. Each and every corner was occupied by a relative tending to some aspect of customization and assemblage of the takeaway gifts for the end of the night. At the dining table, two of her cousins were covering the champagne bottle labels with stickers that had Mabel and Julio's photo with the wedding date underneath. Next to them, Tía ChaCha, always very good with detail, sat with a pair of tweezers, her readers sliding down her nose, affixing rhinestones in artistic clusters around the bottle. These then would be boxed up and taken to the porch where, Olga now realized, Lourdes was put in charge of dressing the bottle necks with tulle ribbon bows. Once dressed, the bottles were taken to the living room, where Tío JoJo and one of Mabel's nephews were placing them in clear gift boxes together with a single champagne flute, which, Olga realized upon closer examination, were also etched with Mabel and Julio's names and wedding date.

Mabel had made her way downstairs, her wet hair dripping onto her Marc Anthony concert T-shirt. Like a general, she surveyed everyone's work.

"Ricky," she barked at one of their cousins, "that label don't look straight to me." She turned to Olga. "Let's get you set up in the kitchen. You can help decorate the gift boxes."

"Wait," Olga said, laughing. "You're adding something else to this?"

"Ya!" ChaCha interjected. "The box can't be plain, Olga! What's wrong with you?"

Mabel, ever eager to be persecuted and judged by her cousin, opined, "Well, Tía, maybe Olga's rich vanilla brides like things more, you know, refined."

"¿Qué?" ChaCha called out, a bedazzled champagne bottle in her hand. "These bottles have hand-placed crystals on them! Who wouldn't find that elegant?"

Tía ChaCha was their Tío Richie's first wife and Mabel's godmother, a role she took seriously enough to adopt all of Mabel's enemies as her own. Olga being their favorite target. They, though, were in the minority. Whether their family worshiped them out of merit for their successes or pity for being parentless, if Olga walked on water it was only because Prieto had already parted the Red Sea. So now that Olga had called into question the style and taste of her cousin's wedding favors, the entirety of the room grew quiet, awaiting Olga's verdict.

Truth be told, Olga's clients never gave out favors anymore, deeming them largely a waste, which was more a matter of mode than money. Since the recession, conscious that weddings were acts of conspicuous consumption, the wealthy had deemed the wedding favor an opportunity to offer an apology for inequity. The tchotchke replaced by "donation in lieu of favor" cards. Graciously announcing to guests that instead of buying a useless favor everyone knew would be chucked into the trash after the wedding, they had chosen to send that money to a charity, where it would benefit people who couldn't even afford a wedding in the first place. In Olga's family, however, these favors — any favors, really — would never be chucked in the trash. The guests at Mabel's wedding would coo over the gift, chill and drink the cheap champagne, and take the flute out again on New Year's Eve. Or, just as likely, place the entirety of the decorated package into a china cabinet, where it would be preserved and lovingly dusted, weekly, alongside the favors from all the cousins' weddings that had come before it. Even Olga, with her fastidious nature, was highly superstitious of throwing away a favor from any family affair, and kept an under-the-bed box filled with crocheted bridal gown toilet paper roll covers, engraved miniature picture frames, and glass swans swimming on mirror ponds whose exact purpose she had never deduced, but of which she had three. She knew Mabel had likely agonized over selecting each label, crystal, and bow. With this in mind, Olga paused, looked around the room, and declared, "Of course, it's elegant, Tía! I just didn't want the packaging to take away from your work!" And everyone laughed and ChaCha, and even Mabel, smiled. New England tact, Olga thought to herself.

"Meanwhile, we can't get any music on in this joint? I get why you've got us working, Mabel, but what kind of sweatshop are you running?"

In this way, with music blasting in the background, Olga sat at the kitchen table while her Titi Lola made arroz con habichuelas blancas — Olga's favorite — and adorned 150 clear plastic boxes filled with bedazzled champagne splits and flutes with teal bows, onto which Ana, her Tío Richie's current wife, then hot-glued a large rhinestone.

King of the Castle

Olga stared at Tía Lola intently as she seasoned beans, boiled rice, chopped onions, and sliced avocado. While she cooked, Lola hummed along to the Daddy Yankee song playing on the stereo system and from across the kitchen Olga attempted to discern something of her aunt beyond her boundless capacity to love. Her mother's baby sister had always bucked convention. In college, she had studied accounting and, once done with school, landed a good job, chopped off all her hair, and took an apartment forty blocks north in Park Slope. Lola then proceeded to stack cheddar in a way that enabled her to care for her mother as she aged, keep Olga and Prieto in fresh back-to-school clothes, and still go on one cruise a year. On Saturdays, Lola, who had been the family chef since she herself was a girl, came and cooked for whatever family showed up. On Sundays, in good weather, she rode with her Puerto Rican motorcycle club. She never married. What she did with her days and nights outside of that, none of them knew. The block had long whispered that Lola was a lesbian, and Olga hadn't ruled that out, but she also wasn't completely convinced.

"If being a single woman made you gay," Olga would say, "then make me Grand Marshall of the Pride Parade."

This would inevitably inspire laughter, because everyone knew that Olga had always been a world-class hetero sucia, a rotating cast of boys and men trailing her since she had first begun to develop. Certainly, her aunt had never brought another woman around the family, minus her friend Lisa, who Lola had known so long, Olga retained no memory of even meeting her. Mabel had lobbied the rest of the cousins hard that Lisa was not Lola's friend at all, but instead her lover, to which Olga retorted that people can and do have friends. "Not the Ortizes!" the rest of her cousins had replied. To a certain extent, this was true. Richie had three kids with ChaCha, two more with Ana. JoJo and Rita had Mabel, Isabel, and Tony. Everybody's kids then had kids, except for Olga and Mabel. What room was there for friends when there was so much family around?

Olga's real confusion about her tía's life was rooted in her grandmother's death. Before Abuelita passed away, Olga could understand why her aunt might feel she had to hide who she was from an admittedly old-fashioned and faithfully Catholic woman. But Abuelita had been gone for twelve years now and Olga saw so little need for a closet that she began to question the hypothesis — that her aunt was queer — in the first place. Her aunt was quiet, but fearless, unafraid to live life on her own terms. To Olga's eye, her aunt's persona simply didn't befit a closeted person. Unlike her brother.

Olga had long suspected that Prieto was gay, but she knew he would more likely die than embrace an identity so "alternative." His private life, in this regard, was one of the few unspoken, off-limit topics between them. Olga, unlike Mabel, did not like to trade in rumor and suppositions, especially where her brother was concerned, and so she kept this thought to herself. Also, no one would have chosen to believe her anyway. Her case for the matter rested largely on circumstantial questions for which her family would have convenient answers.

Wasn't it weird that her brother had never had a girlfriend? *He's too dedicated to his work to have time!*

But what about when he was younger? *Why would a man so handsome want to be tied down?*

Isn't it strange how Sarita is around him? So cold and chilly, no hint of lost passion? *Ay, her family would say, she's just bitter that he ended things.*

Olga was unable to articulate the less tangible reasons for her belief. Things that only she, raised under the same roof with him, noticed. How, when he'd take her to the pool at Sunset Park, she'd find his gaze lingering on the same shirtless boys her own eyes had wandered to. How, when she would clean his room, she'd find men's muscle magazines hidden between the wall and his twin bed, tucked away like another guy might have stashed *Playboys.*

Prieto's relationship with Sarita transformed a nagging feeling into an unconfirmed belief. Olga remembered cognitively registering, the first time he brought her around, how stiff he seemed. Like a robot playing the part of himself. Before his wedding ceremony, when he looked nearly sick, she'd reminded him that he didn't need to go through with it. He'd replied, very seriously, that yes, he did. In a way, she supposed, he was right. To her consternation, her brother's identity was completely enmeshed with the appearance of perfection. And while people weren't outwardly homophobic, she understood that a description of the perfect Latino man did not include the word "gay." Prieto's need to be liked was compounded by his palpable fear of disappointing people: their family, their mother, his constituents. It was, to Olga, his main character flaw. So she said nothing, kept her thoughts to herself. At the end of the day, what did it matter who her brother wanted to fuck?

"¡¡¡Wepa!!!" Prieto called out as he came into the house. "Nothing like coming back to a home full of fam!"

Olga could feel the energy of the place collectively shift, the center of gravity now firmly fixed on her brother. The king returned to his castle. Mabel showed him her favors, Lourdes walking him through the assembly line; her brother doled out hugs and kisses as he greeted each family member in turn. The first time she saw him work a room at a campaign event, she thought of times like this, here with their family — how effortless it was for him to make everyone feel special, how he seduced attention from a crowd.

"¡Oye!" Tía Lola shouted. "What am I? Chopped liver? Come give Titi a kiss!"

Prieto and Olga's father, Mabel would always say, were the only men Tía Lola ever glanced at twice.

Olga's brother bounded into the kitchen, kissed her head, and wrapped their aunt in a big embrace, dancing her around as he did so. From under his arm he presented her with a package.

"Tía, I picked up some steaks. You season them, I'll grill?"

"Bueno, bueno, ¡bendito!"

Olga sat with a beer in their little backyard, watching her brother stoke the charcoal into flames. Impossibly, two more cousins were already out there, hard at work bagging candied almonds into little turquoise net sacks. These, Olga knew, were to go at each guest's place setting. The sight of them made her remember the linen napkins, tucked in a corner of her office, awaiting their debut on Mabel's big day. The recollection curled the corners of her mouth upwards.

"Oh shit," Prieto said. "When I see my sister smile like that, I know she's up to no good. What are you scheming now?"

"Nothing, nothing!" She giggled and sought to deflect. "Hey, you know what I noticed when I was walking up Fifth today?"

Her brother grunted so she continued.

"Bars. Two bars."

"Okay?" he said, stoking the fire.

"Since when do we have bars on this part of the avenue?"

Brooklyn's Fifth Avenue began at Atlantic Avenue, the outermost edge of what eventually became Park Slope, running south until it met the water under the Verrazano-Narrows Bridge at Shore Road, Brooklyn's version of the Gold Coast. In every neighborhood it cut through, the avenue served as a retail hub, full of fruit stands and fish markets, diners, coffee shops, and bodegas. If Park Slope had a "scene," Fifth Avenue would be it, as it was clustered with restaurants, sports bars, and lounges. Bay Ridge, home to *Saturday Night Fever,* long provided the alternative to schlepping to Manhattan for some nighttime fun. But for generations, if you drove through the Polish stretch, which began at Eighteenth Street, and Sunset Park itself, you would not see a bar on Fifth Avenue until you hit Feeney's Pub on Sixty-second Street. Dives peppered Third and Fourth avenues, serving whatever workers remained at Bush Terminal and catering to men hooker-shopping under the BQE, but the Polish and the Puerto Ricans had happily restricted their commerce to the family-friendly variety. In the past decade, however, Olga noticed that, slowly, this too was changing. Hipsters and their ironically named bars had begun to creep further south. First the sailor-themed bar, The Merman, opened on Twenty-first Street, then Gravediggers — right across from the Greenwood Cemetery on Twenty-sixth. Then Twenty-seventh Street, then Thirtieth. Always luring the same patron: skinny, pale kids with NPR tote bags, intricate line tattoos visible under their frilly, ironic sundresses or Bernie Sanders T-shirts with the sleeves cut off. Now, today, on Thirty-seventh Street she'd seen a little wine bar, Sour Grapes, and then on Thirty-eighth a true *bar* bar, named, of all things, *HOLA!,* which Olga found particularly ironic since from a quick glance through the window at the heavy-handed Day of the Dead décor she knew that no real Mexicans were likely involved. It was obvious they were not saying hello to the people of Sunset. Not the ones she knew anyway.

"Those are wypipo spots," Fat Tony, one of her cousins bagging the almonds, chimed in. "I didn't even know there were so many around here, son. But me and my homeboy passed by the other night, and the 'Mexican' joint was bumping. Jam packed. No melanin anywhere."

"Hmpf," Olga said. "How come these bars are there, Prieto?"

"Olga," her brother said, with some exasperation, "I'm in D.C. now. This is a City Council issue. Anyway, there was some rezoning. Makes sense. They cater to those coworking spaces they put up in Bush Terminal. It's not necessarily a bad thing to have a place to stop and get a drink after work, is it?"

Olga did not agree.

"No, but if there's a chance to suddenly open bars in a Puerto Rican neighborhood, Prieto, then why didn't the opportunity go to Puerto Ricans? Or fuck, Mexicans! Hell, why isn't there a Chinese-owned bar up here?"

"See," her brother said, "this is why I want you to be more involved in my campaigns, ya! Actually" — seeming grateful for a chance to change the subject — "the weekend after next, you working? Someone's throwing a fundraiser for me out in the Hamptons. Wanted to see if you could come. You know that's more your scene than mine. . . ."

Olga looked at her phone. "On the Saturday? Ugh, I'm already committed to a thing . . . out east. . . ." She stopped and thought of the party. Her first public outing with Dick. Since she had accepted his invitation, she felt the stranglehold of her commitment. Whether real or imagined, her freedom to ignore Dick, to say yes or no to his requests, had been hampered. True, she had denied meeting him for dinner and blown him off for an impromptu romp after work at the Four Seasons, but after each refusal he had replied with "No matter, we'll have a whole weekend together out east." His words a stake in the ground to which she was tethered. Yes, she could still roam the yard, but at the end of the day, Dick knew she couldn't go very far. Olga wanted to go to this party very badly, but she also wanted to rob Dick of this feeling of conquest, and she wondered if her brother might not have given her the opening to have both things at once.

"Prieto, let's figure this out. Maybe if I do you the solid and go to your thing, you can come with me afterwards to mine."

"Damn, son. That's how it is?" Tony called out. "You got all these cousins up in here, and nobody takes us to shit! How you know I don't want to go to one of your fancy parties in the Hamptons?"

"Tony," Prieto called out, as he threw a steak on the fire, the flame jumping in the air. "Do you want to come out to the Hamptons to my fundraiser?"

"Fuck no, Prieto. You know I get carsick on long rides. It's just nice to be asked, is all."

Novenas

As was her ritual on every visit home, at a quarter to five Olga snuck into her brother's room. She held her breath, and with eyes closed, slid open his closet door, dreading what she might not find there. She exhaled relief immediately, goose bumps rising on her forearms. She could feel its presence without needing to see it: her grandmother's altar. She marveled at its sameness after all these years, an anchor of constancy amid a torrent of change. When Prieto took over the house, and in turn, Abuelita's room, Olga's only request was that he leave the altar. It lived atop a small milk crate covered with a white lace doily, Nuestra Señora de la Caridad del Cobre presiding over empty velas, the faint remnants of red, pink, yellow, and white wax still evident in the glass cases. Around them, photos of Olga's mother and grandfather, her father's mass card, a bottle of Bacardi, a small statue of

St. Anthony, and a photo of Abuelita placed there by Olga herself. Around the Virgin hung four rosaries, and Olga reached now for the black one — obsidian, or so she was told, years and years ago. She stuck it in her jeans' pocket and closed the closet door.

"I'm going to the store!" she called out to no one in particular, and made her way up Fifth Avenue to Our Lady of Perpetual Help, where she slipped into the tenth pew from the front on the left-hand side of the lower level, the bronze plaque on the bench inscribed with the name *Isabel Alicea Ortiz.* How many Saturdays had she come and sat in this very spot with her grandmother? It was impossible to count, but enough that when she died, one of Olga's first acts was to claim the pew — Abuelita's pew — to be marked with her name in perpetuity.

This was their space, her and her grandmother's. In a house full of people, lives crowded with crisis and defined by chaos, this ritual, this place, belonged to the two of them alone. Olga's parents did not forbid her and Prieto from doing much, with the exception of going to church. Their parents felt, generally, that religion was a bourgeois tool for inuring the proletariat to their exploitation, and more specifically, that the Catholic church was the devil's handmaiden, having played such a prominent role in the colonization of Black and Brown people all over the world. Her mother and father were so vociferous about this, so relentless in their critique, that Olga's grandmother moved her altar into her closet, simply to avoid having to hear the two of them go on and on. After Olga's mother left, Abuelita kept it there out of habit. Olga loved the altar. The mystery of it was especially delightful to her, but also the ritual of the prayers, the lighting of the candles. Abuelita would often catch her in the doorway, spying on her grandmother as she knelt and said the rosary. One day she called her over and taught her granddaughter the prayers — the Hail Mary, the Our Father. They were the first and only things Olga could say with confidence in Spanish.

Her grandmother didn't intend to defy Olga's parents' wishes, not overtly. Olga had a curiosity and her grandmother had a faith. Or at the very least, superstition. One Saturday afternoon, when Olga was maybe six or seven, she and Abuelita were running errands when her grandmother looked at her watch and became stressed. Abuelita had long gone to Saturday evening mass, dating back to her days at the factory.

Sunday was her only day off back then, her only day to sleep, even if it was just until seven o'clock. So, she would leave work and go to vigil mass, to pray for her job, her children, the roof over their heads. Then she would come home and see her whole family together, with so much food on the table, in a house that against all odds belonged to them. To Abuelita, the two things were connected. The health of her household tied to her appearance at Saturday evening mass. If it didn't help anything, Abuelita would tell Olga, it certainly didn't hurt anything, either. And so, on this particular Saturday, pressed for time and unsure if Lola was home to watch Olga, she turned to her grandchild and, in a conversation that Olga remembered vividly, asked her if she knew what a secret was. Secrets, her grandmother said, had a bad reputation, like their neighbor, Constantina. Yes, lots of men did come visit Constantina while her husband was away as a Marine reservist, but she also fed many of the stray cats and dogs in the neighborhood and never bragged about it, so she wasn't all bad. That was how secrets were; you heard more about their bad aspects than their good. Going to church with Abuelita was a good kind of secret. Did Olga think she could keep a good kind of secret? She nodded, vigorously, yes.

When Olga stepped inside that first time, she was enchanted. She loved the statues, the ceremony, the marble, the gold, the smell of the incense, the sound of the organ, the sense of order, the veil of secrecy . . . all of it. After everyone went for communion, when the entire parish was kneeling in prayer, Olga shed a tear, so moved was she by the sound of quiet. Abuelita was clearly looking more at Olga than praying, because she kissed her on the top of her head and whispered, "We can come back, you know." And come back they did, without further discussion. Every Saturday they would find themselves out together, shopping for this or that, always winding up at their pew just as the bells rang to begin the five o'clock mass. Afterwards they would race home — sometimes they would buy soda and ice, just to cover their tracks. By then, her father would be over. Her mother, if she was not traveling, there. Her aunt and often her uncles and whatever cousins all gathered at the house. And they would have dinner surrounded by family, feeling blessed that their prayers had worked.

The only time Olga had ever felt pure envy for her cousin Mabel was when she made her First Holy Communion. Olga cried and cried for weeks afterwards. Her mother called her materialistic for being jealous of a meaningless dress, while her father offered to make her a party of her own, just for being her, "No Jesus required." Only Abuelita knew that what she was jealous of was not the outfit or the party, but that now Mabel would know the taste of the Body and Blood of Christ on her tongue. Mabel, who gave Holy Communion no more thought than a bird gives its first flight, would enjoy this privilege Olga had pined for. When everyone could be filled with Jesus, sitting in that beautiful silence in the marble hall, Mabel would be full too, and she, Olga, would just sit there. Still hungry.

When her mother left, Olga grew more brazen, saving her allowance to buy a twenty-inch Infant of Prague statue and building her own altar in her room. Not in the closet, but on top of her dresser. She chose that statue with care, because you could change him into elaborate robes that varied according to the season. When she got a little older, Olga worked for Tío Richie's car dealership on Saturdays and whatever money she didn't spend sneaking into clubs at night she put towards buying outfits for the Niño Jesús de Praga. She would go with her abuela to the Catholic goods store and select a purple Easter gown, a red silk dress for Advent, a baptismal ring too small for even a baby, a miniature crucifix necklace. At her altar she lit candles in front of her mother's photo, saying novenas for her safety, wherever she was.

Her sadness at her mother's departure was tempered by what she saw as an opportunity. She begged her grandmother to enroll her in catechism, reminding her about good secrets and Constantina, the animal lover who used to live next door. Her grandmother obliged. She loved all of her grandchildren, but felt, she would tell Olga as she brushed her hair at night, that perhaps God put them so close together to give her a second chance at raising a restless spirit. Although her grandmother would say that her mother had chosen "a life based on her convictions," she would still sometimes lament that "perhaps she'd have been less angry if I'd been home a little more." And Olga would take the old hand that held the brush and kiss it and tell her that she had just done her best. This was the truth.

It was also true that Olga and Prieto had more time with their grandmother than their mother and aunt and uncles ever had. By the time Olga was in grade school her grandmother had retired from the factory and instead did alterations out of the house for people in the neighborhood. Prieto would make her flyers and post them around and ladies would come with their occasion dresses. Spring was the busiest time. They would learn all the local gossip as everyone needed fixes on prom dresses, outfits for weddings, and, of course, communion gowns. If it seemed like one would fit, her grandmother would lay out a bedsheet on the ground to protect the dress and let Olga try it on. Another good secret. On these occasions, Olga would look into the mirror and practice kneeling and opening her mouth, waiting to receive the Host.

On Wednesdays, public school kids who went to catechism got early dismissal: 2:15 P.M. instead of 3:00. Olga was beside herself to finally leave with those kids, who she knew all walked to Our Lady of Perpetual Help together, stopping for gum and Quarter Waters along the way. She was thirteen and trying to get baptized and make communion all at once, while her classmates were already studying for Confirmation, so Abuelita talked to one of the nuns about giving her special classes. This was a familiar situation for Olga and Abuelita both. Her grandmother had sent one of her girls "away" before, busing Olga's mother to every gifted program the city offered. She'd felt that she'd lost Blanca in the balance. Abuelita wanted to keep Olga closer to home, but also didn't want to stifle her. She aggressively solicited Olga's teachers for special help, pleading her granddaughter's unique case, asking for extra work, anything additional to keep her bright Olga engaged, but close. Olga thought nothing of having private lessons with one of the sisters because she spent her days getting special attention at school, all of her teachers charmed by the ambitious grandmother and her bright granddaughter.

Olga jumped from her seat when the special release bell rang, holding hands with her junior-high boyfriend as they walked the ten or so blocks towards the church's school building. But as they turned the corner, flanked by a pack of their classmates, Olga's blood grew cold. She could hear a commotion, if one man yelling could be called that. She pretended to forget something, told everyone to go ahead, reversed her course just long enough to seem believable, and then hid behind a tree until she saw them all ascend the stairs and walk into the building. The ranting continued. Louder still.

"But what I want to know is, who the fuck told you that my daughter was available for brainwashing? Tell me! Who?"

It was her father. High. Crack this time, clearly. On smack he was like a baby, would just curl up in anyone's arms, looking for proof he was still loved. On crack, he was brave. And angry. And loud. She saw him, at the top of the stairs to the entrance of the school, all up in the face of the nun, Sister Kate, her face stoic under her habit. In the corner, slumped on the top step, was her brother, that fucking Benedict Arnold. That fucking people pleaser. Her father was barely a functioning being at this point, just nerves and synapses either stimulated or dulled senseless. He was, she surmised even at her young age, embarrassing but harmless. Her brother, on the other hand, was of sound mind and body and had brought him here with the sole purpose of ruining her dream.

"¡¡¡Lombriz!!!" she called out to him using the word worm that her parents had always used for sellouts of their own culture. "¡Lombriz!" She pointed, her voice louder than her father's, loud enough to stop her father's rant.

"¡¡Mija!!" He turned to her. "¡Dime! Who put you up to this?"

But she swatted him away, hissing at her brother, "Take him away, you fucking piece of shit."

"Olga," Prieto replied, matter-of-factly, "he's still our father, don't his wishes count for anything?"

She ignored him and turned her attention to Sister Kate.

"Sister," she pleaded, "my father isn't in his right mind. I have wanted be a true Catholic —"

But Sister Kate cut her off. She was an old Irish woman. She had seen this all before. If not crack, alcohol. The vice really didn't matter. Her eyes oozed with compassion. She put her hands on Olga's face.

"Beautiful child. God's timeline is long, and Jesus lives for always, so your time for the Sacraments will come. But for now, I cannot prepare you for them. Your grandmother told me that your parents were dead. You're only thirteen. If your father doesn't consent, I must abide by the law."

Tears streamed down Olga's face.

"But Sister, I will work so hard. So very hard."

The sister blessed her before she went inside.

That night, Olga put Nair in her brother's shampoo bottle. They never spoke of his betrayal again. Abuelita went to confession for her lie, though she did not feel true remorse; she and Olga kept returning to their pew.

When Olga's father did actually die, three years later, with el SIDA, no funeral parlors in the neighborhood wanted to take him. There was a place for bodies with AIDS, everyone said, a potter's field uptown. But Abuelita had an idea, and after digging in her papers to find the proper evidence, spoke about it to Olga. Only sixteen, but armed with her father's baptism, confirmation, and — most shockingly to Olga — a certificate of marriage to her mother from the church, Olga went to visit Sister Kate, pleading that even Catholics with AIDS had the right to decent funerals. Sister Kate made a few calls, and they had to travel into Greenwich Village, but he had a proper wake and religious service at a funeral parlor there. "Lombriz," Olga said to her brother, "thank us later." He never did.

Olga had never had many friends, in part because she loved to spend time with Abuelita, their minds so much alike. Her mother was so black-and-white — rigid with her principles. Her father, a dreamer, lost in impossible ideals. But to Olga, her grandmother was a hustler who actually got things done. She understood the dance, which they did together, often. Both literally, as Abuelita, glamorous and towering in her heels, loved to dance with young Olga, and also figuratively. With her parents absent for such critical years of her life, Abuelita was never afraid to bend the truth, make someone dead or another person missing, in order to procure special tutoring, or a scholarship, or whatever her grandchildren needed. The truth, Abuelita would say, is so much harder to believe than our lie, no? And it's not like we have bad intentions, ¿sí? Yes! Olga would agree. She loved it all. The high heels, the prayer, the laissez-faire relationship with rules and regulations. Whether born that way or formed into shape from necessity, the two women mirrored each other.

When Abuelita died, Olga's mother did not return for the funeral. She and her brother were the only evidence of her mother's existence in their grandmother's life. Olga was twenty-seven at the time and while watching her grandmother's decline had been heartbreaking, the deepest pain came at the funeral mass itself. Sitting there, she felt so profoundly empty, so utterly gutted from the loss, she physically ached for relief.

She'd never done her catechism, never made the official sacrament, but at the funeral mass, Olga was the first to go up and receive. The priest said, "Body of Christ," and she said, "Amen," curtsied, and crossed herself, just as she had practiced for all those years. She made her way back to her seat, her grandmother's coffin just a few feet in front of her. She knelt in genuflection. In this moment, one she had coveted for so long, one she thought would hold the wisdom of the entire world, she felt nothing. She wept, with disappointment and loneliness. A sense of loneliness she hadn't known was possible and one that never truly left her.

Again and again, Olga returned to church after that, hopeful that this visit would be the moment when she was healed. That on this occasion, the anger that so often filled her would be replaced by grace. Eventually, her sense of hope faded into nothing, replaced with ritual. Ritual that brought her closer to her grandmother, that bordered on superstition. Today, with the obsidian rosary being kneaded through her fingers, the ritual felt silly and the empty feeling formed a crater through which she almost slipped. Olga looked up, to the statues, to Abuelita, to her father, to anyone who might be listening, and prayed —

"Dear God, please, let me know what it is to feel loved again."

LOMBRIZ

Inside his D.C. office, Prieto threw his newspaper down in disgust. The op-ed was nothing short of scathing, raking him over the coals for canceling the PROMESA hearing, calling him "the toothless lion" guarding Puerto Rico. He should have known when he saw that Reggie King bought a ticket to his fundraiser that he'd had something else up his sleeve.

"Alex!" he bellowed out to his chief of staff. "Alex, did you see this shit?"

"Well, sir," Alex said as he entered the room, "I was the one who put it on your desk, so, yes."

Some days Prieto detested Alex.

"If it's any consolation, do you think anyone reads the op-eds in the *Daily News*?"

"Actually, Alex, yes. Yes, I do. Maybe not your friends from HBS —"

"Kennedy School, but Harvard, yes."

"Maybe not your friends from Harvard,

but my constituents do. The people on *The Breakfast Club* do. Black and Brown Twitter does. This fucking clown has decided he's the spokesperson for Puerto Rico all of a sudden and now he's trying to come at me for *my* record?"

"I still don't get why you canceled the hearing. This feels like way more trouble than that would have been," Alex said, shaking his head.

"You would think, after knowing me for as many years as he has, he'd have the decency to pick up the phone and call me before he pulled this shit."

The truth was that while yes, the two men had known each other for nearly two decades, it was always a frosty relationship, predicated as it was on Reggie's romantic interest in Olga. Truth be told, Prieto had long eyed Reggie King with a mixture of contempt, admiration, and, more recently, an odd sense of jealousy. A music impresario, Reggie had cultivated a larger-than-life, rags-to-riches persona that, for years, had been confined to the entertainment arena. More recently, though, Reggie had begun wading into the waters of politics or, as Prieto saw it, moving into his lane. It started with his so-called social impact investments. Reggie's first venture, Sanareis, was a biopharmaceutical company focused almost exclusively on developing drugs to target and treat diseases adversely affecting Black and Latino people. Diabetes, heart disease, women's reproductive health. When other music moguls were investing in vodkas and bottled waters, Reggie made headlines for being so community minded. He was suddenly just as likely to be giving an interview to *The Atlantic* as he was to *Vibe.* When he launched Podremos — a company that manufactured wind-energy turbines — he made even bigger headlines, and bigger profits. The cover of *Forbes,* appearances on MSNBC, interviews in *The Wall Street Journal.* Then, a couple of years ago, Reggie, who for the majority of his career never uttered a peep about being Puerto Rican, suddenly adopted the island as his pet cause. Truth be told, the op-ed hadn't taken Prieto completely by surprise. He'd noticed some more subtle swipes Reggie had taken at him in the media. He just never thought he'd come at him like this.

"Seems to me," Alex offered, "he only knows how to operate as a public spectacle. This should make Saturday interesting."

"I'm not worried about it," Prieto said genuinely. "My sister's coming. She's the Reggie whisperer. We'll see who looks like a toothless fucking lion."

"Speaking of lions, Congressman Hurd's office called about that Hurricane Harvey relief package?"

Prieto let out a slightly bitter laugh. "Tell Will, yes, he can count on my vote, because I'm a Democrat and we don't let people suffer just so we can keep our checkbook balanced. I just hope that when the next storm comes to P.R., I can —"

A shriek came from the outer office followed by murmurs and gasps. Alex ran to see what the commotion was. He returned moments later, carrying a small box, a somber, almost frightened look on his face.

"Sir, please don't worry, we've already called the Capitol Police."

"What the fuck is it?" Prieto asked, gesturing for Alex to bring the package to him.

"I . . . I . . . don't really know. But it was sent for you. I just don't know what it means."

But as soon as Prieto looked, he knew. The box was filled with worms.

His mother had not contacted him in over a year, not since he had voted yes on PROMESA, giving financial control of Puerto Rico to a politically appointed board of mainlanders. Yet he knew it was her behind the box of worms. After much posturing, Prieto managed to convince Alex not to involve the Capitol Police, as it was "likely just kids playing a prank." Instead, he had the box and its contents messengered over to the J. Edgar Hoover Building.

When Prieto was first elected to Congress and lobbying for his committee assignments, he shied away from one that might require deeper digging into his personal life, for obvious reasons. While Prieto and his sister had some vague notions of their mother's radicalization, her paper trail — digital and otherwise — was thin. Once on the Hill though, Prieto found himself with increased access to information, and finally, after cultivating a friendship with a rising star at the FBI, a Bronx-born Boricua named Miguel Bonilla, Prieto asked to see his mother's file. It was, he felt, like finding negatives to the photographs of his own life.

The file was thick, dating back to before her days with the Young Lords Party. It started with NYPD reports, trailing her and his father after Papi's arrest for the Brooklyn College takeover. After that, when they joined the Lords, COINTELPRO was almost always on their tail. Despite years of hearing his parents' stories of harassment by the NYPD and the FBI, it was still a trip to see the actual files. To reframe what he'd assumed was the hyperbole of jaded activists as actual fact. Proof not only of his parents' just paranoia, but also a mirror, he realized, to the skepticism he'd clearly held about it.

After the Lords disbanded, the FBI seemingly lost interest in his mother. Through childhood recollections buttressed by findings from the internet, Prieto sketched an outline of her life over the course of the ten or so years that followed. She was still living with them in New York, teaching at Hunter College. She became increasingly involved with a radical wing of the Socialist party, one more global in scope than the Lords. She'd begun going on a speaking circuit, traveling to Mexico, Central and South America, and, from what Prieto could piece together from old Socialist newspapers he found online, spending time in South Africa on anti-apartheid efforts.

Then, in 1989, the year before his mother disappeared from their lives, the FBI file picked up again. Robustly. A man named Ojeda Ríos was on trial for shooting an FBI agent with an Uzi during a raid on his home in Puerto Rico. The raid was part of an attempted arrest for a bank robbery Ojeda Ríos allegedly committed in Connecticut.

Of course, Prieto knew, Ojeda Ríos was no ordinary bank robber, but the leader of Los Macheteros, a militant Puerto Rican independence group that the U.S. government had deemed a terrorist organization. The bank robbery itself was as much about protesting colonialism as it was a money grab. His mother penned a series of impassioned op-eds championing his cause and was immediately back on the FBI's radar.

Ojeda Ríos was eventually acquitted for injuring the FBI agent, but jumped bond on the robbery charge in 1990. He found cover in the hills and forests of Puerto Rico, managing his secret paramilitary army and disseminating, via the local media, recordings to his followers throughout the rest of the island. Humiliated, the FBI launched a manhunt, deploying hundreds of agents in search of Ojeda Ríos. It was in November of that same year that they put eyes on Prieto's mother in San Juan, but she quickly vanished, leading the agents to believe she had joined Ojeda Ríos in the hills. They had been correct. In 1993 she emerged again to claim credit, on behalf of Ojeda Ríos's army, for a bombing at the home of Puerto Rico's then governor-elect. He'd won on a platform of privatization and statehood; the bomb detonated on the eve of his inauguration, leaving the house in flames. No one had been home at the time. Like her mentor, his mother evaded apprehension and for a time, the FBI believed she'd escaped to Cuba. Then, fifteen years ago she was spotted in Chiapas, Mexico, where she'd found refuge with the Zapatistas. Ojeda Ríos, for his part, became a sort of folk hero on the island, living openly in the Puerto Rican countryside, evading the law until 2005 when he was assassinated by the FBI. It had happened on the anniversary of el Grito de Lares — September 23 — fifteen years to the day after he had escaped. On the island there was an outcry.

Reviewing the file, the date stood out to Prieto for different reasons — Ojeda Ríos's murder was just a day after his own grandmother's death. He'd found it difficult to braid this political homicide with such an intimate loss in his own life, of his family's. He imagined his mother planning an assassination as they watched their father's slow descent into death. He pictured her plotting rebellion while his ex-wife was birthing their daughter. While he had sat in mourning for his grandmother, her daughter was shedding tears over this failed revolutionary. A sense of neglect washed over him that turned his worldview quite gray. His thoughts morphed into a feeling of dull pain.

As a young man, with his father a walking zombie and his mother gone, Prieto had to make a choice. Was he going to love them or hate them? He chose love. But in his mother's absence that love became something else. He idolized her, worshiped her. She, who was so committed to bettering the world that she left her own children! In light of this, he began to shape his life so that it reflected the values of this exalted figure. To signal to her that while she was off on the front lines, he was keeping up the good fight at home. The ideal soldier. Discovering that she had left it all behind — left them behind — to follow a fringe figure in an independence movement that would never succeed was, for Prieto, a pernicious blow. Her file recast their abandonment as futile: her cause not only impossible, but the means insane. What did this say about the woman, his mother, who'd dedicated her life to it? What did this say about him, whose life's purpose had been defined, not in small part, to please such a woman? Dwelling on this question took Prieto into dark, existential terrain, and so he packed the information away.

■ ■ ■ ■

His mother had written to him ceaselessly prior to the PROMESA vote, warning of the dire consequences and utter destruction of the Puerto Rican people that it would bring. But he had faced tremendous pressure, both from his peers and of public opinion — to say nothing of Lin-Manuel Miranda. Plus it was, he felt, a matter of common sense. It was the only real choice and so he made it.

Sort of. Truth be told, though Prieto tried to forget the information he'd seen in his mother's file, in the months and years following, he often found himself feeling angry with her. He went through and reread all of her letters, running the dates against milestones in his family's life. He was struck for the first time by her self-absorption, by her single-minded focus on her vision of how the world should be, the lack of interest in their lives outside of what she deemed important about them. Where these letters once filled him with warmth — random reminders that he wasn't motherless, he was loved — for the first time, he began to feel manipulated by her correspondences. So, when she began lobbying him about

PROMESA, he didn't so much vote for it to enact revenge as he didn't give her approval the consideration he historically would have. He didn't care if she was disappointed in him. He was disappointed in her.

For days and weeks after the vote, through the appointment of the panel and the creation of the fiscal austerity plan, he held his breath. Waiting for the angry, scolding missives from his mother that he knew Olga was accustomed to receiving. A waste of his position; a waste of his power. Yet nothing came. After a while, he began to sense that his mother was more than just "a bit" upset. Of course, PROMESA quickly proved humiliating for all who'd supported it. It was nothing more than a private-sector money grab. Whenever the topic of PROMESA came up he'd be flooded with a wave of anxiety, one that was rooted in more than concern for the island. Prieto found himself desperate to apologize to his mother for it. He hadn't realized how much his status as "the good one" had grounded him.

"The actual package was from a compost store on eBay," Agent Bonilla told Prieto over drinks at Le Diplomate. "But I was able to track down the bill-to address on the order: a Karen Price of West One Hundred Forty-ninth Street in Harlem."

Years of hiding — his sexuality, his father's addictions, his compromised position with the Selbys — had perfected Prieto's poker face. Karen Price was his auntie Karen, his mother's first and arguably only real friend.

"Hmm. Not a name I recognize," Prieto said.

"Well, it's an interesting biography," Bonilla replied as he took a sip of his whiskey. The bar was loud, but Bonilla was careful not to raise his voice. "I can't find a direct link, but I can't help but feel she's an associate of your mother's."

"Really? What would give you that idea?"

Agent Bonilla proceeded to walk Prieto through the path of Auntie Karen's life, which had many "common bonds" with his mother's, and yet no direct ties. Not that Bonilla could find. Karen had come from a tame, middle-class family, was radicalized in college, joined the Black Panthers, and defended her own self in court on a false terrorism charge. She, like his mother and father, was involved in the CUNY protests. She, like his mother, eventually became an academic. She'd then lived with a man for a time in Liberia, where she published subversive poems of sex and rebellion under a nom de plume. She never married, never had children. Instead she became a public advocate for jailed veterans of the movement whom she considered to be political prisoners. She was an early public supporter of Black Lives Matter and other activist groups and a private cooperator with more fringe political movements.

What Bonilla didn't know, and of course Prieto did, was that Karen's connection to his mother and radicalization predated all of these things. In an effort to tame her daughter's rebellious streak, Abuelita had sent Blanca to an all-girls Catholic high school. "¿Y instead?" Abuelita would lament. "What happened? She met La Karen." Always *the* Karen, as though she was a force and not a person. Ironically, Karen had landed at the Catholic school for similar reasons as his mother. Her older brother was a Black Nationalist and her parents hoped the nuns might inoculate Karen from this same leftist path. Instead, she and Prieto's mother found each other among, as his mother would say, "a sea of white girls with bleach blond hair" and bonded over their mutual awareness of systemic inequities. Karen would get books from her brother — *The Autobiography of Malcolm X; Black Skin, White Masks* — and share them with Blanca, who, in turn, would come home and proselytize to her siblings and mother. Karen joined the Panthers, while Prieto's parents joined the Lords. But even as the movements faded, as his parents' marriage fell apart, his mother's bond with Karen never waned. When his mother left, to his grandmother's chagrin, only La Karen knew exactly where she'd fled, and only La Karen had a direct channel of communication to her. If the worms came from Karen Price, it was only because she was serving as proxy for Prieto's own mother. To let him know she saw him as a traitor.

"We don't have any direct links to her and the Macheteros your mother was involved in," Bonilla was now saying, "but that would definitely be something up her alley."

"Interesting."

"And you've got no idea why she would send something like this to you now?"

"No. None whatsoever."

"Kooky old hippies," Bonilla declared. "Who knows what sets them off. They don't like the way you vote on some bill or another, and the next thing you know . . ."

Bonilla laughed and Prieto made sure to join him.

"We'll keep an eye on it," Bonilla added, and Prieto just sipped his drink.

■ ■ ■ ■

When he got back to New York, Prieto decided to get to the bottom of things. His mother couldn't just hide from him this way. He needed a chance to explain himself, to make things right. Aunt Karen did not keep a phone, so he decided to pay her a visit. He didn't know how serious Bonilla was about keeping an eye on things, but he took no chances. He donned his Yankee cap, shorts, and a tee, parked his car in a garage downtown, and hopped on the subway, to make the long journey up to Harlem. Because Prieto rarely rode the New York City subway, he found it pleasant. In D.C. he couldn't walk into a restaurant or store without being recognized from TV, so his ability to slip into anonymity despite his close proximity to others was relaxing. So relaxing, he missed his stop and ended up taking a meandering walk through North Harlem. He hadn't walked these streets since he was a kid, when his parents would bring him along for a political meeting or for his mother to visit with Karen. He was shocked at how, just like his own borough, everything seemed so metallic and new. The streets were filled with parents — white parents. Pushing strollers in and out of luxury condos. Up and down steps of brownstones. When he got to Karen's building, a place he hadn't been in years, his hand instinctively went to her buzzer. Muscle memory. She asked who it was through the intercom. He announced himself and waited for her to buzz him inside, but the buzz never came. He was sure it was her; he had recognized her voice. He rang again, and again. He became frustrated, but also nervous. He thought of the box of worms. His aunt had known him since he was born; she couldn't possibly ignore him. Perhaps she just couldn't hear him through the intercom. It was the end of a warm, late summer day; her windows were open. He stood on her stoop and bellowed up.

"Auntie Karen, hey! Wasn't sure if you could hear me through the intercom. It's me — Johnny and Blanca's son. Can you let me up? I just gotta ask you something real quick!"

A few moments passed before he heard the sound of a screen being raised. His aunt's beautiful dark face emerged, older, but still familiar. She looked at him pointedly in the eye, but the softness he had always known there was gone.

"Prieto, no reason to let you up. In case the package wasn't clear: she doesn't have anything else she wants to say to you, nor does she have anything she wants to hear from you."

■ ■ ■ ■

April 2002

■ ■ ■ ■

April 25, 2002

Querida,
Lately I've found myself thinking about the role of women in the world and the important part we play in forcing hands of power to create change. No matter where I've traveled, women, when given space, have excelled at organizing and improving their communities. We're born with barometers in our belly that make us more sensitive to the climate around us and, because we're so often on the lowest rung of any ladder, we're naturally inclined to look out for the least among us. Since we're also burdened by domestic tasks, we're forced to be more efficient. In a woman's world, time is the most precious commodity, and we don't have it to waste.

Of course, the problem is that we don't

live in a world just of women. Not only do men exist, but we are drawn to them and, for complex reasons, they do not treasure time in the same way that we do. It may have to do with an inability to face mortality, or needs of ego, or maybe it simply has to do with the fact that they don't hear the ticking of a biological clock. What I can say with certainty is that a man has no problem wasting time, especially that of a woman. And they manage to do so in such insidious ways we often don't notice that it's happening until it's too late.

Sometimes it looks like passion — they adore us, they treasure us, they want to be with us in the morning, every night, on the weekends. We, our hearts open, eager to give that love back and warmed by the light of their admiration, comply. We make ourselves available at their convenience, never giving another thought to what we might have done with those moments, hours, and days had they not asked for them. We justify it by saying, but what's more important than love? Never remembering that when they ask for your time it's always before and after they've accomplished what they wanted to do with their day.

Sometimes it looks like being supportive — they trust us, they need us, they feel we understand them, they believe we make them better. We, overflowing with capacity to care, flattered that we are so special, so chosen, so intellectually equal and necessary, we again comply. We put our energy — our tremendous energy — into strategizing how to achieve their dreams. How to help actualize their visions. Not realizing that the size of their ambitions blocks the light with which to see our own.

Sometimes love looks like being a savior — they seem lost, confused, without direction. We, ever-optimistic believers in change and the power of unconditional love, again comply. We give them guidance, we offer discipline, we go so far as to loan them our vision until they can find one of their own. All while our own dreams gather dust.

Olguita, mi amor, I have heard that this man — this "musician" — wants to settle down. I implore you to walk the other way. Mija, you're only twenty-five years old! Your own dreams are hardly formed, and I worry that with a man like that — a man who seems so lost himself — you'll spend your whole life supporting his ideas and his career and his children.

Marriage, when I was young, was a permission slip. The only way, in those days, a young woman could cross the threshold into adulthood. But you and your generation have the chance to be truly liberated — and true liberation is freedom from obligation. Obligation to soothe a husband's ego, or a baby's hungry cries.

Your father was brilliant. A dreamer. An idealist. He was a wonderful lover and a wonderful father. I loved him madly. Yet, at the end of the day, I had to accept the choice in front of me: I could spend my time soothing his loneliness and hurt, trying to motivate him back into purpose, or I could spend my time working towards the liberation of oppressed people around the world. Both, you must understand, are expressions of love. The choice isn't necessarily easy.

I worry that you're seduced by the money and the life that this guy represents. I worry that you've been bewitched by the little bit of limelight you get being next to a man who is the actual star. Have you mistaken the cost of the gifts he likely gives you with the value he has for you? Your Papi used to say that the greatest fool is the man of color who defines his success by the White Man's standard. I'll add to that: if he's a fool, then his trophy wife is to be pitied.

I'm sure my family thinks he is fantastic! I'm sure they find his cars and flash and little bit of fame very enchanting! But to me, what a heartbreak to imagine you selling yourself short to be this guy's wife. This thug of a guy who spends all his time making music about nothing. No, not about nothing! From what I've heard he makes music about money. Having it. Stealing it. Needing it to validate himself. Have you forgotten that when money is what centers someone's soul, that soul is hollow? This man is so lost he's ashamed of his own identity — changing his name to hide! Imagine what your father would have said. A man that insecure wants marriage to mark you as his territory the way a dog pisses on a hydrant. A man that insecure will never allow you enough space to find your own way, to express your own voice.

In fact, I can't help but feel that since you've met him, you already seem to have lost your way. What happened to your passion for your photography? What goals are you pursuing beyond spending all your time going where he wants to go with the people he knows?

I won't try to convince you that this guy isn't worthy of you. I remember being young and thinking I understood love, too. But I do have to ask questions, in the hopes that you will ask them of yourself. What are his bigger ambitions for himself? When was the last time he asked about yours? Besides your looks, does he value your mind? Does he ask your opinions in public? Does he support your curiosities in a meaningful way? What is his vision for you as a wife and a mother? What is his vision for himself as a husband and a father? Does he ask you if you want to have kids or does he just assume? Does he know that money can purchase things but not joy? What, besides being Puerto Rican, do you even have in common?

Pa'lante,
Mami

■ ■ ■ ■

SEPTEMBER 2017

■ ■ ■ ■

Bilingual

Getting her brother an invitation for the Blumenthal party had been so easy, Olga couldn't believe how challenging procuring her own had been. Of course, Olga was not a congressperson, let alone one who was on set at *Morning Joe* almost as frequently as the hosts themselves. Adding to this, Olga found out via Dick's assistant Charmaine that the new Mrs. Blumenthal was a self-declared "fan" of her brother. Indeed, a deep dive into Mrs. Blumenthal's Instagram account — @rrriottthespian — revealed that Mrs. Blumenthal had in fact already met her brother, when they shared the stage at the Women's March on Washington. Likely it was not a long meeting, but long enough that they had snapped a selfie together, which Mrs. Blumenthal captioned, *Great politics and easy on the eyes #womensmarch #easyontheeyeshardonsexism fire emoji, fire emoji, fire emoji.*

As she had suspected, Dick, an ardent Libertarian, refused to fork over the $10,000 for entrée into the fundraising fete, sending Prieto a note to say that it was nothing personal, but he wouldn't give him a dollar until he cut government spending and supported deregulation. When Olga read it, she rolled her eyes and almost raised the point that if he really wanted a relationship with her, he would need to see past policy and support her brother in ways big and small. Then she remembered that she didn't want a relationship with Dick and that she therefore didn't really care what he believed or supported. Besides, the entire point of this play, by design, was to ensure that she and Dick would not enter the Blumenthal party together, where surely a *New York Social Diary* photographer would be lingering. Instead she would walk in tethered to her brother's shiny star, enabling her to attract Mrs. Blumenthal's attention *and* rob Dick of the smug satisfaction of diminishing her to arm candy intended to impress some old white guys he liked to slap backs with.

Olga had helicoptered over with Dick on Friday afternoon. As she did not particularly like the Hamptons, or sleeping the night with others, it was her first time out to his house there, an impulse purchase he'd made in the wake of his divorce. It was a lavish bachelor pad, with a game room and movie theater in the basement, and glass walls that looked out on the infinity pool and the ocean just beyond. The kitchen was comically masculine. Walls of dark gray invisible cabinets, a massive wine fridge, and a marble countertop so long and wide she was certain that Dick would want to fuck on it, if only because it invited such unoriginal fantasy. It was a "sexy" house, in the way that pornography is sexy — it screamed the most basic desires a man has while seeming utterly ignorant to how and what might give a woman pleasure. Dick had bought the house, he'd explained to her, as a lure to his growing sons, hoping that they would find the place cool enough to want to come out with their friends, and not mind the "old man" being around. As far as she knew, they had not been out much, either.

Olga found this both funny and sad. She wished her family felt the need to use luxurious real estate to draw her presence. Instead she was lured by nothing more than the promise of a pastel, the timeless power of guilt, and, of course, love. She'd wondered if it was the money or the divorce that had degenerated Dick's family so. Where Dick seemed so lost and lonely, her Tío

Richie, also divorced, now remarried, had ended up with more than ever. Always surrounded by his kids and, whether he liked it or not, both his current and former wives. The sum total of the Hamptons house, and Dick's place in it, made Olga feel a vacuousness that not even sex that night — as she expected, on the kitchen counter — could shake. Indeed, if anything, the sex only succeeded in bathing her in a strange wave of melancholy. The evening left her feeling genuinely sorry for Dick, and nothing was less arousing than pity.

By the next morning, the feeling had not abated. If anything, overnight, it had strengthened and mutated into something more pointed and nagging: guilt. It surprised her. It was her first time sleeping with Dick since she had begun fucking Matteo. It was not the sex that evoked the guilt as much as the stark contrast in how she felt about the before and after. In the moment, she hadn't noticed this with Matteo, but once back in bed with Dick, it crystallized for her: it had been pleasant, a relief really, to fuck someone without the aura of mutual condescension surrounding the act. For the first time, certainly with Dick, but possibly in recent memory, it occurred to her that sex without disdain might be a good thing.

She needed to end things with Dick. Sooner rather than later, and ideally, nicely.

Overwhelmed by the sadness of the house, she asked Dick's driver to take her out at noon, though the benefit didn't start until two. Dick, who had signed up for back-to-back SoulCycle classes, wasn't there to notice. She sat at a bar in town nursing a glass of wine and Googling guests she wanted to meet at the Blumenthal party until her brother picked her up and off they headed to Southampton.

It was a perfect day and the party was centered around the estate's vast swimming pool, which the hostess, or more likely the housekeeper, had decorated with large red and white floating peonies. The cocktail tables had been covered in denim tablecloths with little white vases filled with more red peonies atop them. The entire affair had a casual Americana vibe, assuming that Americana's backdrop was a $20 million beachfront estate. Two of her past clients were there, and Olga was genuinely surprised by how many other people recognized her from *Good Morning, Later.* But, make no mistake, the star of the show was her brother, whom Olga had always envied for his ability, when with his donors or on television, to transform into a person who was white palatable while still remaining very much himself. He wasn't quite code-switching so much as he managed, miraculously, to speak several languages simultaneously, creating a linguistic creole of hip-hop, academia, contemporary slang, and high-level policy points that made Olga marvel. More astounding, he knew exactly when and with whom to finesse which aspect of himself, which proved, as Olga observed her brother, remarkably counterintuitive. He gave one of his older white male supporters a fist dap and slapped his back, and as he walked away Olga heard the man tell his wife that Prieto could be the Latino Obama. He called the hostess of the event Ma, which Olga was certain would offend, if not confuse her, but instead she blushed and kissed his cheek. Yet he was deft enough to know that, when greeting two of his older Black supporters — Prieto's events almost always brought out monied people of color — to call them sir and ma'am, and ask after their children, which inevitably led to the retrieval of a phone and, remarkably, a FaceTime call to their adult children traveling out of state. Her brother had staff for these events, but used no handler, remembering details — from profound to minuscule — about his supporters and constituents.

Olga herself had never learned this linguistic mezcla that her brother had perfected, this ability to be all facets of herself at once. She always had to choose which Olga she would be in any given situation, in any given moment. Indeed, as she watched him work the room, she wondered why he had ever felt that he needed to have her there in the first place; Prieto's "scene" was anywhere Prieto was.

The official program began with her brother speaking impassionedly about bipartisan efforts at criminal justice reform (mild applause), his work to secure more funding and transparency from the EPA to protect New York's coastlines (stronger applause), marijuana legalization (mischievous cheers; a surprisingly salient issue, Olga thought), and finally, the pièce de résistance, his work developing and supporting a wave of midterm candidates to help secure a majority in the next Congress and keep this administration in check (audible whoops). He opened it up to Q & A, which was relatively benign, if perhaps revealing of the conflicted interests of the socially liberal financial elite: feelings on deregulation, the dangers of socialists among us, concerns about big pharma being legally culpable for the opioid epidemic. Then, from the back came a baritone voice Olga recognized immediately and she felt her body tense.

"Congressmen Acevedo, I recognize that no man can be all things to all people, but as one of — what are you? — four Puerto Rican representatives in Congress? And as the head of the Congressional Latino Caucus, how can you explain your recent decision to cancel the oversight hearings for the board implementing the austerity measures in Puerto Rico?"

The crowd, completely ignorant of the subject matter at hand, but hyper-aware that the tone of the question was hardly friendly, grew silent. Olga sucked in her breath and slowly retreated to the back of the crowd, making her way towards the inquisitor, whom she of course knew to be, without needing to see him, Reggie King.

"Well, first, let me say, hello Mr. King," her brother began. "It is, as always, great to see you. As you know, I've been a very vocal supporter of a path to statehood for Puerto Rico. But in answer to your question, the truth is that the PROMESA board is comprised of bipartisan presidential appointees, and our oversight is purely ceremonial —"

"But surely," Reggie interrupted, "even a

ceremonial hearing can help to raise awareness of the neocolonial state that PROMESA has put Puerto Rico in? People are fleeing, schools are closing, and at this very moment people are waiting out a hurricane unsure if the island's infrastructure can survive the season."

"With all due respect, Reggie, I'm very aware of what's happening on my island."

"Our island," Reggie added.

"Gentlemen!" Olga called out loudly for the crowd to hear, cheer injected into her voice. She slipped her hand into the crook of Reggie's arm. "There is nothing that would make my grandma more proud than two people so passionate about their Puerto Rican roots. For those of you who do not know about the fiscal crisis in Puerto Rico, I encourage you to take a moment and speak to my brother," and she waved at her brother, "or to Mr. King here, who are both quite knowledgeable about the issue and would be happy to fill you in during the rest of the reception."

The hostess smiled widely at Olga, grateful to have avoided the actual discussion of politics or policy at her political fundraiser. Her brother winked at her from across the pool, where he was already swarmed by donors, and she found herself face-to-face with Reggie. This was why her brother had wanted her there.

They had met in another era, when cell phones were a novelty and email was for work. Before planes were flown into towers. When everything seemed extremely possible, including the unlikely possibility of being a recent college graduate, hustling at her first job, and being called into VIP by an older, handsome guy who happened to be behind countless songs that she had sung along to as a teenager, in college, and in that very nightclub where they met. He didn't try to take her home with him. Instead they went to Café Express at 2 A.M. and dined on moules frites — the first time she'd ever tried them — and talked until it was nearly time for her to go to work. He drove her home, she showered quickly, and then he drove her to her office. From then on, for nearly two years, it was like this: more than friends, but not quite committed, either. Him chasing his fortune and Olga chasing some sense of satisfaction that always seemed to evade her.

One day, he told her he wanted to get more serious. He was ready to settle down. He knew he would never find anyone else like her. Abuelita was delighted. Her mother, horrified. What was the point of all of that education, all of that insight, just to be an accessory to a man so lost he hides his own culture? A man so focused on money. Eventually, Olga told him she wasn't ready, she was far too young, she had too much she wanted to do with her life, though she wasn't quite sure what. He was the first and last real boyfriend Olga ever had.

Their parting was very friendly, not a hint of animosity. She was surprised by the sadness that consumed her when she read his wedding announcement a year later. She was less surprised when, a couple of years after that, he showed up to pay respects at Abuelita's funeral.

Though he was hip-hop royalty, Reggie's true wealth hadn't come from music, but from several wise, early investments in biotechnology firms and wind farms. And, of course, his real name was, in fact, not Reggie King, but Reggie Reyes. He'd changed it early in his music days when he made the transition from producing salsa and freestyle music to more mainstream pop and R & B. In recent years, perhaps to make amends for having not exactly hidden his Puerto Rican heritage, but not heralding it either, he had become a highly vocal advocate for decolonization efforts on the island. This initially perplexed the tabloids and hip-hop gossip sites, who followed his moves closely, as people seemed confounded that one could be both Black and Puerto Rican concurrently. The result was a bizarre media blitz during which Reggie appeared on various podcasts, talk shows, and CNN segments explaining Afro-Latino identity to the masses, which had struck Olga as surreal. They'd kept in touch, largely on social media, occasionally via text if she saw him in the news or he saw her on TV, just to say hello or "big up" or what have you, but it had been years since they were face-to-face.

Now, he was here before her, again. In the Hamptons of all places. He was older, broader. His face dark and smooth, with an impeccably groomed salt-and-pepper beard. The hip-hop mogul attire of the aughts replaced by a summer linen suit and a button-down.

"Hi," Olga said as she kissed him on the cheek.

"Hey!" He smiled. "You look fantastic. As usual. You don't age."

She laughed. "Please! I've got more La Mer happening on this face than J.Lo uses on her whole body!"

"I dated her once, you know."

"Oh my God." She rolled her eyes. "Always the same with you! The bragging! You think I don't know that date happened when I was in junior high and J.Lo was still a Fly Girl?"

"Pssh! You don't even know what you're talking about, girl. I took her out during the *Out of Sight* era, thank you very much."

They both laughed.

"So, it's good to see you, but . . . what are you doing here? Besides picking a fight with my brother."

"Your brother's wack, Olga, and I've always said that."

"So, because you're consistent, that makes your opinion true?"

"It's a dereliction of duty. He is one of the few people able to call attention to the disaster happening on our island!"

"Ay, Reggie, you and my brother are hilarious. The only island you should be claiming is City Island. Your home is the Bronx. When was the last time you were even in Puerto Rico?"

"Actually, Olga, I have a big-ass house there now, so . . ."

They both laughed. Each could always take what the other had to dish out.

"No, but seriously," he continued. "I came today because I want to make sure your brother knows we're watching."

"And who is we?"

"Just some like-minded individuals who care that our people — United States citizens — are being systemically eradicated by colonialism and neo-liberal policies, that's all."

"Ah. Okay. Just that." She sipped her champagne. "Listen, when did you get so political about all this shit?"

"Well, if you want to know, you woke something up in me —"

"Me?" Olga pointed to herself.

"Ya! When we used to hang out, I couldn't believe how much you just knew about our culture. I was embarrassed by my own ignorance. And I used to make salsa records! Anyway, I started to read, more and more. Then, when me and Grace had Carlos and he was in school, I realized he was very pro-Black, but didn't think of himself as Puerto Rican at all. I had done all this work to get all of this money and my kid was being raised a total alien to the culture I had known. Nothing was the same about us. Not the kind of house, not the beaches he'd visit, not the languages he would speak, not the way he thought of himself. And I figured some of this is just life, but some of this is on me, right?"

"Right." She paused. They stared at her brother working the remaining attendees, the sand dunes in the background. "So, now with all that knowledge and wisdom, you basically spent ten grand just to come and tell Prieto off?"

"Basically," he said. "Seeing you was a secondary goal. I would have dropped another ten G's on that."

Olga smiled, faintly. "I should get my brother. We have another engagement."

"What? You going to that Blumenthal party?"

"We are. And you?"

"Too many creeps under one tent for me, thanks."

She leaned in to give him a kiss on the cheek. He whispered in her ear: "Olga, I know you love him, but watch your brother."

She pulled away. "Thanks Reggie, but we're all good," she said as she walked away, his parting words trailing behind her.

Dick's No Good, Very Bad Day

Dick sighed in the back of his chauffeured SUV as he headed home. Alone. He found himself considering how wildly dissimilar the day's activities had been from the fantasy that he had developed about it. In his fantasy, he strolled into the normally bland Blumenthal party with Olga on his arm, turning the white-haired heads of his colleagues and competitors and then floating her around from couple to couple while she wooed them with her wit and exotic beauty. Instead, he was dropped at the entrance of the party and, right as his driver pulled away, realized that, when on political principle, he'd refused to attend her brother's fundraiser, he had in turn robbed himself of the moment he'd been visualizing in his mind for these past few weeks. How could having convictions result in such punishment? Unwilling to compromise the moment, he decided to wait it out, but, having dismissed his driver, was left with no place to hide. So he occupied himself by calling his senior staff to discuss pressing business that, until now, he'd planned to deal with on Monday. In between his manufactured frenzy, he'd also been texting and calling Olga, with, he would have to admit, a bit of insistence, just to see how quickly she could wrap things up and come and rescue him. For about thirty minutes, he paced back and forth, speaking loudly into his phone and nodding tacitly to partygoers passing him en route to revelry. He'd paused for a moment to catch his breath when, who should appear but Olga's assistant, hand in hand with a brawny young man, both smiling ear to ear.

"Mr. Eikenborn! So lovely to see a familiar face! I didn't think I would know anyone here. Trip, this is Dick Eikenborn, of —"

Trip, the thusly named brawny young man, cut her off and held his hand out to Dick. "Eikenborn and Sons, yes! Of course. What an honor to meet you, sir. I was so impressed with the M and A work you've done in Mexico and the Caribbean. The way you've expanded the brand."

"Ah, thank you . . ."

"Trip. Trip Davidson. I'm a first year at Blumenthal."

The assistant, who was quite perky, chimed in.

"And I'm his date." She looked into his eyes and gently said, "Meegan. Anyway, so nice to be on the other side of a party for a change! Are you waiting for someone?"

"Well, actually," Dick felt unable to restrain himself, "I'm waiting for Olga."

"My boss, Olga?" Meegan said. "She's coming? With you?" He could see her mind working.

"Why? Is it strange? That she would come to a party with me?" Dick heard the insecurity in his voice and regretted being so transparent. But why had she not told this girl about them? Charmaine knew everything important about him.

"No," Meegan said. "Why wouldn't she want to come to a party with you, Mr. Eikenborn?" Whether she felt that way or not, Dick made a mental note that the girl had picked up Olga's social-political skills and he laughed. Meegan continued, "Just surprised that she never mentioned it. She knew I was coming. . . . The only thing on the calendar was a party for her brother —"

"Yes, she's meeting me here, after. Soon," Dick said.

"Well," Trip interjected, "no reason to spend the time waiting out here, when you could go inside and wait with a drink in your hand, right?"

And this was how instead of making his grand entrance with Olga on his arm, he walked in with Olga's assistant and her first-year hedge fund associate boyfriend. It only went downhill from there. No sooner had a waiter put drinks into their hands than they found themselves in Blumenthal's line of sight, his new wife, Laurel, by his side.

"Eikenborn!" Carl Blumenthal called out and they made their way over. Dick awkwardly made introductions to his two new companions, the humiliation compounded by the fact that Carl clearly had never laid eyes on Trip before, so low was he on Carl's totem pole. Then, just as he thought he could make a getaway, the new Mrs. Blumenthal chimed in.

"But Dick, where is your lovely girlfriend and her fabulous brother? I am such a fan of hers — yours truly, a complete *Good Morning, Later* addict! But, more than anything, I just *love* that brother of hers! I was so excited to hear that he was going to stop by."

"They are on their way, actually, Laurel."

"Ah, right! His benefit! If I wasn't playing hostess, I would absolutely have been there. He is just so . . . real! Oh, but why aren't you there, Dick?" Laurel asked, genuinely confused.

Dick was unsure how to answer, as he got the distinct impression that revealing his Libertarian leanings now would be a social gaffe. Luckily, in his moment of hesitation, Laurel continued on with her admiration of Olga's brother.

"Really, I think he could be the Latino Obama. Don't you? Carl, wasn't I just saying that the other night?"

And, just then, the Latino Obama himself arrived. While Dick wondered to himself if a Hispanic version would fuck him with regulations the same way original Obama had, the Blumenthals, and then seemingly everyone, swarmed Olga and her brother. He was no fan of Prieto, whose very name Dick found ridiculous, and refused to use. Dick not only didn't agree with his bumper sticker liberalism, he hated the entire "homeboy" act Prieto put on for the news, and the nickname, to him, was just an extension of an obnoxious persona Dick found, frankly, dangerous. What good could it possibly do young minority men to see someone in Congress using slang and quoting rap music, except to encourage more of the same? And what good could more of that do the country, except to highlight divisions? This guy had a damn law degree from Columbia for God's sake, so it's not like he didn't know how to speak like a normal person. His sister certainly did. Which, of course, compounded his frustrations with her brother even more.

Dick slurped up the signature drink in his hands. A mojito? High in sugar, but he'd chalk this up to his cheat day. He handed a waiter his empty and picked up a fresh one. He made his way to the back of the crowd of guests, mainly women, waiting to take selfies with the brother and gently tugged on Olga's elbow, trying to get her attention. She was already enthralled in conversation with Mrs. Blumenthal, giving her all the dirt on the anchors of *Good Morning, Later.*

He knew that this meeting, this very relationship, was why Olga had agreed to accompany him to this party in the first place. Now that it was budding, he resented that she had found her way to Mrs. Blumenthal on her own. More than anything, though, he resented that just being with him for the day would not have been enough for her.

"Darling," he said, as he slipped a hand around her waist, a bit more firmly than he'd intended to. Her postured stiffened. "There are so many people here that I want to introduce you to."

Olga, Dick noticed, had a way of laughing in public that was not quite her private laugh. It was rounder, going up and then down, like a song she'd practiced. She laughed that way now, as she gently touched Mrs. Blumenthal's shoulder.

"Dick, who could possibly be more important than our hostess?" She paused and Dick simply stared at her. "Prieto! Prieto," she called to her brother and he stopped what he was doing and turned his attention to her, "come here. I told Laurel that you would fill her in on your plan to protect women's reproductive rights."

Dick noticed the way Mrs. Blumenthal looked at Olga with wonder, admiring her ability to command her powerful brother that way.

"You, Mr. Eikenborn," she said to Dick, "are one lucky man!"

"I know," he said as he guided Olga away and scooped two mojitos off a tray, one for each of them. For a moment, a brief moment, he felt the day had been turned around.

Dick guided them towards a step and repeat, where the *Times* society photographer snapped a pic in which he made sure to press Olga close to him. (It was beneath him, he knew, but he loved knowing his ex-wife would see this as she thumbed through the Sunday Styles section.) He then directed them towards some of his old classmates from Exeter, who he knew, once they met Olga, would be gossiping about him for the next month at least. Olga was just engaging in a spirited conversation with Nick Selby over the further development of their waterfront property in Brooklyn when there was a loud commotion, and the evening's true calamity ensued. A service tray came flying out of nowhere, the top half of a cocktail table was severed from its lower parts, and suddenly, sprawled on the floor was a large puddle of mojitos and a tall, lanky Black man in highly impractical shoes. Everyone turned to see.

"Christian!" Olga exclaimed.

"I think you mean Christ, dear," Nick Selby offered.

"I know how to curse, for fuck's sake. His name is Christian."

What followed played out, for Dick at least, in slow motion. Olga was wearing a sensational jade green summer dress that hugged her every curve, and these elaborate high-heeled sandals, but she effortlessly glided over to this Black man on the floor, squatted down, and held out her hand to help him up. Then, once standing, they hugged for a moment. Longer than a moment really, because Dick had enough time to watch her do it and then watch his buddies from Exeter also watch her. She wiped a tear from the man's eye, kissed his cheek, and directed him somewhere. Rather than leave well enough alone — to be content with her act of kindness — she then proceeded to go to the rear of the tent, where the drinks and the food had been coming from, and he could hear her, faintly, barking orders. She reemerged with a small army of staff, some with mops, some just picking things up. On the far side of the tent, where he could spot Meegan and Trip and Mr. Blumenthal (that lucky shit Trip should thank his stars he walked in with him!), he could tell no one noticed any of it. The Brazilian band continued playing their Samba. (Ah! That was the theme! Brazil!) People kept drinking. But in his corner of the tent, the only show that mattered was Olga leading the clean-up crew. In his corner of the tent was Mrs. Blumenthal and her daughter. He wanted to evaporate. It was a feeling he'd never known before.

"Well," one of his Exeter buddies exclaimed, "she's certainly different than the former Mrs. Eikenborn, isn't she?"

He was walking over towards Olga to stop the humiliation, but Laurel and her daughter intercepted him, broad smiles on their faces.

"Olga!" Laurel exclaimed. "Did you know I used to do summer stock?"

Olga appeared confused and nodded no.

"Well, nothing teaches you that hard work is talent's best companion quite like summer stock. I knew you had talent, but you, my dear, are not afraid of W-O-R-K! My husband's friends are lovely, but they don't understand working girls like us, dear."

From where he stood, he could see Olga, his Olga, reassert herself, her shoulders tipped back and her head back up high.

"Laurel, I suppose they can't. You know, I see a problem and I just feel compelled to try and solve it."

"Well," Laurel's daughter chimed in here, "we saw it and were very impressed. If this is how you troubleshoot and you're just a guest . . ."

Dick walked towards them, but not before grabbing a fresh cocktail off a passing waiter's tray. Olga reached for his free hand, tightly squeezing his fingers. He was momentarily delighted. Just momentarily. The rest of the afternoon was a blur. Perhaps they were there for another hour, or maybe it was four. Olga was by his side, then she was gone. Then they were together again. Then they were waiting for the car, and he could hear that the party was still going full swing.

"Why are we leaving?" he asked her.

"Because if we stay any longer, you'll be drunk. Or drunker, I should say."

"It's my cheat day."

She didn't say anything.

"Did you enjoy talking to Nick? He's very interested in Puerto Rico, you know."

Olga laughed. "Is he now? He seems mainly interested in money."

"Well," Dick said, "isn't everyone?"

She didn't say anything.

"Anyway," Dick continued, "I was happy you two met because he invited us down for a retreat of sorts next weekend — for investors on the island. I think it would be wonderful to go to your motherland together, don't you?"

"My motherland," she said flatly as she scrolled her phone, "is a neighborhood in Brooklyn, which your friend Nick and his family have slowly begun to destroy."

Dick laughed.

"Let's not be dramatic, Cherry. Anyway, it's a little time at the beach together. I can show you how to surf." He tried to nuzzle her neck, but she was unresponsive. "We'd fly down Friday, maybe Thursday, if you think you can —"

"I can't," she replied without skipping a beat. "I have my cousin's wedding that weekend."

"Your cousin is getting married? Which one? Why didn't you tell me? I don't have to go to this thing with Nick, you know. He has these little gatherings all the time."

"I didn't tell you," Olga said, some distance in her voice, "because it doesn't concern you."

"But it concerns *you,* so then I'm concerned. I want to go and meet your family."

Olga paused for a moment. "No, Richard, you don't. Not really."

Dick considered this. The truth was, if her family was anything like her brother, he didn't want to meet them, but he didn't want her being embarrassed of them, either.

"Olga." He cupped her two hands in his and looked her in the eyes. "I love you. There is nothing I could find out about your family that would send me running away."

Olga looked at him and let out a cackle. Not her public laugh, but not her bedroom giggle, either. It was, he felt, a cruel laugh.

"That's fantastic." She shook her hands free of his grasp. "Of course you think I'm worried about your impression of them. Why would you ever consider that I'm worried about their impression of *you*? Who would ever not like you?"

It took him a second to register her sarcasm, which was more a result of the multiple mojitos he'd consumed, not because her voice wasn't thick with it. Dick's car pulled up in front of them, but neither moved to get in. He could not believe that after the day he'd had, that she had put him through, she was now insulting him to his face.

"Let's change the subject," he said sharply. "Why did you do that today?"

"Do what?"

"Why did you embarrass me?"

"Excuse me? I embarrassed you?"

"I brought you here as my guest and you were off acting like a maid, in front of all of my friends."

"Like a maid?"

"Yes. There were some very prominent people here. People I know and do business with, and you were down on your knees helping that waiter off the ground, directing people with mops. It was embarrassing —"

"That embarrassed you? That embarrassed you. Okay. Well, you know who didn't find it embarrassing? The hostess! There is no way that I don't get hired for Laurel's daughter's wedding."

"Well, that's exactly my point! This was a party, not an audition. You acted like a maid and now you'll be hired as one."

"So, that's how you see me?" Olga said to him.

This was the moment, Dick realized in the car ride home, when his answer should have been different. He should have said anything but what came out of his mouth next, but he didn't.

"I only see what you present."

"Richard," she said, with remarkable calm, "and I mean this very sincerely. Please get in this car and go home and fuck yourself."

■ ■ ■ ■

October 2006

■ ■ ■ ■

October 5, 2006

Querida Olga,

When I was a girl, my father told me that I'd been named for Blanca Canales, the revolutionary, and that she was the one who gave me my fighting spirit. So, when I was pregnant with you, your father and I put together a list of names that would instill you with the spirit of your ancestors as well. It was your Papi who suggested we name you for Olga Garriga, who was born in Brooklyn like you, but dedicated her life to liberating la Matria. She had the wisdom to understand that as long as the people on the island were bound by colonial rule, no Puerto Rican anywhere in the States would be a truly equal citizen. I liked this choice because Olga Garriga could have had an easy life, blending in as a

New Yorker, meeting a man, raising children to think that they, too, were American. But instead, she chose the hard path, because that was the right path.

Still, in the back of my mind, I couldn't help but think of another famous Boricua named Olga. One much less admirable. And this gave me pause.

When we were young, me and your Papi used to visit his old friends in Loisaida, where he'd grown up. That area was full of artists, writers, poets. All Boricuas. All into uplifting our people. One night, we heard this Brother perform this poem, and it broke my heart. In his verses I heard my family's life. They were characters — Juan, Miguel, Milagros, Olga, Manuel — but as far as I was concerned he could have named them Isabel, Richie, JoJo, and Lola, because he — Pedro Pietri — captured my family. All of them chasing an impossible dream: to be accepted by a nation that viewed them with contempt. So willing — eager, almost — to shed our rich culture for the cheap thrill of being seen as "American." Thinking that if one day they accumulated enough stuff, if they learned to act the right way, they could wipe the "Spic" off of them and be seen as "the same." And because of course white America will never see them as equal, they die owning lots of things, but having lost themselves.

So, although I admired Olga Garriga greatly, there was a part of me that worried this name might be inauspicious. That instead of imbuing in you the spirit of a fighter, it would render you like the other Olga. The one whose obituary had already been written: destined to spend her life chasing a love she'd never fully have.

I hear from my friends that you are on a reality television show now working for rich white people. Planning parties for them. Like a secretary. Or, maybe worse, a maid! Someone sent me the tape and I almost don't want to watch. Is this a business? Is this a job? Or are you trying to be famous? Because the world needs to see another Latina girl sweeping the dust from white people's feet? I'm struggling to understand how this happened and what about this path was appealing to you.

Your father was beaten and put in jail to raise his people up. I gave up my life and family to liberate the oppressed.

Even your brother has committed himself to this cause. It's hard for me to understand how you've wandered so far astray. When you see your brother out there, fighting for his people, while you flail your arms to get a few dollars and a little bit of attention, how do you feel?

Mija, it's not too late to choose which Olga's path to follow.

Pa'lante,
Mami

SEPTEMBER 2017

THE LIFT

"Thanks for coming back," Olga said to her brother as she climbed into his truck.

He barely waited a beat before he pulled right back onto the Montauk Highway. Olga hadn't even asked him to come up the driveway; she met him out by the side of the road, just near the Blumenthal estate.

"Listen, sis, I'm not sure why you couldn't call a fucking Uber, but I'm your brother, so you call, and I guess I come? Even when I'm already thirty minutes out of this fucking — holy shit! Olga! Olga, have you been fucking crying?"

The late evening sun, blindingly bright, had illuminated the saline outlines of dried tears just beyond the rims of Olga's gold-edged Ray-Bans.

"Cry!" she said, looking straight ahead. "Cry? Prieto, I didn't cry when we put our grandmother in the ground, you think I'm gonna cry because of this fucking pendejo?

I was bored waiting for your ass, so I smoked a little weed with the valets."

Prieto glanced at her again. She pulled down her sunglasses and widened her eyes. He shrugged his shoulders.

"Please," Olga said. "If I ever cry again, I promise it will be about something more important than some dumb shit Dick Eikenborn said."

Prieto just shrugged again.

"It's fucking *Visine,* okay?" Olga said. She put her sunglasses back on and stared straight ahead into the road, feeling her irritation beginning to bubble up just as she'd calmed it.

In fact, she had been shaking with rage following her fight with Dick. She could barely walk down the driveway after he pulled away. The adrenaline had caused her muscles to spasm. She had to stop a couple of times to simply calm herself enough to proceed and, during one of these brief pauses, she was shocked to find water trickling down her face. They had been involuntary, the tears. Which is why she didn't admit to them. Also, they were tears of anger, as she thought over and over again, who the fuck did Dick, who had never actually earned, outright, a single thing in his entire life, think he was to speak to her that way? Every single thing she had done with her life she had figured out for herself. Going to an Ivy League college. Every internship. Her first job. Her second job Reggie King had helped her get, but how many other bitches did Reggie meet and then never talk to again? Her business was all her, too. She designed the logo. She built her fucking first website. Her first clients? No one brought those people to her door, she sought them out. She closed the fucking deals. She got her own shot at TV. She pitched her own press. No one had fucking helped her get to where she was, and here this corny motherfucker who can't tie his own shoes without calling for his assistant was telling her that she acted like a fucking maid? Because she was trying to be a decent human being? Because she has actual fucking skills and knows how to get shit done?

"What the fuck are we listening to, Prieto?" she blurted out, the music suddenly piercing her thoughts. "I can't do three hours with your golden oldies of freestyle, dude. . . ."

"What? You don't like Lisette Melendez?" He turned the dial louder. "Where's your pride, sis? Freestyle is one of the great Puerto Rican art forms. Did you know that —"

"— freestyle music is where Marc Anthony got his start? Yes. You tell me every time we listen to this shit."

"Come on, you don't like this one?" Her brother pushed to another track, raised the volume, and began singing "Dreamboy/ Dreamgirl" at the top of his lungs, which Olga could not help but laugh at.

"This should be your next campaign video! Congressman Acevedo: Reppin' the Old School, Reppin' YOU!"

They both cracked up, and her brother lowered the volume and changed the music to an old Brand Nubian tune.

"Sis, you did me a real solid with Reggie today, so as a thank-you, I'm gonna put on some music more to your liking."

"I should be pissed you didn't tell me he was gonna be there. What the fuck?"

"I couldn't take the chance you wouldn't show."

"Did you know he was gonna come at you like that?" Olga asked.

"Suspected . . . after that op-ed, I'd have been shocked if he didn't. Look, it's his right to ask, but as you can see, no one in that Hamptons crowd gives a shit about P.R."

"Well, I don't know about all that. Richard has crazy money invested in stores down there and just today he was telling me Nick Selby apparently —"

"Hold up. Were you hanging out with Nick Selby?"

"For like, ten minutes at the party, it was more that Dick told me —"

"Olga, stay away from him. Him and his brother. Please. They're into some fucked-up shit."

"Really? Nick made it sound like you guys were friends."

She watched her brother's hands stiffen around the steering wheel.

"Half of New York thinks we're friends, Olga. It's not always a two-way street. He's a bad dude."

"Well, he seems exactly the same as the rest of those developers, as far as I could tell. As I suspected, he thinks his fucking mall is the greatest gift to Sunset Park since the public pool —"

"Jesus! Olga! Enough with this pendejo, okay? How much clearer do I need to be?"

But he wasn't being clear at all, Olga thought to herself. Literally hundreds of shady developers, lobbyists, bankers, and financiers tried to curry favor with her brother in any given week. Why did her brother find this particular guy so unsavory? It wasn't just his words; his whole body had tensed. She heard Reggie's parting words in her ears. From under her sunglasses she eyed her brother as she very gently asked, "Prieto, why did you cancel the PROMESA board hearing?"

"It's just what I said to Reggie — it's ceremonial, we have no real authority. What's the point of wasting everyone's time just for them to pay us lip service? The president appointed these people and we can't fire them. Puerto Rico got screwed with this whole thing, but what choice did we really have, right? They had this massive debt. We couldn't let them default, for any number of infrastructure reasons; if they defaulted, they would have to shut the power company and we literally wouldn't be able to keep the lights on for the people there. PROMESA, and this oversight board, was the only structure the Dems and R's could agree on.

"Of course, the people on the island, and people like you and me, and I mean, I guess Reggie, since he's all down with la raza now — we know that this mess is the result of fucked-up colonial policies that leave them victims to the mainland's whims. But, to the rest of America? Puerto Ricans look like they just can't handle the little bit of government we've been given. So, to me, I didn't feel like it helped our cause to let this figurehead get in front of my committee just to make us look like we can't manage our bills without help. And, as you know, optics are what win the day, right?"

Her brother's demeanor had been relaxed through his whole reply. His white knuckles from moments earlier gone from the steering wheel. He was thoughtful and his argument lucid. But she noticed he never once broke his eyes from the road as he delivered his soliloquy.

"So, listen. Mabel said after the wedding she and Julio are moving out?" Olga asked, changing topics. She had another item on her agenda with her brother, and this seemed a good time.

"Ya. You know Mabel. She's been paying, what? Like four hundred dollars a month for the past five years. Taking trips with all the scrilla she's saving, buying every Coach bag she can get her hands on, and now that she's gonna be married, she's too good for the place. Says she and Julio can't be in some shitty rental in Sunset Park."

"That bitch has never even paid market rent!" Olga laughed. "Let me guess. They're moving to Long Island?"

"You know it! Bay Shore. 'Es classy,

Prieto. Lots of little bars y lounges, not like here.' "

"Ah, well, she's nothing if not predictable, right?"

The siblings belly laughed.

"Anyway," Olga continued, "I guess that means the apartment is available again."

"Why?" Prieto asked. "You wanna move back? Because I was figuring Tony was gonna ask for it."

"Me?" Olga asked, slightly wistful at the idea. "No. I'm fine where I am, but I saw a friend of mine today, he's in a bit of a hard way. I'd like to do him the solid and let him take the place to get on his feet for a year or so."

"Oh yeah?" Prieto asked. "What friend did you see today? Because I know Reggie's not looking for a two-bedroom walk-up in Sunset."

"Do you remember my friend Jan? You met him at my birthday thing last year?"

"Um, I don't know. I meet so many people. Polish?"

"Yeah. That's him. Well, not to be morbid, but he died. Anyway, he had this long-term boyfriend, this guy named Christian —"

"What the fuck? That guy died?"

"Jan? Yes. See, you do remember him," Olga noted. "It was really shocking. So, and

I should have thought of this, but basically Christian has been trying to cover —"

"Wait, Olga. This guy died. Out of nowhere?"

Olga glanced at her brother from the corner of her eye. He was agitated.

"Jesus," she said. "Calm down. You only met him for five minutes."

"He's a young guy, Olga. My age." He was speaking quickly. "All of a sudden he's just dead? Yeah, it's a little shocking. It doesn't happen for no reason."

"Well, that's true." For a second she paused. This had clearly touched a nerve. "So, ugh. It's so sad. Not to make this story worse, but he'd tested HIV positive and I guess —"

"He died of fucking AIDS?" Prieto banged the steering wheel.

"Prieto! Why are you so hyper? Let me finish the fucking story!"

"He was just . . . he was just so young, Olga."

Olga eyed her brother, trying to size up this response that had taken her by surprise.

"Super funny guy," Prieto offered as he looked out to the road. It was dusk now, the night sky going pink into mauve, the streetlamps on the LIE illuminated against it. "Just such a sharp sense of humor. I cannot believe he died of fucking AIDS."

"¡Coño!" Olga said. "I know you're traumatized from Papi and shit, but you're an elected official. Educate yourself. Not sure if you heard, Prieto, nobody dies of AIDS anymore. At least not in America. You just get stuck taking a shit-ton of meds that might leave you broke and not feeling amazing, but you can literally end up undetectable. Let me finish my story before you start fucking rumors."

Prieto paused. "So then how did he die? If he didn't die of AIDS?"

"He killed himself," Olga said. Her brother banged the wheel again. "He hung himself in his fucking closet when he found out. Can you believe it?"

Prieto stared at the road ahead, silent.

Here, Olga saw a long-closed window and decided now was as good a time as any to attempt to pry it open.

"It's crazy because even though he lived with another man for almost two decades, he was still in the closet. Can you believe it? When I went to his funeral, no one in his family 'knew' he was gay."

"Why do you say it like that?" Prieto said. "With your hands like that. They didn't 'know.' "

"Because, Prieto," and she turned her full

body towards her brother now, and with frankness said, "everyone always knows, all right? They just never say anything. They might all want to go along with the story forever, if given the chance, but if told the truth, they would never be surprised. Don't you think?"

Her brother glanced at her. There was silence for a long moment. The window would stay closed, and so she moved on.

"Anyway, you're acting so crazy, you made me forget the point of even telling you about this."

"When did it happen?"

"Five, six weeks ago?" Olga continued quickly so as not to get derailed from her objective. "His boyfriend Christian realizes, after the funeral and the celebration of life and the dust of the whole thing settles, that the only way the math on his life — the apartment, the jobs he has, his Obamacare, all of it — the only way it works is if there are two incomes in the house and now he's down to one. So, he calls Jan's old boss to see if he can pick up a couple of shifts, but the guy is a performance queen — I mean, he's done some light bookkeeping and reception work — but he was not cut out for that waiter life. They gave him a chance and I can tell you it was a first and last because he was working the party today and did a face-plant while carrying a tray of caipirinhas."

Olga looked at her brother, who seemed lost in his thoughts. She figured she would make the suggestion now, while he seemed distracted, to see how it landed.

"Anyway, he was so distraught, I felt like I had to try to help and the easiest way to do so was finding him a cheaper place to live, so I offered him up the second-floor apartment as soon as Mabel gets out of there. We can give it a fresh coat of paint, ya?"

There was a pause and Olga was about to move on to another topic, patting herself on the back for how smooth this had been, when Prieto turned off the music.

"Olga, that is so not cool. We always said that was our family apartment."

"Yes, for when our family is in need, Prieto, and, God bless, we're all good right now. Tony might want the place, but he'll still want it next year. Lord knows he's not getting a spot on his own between now and then. There's no way Christian will want to live all the way out in Sunset for more than a year and —"

"And my daughter lives in that house, Olga. And he's a stranger."

Olga felt her throat get tight.

"He's a stranger to *you.* And it's a separate fucking apartment, Prieto, with its own doors and its own locks. He has his own life and while I love Lourdes dearly, I don't think hanging with a twelve-year-old is his schtick, you know?"

There was a thick silence. Her desire to do a good deed was now situated in opposition to her brother's fears. Olga could feel her anger quickening, the vexation overtaking her rational mind. She tried to calm herself before she played the card they both knew she held in her back pocket.

Though Olga normally delighted in advantages, this was one that made her uncomfortable: the knowledge that the house, the epicenter of the Ortiz clan, had not been left, as one would have thought, to all the children, or even all the grandchildren, or even to just the two grandchildren who had lived in the little limestone on Fifty-third Street for their whole lives. Instead, Abuelita had decided that the best way to keep the house, and thus the family, intact was to leave it in the hands of just one person, and that person was Olga.

Their Tía Lola had been the executor of the will, a wise decision on Abuelita's part. She, of everyone, not only didn't need anything Abuelita had, but was also of similar temperament and therefore understood her mother's thinking. Additionally, Lola was savvy enough in Ortiz family politics to know when a white lie was appropriate. Upon evaluating the will, she pulled Olga and Prieto aside simultaneously and reasoned that, if they wanted peace in the house and the family, they would need to keep this conversation private. She explained that this was the kind of thing that could tear other siblings apart, but that she, and Abuelita, expected more of them. It was clear to Lola that of everyone, Olga, being single, would have the greatest likelihood of needing the home. In other words, she was the least likely to sell. Prieto, who was married to Sarita at the time, nodded politely. Olga, terrified that this burden might draw a wedge between them, relinquished it. Prieto, she had said, I may own it, but the house is yours and upstairs is for whatever the family needs. This, her aunt had said to her later, was exactly why Abuelita had given it to her in the first place. Tía Lola told the family that the house now belonged to "the Estate," which made everyone feel just fancy enough to not ask too many questions. Richie, the usual troublemaker, was too grief stricken to make waves, and neither Prieto nor Olga had ever spoken about the true ownership of the home again. Olga knew that bringing it up in anger would inflict the kind of wound not easily healed. She hoped her brother wouldn't get the better of her.

"Olga, the bottom line is, I don't want some pato living in my house."

This comment, for Olga, confirmed more about her brother's sexuality than any full-throated confession ever could have done. And it was this comment that caused her to go blind with disgust, which quickly morphed into fury. Fury at his self-loathing, revulsion at his selfishness, and animus towards the weak character this conversation had laid bare to her. She forgot about the house. Her mouth flew open and she spit out, "Because you're afraid of what he'll do or what you'll want to do, hermano?"

For several minutes Prieto did nothing, eventually reaching over and turning the music back on, louder and louder until the thumping of the bassline left no room for thought. Outside, the LIE ran into Queens and curved in such a way that the entirety of Manhattan was before them, twinkling. Up for grabs.

What About Your Friends

Because her list of acquaintances, contacts, colleagues, and clients was so extensive, it took Olga a long time to realize that she didn't have any actual friends. At least not as defined by Webster's: bonds or mutual affection with individuals exclusive of one's relations. In fact, the only stranger with whom Olga had ever shared her intimate thoughts and feelings had been Reggie King. Beyond him, the closest people in Olga's life had been her grandmother, her cousin Mabel, and of course her brother. Olga was generally not an anxious person; her profession had worked much of that out of her system. But, in rare moments such as this one, when she and her brother found themselves with a cavernous gap between them, existential anxiety would grip her tightly. As they drove in silence, she had to fight her immediate impulse to reconcile quickly.

She tried to trace how this had happened — how she came to find herself awash in party invitations and drink dates but devoid of actual intimate relationships. It wasn't always this way. When she was younger, she and Mabel ran with a big group of kids from the neighborhood, in and out of everyone's houses, everyone up in one another's business. Like a big family. When her mother left, and her father was running the streets, Olga was aware that she was undoubtedly the subject of neighborhood gossip, but in her crew, she never heard about it. Once, they were kicking it on Mabel's block and some boy tried to make a crack about her dad and Mabel dressed him down so fast, so viciously, that nobody ever talked smack about Olga, Mabel, or anyone in the Ortiz/Acevedo clan ever again. At least not when they were around.

But when high school came, everybody went to one of the two local schools except for Olga, who had taken up photography and ended up at LaGuardia in Manhattan. The commute was long and she spent her afternoons in the dark room, so she missed all the after-school trips to the Fulton Mall or drinking forties on Shore Road. She knew, because Mabel told her, that their neighborhood friends thought she was stuck-up now. That she thought she was better than everybody else because she went to school in Manhattan. Olga only sort of cared. Prieto was already up at college and Olga was too focused on how she could also get out. Her house was emptier than ever, yet she felt smothered by her short life.

LaGuardia was a public school, but Olga was surprised to find the student body quite different from her neighborhood schools in Sunset. She was shocked how many kids in the art program lived in Manhattan. Whose parents were not rich, but were professionals: public defenders, college professors, government officials. She felt too embarrassed to ever let anyone know what fuck-ups her parents were. It was easy enough to avoid since most socializing outside of school was spent going to raves or sneaking into the Limelight. Places where the music drowned out the need for intimate conversation.

Olga had hoped college would be a way to reinvent herself on her own terms. She had been unprepared for the culture shock. The place was implausibly white, and implausibly wealthy. Most students attempted to mask their wealth, which, for Olga, only made the revelations more jarring. Like when her hallmate, who wore sweaters with holes in them and once asked Olga to buy her falafel because she was "broke," casually mentioned that her father was taking her to Paris on the family jet for the weekend.

There were so few minority students that they clustered together and, in the face of such white cultural dominance, attempted to "out-'hood" each other by any means necessary. She couldn't tell if it was a performance for her benefit — because in those days saying you were from Brooklyn had an edge to it — or if it was just generalized identity exploration, but here too, she met with a kind of duplicity. The girl who made a show of dating a member of the Crips turned out to have been a Jack and Jill kid whose parents owned ten McDonaldses. The guy who told a story about his best friend "doing a bid" for dealing — a story Olga immediately recognized as paraphrase of Nas's "One Love" — was an alumnus of Phillips Andover, a place Olga had never even heard of until she got to campus. When Olga asked him about it, he got in her face saying, "You don't know my life! I did Prep for Prep!" One weekend, Mabel, curious what it was like to go away to school, came up to visit. She loved the campus and the bookstore, and even came to a sociology lecture — the subject that day was infidelity — and was riveted. But when Olga took her to an off-campus house party the BSU was sponsoring she took one look around and declared, "These people are mad corny. Let's bounce." Olga felt validated. They ended up at a hip-hop club downtown where Mabel commanded attention, as per usual, on the dance floor. It was ironic how close she and Mabel were during her college years, given the physical miles and the cost of long-distance calls, but for Olga, feeling lost amid all the posturing, Mabel's authenticity was a touchstone.

Her brother had loved his Greek experience so much that Olga briefly considered pledging — there was a chapter of his sister sorority on campus — but their first recruiting event was a screening of a film about the Young Lords and Olga decided she'd been indoctrinated enough in this area and bailed. After not finding her place with the students of color, Olga took to hanging out with the international kids. She found it ironic, then, that the minority students branded her a "sellout to the community" because of this. What she wanted to say, but didn't, was that she'd already sacrificed more for the "community" than they could possibly understand. She brushed it off. Olga liked the international students. They were the only other people who seemed to find the place as alien as she did. Olga found it refreshing that those who were rich were unapologetically so: driving luxury cars, putting up oil paintings in dorm rooms, hiring personal chefs to cook elaborate birthday dinners filled with wine and arguments about film and literature. This, Olga felt, was what you were supposed to do with money. The friendships were never particularly deep, but they helped to pass the time, and they expanded her world.

When college was over, Olga again struggled to find her way. She floated between Mabel's world and the Eurotrash dinner parties — now being held in Manhattan pied-à-terres — enjoying both, but never feeling like she fully belonged in either place. Mabel, having stayed in Brooklyn, had a vast network of friendships and club hookups from school and work that she afforded to her cousin. It helped Mabel too, Olga realized. Having a cousin who was "artsy" and "cool" offered her a differentiation point, though, in those days, Mabel's body was so banging that she differentiated herself well enough on her own.

She was, in fact, out with Mabel when she met Reggie King and for any number of reasons, Mabel was a fan. First, Mabel had always been a big freestyle head, so she was already an admirer of his work, but also Reggie's flash was very much Mabel's style. And Mabel's sense of humor was right up Reggie's alley. Plus, Mabel loved the VIP access that Olga's relationship granted her by extension; the night that they all met, Mabel ended up going home with one of the hype men from Mobb Deep. When Olga broke things off with Reggie, Mabel was furious. She was as mad as if she had been Reggie's cousin. Her anger irritated Olga, who felt she was encouraging her to stay with Reggie to keep her own VIP status, which made Mabel curse her out, screaming about how a pendeja like Olga didn't deserve happiness. And although, with Abuelita's intervention, they eventually squashed their beef, it wasn't ever really the same after that.

There were moments of closeness, here and there. When Prieto married. When Lourdes was born. When their grandmother died. But generally speaking, when Olga lost Reggie, she also lost Mabel. She wished she could call her cousin now, but things had been too weird for too long at this point to trust her with such sensitive information about her brother. Days like today made her feel so lonely.

She picked up her phone and texted Matteo.

Prieto dropped her off at a bar where she said she was "meeting a friend."

"Olga," he said through the window, with a weary smile. "You don't have any friends."

"I know. It's why I hate when we fight."

"At the end of the day, it's your house."

She walked around to his side and leaned in. "At the end of the day, it's the family house, but I wouldn't have offered it if he didn't need it, Prieto."

He put his hand on the top of her head.

"I don't know who you've got more of, Abuelita or Mami," he said, and drove away.

Stoops

Olga teetered into a bodega and picked up a six-pack of beer, desperate to get out of her uncomfortable heels. A white girl, she thought, would just walk barefoot the half block to Matteo's house. She had seen them, the girls, barefoot on the filthy sidewalks. Her grandmother would roll in her grave. He had wanted to meet at a bar, but she had texted that after the day she had she really didn't want to talk to anyone, not even a bartender. She realized, after she hit send, that implied that she didn't consider him "anyone," but she was too weary to overthink it.

He was waiting for her on the stoop, also with a six-pack, a small speaker by his side pumping out an old Spinners tune. She felt happy when she saw him in a way that was new to her. He was soothing. Like sweet fried plantains. They smiled at each other in silence as she walked up the brownstone steps to the top of the stoop, sat down, rested her back against the banister, and swung her feet up onto Matteo's lap. He unbuckled her sandals while she opened a bottle of beer, giving each foot a squeeze as he did so.

"This is a good song," she said.

"Ah, the best. But you know what?"

"What?"

"It sounds better on vinyl."

"Well, shit," she said, "tell me what doesn't?"

"Fair point."

A skinny old man in a muscle tank and basketball shorts pushed a reappropriated IKEA shopping cart piled high with his possessions — framed art, bags of clothes, a folding chair, an old-school boom box — up the street past them. He called out to Matteo.

"Yo! My man! You got something you can contribute to my battery fund? I've got no juice." He gestured to the boom box.

Matteo slid out from under her feet and bounded down the steps, slipping the guy a bill. He quickly resumed his position as her footrest.

"You think he'll really use the cash for batteries?" Olga asked. The man had reminded her of her father towards his end, and the melancholy of the car ride blanketed her again, thick as the summer air.

"Freddie? Yeah. He loves that friggin' boom box. He'll stand in front of the bodega all day with that shit blasting. He's harmless, but you know, the new blanquitos . . . he creeps them out a little bit."

"Yeah. My dad, at one point, was kind of like that." Olga could feel Matteo's attention on her. She continued: "But he definitely wouldn't have used the money for batteries, as much as he loved music." She laughed, though the memory was not funny to her.

"Did I tell you my dad was a junkie when he died?" she asked, knowing fully well she had avoided the subject deftly to this point. "Basehead, too. A long fall from his Young Lords days."

"Overdose?" Matteo asked quietly.

"Nah. People didn't OD back then like now. AIDS, though, that was a different story. Death sentence. My Papi was a functioning addict for a long time. Kept a job, would still come and see us, like normal. But then, you know, the same old story. Starts missing shifts, loses his job, starts coming around high, then he's pawning shit, then he's stealing shit to pawn. But! In all that time, the only thing he'd never sell were his records! Anyway, one morning, Abuelita found all the albums in crates in the front yard of our house. His landlord heard he was sick and kicked him out. Papi carried out his records and the landlord burned everything else in the backyard. Magic Johnson had already played in the fucking Olympics with HIV, but this guy was afraid of a mattress. Coño. After that day, for a couple of months we couldn't find him. Then, we got a call from the hospital.

"This was ninety-four? The people still dying were mainly like Papi — junkies. Brown and Black addicts. Some gay men, trans girls. But by this time, they, too, were all Black and Brown. I don't know what it was like in the eighties, but the doctors and nurses treated them fine — shit, for lots of people, sadly, the hospitals were more stable than their home situations. But these people were lonely as fuck. No one was visiting these homies. The hospitals were like ghost towns. But we would go, religiously, and see Papi. My aunt Lola would bring him food, though he couldn't eat by then. My abuela would give him sponge baths. Even my uncles would come — which, honestly, I have to remind myself often these days, since my Tío Richie's become one of these nutty Make America Great Again people, which I can't even get started on. Anyway, my brother never went. Not once. At first, I thought it was because of my mother. But then I began to think it was something else."

Olga could feel the weight of her words in the air, but felt a heaviness move off her chest a bit. She smiled at Matteo very faintly, felt her cheeks get flushed.

"What'd make you think your mom wouldn't want him to visit your dad?"

"I assumed she sent him a letter like the one she sent me. She sort of took a 'don't let his shit weigh you down' tack. But my brother and I? We think she was angry. Like legit pissed. The way she saw it, she'd fallen in love with a powerhouse activist who wanted to change the world with her, and then he goes and lets himself become another tragic Puerto Rican statistic."

"And how did you see it?" he asked as he rubbed her legs. She pretended not to hear.

"Prieto never came to the hospital and he'd tell my grandma and anybody who was listening that he was just trying to preserve his good memories of Papi. Which was Mami's advice, I knew. But, in the back of my mind I'd always wondered if he didn't go because he was afraid."

"Of AIDS?" Matteo asked.

"Of fucking everything," Olga said, her

head shaking in disbelief. She sat up straighter. "We had a big fight today —"

"About his fundraiser?"

"No, about a favor I wanted to do for a friend. It's a long story . . ."

"You see me trying to go anywhere?" Matteo asked.

Olga sighed. "Okay. Have you ever been talking to somebody about, ostensibly, one small, specific thing, but the implications of what you're saying shift the way you perceive everything that came before and after it?"

"Absolutely," Matteo offered flatly. "When the doctor told me my mother was dying. We were having a conversation, but in my mind, I was revisiting her taking me to school for the first time, trying to give me a haircut at home, going to look at colleges. Within seconds, I was also imagining her funeral and sitting shiva and how impossible that would be."

Olga sat up and rested her head on his shoulders, taking one of his hands in hers. They sat silent for a moment.

"I wasn't trying to bogart the conversation or anything, it's just that I knew what you meant. Please keep going."

Olga had never aired family business to a stranger before, but her only real-life confidant was, in this moment, the person she could not talk to. She took a breath.

"See, my brother cares so much what other people think. He wants to be liked so badly by everyone. It's something about him that's irritated me since we were kids. I'd always thought my brother was probably gay. I thought it was stupid for him to not just say who he is, especially these days, but, like I said, he gives so many fucks about his image and well, he's kind of boxed himself into this persona. Today, we're driving home, right? And I ask him for this favor — we have a rental unit in our house, it's about to be vacant, and I want to offer it to a friend going through some shit. Anyway, in this one conversation, my brother basically confirms that yes, he is gay, and is completely closeted about it —"

"Shit," Matteo interjected.

"That's not even what I'm really tripping on. See, at his heart, Prieto's an intensely compassionate person. The things he did for my father, the way he would care for him when he was just even dope sick, were ridiculous. But, he's like that about strangers, too. Every person with a sob story in the neighborhood goes to him because they know what a sucker he is. If someone's WIC gets screwed up, he'll buy them milk and eggs to hold them over. So, here's my friend — the boyfriend of my friend who killed himself. My brother's met him before, the poor guy is grieving, he's broke, he's in need of a cheap apartment. To help him costs my brother nothing. And I was like, damn, this is a first, my brother turning his back on a sob story."

"Because he didn't want a gay guy in his house?"

Olga nodded. "More or less. I let my temper get the best of me and I just outed him. It got ugly. But here's the thing, it struck me as out of character for Prieto, but somehow it also felt familiar. Suddenly, I remember being at the hospital with my father, feeling pissed at my brother for not showing up and seeing all the lonely people there, dying. And it was all so clear to me that my brother was afraid. Scared that if we saw him there, near all these gay guys, we'd recognize something about him in them. Which is irrational and crazy, I know, but I've always thought that's really why he never came."

"Not that crazy," Matteo offered. "How many Christian fundamentalist homophobes who won't even buy a wedding cake from someone gay end up being outed? Fear, self-loathing. All of it."

"Right. So, the question I'm now asking is, if my brother's need to protect this secret is so intense he'd turn his back on his own dying father, what else would he do? I'd always thought my brother's goodness defined him, but what if it's actually his fear? If protecting his image eclipses his impulse to do good? What would that mean about who my brother is?"

"What it would mean, Olga," and this Matteo said with a wry smile, "is that your brother is just like every other politician."

"Well . . . fuck," Olga said, and swigged her beer.

Be Kind, Rewind

"I need to pee," Olga declared after a couple more beers. "Show me where your bathroom is."

Matteo straightened up. Olga started towards the front door and Matteo rushed to block her.

"Let's go out and eat," he offered. "There's a great Peruvian spot literally around the corner. You can use the bathroom there."

Olga looked at him quizzically for a moment. His eyes, round and brown, were glistening and wide and she saw in them his fear. The hoarding. He made it so easy to forget. It had been a long day and she collapsed her body against the doorframe.

"Matteo, I know, intellectually, that we should probably have a formal conversation about your . . . issue, but the truth of the matter is, I'm too damn tired and need to pee too badly to do that right now. Please, just let me in."

Matteo looked straight at her, somewhat imploringly. He turned and rested his head on the door, slowly removing a set of keys from his pocket, then opening one side of the heavy oak and glass double doors.

"Wait here for a second," he said, with more force than she expected. He grabbed the six-pack and the speaker, walked inside, and Olga could see several lights flicker on, a warm glow emerging from the foyer. Olga closed her eyes, her stomach suddenly sinking in the way stomachs do when one dreads the arrival of bad news. She understood the fright in Matteo's eyes and felt it now, too. How long had it been since she felt so comfortable around someone she wasn't related to? When, if ever, had she spoken so openly about herself with anyone, let alone someone she was sleeping with? It should feel uncomfortable, even terrifying, but with Matteo, it felt like relief. In his presence she felt the coil of herself unwind, physically and mentally. The human equivalent of the wonderful rum they had sipped together at Sylvia's. Olga was not one to deprive herself sensory pleasure — sex, food, drink, travel. Emotionally, however, she had long been malnourished. Time with Matteo felt wildly indulgent. Six-course-meal-at-Le-Bernardin indulgent. But now practicalities inserted themselves. Practicalities, even as mundane as relieving one's bladder, have a way of upending indulgences carried on for too long. A threshold stood between her belief that nothing this nice could ever last and her hope that maybe she was wrong.

"Okay," Matteo said, poking his head out the door. "Come on in."

The warm light, Olga realized, was the result of the four to five light fixtures Matteo had hanging over the space: one a crystal chandelier, the others a hodgepodge from various eras that he had clearly jury-rigged. The light reflected off a collection of mirrors and picture frames of various sizes, most empty, some not, that lined the entryway on one side and continued up the wall along a flight of steps to the second floor. To her other side, the walls opened into pocket doors, to what would normally be, in a house like this, the living room. Here, Matteo had arranged, as best as she could tell at her quick glance, a makeshift furniture museum. The walls were flanked, from floor to thirteen-foot-high ceiling, with distinct side chairs and dining chairs hung neatly on wall hooks, ranging in style from Victorian to Bauhaus. She stole a glance at two or three furniture vignettes featuring sofas and side tables but could hardly make out more before Matteo called out to her, directing her to a small half bath under the stairway. It was preserved from another era, an addition or redecoration from the late '70s, with its bright yellow porcelain sink and matching toilet. A light plaid wallpaper peeled slightly at the edges, she noticed as she peed. Here, the walls were surprisingly bare. A large stack of *New Yorker* magazines sat in a corner, though, Olga noted, hardly more than any normal subscriber had in their home. She flushed and washed her hands and made a note that the hand towels were clean. When she didn't find Matteo waiting outside the door, she took her chances and wandered across the hall to where, traditionally, a dining room would be. This, Matteo had repurposed into a music room, of sorts. The largest wall — the one that connected to the parlor space — was lined with shelf after shelf of records, even the fireplace repurposed for record storage. Against the windows, which she knew likely looked out into the backyard, was, of course, a record player, as well as any number of nearly extinct mechanisms for playing recorded music. An eight-track player, CD players, cassette decks, and, of course, speakers of various shapes and sizes. Olga had just turned to take in the rest of the room — rack storage for said eight-track tapes, CDs, and cassettes — when Matteo appeared, two beers in hand. She startled.

"Well," he said, "since you haven't run out of here yet, I figured I should at least offer you a beverage."

"This is . . . unreal. Is this what the rest of the house is like?"

"Um, kind of," he offered sheepishly. "I, um, like to keep the stuff categorized, I guess. This is . . . music. Upstairs, I have a lamp room — lamps are hard for me to pass up, personally, and um, well, I know I said I don't keep papers and stuff, but that wasn't totally true. Downstairs is comics and magazines — but what I'd like to think of as good stuff, you know? I've got two decades' worth of *Rolling Stone* and every issue of *Vibe.*"

His sheepishness began to recede as he started talking through the various rooms, his enthusiasm for their contents clearly shining through. Rather than find this repulsive, Olga was surprised that it endeared him to her. She wanted to know the size and shape of the hole that had been left in his heart that required so many objects to fill it. She found herself envious that he had identified something to pack it with.

"The TVs . . . they're in my bedroom," he continued, "I mean, I don't watch a ton of TV, but I have a lot of them. Different models and stuff. They all work. I just keep them in there and sometimes the light can be soothing to sleep to, or to pop in an old movie. And then, I keep a Christmas room, but it's small . . ."

"I thought you were Jewish."

"Yeah, but who doesn't like Christmas, right? Like, if you're having a bad fucking day, what's better than sitting near a Christmas tree and listening to some carols? Actually, there are more records up there, because I don't mix the Christmas music."

They were standing a few feet apart. A silence fell between them.

"No one has been in this house in eight years besides me, Olga."

He offered the words to her, loaded as they were with meaning. And she accepted what he said with gentle care. Fear and affection bubbled warm in her chest. A sensation of intimacy innervated her body from the root of her sex to the roots of her hair. She wanted to tell him that she was honored that it was her. That she was happy he'd talked to her that sad day at the bar. That she thought the house was actually kind of fucking cool, even if it wasn't perhaps psychologically healthy. She wanted to say that she was sorry his mother had died, that she was sorry he had felt so lost. That she understood pain like that. That, for her, instead of filling her house, she had slowly stripped herself bare, until there was nothing. But she was too out of the practice of loving, in that moment, to say those things.

"Thanks for letting me use your restroom," she said with a smile, frustrated with her own inadequacy, and desperately hopeful that he understood.

He closed the distance between them, kissed her cheek, and pulled away with a smile.

"Girl, do I have a record that's gonna blow your mind! Let me find this shit."

He quickly made his way to a spot on the many shelves of records and, with slight smugness, made a show of his find.

"That's right! Fania All Stars, San Juan seventy-three!"

"Shit!" she said, with genuine delight.

He laid the needle on the record and Olga immediately recognized the piano opening of "Mi Debilidad." Matteo cleared a coffee table from the center of the room and they began to dance.

"Tú siempre serás mi debilidad," he sang

along to her.

"Ha! Do you even know what you're saying?"

"Mami, I'm very, very fluent in Spanish. Shit, I bet my Spanish is better than yours."

Olga smiled, knowing this was likely true. The song changed and she collapsed on the sofa. Matteo lay down next to her and she rested her head on his chest as the music washed over them.

"Papi loved this record. We used to have these amazing dance parties when I was little. It was just my family getting together, but I was a kid, so they felt like parties. My dad would put on music, maybe take out his congas. It was the best part of growing up, for real. Before it all changed."

"What happened to the records?"

"Why," she asked playfully, "growing your collection?"

He pinched her stomach, lightly. "Har, har. No, I just meant, he left them, but what did you do with them?"

Her hand had been tracing Matteo's stomach, but now she stopped.

"I broke them," she said, taking a breath. "After he left them, Abuelita put them in the basement. No one felt like playing music much in those days. But when he died, after the funeral, I missed him real bad. I kept thinking of all the times I'd see him in the streets, high, and would cross so he wouldn't see me. I felt so ashamed of that. And mad that I couldn't see him again. You asked how I felt about my dad being a junkie? I guess I felt pissed off about it, too. At him for using, at my mom for giving up on him. At my brother for enabling him.

"So I went downstairs to just listen and remember. And at first I was crying, but then, I just felt . . . rage. And I took the record off his record player — it was *Still Bill* — and I just threw it across the room."

"Damn, you did that to Bill."

"It felt so good to break something. I could never have hurt him or his feelings — he was too gentle — but it felt good to hurt these things he loved. And so, I just kept going and going. Just smashing them all. My grandmother heard me and she came down to try and stop me, but Tía Lola held her back. I think my grandmother was angry. Actually, I know she was. These were the only things my father never sold for drugs. And I fucking destroyed them.

"Records don't shatter, you know? They just end up in these big pieces. So after, I'm seeing all these pieces, remembering how he liked this song, or my mother loved that song. And I realized that I won't be able to visit those memories again, because I destroyed them. And I was even more pissed off now, but with myself. I cried until it hurt my insides and I pounded my fists on the basement floor until I bled. I guess eventually I tired myself out. I actually don't remember. I just know that I never really cried again. Not since. I had let out all my tears for a lifetime."

Matteo rolled on his side to face her, caressing her face. He was silent for a moment.

"You know what?" he offered softly. "I bet I've got a lot of what he had here. You tell me titles, and I'll pull them out for you. I have at least one other record player. We can take it all over to your place, and you can sit and remember whenever you want."

Olga pondered this for a second, warmth filling her insides.

"Okay." She sat up and smiled. "I'll tell you titles, but you know what? Let's leave them here. This is a nice room to listen to music in."

"Oh yeah?" Matteo asked.

She nodded. For the rest of the night, until day broke, she called out record titles and he found them on his shelves and played them for her. Some they listened to quietly, others would spark a story or memory too big not to share. Sometimes, they just danced.

"I have to tell you," Olga offered up during *Earth, Wind and Fire,* "you really are a good dancer!"

"Do I lie?" he offered up with a laugh.

For a moment she imagined what it would be like to spend a whole night dancing with him. To show up to a family affair with a real date. To have someone to sit with that she might actually want to talk to without biting their head off. Someone who might actually make her laugh. She wondered.

"Listen," she said as the song wound down, "do you, you know, have a suit?"

"Oomf! That hurts," he said, putting his hand over his heart. "I'm a pack rat, not an animal, girl. As a matter of fact, I own many suits! And they're not some Men's Warehouse joints, either. Zegna's my shit, for your information. Sometimes, I wear one for closings . . ."

"Sorry! My bad! Of course you own a suit. You worked on Wall Street, for fuck's sake." She inhaled. "I was just wondering because, ugh, well, I've talked about my cousin Mabel?"

"The one you don't like."

"Is it that I don't like her?" Olga asked, to herself as much as to Matteo. "She pushes my buttons, you know? So, sometimes I avoid her, and sometimes I like fucking with her. Typical family shit. But we grew up together. Like, really grew up together. And now she's getting married."

"Do you like him?" Matteo asked.

Olga thought about this. She had never considered whether she liked Julio before, he just was. "He's fine. Lazy. But she's happy, so, I'm happy for her. More than anything, we haven't had a party in a while, my family. We see each other all the time, and it's always a little crazy, people get a little loud, but we don't just do this — like we just did — anymore. I've been acting whatever about it, but I'm excited for Mabel's wedding."

"And? I need a suit because . . ."

"¡Coño! You're gonna make me ask you? Like, all formal?"

"Yes." He grinned, seeming to take a bit of pleasure in it.

"Matteo, will you come to my cousin Mabel's wedding with me next weekend?"

"Por supuesto, mami."

■ ■ ■ ■

JANUARY 1994

■ ■ ■ ■

January 24, 1994

Mijo,

I was sad to hear that you moved back to Abuelita's to finish school. It was a nice thing to do, I suppose, to be there for your sister. But I don't believe in making ourselves sacrificial lambs for our families. Of making ourselves smaller. I'm glad you've found things to keep you engaged, ways to give back, but this move, I fear, sets a dangerous precedent.

When I met your Papi, he was just twenty-one, the same as you now. He was guapo, like you, with such a young face, I couldn't believe he'd already been to war. I was only seventeen, and though I was against Vietnam, he'd enlisted and I found that brave. I had passion about inequity and oppression, but your father was already putting these things into practice. I remember, the night we met, we went walking in Sunset Park. He was studying education at Brooklyn College and had such big ambitions. To him, history books had been wiped clean of our existences and he wanted to change that. He wanted to change curriculums. To get more Black and Brown teachers in our classrooms. To change the way Black and Brown kids saw their educators; how they saw themselves. His vision was at once practical and expansive. I was excited and in awe and we were together from that day forward. And because of his dreams I started to have my own. Of us. Side by side. Changing the world.

But, Prieto, I was young and naïve and completely swept up in your father's energy. Unable to see the trouble laid out right before me. Vietnam offered your Papi a chance to escape his station in life, but it also tethered him to a terrible demon. Like many others he returned a heroin addict. He hid his problems well. It was months before I discovered it and by then I was so in love, the idea of us parting? Well, it physically pained me. He thought I could heal him and I thought I could, too. Thought that if I believed in him enough, he could overcome this and live out all those great ambitions he had for himself.

When he found the Lords I was so grateful. They helped get him clean and keep him clean. They provided him the camaraderie and discipline that your father had loved about the army. The times then were so exciting. For us. For our people. For the world. We were working hard and making a difference. Taking over hospitals, marching at the UN. We were calling attention to public health issues, to colonialism, and most importantly, we were educating and waking up our community. This, I thought, was what life with Johnny Acevedo was going to be about.

Eventually though, the movement collapsed — was ripped apart, really. By the time you were born, I had left the Lords, feeling they had lost their way. Frustrated with what this great organization had become. Your father didn't agree. They wanted members to take factory jobs — to work directly with the proletariat — and he did. Went down to Bush Terminal and got a job in a plastics factory there. And I watched his world get a little smaller. Suddenly we had two children and his world got smaller still. People with big visions, Prieto, aren't meant to shrink themselves.

Your father didn't discover drugs then, he just revisited habits I had thought were long gone. A familiar way to expand his interior world once he decided to narrow his physical one. He'd been clean for years, but to me, when he gave up on his dreams, he lost his discipline. Started partying. Started with the crack, then back to dope. He lost the strength to say no to temptations. And now, because of this weakness, he is being eaten by this disease.

For years while this went on, I sacrificed my own goals and priorities to try and salvage his. In truth, I should have left right away. I didn't fully comprehend, back then, that the only person who can chart your course is you. No individual can save another, certainly not anyone who doesn't want to be saved. So, yes, it's nice that you are there, close to home, for your Papi and your sister — but this sacrifice of yours will not change anything. Your Papi is an addict and has AIDS. He is not rich; he is not white; he is not Magic Johnson. No cure is going to find its way to him, certainly not in time.

When I hear about all that you are doing in Sunset Park — for the community, for Puerto Rican people, for working people — I'm reminded of the best of your father. That spirit of wanting to lift everyone up. You must be careful not to let anyone, including your family — even your own dying father — distract you from your bigger ambitions for yourself. You are a person of great potential, already on your path. Don't make yourself smaller for anybody.

Prieto, your real Papi died several years ago. What is left now is just a body dying of this pato disease. Don't make his shame your shame. Put a wall up between you and his last days, if for no other reason than to protect yourself. To preserve your own dreams. Keep the best of him close to your heart. Remember the lessons you learned when he led by example, and leave these days, these last years of his life, in a trash can. Set it on fire so you can't visit it again.

You must remember, mijo, even people

who were once your sails can become your anchors.

Pa’lante,
Mami

■ ■ ■ ■

September 2017

■ ■ ■ ■

Shore Road

As day broke and illuminated the bedroom, the ceiling fan spinning above him offered Prieto a resting place for his eyes — a marked improvement from the hours prior where he stared, aimlessly, into the dark. No shadow could claim his attention, so instead his eyes flitted here and there, mirroring his mind and leaving him exhausted. Now he lay, naked and flat on his back, counting the rotations of the fan, feeling his dark olive skin begin to goose pimple in the cool morning air. He instinctively rested his hand on his dick thinking masturbating might calm his agitated nerves, but his mind immediately went from Jan to disease to his daughter. What the fuck would he tell her? His penis remained a soft sack of skin, and his body, instead of feeling release, was, once again, pumping fear and anger.

Where, he thought to himself, could he possibly go to get an HIV test without anyone recognizing him? He could hit up the Attending Physicians office, under the guise of a physical, but what if the result was positive? Who could he trust there not to leak? He didn't even have a doctor in New York. And even if he did, how could he trust that they — or any doctor — wouldn't be approached by one of the Selby brothers' goons? One more thing in their arsenal.

To fucking have AIDS, he thought, would be the most fucking miserable, hijo de puta, piece-of-fucking-shit legacy he could imagine. After all he had endured in his life, all he had accomplished, all he had withstood, to be marked with the same stain that his fucking junkie father had ended up with was simply too much. Logically, he knew that his sister was right. People lived long lives with HIV now. But he felt fear anyway. And shame. He loved his father, but his end was hardly something Prieto had been proud of. And now, here he was, on the edge of the same.

He thought of Jan.

"Fuck you, Jan, you fuck!" he said out loud, to no one. The apartment was empty, Lourdes with his ex-wife, Mabel and her fat fucking fiancé sleeping upstairs. "Do you realize I don't need this shit?"

Jan had been intensely sexy. Olga had

always been surrounded by sissies, from grade school when she would stand up for the girly boys who would get picked on by the hard kids in the schoolyard. He had never allowed himself to notice these boys, not even as they aged and became men, often handsome. It was territory much too risky, too dangerous to enter, but somehow Jan had lured him in. They'd met at Olga's birthday party. Jan had been there with his boyfriend, but the way Jan started flirting with him, Prieto knew they must have an agreement. At first, Prieto had thought he was fucking with him when he started asking him what Prieto was doing for his queer constituents. Prieto had given some sort of pat response about having supported same-sex marriage legislation, and then Jan very pointedly asked, "But what about all those men out there living double lives? What's the street slang for that?" He had raised his eyebrows mischievously and Prieto knew he'd been seen. It scared him, but thrilled him, too, and as clandestinely as possible, they exchanged information and met up the next day. They had laid in bed for a long time afterward talking; Jan was funny as shit and bright. Prieto had imagined what it would be like for this to be real life — to go to a bar and meet someone and get to know them and just be. Together. To have someone like that in his life every day.

He smirked now, thinking of the machinations he'd gone through over the years to keep his secret when his fucking bitch of a sister had known the whole time.

He decided to go for a drive.

In his car, the sound of his loudening stereo pierced the early morning quiet. A dick move on a Sunday, he knew, but in this moment, for once, he didn't care. As he drove over to Fourth Avenue, Prieto thought how at no point in his life could he recall anyone in his family ever explicitly saying anything bad about gay people. Maybe the occasional observation about the way a neighbor's son walked or speculation about a certain distant cousin who was still a bachelor. If they had an inkling, they certainly didn't try to shame him into a closet. Not explicitly. No, he kept himself there not because he was told his feelings were wrong, but because he understood that they were not exactly right. That was made clear to him in ways big and small for as long as he could remember. His grandmother couldn't talk about how handsome he was without immediately predicting how he would surely "drive the girls crazy" when he grew up. He was only in the first grade when his aunts and uncles started asking if he had any "little girlfriends" at school. Even his mother, the ardent feminist, couldn't help but try and push the daughters of her activist friends on him. So, while no one said that "being gay is bad," what he certainly heard loud and clear was that liking girls was good. Affirmation by female affection was a way to prove himself to his family, a way to live up to their ideal of who he was.

He hated disappointing people. For reasons more complex than his sexuality. He was only ten or so years old when his mother began traveling — to conferences, protests, to give lectures. His father had by now moved out, leaving Abuelita as their primary caregiver. He felt grateful for the sense of security she provided but also guilty that he and his sister were a burden on a woman whose life had already been hard. So, he strove to make her as happy as possible. To prove to her that he was worth the sacrifice. By doing well in school, by keeping an eye on his sister, by keeping an eye on his father. The more he did, the more she idolized him, bragging about what a strong young man he was becoming to anyone who would listen. The more she bragged — to neighbors, to family — the more he felt obliged to never disappoint her or anyone else.

Of course, the rational part of him that looked back on it, the part that was now a father himself, recognized that disappointments — large or small — don't eradicate that kind of love. What could Lourdes tell him about herself that would ever make him love her less? Nothing. He wondered if she knew that.

He stopped at the bagel store on Sixty-ninth Street, surprised that he was hungry. The girl working behind the counter recognized him from the news, asked for a selfie, and tried to give him his bagel and coffee for nothing. Her hairstyle and dress were obviously different, but he was struck by how similar she was in mannerisms and speech to the kinds of girls he'd grown up with. The kinds who used to flirt openly with him in his junior high schoolyard, whom he'd pretend to like back knowing full well they were not the ones who gave him that butterfly feeling he sometimes got. He always was sure to have the name of a girl in his class ready on the tip of his tongue for when his homeboys asked who he thought was hot. He strung the girls in high school along just far enough to guarantee them always calling the house, so that Abuelita's prophecies would seem true.

If he'd harbored any fantasies to be more open and honest about himself, they were tamped down by two things: Tía Lola and, more dramatically, the disease.

As Prieto became aware of his own sexuality and his subsequent efforts to avoid suspicion and detection, he began to reappraise his aunt. Even at a young age he sensed that they, his family, were only getting a part of her. That a chunk of her was hidden. As he grew older and heard people throw the word "lesbian" around — derisively and otherwise — he saw aspects of his aunt in the women they described. He recognized then, clearly, that whatever she kept concealed from their family, it was because she felt she was compelled to. He understood the sentiment and it reaffirmed his own instincts. He wondered now if she had sensed his truth as well.

But that was mere behavioral modeling. More than anything, for years, really, what had made the idea of calling himself gay or queer or bi or any of these things impossible was the disease. He had just developed his first crush — on a boy named Anthony who lived on the block — when suddenly all everyone was talking about was AIDS.

But it wasn't just called AIDS, it was the gay disease. They were dying, they were dying alone, and people seemed to feel they deserved it. When famous people started dying, he remembered his uncles and aunts talking about it: "Can you believe so-and-so was gay all this time?" Completely ordinary people were dying and he would hear the gossip: "Who knew he played both sides . . . ?" He remembered how, when word got out about his father's diagnosis, he went out of his way to tell people his father had been a junkie. As if somehow that was better than them thinking he was gay?

The disease made had him feel frightened and ashamed, all at once. And yet, also reckless.

The night he realized his father had AIDS, the first night he allowed himself to go to the Piers and meet someone, it was Prieto who was willing to consent to unprotected sex. It didn't get that far, not that night. But, over the years, on certain occasions, despite his fears or maybe because of them, he took risks that defied logic. It was on one of these such nights that he met up with Jan.

He parked his car on Shore Road, grabbed the bagel and the coffee, and made his way across the pedestrian overpass to the waterfront. He remembered for a moment crossing this same bridge one night with his friend Diego. It was that summer he realized Papi was going to die. The summer before he started college. He and Diego had smoked some weed down by the water and were crossing back to head home, play fighting each other. He didn't know if it was the weed or what, but he felt the feeling behind their play shift, and in a brief moment he felt so free, he leaned in and kissed Diego and Diego kissed him back. When he pulled away and opened his eyes, he could see the cars on the Belt Parkway below, their headlights shining through the bridge's chain-linked enclosure and into his eyes. How quickly his euphoria turned to terror that someone might have seen what they had done. He and Diego never spoke about that kiss again. Prieto wondered what had happened to him.

The promenade was empty now save a few joggers and bright-eyed fishermen. Staten Island was still concealed by a bit of mist coming off the Narrows. Looking at the water often took his mind off things, but he now found himself reaching for his phone. He needed to know where he stood. He went to look for clinics out of state —

maybe somewhere en route back to D.C. — when he had an idea. One he knew immediately would resolve his dilemma and possibly produce some pretty good political theater, which he hadn't had very much of lately. He would sponsor a men's wellness event in his district — center it around men of color and HIV, blood pressure, and diabetes. He'd make a big fuss of getting himself tested and checked. Talk about how it's not about being gay or straight, it's about knowing your status. Yes, he might still get bad news, but now it would come with a wave of public sympathy. He was contemplating his worst-case-scenario public statement when a text message came in from Alex.

Hurricane Irma hit. Damage light, but power out in P.R.; should probably release statement/tweet? Pics from Cuba not looking good. Send prayers?

He scanned the articles Alex had linked to and typed a reply.

Pls. fix grammar — Praying for the people of Cuba; grateful P.R. spared worst, but as 70% of the island sits in darkness, Irma reveals how government fails Borinquen again and again. Privatization not the answer.

The mention of the islands turned his mind to his mother and his mother's mother. He thought about what his sister had said. How everyone always knows. If that was true, he wondered why none of them had ever told him that it was okay. Okay to be who he was. He wanted to call his sister and ask her. He couldn't bring himself to pick up the phone.

They used to come here a lot, he and Olga, at one time. When she was younger, he'd take her and Mabel over to Ceasar's Bay Bazaar, where he'd thumb through freestyle mixes while she and Mabel flirted with the guy who ran the Sergio Tacchini kiosk. Afterwards, they'd always get ice cream and sit by the water, boy watching the skateboarders for a bit before he took them home. After Papi died, they came out here together — him and Olga — with two forties of Heineken — and told each other every good thing they remembered about their father so the other would have their own memories and then some. Olga was only sixteen and got so drunk Prieto had to carry her back to the car.

He felt exposed by her. Angry with her for exposing him. But, more than anything, he was angry that she had known all this time and just let him suffer in this secret alone.

He took a sip from the coffee as he looked

out onto the placid water.

The mist had lifted.

Champagne Dreams

On Monday morning Olga awoke and found herself not only still at Matteo's house, but reluctant to leave. He brought her coffee in bed as they watched reports of Hurricane Irma's wake: flooded streets in Cuba, ports destroyed in the Virgin Islands. In Puerto Rico, damage was minimal, but its frail power system buckled quickly, the island now left in the dark. It might take weeks to restore power, the news said.

"How long do you think they'd let Rhode Island or Virginia sit in the dark?" Matteo asked rhetorically.

Outside, the weather was as gloomy as the news, but Olga felt more buoyant than she had in ages. The first night she'd slept over, she awoke with a panic attack, in disbelief that she'd revealed so much of herself, of her life, to the person lying next to her. She wanted to leave as quickly as possible and, in the gentlest way, Matteo wouldn't allow it. He made omelets and coffee and got the paper from the stoop, and they read the *Times* on one of the sofas in the living room. Later that morning, when they had sex, she recognized it as a completely new, terrifying but exhilarating experience: physical intimacy with someone she actually decided to let in. To know. In contrast, she recognized that sleeping with Dick had never been about feelings, or even pleasure, but rather a repetitive attempt to use sex to try and prove that she was, in fact, worthy. She had not realized the weight this had been on her, one she was relieved to be rid of. By Monday morning, she was so content she lost track of time and found herself running late to start her day.

Although Mabel's wedding was less than a week away, Olga had not only failed to have her bridesmaid's dress altered, she had yet to even claim it from the Midtown bridal salon Mabel had ordered the dresses from. This morning, they'd explained, was the last possible chance she could come in and be properly fitted. Before that, however, she was due to the office for her quarterly champagne exchange with Igor. By the time she hurried down the Chelsea street her office was located on, he was already impatiently waiting outside of the building with two guys she had not seen before.

"Who are they?" she asked.

"These," Igor said, "are my OTBs — off the-boats. Just came from Ukraine a few weeks ago. Know almost no English but will do any kind of work I need. Very helpful for stuff like this."

Olga eyed them. They were beefier than his last set of hands, but somewhat typical of the Russian-Ukrainian wannabe gangsters she was used to Igor bringing around. Tight black T-shirts, suit slacks, pointy leather oxfords that refused to acknowledge the manual labor that was being asked of them, as though their footwear saw a future when they would not be pushing hand trucks full of stolen champagne, but rather sitting at a café off Brighton 6, calling the shots. Or, at the very least, knowing what the shots were.

Olga had met Igor seven or so years before, when her services had been retained to produce the elaborate nuptials of a Russian oligarch's daughter. She had a limited understanding of how the family made their money in Russia — the vague term "energy" was tossed around quite a bit — but stateside, it didn't take Olga long to observe that they had clearly diversified. Family meetings around the wedding were continually interrupted by "business associates" ranging from restaurateurs to home health aide empresarios, often bearing gifts. Though they kept an apartment at the Four Seasons, when in New York they mainly held court in an externally forgettable, but internally lavish Russian restaurant off Coney Island Avenue. Every meeting was an occasion that involved copious amounts of salmon, caviar, pelmeni, and vodka and equally copious amounts of family. Igor, who served as a chief of staff of sorts, was always there. Though shrewd during the contract negotiation, the family was warm and gracious once the planning was actually under way. They spared no expense for what they wanted, treated workers fairly, tipped generously, and had a strong sense of their own style. Above all, they wanted people to have a good time. Olga hadn't enjoyed her job as much before or after them.

She'd landed that gig during her reality TV years, which meant the period when she was busier trying to be famous than rich. Which meant she was running her business honestly, transparently, and with little profit. The oligarch was charmed with the way she sagaciously negotiated his contracts and bemused by how hard she protected money he was happy to spend. He warmly abused her for what he called "her miserable sense of business." After the wedding, Igor came by the office to drop off her tip — $9,000 in cash, a new Chanel watch, and ten cases of Veuve Clicquot champagne.

"The boss said to enjoy this however you want, but if he were you, he'd keep the watch, invest the cash, and sell the champagne to one of your WASP clients."

Olga decided that was exactly what she was going to do — though in truth some of the cash was tucked into Lourdes's college savings account. She was unsurprised by but keenly aware of the sum the champagne earned her. She'd been able to present it as discounted product to the client, when for her it was all profit. Her wheels began to churn. This seemed a harmless way to earn a few extra dollars and her clients all loved good wine and champagne. Olga began to overorder, just a bit at first, and then more and more, when placing her clients' champagne orders. Then, when she had amassed enough inventory to cover a whole party, she would offer the product to her clients at a discount.

A couple of years later, when the oligarch's daughter was having her baby shower, Olga planned it gladly, free of charge. She was grateful for the new revenue stream they had opened up for her. Igor suggested more ways that they could work together, as the family restaurants sometimes found themselves with extra product — caviar, vodka, expensive whiskeys — but sometimes found themselves short on other extravagances, like hard-to-find wines. Though Olga was mildly apprehensive about forging an ongoing alliance with the Russian mob, the opportunity seemed too good to refuse. In this way, their exchanges began. Olga would tag onto her clients' liquor orders a few extra cases of champagne, but also an additional case of Stag's Leap Cask 23 here, a case of Penfold's 2013 Grange there. In turn, Igor would deliver below-cost cases of Russian vodkas and Johnnie Walker Blue Label, which Olga could then, of course, resell. Once every couple of months they would exchange product and cash, as the relationship proved symbiotic for all parties.

Had she stopped to think about it from a purely catechistic perspective, the wine enterprise was clearly a form of theft. Morally and possibly criminally wrong. But Olga did not stop to think of it this way, instead viewing this as a present of unquantifiable value that the oligarch and Igor had given to her. Prior to meeting them, Olga was eking out a living, believing, mistakenly, that if she provided quality services the money would eventually work out. They gave her a new lens through which to see her day-to-day operations: apply big-business thinking to her mom-and-pop shop.

"You know," Igor said to her today, "there are a lot of people in my line of work making weddings, birthday parties, all of the stuff you do, Olga. They have cash, not so much to burn, but to . . . well, clean up. Simon thinks, why not kill two birds with one stone by working with a nice girl like you, who understands how the world works? Do you get what I'm saying?"

Though a lover of risk and cash in equal measure, Olga's gut instincts told her that this was a bridge too far for both. Exchanging product was one thing; cleaning people's money could quickly turn friends into enemies. She did not want to become the oligarch's enemy.

"Igor, please tell Simon I appreciate him thinking of me, truly, but things are looking up for me these days, and, well, cash is tricky. The IRS and all."

"What do I know of the IRS?" he said, looking at her with mild disdain, as though he had sized her up as admirable and now needed to reassess not only her, but his own judgment. "If you change your mind, you know where I am."

And with that, Igor and his two OTBs, hand trucks loaded with several cases of Cakebread, headed out the door, passing Meegan who was on her way in.

"Who were those guys, Olga?" Meegan asked as she placed her bag down.

Olga sighed. It had been a long weekend and she was too tired for Meegan this morning.

"Russian mobsters coming to buy hot goods to resell on the black market in Moscow, Meegan."

Olga turned to her computer. There was a moment of silence and Meegan started to laugh.

"What's so funny?" Olga asked.

"You said that about those guys as though it could be true!"

Something about her failed attempt at honesty gave Olga the giggles and soon both women were wiping tears from their faces. The moment softened Olga towards Meegan, at least momentarily.

"Did you have a good time at the party?" she asked.

Meegan hesitated.

"At first, I guess." Meegan sighed. "But then Trip ended up in a pack of his sweaty coworkers doing shots off an ice sculpture, and I got stuck making conversation with all the other girlfriends."

Olga smirked, more with familiarity than malice.

" 'It's not the life I chose, it's the life that chose me,' " she said.

"What?" Meegan asked, earnestly.

"Rap lyric. But the point is, in my opinion, when it comes to men and relationships? We're all born with our lives set on certain tracks. On your track, unless you go out of your way to buck convention, you will encounter Trip after Trip, always ending up outside of a shot circle with the other girlfriends, who eventually will become wives and then moms. Making small talk, or as you called it, 'conversation.' "

"What a remarkably cynical assessment," Meegan offered while collapsing onto the office sofa.

"Let it marinate for a minute, see if it rings true, and tell me later. Or, in a few years." Olga smiled. She hadn't meant it cynically at all, in fact.

"Well, so, what about your 'set track' then?" Meegan said with a sly smile. "It clearly has Mr. Eikenborn on it."

Olga looked at Meegan for a moment, her face purposefully blank, before she coolly turned back to her email without saying a word. She was only faintly aware of Meegan rising from the sofa and noisily slamming cabinets while she made coffee before opening her laptop with a loud huff.

"So," Meegan pronounced, "I've worked here for over a year and I have to ask. Why the fuck do you do this? This job, I mean. You don't have a single, actual romantic bone in your body. You seem to have little respect for marriage, and from what I can garner, only passing regards for the feelings of a man who seems as vulnerable as Mr. Eikenborn."

Olga stopped for a second to take in her prey. She could easily eviscerate Meegan by telling her that she had watched too much TV as a little girl and that marriage has, historically, never been about romance. She could destroy her intellectual argument by explaining that respecting marriage and planning weddings had nothing to do with each other, and that she pitied her for not grasping the difference. She could ruin her sense of optimism by explaining that Dick was just Trip, but old, the vodka luge antics replaced by circles of self-congratulation for growing their inherited wealth. That she had contorted herself for years to get onto a "track" to meet these very men, only to make that horrid discovery. But before she could answer, she felt her tongue slacken in her mouth, softened by the initial question, and the naïve girl who'd asked it. Meegan, who from Olga's vantage point had struggled for nothing but to maintain her rose-colored glasses, was asking the question that Olga had not dared to query herself: why the fuck was she doing this work?

She had been a talented photographer. Perhaps not good enough to be a working artist, but surely she could have become a gallerist or a curatorial assistant. What would have happened had she not been so afraid of making her student loan payments? If she'd been a bit more courageous and self-assured? Instead, she took a job with a nice paycheck in a communications department at an ad agency. Not even making the ads. No, she did promotions for the ads, which, even without her mother's reminders, was so meta it felt useless. But it paid well. Eventually, after she met Reggie, she tried her hand at real public relations. It was then, when one of their celebrity clients was getting married and appreciated her ability to manage events well, that she was asked to do her first wedding.

After her grandmother died, without that unconditional love, Olga did not know who would ever love her again or what would make her feel worthy of being loved. Weddings, Olga felt back then, could do this. Making people's dreams come true, Olga reasoned, would provide countless opportunities to be adored, to be valued, to feel important. She reflected now, with Meegan before her, what a wide-eyed assessment that had been. Weddings, she quickly discovered, were about everything except the health of a couple's relationship. They were social performances, the purpose of which varied from family to family. And they were competitive. Clients wanted to appear more tasteful, more unique, more extravagant, than the hosts of all the other weddings they had been to before. Olga's success at work, therefore, was not evaluated against how many of her clients' dreams she could bring to life, but on scores of emotional calculations far beyond her control. It was the ultimate in conditional love. She had grown, she realized, to resent the constant cycle.

"I'm not avoiding your question, Meegan," Olga replied, "but I'm curious why *you* think someone should be in this line of work?"

Meegan beamed. Olga rarely offered the

opportunity to expound on personal opinions.

"Well, I guess the biggest reason is that this world is so fast and crowded. We all do a hundred things a day, and post photos of it all, too. But weddings? They still make you take a breath and take things in. People don't forget them. No one ever says, 'Tim and Tina's wedding? I don't remember that one!' They always remember. So, in this time when memories are so hard to keep because our lives are so cramped and disposable, weddings stick. And we help create the memories that stick for these people. And that feels really special. And really important."

Olga glanced at the clock. The bridal shop would be opening soon. On another day she might have reminded Meegan that Muslims were being banned in their country and children being shot down in schools, and maybe that ought to take up a bit more mental space than a dramatic centerpiece. Or pointed out that many people, like her cousin Mabel, threw weddings all the time with no professional help whatsoever, at pennies on the dollar of their clients' budgets, and that those parties were just as memorable. But today, perhaps softened a bit by the events of the weekend, Olga was touched by her earnestness. Why poison Meegan's happiness with her own dissatisfaction?

Olga closed her laptop, gathered her purse, and looked Meegan in the eyes.

"Meegan, you're in this for all the right reasons. You'll go far."

Meegan smiled and went to lean in to give Olga a hug, and Olga bolted for the door.

In the elevator, she rested her head against the cool metal and thought, What the fuck am I doing with my life?

Los Pañuelos Negros

Though it had been merely overcast when she had gotten to the office — a space meticulously designed to conceal the fact that there were few windows — as Olga stepped out of the elevator and into the lobby, she could see the downpour. Of course, she had no umbrella, nor the will to go back upstairs and see Meegan's earnest face again, so she stood for a moment calculating how fucked up her blowout would get if she made a sprint towards Sixth Avenue, where she was certain the Sudanese guy who sold umbrellas would be set up. They should put you on TV, she'd told him, a few weeks back when she saw him doing brisk trade after a sunny day turned like a race car and the skies had opened up. He said he'd learned to smell for rain where he was from and Olga quipped that her only learned olfactory instinct was which subway cars to avoid. She thought about the subway ride up to the bridal salon. It should be just a quick shot on the 2/3 uptown, but now, with the rain, who knew how or when she would get there. New York had a shocking way of spiraling into chaos whenever met with precipitation, as though the entirety of its infrastructure was actually made of sugar, and the water triggered dissolution. She could call a car, but not only would that take longer, it would cost a fortune. For her bridesmaids' gowns, Mabel had selected an ensemble look; Olga felt confident she'd been purposefully assigned the ugliest of the style variations and at $450 *before* alterations, Olga refused to sink another penny into this frock. Resolving to stick with her original plan, Olga placed her purse over her head in a symbolic attempt to preserve her hair, and charged out the door as fast as she could, immediately running full force into a mountain of a man holding an oversized umbrella.

Underneath his fitted black suit his body was pure muscle, and Olga rebounded off in such a way, he needed to use his one free arm to steady her. In her confusion, she looked up, ready to apologize, but he began speaking before she could open her mouth.

"Ms. Acevedo?"

"Yes," she said, surprised.

"Sorry to startle you, but Mr. Reyes would like a word with you."

"Reggie?" she asked, equally surprised by the use of his legal name as she was his impromptu appearance.

"Yes, ma'am. He's waiting in the car, just up the street. So, if you don't mind following me . . ."

The mountainous man's name turned out to be Clyde. Olga learned a remarkable amount about him on their relatively short walk. He'd been a linebacker at Howard, Reggie's alma mater, before getting sidelined with an injury and losing his scholarship. He was working Reggie's security detail to earn tuition money, though he was enjoying it so much, he wasn't sure he would go back. By the time the driver opened the door to Reggie's military-grade luxury SUV, Olga felt deeply invested in his future.

"Clyde, you've got to go back to school, okay?" she said as she slid into the rear of the vehicle.

From under the umbrella, Clyde smiled. "I'll definitely think about it, Ms. Acevedo."

The driver closed the door for her, and Olga turned her attention to Reggie. She wasn't certain what he could possibly want but was fairly sure he had more to say about her brother, especially with the Hurricane Irma damage in P.R. Still, it was unlike him to use her, or anyone, as a go-between. Reggie's style was more combative: to call someone out on social media or just roll up to her brother's congressional office with a camera crew in tow. What on earth could he want from her?

"Clyde's sweet," she said as she turned to him. She was surprised to find him not on his phone but sitting fully upright, his attention focused on her.

"He's a good kid."

"You have to pay for him to go back to school; his tuition is like, five dollars for you."

Reggie laughed.

"You act like a bitch all the time, but you have this heart of gold, Olga. Of course I'm gonna pay his tuition, but it's not a bad thing to let him work for it a bit, is it?"

Olga shrugged. "How come only Brown and Black people have to learn to work for everything? Why can't we get some stuff just handed to us once in a while?"

"Fair point," he conceded.

There was a silence.

"So," Olga offered, with suspicion, "what's up with the stakeout . . . Mr. Reyes?"

Reggie chuckled. "Well, Ms. Acevedo, as

it happens, I'm using my government name in personal settings these days. Considering changing it professionally, too."

"Bad for your brand," Olga offered.

"But good for my people — our people — to see that a Black man, an Afro-Latino man, did all this." Reggie gestured around at the car, which — only now did Olga notice — was intensely lavish: vast space, mother-of-pearl inlays, and a leather interior she could not quite place the texture of. She fingered the seats.

"If you're wondering, it's whale dicks."

"That's fucking nasty, Reggie," Olga said as she jumped off her seat.

Reggie belly laughed, hard.

"Nah, I'm kidding. I'm kidding. The original Dartz had them though! No joke. Sheiks were into it. Had diamonds and rubies in the gauges, too. That sounded over the top, even to me, but God do I love this fucking truck! Bulletproof. All of it, windows, sides. Safer than Limo One."

"It's very subtle," Olga offered with a smile.

"Just like me, mami, just like me! Anyway, all I'm saying is, when I started using 'King,' I was thinking of my own self. How do I advance my own shit? Now, my focus is on advancing my people — Puerto Ricans,

Latinos generally, and of course Black people. You can't be it if you can't see it. So, I want people to see that while this clown in D.C. is trying to round us up and ice us out, a man named Reyes could buy and sell this motherfucker."

Olga looked out the window and realized that, even in the rain, people — mainly teens — had stopped to take pictures of the monstrosity. She remembered seeing photos of Reggie and his kids hopping out of this same truck on one of the hip-hop gossip accounts. These kids probably saw it, too. Now they were scrambling in the rain just to get a picture of his car. Not even him. He was a mogul, and he looked like them. Reggie hadn't had anyone to look up to. His pomposity had not changed; his ego was, if anything, larger than ever. But she was moved by his sincerity.

"I'm here for all of this," Olga pronounced. "But I also need to get on with my fucking day, Reggie, so do you want to tell me what's so important that I get to see you twice in one week? In fact, better yet, take me uptown while you do."

Reggie lowered the divider and instructed the driver to get going, and the tank-sized vehicle began to pull out of its oversized parking space. When Clyde disappeared from view, he began to speak again.

"Olga, first I want to say, I come with good news. It's the only reason I snuck up on you like this."

Olga tried to imagine what good news Reggie could possibly have for her, of all people.

"You're renewing your vows and are going to hire me to plan the whole thing?"

Reggie laughed.

"You're hilarious. First of all, no, we aren't. Second of all, if we were, I'd never hire you because it would be too awkward."

"If you're paying money, nothing is awkward about it, Reggie. I'm a professional."

"Listen," Reggie said, his tone becoming more serious. "The thing is, before I can tell you the good news, I need a guarantee of your secrecy here. Because the information I'm about to share with you could really fuck up people's lives, mine included, okay?"

Olga stared at him with intense curiosity. Her stomach fluttered. She took in the scene outside the car.

"We're going the wrong way," she said. "I need to go uptown."

"Olga, you need to go home, so we are driving you there —"

"Reggie? What the fuck?" Olga interrupted, her hands rising unconsciously to illustrate her anger. Reggie gently clasped them in his own.

"And once you get there, you're going to stay home for the rest of the day, and then tomorrow, you're going to go to work, like everything is normal."

"Everything *is* normal, Reggie," Olga said, though, already for the past few days, life had been anything but.

"Did your brother tell you he'd gone to see your aunt Karen a few weeks back?"

Adrenaline inundated Olga. She was trying to reconcile Reggie and her aunt Karen and her brother in her mind in a way that would make sense.

"What? No. We haven't seen Aunt Karen in years."

"*You* haven't." Reggie scoffed. "But you should ask him about it and see what he says."

Olga took this in. Why would Prieto go to see her? And why wouldn't he mention it to Olga?

"How do you even fucking know this?"

"Karen told me, and when I heard, I figured he would be too much of a pussy to tell you."

"Why is my aunt talking to you? How does she even know you?"

"I'll get into it, but I need you first to promise me that this conversation won't go beyond this car."

"I can't promise that without knowing what we're talking about."

"That's the only way to promise. It stays between me and you. And I will talk to you about this anytime you want, day or night, that I promise you. But you must swear on your grandmother's grave not to discuss this with your family, and especially not your brother."

Olga paused. Her hands still in Reggie's grasp, she noticed now they were trembling. She nodded.

"Olga, your mother sent me here to talk with you today."

Her mouth dropped open.

"How —"

She started to form a question, but Reggie put a finger over her lips, his body fully turned towards her now in the back of the truck.

"Your mother is a very important part of a group of patriots aiming to claim dignity again for Borikén, and all of us —"

Olga's full body was now shaking. She shook off Reggie's grasp.

"I don't give a fuck about Borikén right now Reggie! Where the fuck is my mother and why the fuck do you know where she is, when me and my fucking brother don't?"

"I'm trying to tell you, Olga —"

"I need you to tell me without the fucking political rhetoric, okay?"

Reggie put his hands on her arms, to try and stop her body from shaking, but she had lost control over herself. She felt sick from the pit of her stomach. She wanted to cry, but no tears would come. Did she feel despair? Betrayal? She certainly felt rejection. Her mother, so far from her, such a great and powerful Oz, yet fully realized to . . . Reggie? Reggie whom she had despised. Whom she had advised Olga herself to avoid. It made no sense.

"Tranquila, tranquila, tranquila," he began to whisper. Her grandmother would always calm her that way, in the nights following her mother's departure, when she would wake up crying. She would come in and lie next to her, stroking her hair, whispering the same words. Had she ever told Reggie that? She found herself responding to his command, her body slowly quieting itself. When her shaking stopped, Reggie took his hands off her shoulders. Though it was not quite 10 A.M., he leaned forward and pulled from a cabinet two heavy crystal tumblers and filled them each with a heavy pour of rum. He handed her one, and, locking his dark eyes with hers, clinked her glass.

"¡Salud! This will make us both feel better."

She took a sip, but he took a swallow.

"A few weeks after you ended things with us, I got a package in the mail to my home. It had no return address —"

"My mother."

"Yes. It was not a terribly long letter, but I was shocked to get it. You had told me small bits about her, but honestly, that she had tracked me down weirded me out. Still, the letter, it was very poignant to me. No one had spoken to me that way before. She started by telling me that she didn't feel I was appropriate for you, because you were a brilliant mind who had been raised for liberation, while I, like so many Puerto Ricans before me, was an anchor for our people. My mind had been colonized. She went on to articulate what she thought someone like me, who clearly had the ability to visualize futures for themselves that seem impossible, could do if they could look beyond the White Man's goals. She didn't say anything else about it, but she enclosed three books. One was a collection of essays by Hostos, a biography of Che Guevara, and a book of poems with Julia de Burgos and

Pedro Pietri.

"A few weeks later, I got another letter. She was curious what I thought about the books, and she invited me to write to her. She gave me a name and address of a person — I don't remember who or where, because it would always change — but she had people willing to receive mail for her. She instructed me not to use a return address, and to mark the envelope with a small black triangle, so that this person would know the letter was for her."

"And so, you wrote to her?" Olga asked, flatly.

"I wrote to her. I had been really moved by her letter, by the essays, and mostly by the poems. I read *Puerto Rican Obituary* at least a hundred times and I was embarrassed to see myself in it. I hated the way we lived when I was a kid, piled into a fucked-up apartment in the Bronx, cleaning up after people, the only things to show for it some scratch-off tickets, everyone dreaming of going back to some island I'd barely known. I wanted the American dream. I wanted the house on Long Island, I wanted to be on the all-white block. I didn't realize I was rejecting myself, my own heritage.

"I wrote her all this and she sent me more books and the letters and things continued for a while — for years, actually —"

"So you became pen pals? You and my mother."

"At first. Then, after that whole thing happened and I began to publicly claim my heritage more, she sent me a note. She felt it was time for me to go beyond general education and become more proactive. She told me to reach out to Karen."

"My aunt Karen?"

"Yes. So, this is how I know Karen. I went to pay her a visit and it was actually Karen who told me about the Pañuelos Negros. Who invited me to join." He went to take another sip of his rum, but Olga stopped him before he started talking again.

"What the fuck is that? Black bandanas?" She shook her head but did not raise her voice.

"Well, you said you didn't want me to get political in talking about this."

"I just wanted you to talk to me like a fucking person, whose life this affects, not like you're trying to recruit me into a revolution."

He looked at her and shrugged.

"Lo mismo, ¿no?"

"Reggie, just fucking tell me what this thing is."

"The media wants everyone, especially

people on the island, to think that an independent Puerto Rico is a fringe fantasy that only radicals subscribe to. That the real force is behind the centrists who want statehood."

Olga was at the end of her patience but promised herself not to interrupt until Reggie was done.

"And with good reason. In the eighties and nineties the government, in cooperation with complicit Puerto Rican sellouts on the island, systemically stymied a strong and growing independence movement. They imprisoned all of the leadership, branded them terrorist organizations, drove people underground. Those they couldn't imprison they drove into hiding in the mountains of the island. But, as you know, Olga, the wealthy and powerful are lazy, and think that if you can't see something, it doesn't exist. Back in oh-five, the Feds finally managed to assassinate Filiberto Ojeda Ríos, the most visible revolutionary that Borikén had known in modern times. He'd evaded their capture for nearly fifteen years, in small towns, in the mountains, sometimes in the bigger cities. With his assassination, every leader of every public movement for independence was either dead or in jail. Or so the government thought. And with no visible resistance, they were able to further pillage and sell off our island to the highest bidder.

"This was the White Man's fatal flaw. They murdered Ojeda Ríos, thinking that the idea of the revolution lived within *one man,* without ever stopping to consider *how* he had evaded them for so long. Do you understand what I mean?"

"The peoplc," Olga said. "The people helped him hide."

"The jíbaros. The regular country people, for years, shrugged their shoulders when agents would come around asking about this man. 'No sé, no sé,' they would say. They adored him, they took pride in his ability to evade the law, because they knew this was foreign law that was looking for him. They understood that he was standing up for them, even if they couldn't articulate it. It didn't have to do with him and his personality, it had to do with an idea."

Reggie's argument had become abstracted again; she was on the verge of losing patience.

"The people who followed Ojeda Ríos were devastated by his loss and all of Puerto Rico was mourning. We were too blind with grief and anger to see that the revolutionary spirit had already taken root on the island.

But not your mother. Your mother saw the opportunity there, and despite putting herself at risk of the law, she made her way back to Puerto Rico to help her people. Revolution, in the past, was meant to be armed. Acts of war and protest claimed by an organization — FALN, the Boricua Popular Army. Your mother, however, understood that such public organization only put a target on our backs and that revolution in the digital age could look different. This is how the Pañuelos Negros were born.

"Our name comes from the bandanas we wear whenever we might be out in public. We don't even really want to know who our own membership is. Perhaps your mother is the only one who knows every member of our movement."

"So, if you aren't violent, what do you do?"

"I didn't say we aren't violent, Olga. I just said that revolution is different now."

He paused.

"You mother reorganized all of the supporters of every other independence group — those both above and below ground. She quietly began recruiting people like me to her cause — strong people with influence who had not turned their attention to what was happening to our gente. She went after the students — the angry and the disaffected, the brilliant chemists, engineers, and computer programmers forced to leave the island because there was no work for them at home anymore. Quietly, over the past decade, your mother has assembled a decentralized organization all over the diaspora, hungry for revolution, just waiting for the right moment to rise and topple a hundred and nineteen years of American colonial rule and take back our land."

Olga took a sip of her rum and then found herself giggling. The giggle became a laugh and the laugh overtook her until she was doubled over in her seat. Reggie did not join her.

"Reggie, wow." She finally calmed herself enough to talk. "I know you aren't making this up, but wow, has my mother got your number if she's convinced you that somehow she has amassed an underground revolutionary army gearing up for independence. The rational businessman in you has got to know how fucking nuts this sounds! If there are so many people interested in a free Puerto Rico, why the fuck did these homies not vote for independence in this last election? When was the plebiscite? May? Where were these 'revolutionaries' at the polls?"

"Olga, revolution cannot happen on the terms of the oppressor. The very idea of the plebiscite is flawed."

"So, then when is the time for revolution, Reggie? Tell me. Because the last I saw the whole island was in the dark."

Reggie smiled at her. "Exactly, Olga. Our network of Pañuelos Negros is broad, their commitment deep, but as with everything in our history, nothing happens without the jíbaro. The Yanqui is currently doing the work that we, the leaders of revolution, could never do quite as effectively. They are letting the jíbaro know that they are seen as a piece of trash, dispensable. Between PROMESA's austerity and PREPA leaving everyone sitting in the dark, the island is finally recognizing what the Yanqui thinks of them. The Yanqui has counted on us being asleep for years, but their neglect and exploitation is slowly waking up all of Borikén, and when they rise from their nap, we will be there."

They had pulled up outside of Olga's building. The rain was coming down in sheets over the car. Olga looked at Reggie and a smirk took over her face.

"Why now? Since I was thirteen, I've gotten nothing but some fucking self-righteous letters. Literally, nothing but one-way conversations. She never sent *me* an address to write to her. Never felt, for all these years, that I needed to know all this. So, why does she send you now?"

"Olga, you need to understand, revolution —"

"Requires sacrifice? Oh Reggie, I know. What I don't know is, why now?"

"Because your mother needs you."

Olga felt a pull in her chest at his words. She should feel indignation at this. Rage, even. That this woman who was a stranger to her, who didn't know the difference between missives and mothering, would have the audacity to approach her for the first time in decades with a need. To ask for something. To present herself to Olga in this way. She should feel this way, but she did not. Instead, she felt a long dormant affection bubble up clearly in her chest: the idea of having a value to her mother warming her insides.

"What does she need?" Olga asked.

"She'll let you know," Reggie said. "If she wanted me to know now, she would have told me."

Olga shook her head. "I can't keep this from my brother."

Reggie hesitated. "If your mother wanted Prieto involved, she would have sent me to see him instead."

This irked her. "Reggie, I know my mom is like your best friend in arms right now, but please don't forget that when she bounced, it was my brother who helped take care of me. He deserves to know."

"I wouldn't suggest you break your mother's confidence."

A surge of anger pulsed through Olga's body. She went to let herself out of the car, but the lock was on.

"Unlock the fucking door, I want to get out of here."

"Olga, let Clyde walk you, it's pouring out!" Reggie went to lower the divider to ask Clyde for help, but Olga was too quick and had unlocked the door and ran out into the rain, the curls of her hair released from the straight by the steady stream of water.

Final Payments

Since Abuelita died, Mother's Day was one of nearly unbearable torment for Olga. Normally, days, weeks, and sometimes even months would pass where, barring receiving one of her letters, Olga could, more or less, lock her mother, and her absence, inside a deeply buried mental safe. One where the hurt and pain she caused could not contaminate the other aspects of Olga's life. Mother's Day, however, was an unavoidable reminder, and without Abuelita to shed affection upon, the "holiday" left her with idle, nervous thoughts run rampant, infecting her perceptions of all other matters of her life. Assuming Prieto felt the same way, they had, on a few early occasions, convened, but somehow being with her brother made her feel all the more motherless. Their orphan state emphasized by the other's presence. Instead, she began, on that day each year, to isolate and drink until she could not possibly think cogent thoughts about this woman she barely knew, nor feel shame for having been left by her. This is what Olga did immediately after she left Reggie King and the next day that followed, feigning to Meegan that she was "working from home" while actually blackout drunk in front of her TV. It wasn't until the Wednesday before Mabel's wedding, when Tía Lola called, repeatedly, that Olga was forced to snap out of it.

"So, listen," Lola began, not bothering with formalities, "Mabel got herself into a bit of a situation with the catering hall . . ." Her voice trailed off, but Olga already could tell where this is going.

"How much does she need?"

"If me, you, and your brother each kick in three, she should be good."

"¡Coño! She's short nine thousand? What hap—"

"Ay, ten, mija. Pero my brother JoJo, God bless, had some cash he was going to give her as a wedding gift. So, can you come with me later to take it?"

"Take what?"

"The cash! That's the whole issue. The last payment is due in cash, and Julio was supposed to take care of it since he mainly gets paid in cash, pero" — and here her aunt dropped her voice — "I guess he got fired two months ago and never said anything. Mabel just found out last night. The venue called looking for their money and so she confronted him about it."

Olga sighed. What a prize my cousin won, she thought to herself. She looked at her watch.

"I'll go to the bank. Come get me when you get out of work."

Olga knew that in New York, even a budget catering hall wedding like her cousin was having could set a couple back forty, fifty, sixty thousand dollars. Olga also knew, of course, that the venue couldn't possibly be the last payment Mabel had to make. Hair and makeup, the DJ, and who knew who else was owed their final balance on the wedding day. To say nothing of tips, which they all expected (and deserved). She knew Mabel had paid for her honeymoon, plus first, last, and security on her new apartment in Bay Shore, plus all the deposits on all the vendors. And yes, while her cousin did have a decent job at Con Ed, she also had a spending problem and, Olga knew, wasted too much time at the slots when she'd go to the casinos to see freestyle shows. Which was, by matter of fact, where Mabel had met Julio in the first place. He was working as a bouncer for these nostalgia showcases in Atlantic City; one-hit wonders of the dance genre would perform for the people who loved them. Mabel was, by all accounts, an excellent dancer who commanded attention on the dance floor. So, when Julio came out to get Timmy T to cede the stage for Judy Torres, he spotted Mabel immediately. According to Mabel, they locked eyes from across the room and it was over. It was also over for Julio and that particular gig. Timmy T went into his third reprisal of "One More Try" and Judy, known to be a bit of a diva, complained to the promoter that he had eaten into her stage time. The job went poof, but a relationship blossomed.

He made Mabel very happy. Obnoxiously so, in fact. But Olga was hardly the only one who noticed that it was always Mabel who paid the bills for the romantic getaways that Julio planned. Her sister Isabel, Fat Tony, Prieto, Tía Lola, they all got in their little comments. It didn't escape their attention either that his proposal, with a ring Olga was almost certain was a CZ, came right after Mabel's promotion, which included better benefits and a pension plan. If Mabel noticed, she was too scared to give the thoughts any oxygen, but Olga knew her cousin was no dummy. She also knew that Mabel would rather die than let the rest of the family find out about this latest predicament, and that the money for the venue would not be enough to get her through the day she had planned for herself. Olga withdrew an additional $3,000, which she handed to her Tía Lola when she got in the car later that afternoon.

"Querida, you're all sugar."

Olga shrugged. "Nobody's all anything, Tía."

She felt her aunt's eyes on her. She had been intrigued at the prospect of time with her tía, her mind brimming over with thoughts and questions about their family that she'd never considered raising before.

"Pero," her aunt continued, "it's nice, Olga, to be there for your family. We're all each other has."

Olga sensed an opening and decided to test the water.

"The way you were there for my parents?"

Her aunt put a hand over her heart and grimaced for a second.

"Well, yes, mija. It was hard what happened to Johnny. We were all happy to help. I'm sure things like a wedding make you miss him. I know I do. . . ."

No one in her family ever talked about

her mother's disappearance. (Abandonment, Matteo had called it, an expression that made Olga wince.) Yes, they would pray for her mother, occasionally tell stories about her, exclaim over some trait Olga or her brother had obviously inherited from her — ranging from noses to hand gestures to attitude problems — but the circumstances surrounding her leaving and the fallout of that act were never discussed. Noting this now vexed her and, in her irritation, she found the courage to continue.

"But, what about my mom? Papi was sick, but she just kind of left. Abuelita took up most of the work, but you got stuck holding the bag, too, Tía. Clothes, school trips, money for textbooks, art supplies."

They were on the highway now and her aunt was silent for a second.

"Olga, listen," she said gently. "When I was born, there were very few choices for women. You liked boys, you got married. Then you could leave the house. Then you had babies. It's hard to understand, I think, because things have changed so fast. But, when I was younger, it wasn't possible to live the life I needed to live and also be a mother. At least not with our family and our ways. Even your parents, as anti-establishment as they were, had a church wedding. So, while I knew I didn't want to be a man's wife, that didn't mean I didn't want to be a mother. When your Mami left, honestly, for me, I thought I hit the jackpot. I could cook for you and your brother, take you places, hug and kiss you when you needed it. Pero, also still get to be me. Live how I wanted to live. So, that's all to say, I never feel I got stuck holding a bag, because I felt blessed by God to have a chance to be so needed."

Since her talk with Reggie King, Olga had found that tears, which had for so long evaded her, now came in endless cycles. She pulled her sunglasses from her purse and put them on, taking a deep breath as she did so. She was overwhelmed with love and gratitude for her aunt, but also sadness for her. And anger. At herself, at her family, for making her feel she had to live this way. If she looked at her aunt, she would not be able to hold back her tears, so she placed her hand on her shoulder.

"Titi, why didn't you ever tell us?"

"What would it have changed about my life, mija? I've never really hid myself, never pretended to be anyone else. No offense, but you young people think just because you don't know something, it's a secret. The women who I wanted to know, knew. Trust."

And here she laughed. "My generation isn't like you kids. You want everyone to talk all about every bit of themselves all the time. On the Facebook. So stupid."

Olga laughed. "Tía, I'm forty years old. I'm hardly young."

"You're not old, either!" Her tía smiled, cautiously. There was a pause. The oldies station was on, which Olga realized was playing music from when she was a teenager, Jade singing about not walking away.

"You know, mija, like I said, things are very different now. It's not too late for you to have a baby, you know."

"Tía, I don't think that's in my cards. All I do is work —"

"So, get a different job. You're smart. You're on TV. You know people. Olga, you don't even need a man anymore — it's amazing!"

They both giggled.

"Titi, can I ask you something?" Olga asked, an earnestness coming through her voice. "Do you think I'd be a good parent?"

"Absolutely. I know what good ones look like and what bad ones look like. My father, even when he was around, that hijo de puta, didn't care about anything but drinking and chasing skirts. But my mother, my mother would have died for us. Your father, in my opinion, yes, ended up with all his problems with drugs, but my God, did he love being a father! Get out of here! Making you and your brother feel good and loved. Teaching you about the world. Spending time with family."

"And my mother?" Olga asked.

"My sister? Look, she loved you both — wherever she is, she loves you both — don't get me wrong. But from day one, the world was about her and her agenda. Selfish.

"I remember when my mother was buying the house from Mr. Olsen, all the trouble your mother caused. See, Mr. Olsen loved our Mami and he loved us — bought us Christmas presents, let us hunt for Easter eggs in his backyard. But he was no fan of Puerto Ricans, generally. He felt they were pushing people like him out of his neighborhood. Obviously, Mami raised us to be polite, to show respect. But anything we did — hold the door, bring in the mail — he'd always make a big fuss and say, 'If only all Puerto Ricans were like your family!' This drove my sister crazy. She would come into our apartment going on and on about how he hates us, how it was an insult disguised as a compliment. And then one day, your mother just went off. 'Who the fuck did he think he was?' and 'Do you know we descended from the Taíno?' All that kind of shit. I never knew how Mami smoothed it over. . . . The crazy part is, she wasn't wrong, mija. Mr. Olsen *was* prejudiced. But my mother saw something to gain that was good for her family in the long run. Your mother? She needed to prove a point. And she was never happy unless the rest of us agreed with her. She never grew out of that. Even when you and your brother were little, if you didn't parrot her, she found flaws. No room for you to be your own people. In my opinion, that doesn't make for good mothering."

Olga was shocked at Tía Lola's candor. The floodgates were suddenly wide open. Tía Lola continued: "You have to understand, Olga, I don't know how you remember things, but the last few years, she'd barely been around. Traveling constantly. When she left, we thought she was going to Panamá, to give a speech. We were expecting her back! Days go by, two, three, finally a week, then two. We were going crazy with worry. Then, finally, the letter came. To your father. Saying she wasn't coming back. No address, nothing. My brother Richie wanted to call the FBI, to track her down and bring her back. Mothers can't do this kind of thing, he kept saying. But fathers can? I asked. Eventually my mother went to find La Karen. She knew Karen would know how to reach her. I don't know if my mother ever spoke to Blanca or not, but when she came home she said that maybe this was for the best, Blanca didn't have the mothering gene.

"Which is my point, Olga. You have that gene in you. You care for people. You see them. You see their flaws, but you can accept them as they are."

She thought of Matteo. He had been calling her for the past two days and she had been too drunk and sad and confused to pick up. Unsure how to explain her state without explaining what she now knew. She'd left him hanging for almost three days. It was wrong and she felt badly. She took out her phone and texted him to apologize, letting him know she would explain herself, though she wasn't completely sure how.

"¿Y quién es that you're texting?" Tía Lola asked. She was a low-key bochinchera. "Maybe someone to make a baby with? You make a nice living, you don't need them to stick around, eh? Cheaper than science!"

"Titi! You're so crazy!"

The phone rang. Matteo was calling her.

"Hey!" she said, relieved all was still well.

"Hey." He was stern and her face fell. "Listen, I'm calling you because I didn't want to do this over text, but really, what the fuck?" He wasn't raising his voice, but there was a tightness in it. She lowered the volume so her aunt would be less likely to hear.

"I know." A panic welled up in her chest. She wasn't used to being the confronted. "Like I said, I am really sorry. Some stuff came up and I got overwhelmed and shouldn't have just disappeared like that."

"I texted you. I called you. You couldn't reply? Not even to just say you were okay? Because at first I was worried."

"Oh," she said. It hadn't occurred to her that he would be worried. It had been so long since she had tried to have anything resembling a real relationship, accountability had not occurred to her.

"But then after the second day went by, I decided I had been wrong about you and that you were just a dick."

She started to feel mad, or maybe it was frustrated. "I'm not a dick. I just have some crazy stuff happening. I told you I had that fight . . ." She censored herself, lest she have to then explain herself to her tía, who was feigning disinterest. Poorly.

"Look. I told you when I let you into my

house that no one had been there for eight years. Do you know how that feels to open up to somebody and then have them ghost you?"

"I didn't ghost you." She paused. "I never thought we weren't going to talk again."

There was a moment of silence.

"You know, Olga, you're not the only one with abandonment issues. You know that, right? My pops bounced, too. I'd have thought you of all people would understand how fucked up it feels. To be waiting by the phone."

Olga felt sick. She did know. Too well. She just hadn't thought about it like that. She suddenly wanted to cry.

"Matteo. I don't know what to say. I didn't call you because I didn't even know where to start. Not because I'm not interested in you. And I promise when I see you, I'll explain as much as I can."

She waited for him to say something. He was on the street. She could hear traffic and his breathing.

"Olga, I really dig you. You obviously know that. I haven't been trying to hide it. But I don't know that I have this in me."

"What?" she said, genuinely shocked.

"I don't know if I can mentally handle a hurt like that. You have to understand. I thought that I could try, but this just got me thinking. . . .”

“But what about Saturday?” The high pitch of her voice surprised her. Even Tía Lola couldn’t pretend to not be listening anymore, lowering the volume of the radio.

“Mabel’s wedding,” Matteo said, with a bit of a sigh. “Look. Olga, I’m not the kind of guy to show up and meet a girl’s family if I’m not trying to be serious. But how can I take you seriously if you treat me like I’m disposable?”

Her stomach became a lead ball dropping down into the car seat. She felt sick and dumb for thinking that this would be no big deal. That she could just say sorry and he’d just shrug it off. This was more than about losing a date for the wedding. She felt scared of losing this chance. At something. With a real someone. She was so angry with herself.

“I’ll never do this to you again,” she blurted out. “I’m just very, very out of practice here. Please, have patience with me. I can do this. I take you seriously.”

There was quiet on his end, and in the moment Olga composed herself, her tactical brain taking over.

“Look, Matteo,” she continued, gently. “You’re a grown man. You know yourself.

And you're right, this was bullshit. But, on the other side, if this is something real, should one fuck-up spell total doom? Don't commit one way or the other right now. Don't decide during this call. I'll text you the information and if you believe I can do better — that I will do better — you come. Okay?"

"Okay," he eventually replied, and they both waited a second before they hung up.

A heaviness filled the car. Olga stared straight ahead and raised the volume on the radio, but her aunt quickly leaned forward and lowered it again.

"¿Y quién es?" she asked, knowing her niece well enough to avoid eye contact while she pried.

"This guy. I . . . I like him. And I was going to bring him to the wedding, but I think I fucked up."

Her aunt raised her eyebrows and patted Olga's knee. "Okay . . . well, nena, we all mess up sometimes. I'm sure he'll give you another chance. You can be very persuasive."

Olga sighed. They were on the Belt Parkway now and the sight of the bay was soothing. She lowered the window to inhale the saline breeze and hoped her aunt was right.

The Rolls

A gaggle of girls in coordinated but non-identical turquoise dresses filed out of a white Escalade SUV stretch limousine and up the stairs to the main Cathedral of Our Lady of Perpetual Help, bringing a cacophony of laughter, gossip, and jitters with them. Olga herself hung back, nervously searching down Fifth Avenue for the classic white Rolls-Royce that would be bringing the bride, Mabel, and her parents. The drive from their house on Fifty-third Street to the church was short, almost impossible to fuck up, really. Yet Olga held her breath until she saw the vehicle approach.

The car was Tío Richie's. Ever entrepreneurial, he had a number of side hustles, including renting vintage cars out for weddings and film shoots. He'd made a big fuss about loaning Mabel the Rolls for the day as her wedding present — a pretty cheap gift in the first place, Olga felt — but then the driver, who didn't have a working cell phone and had never driven in Brooklyn before, showed up late to pick up Tío JoJo. When JoJo called Mabel to say he was running late, Tía ChaCha, who'd been getting ready with all the girls on Fifty-third Street, was all too happy to launch into a diatribe about how this was typical half-assed Richie shit and how Mabel would've been better off paying for this herself. This, of course, set Mabel off. She asked what did ChaCha know about paying for weddings since she'd never done anything but go to City Hall? ChaCha, not one to take things lying down, then commented that maybe Mabel wouldn't be so stressed if Julio carried his very large weight and Mabel didn't feel like she needed to be so extra.

Since she was a kid, before Mabel would start to cry, she'd begin to sweat. First across the bridge of her nose, then around her temples. So when Olga looked over and saw her cousin's baby hairs begin to glisten with moisture, she knew the waterworks were on the way. She intervened before her cousin completely wrecked her edges, suggesting Tía ChaCha take the programs over to the church; a walk might do her good.

"Olga, ven acá." As ChaCha left, Mabel called her cousin over to where the hairdresser was just fixing her tiara and veil onto her updo. She looked ahead into the mirror and made eye contact with her cousin. "Thank you. Por todo."

Olga knew she meant it. For more than just getting ChaCha out of the room. They never spoke about the money, but Mabel pulled the cash to pay for hair and makeup out of Olga's bank envelope. She felt a deep closeness with her cousin then that she hadn't felt in years. Since they were girls, even. Before society's apparatus began to sort and place them onto different life paths. One deemed clever, the other coarse; one anointed pretty, the other told to keep out of the sun. Over and over again, Olga realized, they'd been told these things in different ways, by teachers and at home — implicitly one a little better than the other — and eventually, they had come to believe and resent it. As she looked at her cousin in the mirror, she could feel Abuelita's warmth on them, happy. Olga wanted this moment to last. She wanted to hug her cousin, kiss her perfectly airbrushed, made-up face, but she could see the beads of sweat forming on Mabel's forehead again.

"¡Ay, Mabel! You're gonna jack up your whole face if you don't stop!"

Mabel laughed, pressing her undereyes

with her fingers to stop the tears.

Though the early part of the day had been smooth and lively, full of laughter, music, chisme, and mimosas, the family was, admittedly, on edge, the week's events having compounded the heightened emotions wedding days always elicit. Both Tía ChaCha and Mabel's mother still had family in P.R. living without power from Hurricane Irma. Maybe an hour before JoJo called about the trouble with the driver, everyone's phones had buzzed with news alerts. A new storm was approaching, this one named Maria, Puerto Rico again in nature's crosshairs. ChaCha had tried in vain to reach her mother in Ponce while Mabel's mom knelt to pray. Olga, thanks to Reggie's assurances that her mother was safer and more secure than 99 percent of people on the island, was relieved of worry. At least regarding the storm. For most of the day, her mind had been preoccupied by Matteo.

She had no idea how to go about making up with a guy. It wasn't that she'd never fought with Reggie, or even Dick. She just had never wanted or needed to do the work to make it right. Eventually, they would come around. This time, though, she wasn't so sure. She had sent him all the details for the ceremony, and he had simply messaged back that he got it. In a panic, she sent him a dozen roses. He texted her thanks. She called and left lengthy voicemails saying she hoped he'd give her a second chance. She got nothing back. She was unsure if he'd decided to come and was making her sweat it out — give her a taste of her own medicine — or if he'd simply decided she wasn't worth the trouble. She tried to keep herself busy being helpful so as not to drown in the anxiety of wondering which of the two it was.

Mabel's morning was burdened by more material concerns. Olga watched as she repeatedly checked the bank envelope thick with cash, mentally making calculations. Tía Lola told her to stop worrying, it would just ruin the pictures, reminding her that she could always dip into the gift envelopes if need be. This seemed to do the trick. Mabel stood up, downed a mimosa, and proclaimed herself ready to get married.

In the limo, the other bridesmaids — cousins and a couple of girls from Con Edison — snapped selfies and posted to Instagram. Olga, her niece on her lap, thought of how this was yet another family milestone her own mother would miss. She pondered if she herself ever married, or equally unlikely, had a baby, would those be events of enough import to call her mother home? Then Olga remembered that Prieto, her mother's favorite, had lived these very moments without her presence or support. Her question was answered. It was dumb, irrational even, that despite her awareness of this neglect, a small part of Olga anxiously wondered if and when her mother might reach out to her again.

Mabel's limousine finally approached. Olga wanted this day to be perfect for her. She helped her tío and tía out of the car and when Mabel emerged in her Vera Wang for David's Bridal strapless princess gown, Olga carried the detachable train as they walked up the stairs. While Mabel waited for her grand entrance, the one she had been waiting to make for most of her adult life, Olga fluffed and placed the train against the marble floors of the vestibule. She pulled her cousin's veil over her face and told her that she looked beautiful, which she did. Then Olga adjusted her own ill-fitting turquoise bridesmaid dress — she never did get it altered — and headed down the aisle.

On her way, she spotted Matteo, positioned in an aisle seat on the bride's side, looking handsome in a black suit, which fit him like a glove. He'd gotten a shape-up and shaved. The sight of him electrified her. Filled her with relief and joy. For the first time in a long time she was excited. To dance with him. To introduce him to people. To gossip with over who was drinking too much and who was talking about whom in the bathrooms. To have been given a second chance.

He spotted her, and, improbably, took out an old-school disposable camera. She grinned, widely, in his direction and the flash went off.

Report to the Dance Floor

"Hold up!" Matteo exclaimed as they entered the reception room. "Your cousin got Fatman Scoop to DJ her wedding?"

"That guy?" Olga answered. "Nah. That guy's a Fatman Scoop impersonator. He just kind of looks like him and will hype up the crowd, you know? It was an add-on the DJ offered. They had a Funkmaster Flex option, too, which, personally, I would have picked since Fatman Scoop wasn't even a DJ, but whatever, Mabel was into it."

The bride and groom were off taking photos and guests had barely begun to find their seats in the reception room, but already a small group had claimed spots on the dance floor.

What's your zodiac sign? What's your zodiac sign? the Fatman Scoop lookalike asked from the small stage.

"Virgo!" Tía ChaCha kept calling out, swerving her hips to the music.

"I always liked Fatman Scoop," Matteo offered, "he had something for everyone. Long hair, short hair, hundred-dollar bill, ten-dollar bill. Very inclusive."

"Funny, that's exactly what Mabel said! She got conga players, too, for later."

Fauxman Scoop was asking for an *Ooo-oo* and a *What? What?* And Tía ChaCha was all too eager to comply. She was in a skin-tight spaghetti strap, gold sequin dress with sky-high stiletto heels, and Olga could see her Tío Richie over by the bar, leering at her while he sipped his rum and Coke. As she directed Matteo's attention to her uncle and the drama potentially about to unfold, Prieto made his way to their table and took a seat next to Olga.

"This is about to be a hot mess!" he said. "I personally got her two drinks at the cocktail hour, and the night is young."

Olga smiled faintly. She'd been avoiding her brother's calls and texts all week and, fortunately, had been busy enough with the chaos of the day to have avoided a real interaction with him. Now though, they were seated at the same table for the rest of the night and she was not quite sure how to behave. She was still unpacking their fight the weekend prior, unsure how to reconcile the cracks in her brother's character that the argument had revealed. Yet, this all took a back seat to the guilt that gripped her for withholding what she'd learned about their mother. When she got out of Reggie's car, a part of Olga had thought, Fuck you guys. Keep this a secret from my brother? This is my family. Not only did her brother deserve to know, he was the only other person who could understand all that she was feeling. The anger, the betrayal, the confusion, and frankly, the yearning for this phantom presence. Yet, something kept her from calling him: a palpable sense of fear.

She was anxious, given his public role, that sharing this kind of information with Prieto might put him in some sort of compromised state. Of lesser concern was fear *of* her brother himself. Although Reggie clearly had reservations about Prieto's trustworthiness that it seems her mother shared, Olga ultimately believed that whatever secrets and lies Prieto kept, her brother's heart was incapable of inflicting intentional harm. Except perhaps upon himself. No, Olga's largest and most pronounced fear was the Pañuelos Negros themselves, and by extension, her mother. In the past, liberation groups like FALN were not afraid to employ violence in their quest for independence for the island. What Reggie described, these

Pañuelos Negros, didn't strike her as much different. If he or her mother caught wind that Olga breached their trust, she had to admit that she was uncertain where their loyalties would lie. If, somehow, her brother now found himself on their bad side, Olga certainly did not want to feel responsible for pushing him further over the edge.

All of this pressed on her now as her brother tried to make small talk. When Olga didn't immediately answer, Prieto continued.

"Hey man," he said, as he leaned over to offer his hand out to Matteo. "Sorry we didn't get to meet earlier. Prieto Acevedo, Olga's brother."

"Hey, yeah, man! I wouldn't be a self-respecting New York 1 watcher if I didn't know who you were! I'm —"

Just then Matteo was interrupted by Fauxman Scoop, who blasted an air horn as the dated ballroom went dark. Seconds later, LED lights bathed the guests in turquoise blue. "Despacito" boomed from the speakers as the double doors opened and a trail of waiters and waitresses clad in black polyester vests and clip-on bow ties entered the room, assembling themselves in two facing lines, each holding what appeared to be a massive sparkler.

And now, ladies and gentlemen, Fauxman Scoop declared, *I want everyone on their feet because it's the moment you've all been waiting for. Let's get your napkins in the air, and wave 'em like you just don't care! You've known them as Mabel and Julio, but now I present them to you for the first time as husband and wife. . . .*

Just as Luis Fonsi began the song's first refrain, the waiters lit their sparklers, more or less simultaneously, and raised them into the air, forming a flaming archway through which, Olga realized, the newlyweds intended to walk.

Mr. and Mrs. Julio Colón! Put 'em up! Put 'em up!

Mabel and Julio, beaming and holding hands, now danced into the room, a follow spot on them, squeezing their rather corpulent selves through the human archway. Julio bumped his hip on one of the more petite waitresses, nearly knocking her over.

"This looks dangerous," Prieto muttered.

"I've never seen this done indoors before," Olga replied.

Around them, the rest of the guests did not share their concerns, as everyone, including Matteo, was spinning their napkins — their beautiful, hemstitched, linen napkins — in the air, either cheering the couple on or singing along with the song. The waiters cleared the dance floor, and suddenly Mabel and Julio were swarmed by their bridal party, Lourdes, and Tía Lola, who got into formation behind the newly-weds, and began to re-create, with remarkable precision, the exact choreography from the "Despacito" video.

Prieto, who like everyone else had been singing along, turned to his sister. "Hold up. You're a bridesmaid. Why aren't you up there? Too good for choreography?"

"No! Dude, Mabel kicked me out! I missed too many practices. She gave my spot to Lola."

The chill between the siblings melted a bit as they laughed at their cousin's strict quality control efforts.

Aright now, who out here is ready to get loud?

This seemed to Olga a stupid question since the answer was clearly everyone. Nevertheless, she was amused as the crowd all cheered in response and, after dropping another air horn, "Let's Get Loud" commenced. This was a crowd-pleaser at even the most uptight of WASP affairs, Olga knew, but here, in this setting, it whipped up near pandemonium. Guests of all ages pushed aside sateen-slip-covered banquet chairs as they swarmed the dance floor.

Though it was, indeed, loud in the room, Matteo picked up where he left off, leaning over Olga and offering his hand out to Prieto.

"Matteo Jones, Olga's bae."

Prieto smiled and raised his eyebrows, looking over to see how his sister would react, but she could only blush and swig at her glass of wine.

"Name it and claim it, man!" Prieto laughed, obviously amused at Olga's discomfort. "Don't mind my sister. She hasn't brought anyone to meet our family since the Bush administration."

At this time, we're gonna ask everyone to find their seats for the first course.

"For the record," Olga chimed in, "it was Bush two, not one, okay?"

"Right, right. Bush two. Anyway, you must be doing something right that she decided to show you the full circus."

A waiter passed and took their drink orders just as Tía Lola and Tía Ana made their way to the table.

"Before anyone gets any ideas, that centerpiece is mine!" Lola proclaimed.

Tía Ana collapsed onto a banquet chair.

"¡Ay! I can't keep up with your Tío Richie, kids! He still can dance like he's thirty years old!" She grabbed the waiter, ordered a cocktail, and went mindlessly to place her napkin on her lap when she stopped suddenly to appraise the piece of fabric. "¡Qué elegante, Olga!" she said as she raised her eyebrows. "You always know the right touch."

As Olga's smile broadened to a cat's grin, her aunt's face fell. Olga followed her gaze to the dance floor, which had been cleared of all bodies save two: Tío Richie and Tía ChaCha, who were engaged in a salsa to an old La India song. This was nothing new at family affairs. The former spouses argued at the drop of a dime, but on the dance floor, they couldn't stay away from each other, much to Tía Ana's horror. Olga could see her aunt moving to fetch her husband, which she knew would devolve into a scene.

"Titi, no. The song's almost over, you know they don't mean anything by it."

"Do I, Olga?" Ana replied, her voice tight. "I'm tired of this shit. If he likes the way she dances so much, he can go back to her!" She started to rise.

"¡Ana, siéntate!" Lola said quietly as she grabbed her sister-in-law's forearm.

Matteo, who had been quietly looking on, whispered excuse me and got up from the table. Everyone's eyes followed him as he casually walked onto the dance floor and asked to cut in. Richie demurred, leaving his ex-wife to dance with Matteo while he found his seat next to his current wife. He kissed her cheek as he sat down and, from the smile on Ana's face, everyone exhaled knowing the storm clouds had passed, at least for now.

"That was smooth," Prieto declared.

"And," Titi Lola chimed in. "¡Mira! He's a good dancer."

She was right. On the dance floor, Matteo effortlessly guided ChaCha into a cross body lead with a double inside turn, followed by a copa.

"You know what they say about good dancers. . . ." Lola giggled mischievously. "I told you it would be fine, nena."

"So, what's wrong with him, hermana?" Prieto asked.

Olga sighed. "So, so many things. Which, I think, is why he might be perfect."

For the rest of the night — a blur of golden-era hip-hop, freestyle, salsa classics, Motown, and disco — Olga barely had a chance to dance with her date, such was the demand for his skills among the tías and primas. Not just in her family, but Julio's, too.

This one's for the lovers out there! Can I get

all my lovers up here right now?

Olga was at the bar chattering with one of the other bridesmaids and could see Matteo looking for her from the dance floor, where he tried to pry himself away from Mabel's sister, Isabel. They made eye contact just as Luther began to sing "Here and Now" and Olga walked over to join him.

"Damn, girl, I've been waiting for my chance to slow dance with you all night!"

"Well, you can't help it if you're a hot property!" Olga laughed.

"Everyone's really cool. Making me feel very glad I came."

"So," she asked with a bit of trepidation, "we're good, then? Beef squashed?"

"You didn't hear me say I was your bae back there?" he asked.

Olga laughed. "Yes. And it made me happy. And relieved I didn't run you off."

"The flowers were a nice touch. Besides, how could I run from all this?" He gestured towards her, which made them both laugh since not even Matteo could not pretend that this bridesmaid's dress was a good look for her.

"Well, I mean, I know what's *under* that dress, right?"

She giggled and as the song faded into "Off the Wall," Prieto approached them.

"Hey sis, can I talk to you for a minute?" Prieto asked. Olga had been wondering when this would happen. Mabel had already made her way to the dance floor — this was one of her favorite songs — and was all too eager for her chance to dance with Matteo, practically pulling him from Olga anyway.

"Sure," she said. They each grabbed a drink from the bar and made their way through the mirrored lobby of the catering hall, out to the parking lot, which overlooked Sheepshead Bay. They sat on the front steps of the venue, out of earshot of the valets. The carpark was brightly lit and she could, for the first time, see how bad her brother looked. His eyes dark with exhaustion, the emotion drained from his face. She understood immediately that his cheer had been put on for the day. A show for everyone else.

"Prieto. What's wrong?"

Her brother buried his face in his hands.

"Olga. Fuck. I don't even know where to start. I know you're still heated with me about last weekend — but fuck. Fuck. I have this whole other problem and I don't know who to talk to because I can't fucking talk to anyone about this."

Any sense of misgiving she'd had towards Prieto was now pushed away by the sense of contrition she'd been feeling since their fight. Truthfully speaking, after her conversation with Tía Lola she reassessed and regretted the harshness with which she'd judged her brother's personal choices. She thought about Jan's sister at the funeral. At the end of the day, however much her brother wanted to reveal about his sexuality was his choice, and she'd support that.

"Look," she said, "about the other day. The truth is, it doesn't matter who you —"

"Olga, I'm worried I've got AIDS." He buried his face back in his hands again, and she could see him shuddering.

"Prieto. What happened?" Though it immediately became clear to her. His reaction to Jan's death had been strange. Disproportionate. She just couldn't imagine when they would have gotten together.

Her brother looked at her.

"It was just one time. After your birthday party."

"No rubber?" she asked.

Prieto shook his head no.

"Ay, bendito, I'm certainly not one to judge, because I've taken my chances, but for a guy trying to stay in the closet . . ."

"Please, don't."

"Sorry. I'm sorry." She put her hand on her brother's knee and patted it. "Have you taken a test yet?"

He shook his head again.

"I'm scared. Of a leak. I don't know who I trust."

"Okay," Olga replied quietly, her wheels turning.

"I, uh, had an idea though. Like, do a public health day in Sunset. A 'know your status' kind of thing, and —"

"Prieto, get the fuck out of here! You can't do something like this in public! That is one of the craziest ideas I've ever heard."

"Well, ¡coño! What should I do then?"

She was silent for a moment.

"I'll ask my gyno to do it. She's an old client, she'll do me the solid."

He sighed and put his arm around her, drawing her close and kissing her head.

"But we have to take care of it this week, you hear me?"

"Yes." He paused. "Fuck."

In that moment all Olga wanted to do was to quell what she knew must be her brother's fears. To be there for him, completely. To do so, she realized, she must first clear the fog of doubt that Reggie had cast over him.

"Prieto," Olga said gently. "I've got to ask you something. When was the last time you saw Auntie Karen?"

He looked her in the eyes for a moment without saying anything.

"How do you know about that?"

Olga wasn't quite sure how to answer, how much to reveal. Before she could though, Prieto continued: "Mami's been pissed at me since the PROMESA vote. She'd been lobbying hard for me to vote the other way. I figured she'd be upset, but" — his voice began to break with emotion — "I haven't heard from her in over a year. So, you know, then I, uh, canceled that hearing — the one Reggie'd been all up in arms about. After, I, uh, got this box in the mail. Anyway, it was obviously from Mami. If not directly, indirectly, you know?"

"Wait? No. What was in the box?"

Prieto scoffed and shook his head. "Worms. She sent me a fucking box of worms. Sometimes I wonder if maybe she's just fucking crazy. . . ."

He let out a slightly bitter laugh, but his sister could not join him because a chill had come over her. The sense of fear that had been lingering in the back of her mind about Los Pañuelos returned, now a concretely formed thing. Lombriz. She knew, as well as her brother did, what the worms meant. Somehow, this information framed everything else — Reggie's presence at the fundraiser, the timing of her mother's approach, the demand for her secrecy — far more ominously.

"Anyway," Prieto continued, "I wasn't as freaked out as I was frustrated. I don't know, maybe I wanted a way to make it up to Mami. . . . It's all so fucking twisted. So I went to see Karen just to see if I could fucking communicate with her somehow."

"And?" Olga asked, cautiously.

"Karen wouldn't even see me. Mami's next-level angry."

Her brother had tears welling now and Olga put her hand on her brother's back and rubbed it the way Abuelita used to do. She felt a sense of relief. Prieto had proven Reggie wrong. She'd asked him about Karen and he'd told her. Because why wouldn't he? After all that they had been through together. Just the two of them. Now, she resolved to be there for her brother in this moment, fully. Her brother who helped raise her, who bought her prom dress, moved her in and out of every college dorm she'd lived in, who took her, at twenty-five, to have an abortion and asked no questions at all. Her brother who was, she knew, her only real friend. Olga deeply resented her mother for injecting this wedge of secrecy between them. She wanted to tell him everything that she knew, in the hopes that together they could make some sense of it, and, perhaps selfishly, to unburden herself a bit. A lump formed in her throat. Instead, she said, "Mami's gonna be fine. She'll get over it. We'll think of some grand gesture to make it right. So, don't worry about that. Let's just get you this test, okay?"

It was a lie, she knew. But she needed this lie right now. To protect her brother from fear: of disease, of losing their mother's love, of perhaps something more nefarious. To protect herself as well. From what exactly, she did not know. What she felt though, in her gut, was that for now, the less he knew, the better.

There was more she wanted to say, but they were interrupted by the sounds of laughter coming out of the reception hall. Tío Richie, Mabel, Julio, Fat Tony, Matteo, Titi Lola, Tío JoJo, and Titi ChaCha emerged, drinks and cigars in hand, lighting up before they could even get outside. ChaCha had her arm around Tío Richie's ample waist and Prieto swatted his sister's arm as they knew the parking lot fight that would ensue whenever Ana noticed that they both were missing from the ballroom. Olga raised an eyebrow at Matteo, who just shrugged at her with a smile. She was walking over to him when Mabel grabbed her arm and pulled her to the side. She'd been dancing all night and Olga was impressed with how well the airbrushed makeup had stayed.

"You brought those napkins, didn't you?" Mabel asked.

Olga wasn't going to lie, but at the same time, after their exchange this morning, she didn't feel the sense of joy she had thought this moment would provide her. Olga sighed. "I did, Mabel. Pero . . ."

But it was too late.

"Listen, puta, I'm no dummy. I know you. You did this to try and show off to la familia, but guess what? All you did was play yourself! My mother-in-law was so impressed by those fucking napkins! And since she has no idea who the fuck you are, she figured it was me. She was all 'What great taste you have, Mabel! They don't even leave any lint. This is real European style, Mabel.' You know she's Italian and thinks she's fucking better than everybody."

Olga sighed, regretful that she'd already fucked up their truce. "Mabel, I really want to start on a new —"

"Prima, listen, we're all good. But in the spirit of a clean slate, I just needed you to know that I saw what you were trying to do and let you know that it backfired, okay?

You wanted to make me look like a chump and instead I looked like a champ!"

The cousins stared at each other in silence for a moment, and Mabel took a puff from her cigar.

"So," she continued, "we'll call it water under the bridge now. Pero, Olga —" She gestured her cousin to come towards her, and whispered, "What I really want to know about is your new man. I mean, I'm a married woman now, but a girl can't help but notice . . ."

The doors to the hall opened and they could hear Fauxman Scoop call from inside,

Aiiight, Imma need all my single ladies and all my single fellas to report to the dance floor. Report to the dance floor!

Olga reached for Matteo's arm.

"That's us; let's go."

Swallow

The Wednesday after the wedding Olga awoke with a start from a dream. She was a little girl again, holding her father's hand as they exited the subway. He was taking her to the circus — not the cheesy one at Madison Square Garden that Prieto liked, the good one. The one behind Lincoln Center. They exited the train and walked past the fountain and when she could see the red-and-white-striped tent lit up before them, she squealed and looked up at her father with delight. Inside the tent was an old-fashioned arena, the crowd seated on bleachers around the bright blue ring, a big white star radiating from its center. Olga and her father found their seats and the tent went dark for a moment before a single spotlight shone on one side of the ring, revealing, in a gilded cage, a lion. The lion swiped at the bars and roared, vexed at its captive predicament. On the other side, a second spotlight. A woman dressed in a red tailcoat and top hat, black leotard, and knee-high boots, one of which was resting casually on a small black stool, stood illuminated. In one hand she held a whip. Her other rested with ease on her hip. She grinned at the crowd and the gold of her hoop earring caught the light, making her appear to glow. It was her mother.

"If anyone can tame a lion, Olguita, it would be your Mami!" her father whispered to her. Olga beamed and her mother cracked the whip on the ground as she approached the lion, who roared in irritation, pacing before she opened its cage. The crowd held its collective breath as she commanded the majestic beast towards the impossibly small stool. The lion bared its teeth. Olga's mother cracked her whip again, repeating her command. The big cat hung its head for a moment before he galloped to the stool, assuming an awkward perch. The crowd cheered. Someone handed her mother a torch, which she brandished before the crowd, and the lion met it with a swipe of his large claws before leaning away from the flame. With a flourish, Olga's mother set a metal ring on fire and the crowd again gasped. She cracked her whip. The lion sat still as a statue, the crowd silent. Waiting. Then, in one movement it leapt from the stool, bounded onto the floor, and jumped through the ring, unscathed. The crowd went wild — people jumped up, including her father — popcorn spilling in the excitement. Her mother commanded the lion back to the stool, approaching the beast with swagger. She winked and offered her hand to the lion, gesturing for it to give its paw. The lion complied, bowing its regal head bashfully. The audience laughed. Now her mother smiled coyly at the crowd, as if to say, watch this. She raised her whip in the air, dancing it over the lion's head, snapping the fingers of her free hand to the beat of the background music. Slowly the lion rose on its hind legs and, the crowd realized with delight, began moving to Olga's mother's beat. The crowd joined in, clapping as the lion danced. Her mother sliced her hand through the air. Stop. And they did. An *ooooh* of wonder emanated from the crowd. She motioned for the lion to wave. He complied, the audience breaking into a coo of *aaaahs.* Her mother then began to bow, tipping her hat and turning to address every corner of the audience. Then, just as her show was coming to a close, Olga's mother snapped her whip one last time, gently, and

beckoned the lion to give her a kiss.
It swallowed her whole in one bite.

Olga bolted upright, her mother's name on her tongue. She checked her phone. It was just before five in the morning. Maria had made landfall in Puerto Rico. She slipped out of bed, careful not to wake Matteo, and scrolled social media as she made her coffee. People, either unable to believe their own eyes or certain that later they would be doubted, were posting videos of the storm's fury. In one, a woman in Utuado screamed as Maria ripped the roof off her home, in the background the wind knocking the crowns off her royal palms. In another, a family in Humacao cowered together in a bathtub while Maria, with the ferocity of a vengeful lover, pounded their glass patio door determined to make her way in, indifferent to the shattered glass eventually left in her wake. The locations varied — a hotel ballroom in San Juan, a flooded street in Guayama — but the constant of them all? The trembling of the hands wielding the cameras, the physical manifestation of fear across the entirety of the island. The star of the spectacle was the wind, which roared like a menacing vacuum, sucking away leaves, trees, homes, cars, lives. Then Maria ripped down the cell towers, so the videos stopped, but Olga knew the terror had not.

Olga had only been to Puerto Rico once, for a long weekend back when she was dating Reggie King. Reggie was, in fact, born there, but left when he was two. As a kid he'd gone back to his grandmother's a couple of times in the summer, when his mom's hands felt too full. But he'd not been back as an adult and, as he'd kept emphasizing, had not been back rich. He was only a little rich in those days, but it clearly meant something to him to return with his shit in a Louis Vuitton roller instead of a shopping bag, staying in a suite at the Ritz in San Juan instead of a concrete three-room in the campo. While Olga took pleasure in watching him enjoy this, she also couldn't help but see that, though this was "home," they didn't exactly fit in. What Olga had thought of as looking "New York," she realized, down there, just looked "American." Her Spanish was wack at its best, so every time they sat down to eat or get a drink the waitstaff would hear one word out of her mouth and switch to English. Reggie loved this, of course, because he delighted in making a big show of speaking Spanish — surprising them that he was one of them and not an African American — and they'd switch right back. She shouldn't have been surprised to hear that he'd built a house there, because even at the time, he'd enjoyed the trip much more than she did.

What Olga had loved, though, was the music. Everywhere. Salsa, plena, and bomba. They went to a street performance and the circle must have had thirty drummers. The first dancer was a dude so big, Reggie joked that he could have been the reincarnation of the late, great Biggie Smalls. Women, complexions ranging from the inside of an almond to the outside of a coffee bean, each more beautiful than the next, danced in these fantastic white skirts. Teasing the drummers with their fabric and hips. Delighting in their own existence. She felt the beat of the bomba in her chest, bigger than that of her own heart. As big as the whole island.

It occurred to her now that during that trip she and her mother were likely mere miles from each other. Together on that tiny island. Would her mother have known she was there? She felt about her mother much as she felt about Puerto Rico itself: mysterious and unknown entities. Her only certainty about either was that they, somehow, were both a part of Olga.

■ ■ ■ ■

The more time Olga had to recontextualize Reggie King with the information her brother had given her, the more uneasy she felt. Still, he was her only conduit to information. She texted him a series of question marks. Reggie sent a *nada por ahora* in reply. This grated her. Not the lack of answers, but that she was reliant on him in the first place. Discovering that her mother had given Reggie a way to reach her — something her own children had been desperate for — had quietly crushed her. It saddened her that the most important woman in her life was effectively a stranger. To her, but not to everyone.

By the time Matteo woke, Olga was parked on her sofa, transfixed by the news. Though the storm had barely begun its cross-island journey, on all the morning shows they heard Gayle King and Matt Lauer and Pat Kiernan and even Rosanna Scotto all saying the same things — Puerto Rico was "likely destroyed," the phrase feeling like a shot in the heart each time she heard it. A strange sense of dread welled up in her chest.

For so many years their mother existed as a floating entity, whose only location was inside the many envelopes that arrived from destinations unknown. Now, Olga was able to firmly fix her in a place. To imagine her with surroundings, as a real person in a physical body. A body that had inevitably aged. A body that could be washed away by floodwaters or hit by a falling tree or . . . It was a new sensation to not only have her mother such an active part of her thoughts, but a subject of her concern.

"Are you okay?" Matteo asked.

"I don't know," she said flatly. "My mother is there."

"What?" Matteo said, surprised. "I thought you —"

"It's . . . it's pretty new information. Well, to me at least."

After their reconciliation at the wedding, Matteo hadn't pressed too hard on why she had gone dark in those days before. He took her affirmation that it would not be a repeated mistake at face value. In the moment, Olga had been filled with relief. But now, overwhelm consumed her and she needed, she recognized, help unpacking all that had transpired. She danced carefully around the details.

"One of my mother's . . . associates came to see me last week. At my office."

"Okay. Is that normal?"

"Anything but. Apparently my mother needed my help."

"Is she okay? Like, physically?"

Olga laughed. "I mean, I don't know about mentally, but yeah, she doesn't need a kidney or anything like that, if that's what you mean."

"So, she bounces for, like, decades and then shows up looking for a favor? I hope you told her to fuck off."

Even though Matteo reflected back a thought Olga herself had had, she still felt annoyed.

"It's still my mother," she said defensively, "I'm not going to just tell her to fuck off if she comes looking for my help specifically. I'm going to at least hear her out."

Matteo walked over to where she was sitting on the sofa and leaned down to kiss her on the head.

"Listen, Olga," he whispered in her ear, "it's your mom, I get it, it's complicated. I just get upset when I think about you going out of your way at all for a woman who never did the same for you."

There was a silence between them.

"What does your brother think?"

"I haven't had a chance to tell him," she replied defensively. "Besides, it doesn't even matter. They didn't say what she wanted and whatever it was, it's probably irrelevant now."

To other people, Olga imagined her brother seemed lucky.

People often mistook fame for fortune, not understanding that even those with some renown are vulnerable to miseries. Olga felt Prieto had been born under a difficult star. Too early to feel entitled to be himself in society. Too affected by their parents' influence to ever be avaricious. He had a child to care for and protect. Enemies that she knew of and others she knew she could barely imagine. She remembered her brother's blood test was that morning. If her instincts were right and the results were positive, her brother's constitution worried her. She could see no way for him to keep his life intact without bold honesty, and she wasn't sure he had the courage that would require.

They met in the waiting room of her gynecologist's office. CNN played on a TV in the corner of the room, alerting anyone paying attention that the lights were out again in Puerto Rico, though anyone paying attention knew that had been inevitable.

"This will be worse than Katrina," Prieto said.

She nodded. "Louisiana's a state."

The hurricane had only amplified Olga's discomfort at withholding their mother's whereabouts, yet she couldn't bring herself to add to her brother's already full plate of troubles. She had nothing to offer but worry, and he had enough of that already. No sooner was Prieto's blood drawn than his phone rang. It was the governor's office. They were trying to negotiate a trip down as soon as Friday, to bring supplies, assess the damage, and see what state-level relief they could provide. They wanted Prieto on the plane, and he was eager to help. He was then engulfed in triage — with his staff, with his colleagues, with his contacts. She could hear him: sourcing water, medicine, batteries, flashlights, radios. Their preparations made her anxious. They were looking for things she couldn't believe FEMA hadn't put in place. It disturbed her that people might be dependent on an ad hoc goods drive being run on Prieto's cell phone from her OB-GYN's office.

That night, back at her house, the news showed an aerial of the island in darkness and predicted it would be months — maybe years — before they had power again. By the light of the next day, more videos emerged: collapsed roads, flooded homes, mudslides. Tears came to her eyes. She could not stop watching. She remembered doing this after 9/11, too. Her grandmother told her to go out, get away from the news, but she couldn't. The bodies jumping from the building then, the people moated by floodwater now. This could only get worse.

Olga's breakup with Dick had only one true lingering effect — she'd lost any and all enthusiasm for her career, recognizing, she supposed, that his comment would not have stung so acutely had she not, in some part, agreed with him. Maria served as the perfect excuse to ditch work and wallow in televised misery. For the next few days, while her brother was servicing the actual people, Olga was on her sofa, observing, in slow motion, all the ways in which the island was now truly fucked. There was no power, there was no water, the sun was back out and people were hot. Sick people didn't have medicine. Food was spoiling. People would go hungry. People would panic.

In all of the hours of footage that Olga viewed, she could count the number of times she saw a soldier or federal officer. Where were they? Online, the president was busying himself with the patriotism of professional athletes and rallying crowds around a pedophile. It took his political opponent to remind him, on social media no less, that there was an entire Navy vessel intended for supporting crises like this, if only he would deploy it. Towns were trapped within themselves — roads cut off by downed trees or power lines, or the roads themselves simply having disappeared. Buckling under the weight of floodwaters after so many decades of neglect by the government. Yet how did Olga know this? The news crews, with their helicopters, managed to get into each nook and cranny of the island, which somehow FEMA hadn't managed to do. As one day turned into two into three and four, in each town you would hear the same refrain: We need help, where is the help? We are American.

"They're going to let them die," she finally said to Matteo on Saturday evening, three days after Maria left. "It's impressive."

"What is?"

"They've figured out how to commit genocide without getting their hands dirty."

"Babe," Matteo said cautiously. "We have got to get you out of this apartment."

Earlier that day he had, in fact, gotten her out of the apartment and it hadn't gone very well. Matteo convinced her to walk to the Atlantic Center to buy supplies to send down, but when she looked at the needs list and found herself filling their wagon with diapers, baby wipes, and formula, she burst into tears in the middle of the store. The phantom cries of babies waiting for formula and clean diapers were ringing in her ears, knowing that no one in charge cared if and when they received them.

"White babies would have had diapers yesterday!" she cried.

"It's okay, it's okay," Matteo said, trying to console her.

"She's right though," a Black woman pushing a cart past them offered. "The government's never in a hurry to help anybody like us, so it's on us to help each other."

Olga noticed her cart was also filled with the random needs of disaster victims.

"¿Puertorriqueña?" Olga asked.

"Girl, I don't need to be Puerto Rican to want to help out. That's the problem right now. People think they're only responsible for people exactly like them. I don't feel that way. They left my people to die after Katrina. It's the same. Like I said, it's on us to help each other." And the woman, and her cart, kept it moving.

On Sunday, she found herself hunkered

down at Matteo's, planted firmly on the couch. Matteo hadn't convinced her to go out so much as to switch locations, and they were now, at Olga's insistence, watching the news at Matteo's.

"Look at that," he said. "These homies are like, 'Fuck the government, we're gonna take this shit into our own hands.' "

On the TV screen, Olga saw them, the men and women with machetes, hacking away at the fallen trees and clearing their own roads. She could see that a few of them — the ones organizing the others — wore black bandanas over their faces. All you could see were their eyes. On another channel, a group had gathered around a single small solar lamp — a woman with a hot burner salvaged rice and beans and managed to cook for the entire neighborhood. Then another clip: in a town plaza, among the still fallen branches, a bomba circle had formed, and, taking a break from waiting for gas and waiting for water, people had stopped to dance. In her chest she felt a pride well up, a pride connected to an ancient something programmed to survive. For the first time in days, she felt something other than a deep, endless well of sadness.

Her phone buzzed. It was Reggie.

"¡Pa'lante!"

And she knew her mother had stared Maria down.

Always Keep Going

The Friday after Maria passed, the New York gubernatorial delegation made their way to San Juan. As their plane began its descent, Prieto glanced out the window and gasped. The island, normally a slab of lush malachite floating in a clear aquamarine sea, was now a brown scab in a gray shadowy abyss. The trees were stripped raw, the foliage victim of Maria's rage. He felt his heart rip a bit, imagining nature's arduous journey to restore color to the island. It was only when he landed that he understood the practical implications of the island's lost verdure. Without the shades of the palms and cool green of the hibiscus plants, the sun burned the earth and the people trying to salvage themselves under its rays.

The first time Prieto had gone to Puerto Rico was for the national convention of his fraternity back when he was an undergrad.

It was the mid-'90s and an infusion of capital from mainland businesses had caused San Juan and the environs to boom. There was a banquet for the three hundred or so brothers who had gathered from cities up and down the East Coast. They were greeted by scions of local industry: pharmaceutical company heads talking about job creation by and for Puerto Ricans, hoteliers discussing the ability of tourism to unify the diaspora. The keynote was the newly installed governor, the same man whose son was governor now. He gave a sweeping speech about the next phase of Borinquen and how privatization of the island's municipalities would pave the path to Puerto Rican statehood.

Prieto remembered lapping it up at the time — giving the guy a standing ovation and waiting, eagerly, to shake his hand and take a photo afterwards. He had no idea that in three short years President Clinton would end the tax incentives that had brought those companies there in the first place, and that along with the tax breaks would go the jobs. He didn't yet understand that American companies weren't motivated to create meaningful work for anyone anymore, least of all Puerto Ricans. Since then, each time Prieto returned to the island — and over his years as a New York public servant, his trips were many — he noticed that San Juan was a little less shiny, the sense of possibility less ebullient, than what he'd seen that first trip.

On that first trip, Prieto had wandered off from the convention group and made his way to an address in La Perla, right on the water in Viejo San Juan. His Spanish, clumsy back then, helped him make his way through the narrow streets. On arriving, he could hear a mom yelling at her kid about cleaning up after themselves. He knocked, unsure if his language skills were good enough to explain what had brought him here: that his father, Juan Acevedo, had once lived at this house before he left for Nueva York. He'd brought a photo of his pop — in his military uniform — just to see if that might spark a memory or recollection and if he might still have family around. It didn't. But the woman, Magdalena, was so touched by this poor Nuyorican so interested in meeting his family that she wouldn't let him go without feeding him and introducing him to her children and neighbors. After they ate, she took him to meet every Acevedo that she knew in the area, just in case his father's name and story meant anything to them.

He thought of her now as he glimpsed La Perla through the window of his military escort vehicle.

"Can we stop here for a second?"

"Congressman, I'm sorry, but we can't take you there. La Perla is a mess and we've got to get you back for the helicopter tour."

"We'll be fine," he offered firmly.

They could not make it into the barrio by car, their path blocked by a downed phone line. While the National Guardsmen assessed the road, Prieto jumped out, winding his way down a sloping footpath covered with leaves and debris towards Magdalena's, and his father's, onetime home. Had she been home during the storm, she surely couldn't be there now. The roof was torn off, the windows blown in, and half the second floor had collapsed onto itself. Down the street he saw an old man wearing the apron of a bodeguero coming out of his building with a broom. Given the state of the street — fallen branches, scattered leaves, shattered car windows, rubble from buildings — the broom seemed a laughable tool. Nevertheless, the man began to sweep. From the top of the steps, one of the National Guardsmen was beckoning Prieto back to the car, so he called out to the man in Spanish —

"Does Magdalena still live here?"

"Yes, but her sons took her to the mountains before the storm. To the Pañuelos Negros."

Prieto was unsure what that meant. The National Guardsmen were approaching now, calling his name.

"If she comes back, tell her that Prieto came to check on her."

The man nodded and put a thumb in the air.

"Pa'lante," Prieto called out.

"Siempre pa'lante," the man called back.

Keep going. Always keep going.

Two days prior, Prieto did not think that anything — not even a catastrophic Category 5 hurricane — would ever take his mind off his HIV test. From the moment he allowed his sister to schedule the appointment, it was his near singular obsession. He was haunted by the idea of leaving Lourdes without her father, inflicting a pain on her life that he knew all too well. He knew dwelling on death was irrational, but found himself unable to pull his mind back from wandering these dark alleys. The night before he'd been unable to sleep. He was high-strung when he arrived at the doctor's office. He felt like the nurse gave him a screw face when he got up to follow Olga into the exam room. His heart had been racing, confident that this was a terrible idea.

At first, it certainly seemed that way. His sister had told him that the doctor was cool with her plan, that it was a simple favor. But it became apparent that Olga hadn't told anybody shit. First, the nurse tried to take Olga's blood, which made his sister insist on seeing the doctor personally, which then, understandably, made the nurse feel insulted.

Prieto could hear her muttering to the other nurses about how the doctor probably hadn't drawn blood since med school, but Olga wasn't paying attention and, at the end of the day, it wasn't Olga's arm that was about to be poked.

"I can't believe they already lost power," she said while she scrolled her phone.

"Honestly? Most of the island didn't have power back from Irma. . . ."

"What's going to happen?"

"They were already fucked, now they will be fucked in the dark."

"Jesus, Prieto! Way to be a Debbie Downer over here!"

He pinched his eyes as he appraised his sister. Did she think, moments before having to get a fucking AIDS test, he was going to muster the energy to play Mr. Optimist? He was tired of this role. Before he could reply, the doctor walked in. Prieto watched as she absorbed his presence and realized that she had no idea of the favor they were about to ask. While it had occurred to him that perhaps this scheme of Olga's violated some sort of ethical code, it suddenly dawned on him that Dr. Gallagher might be the type of person to be affronted by the request. He and his sister could very well be thrown out in a matter of moments and he'd be back where he started.

"Congressman Acevedo!" Dr. Gallagher exclaimed. Her expression transitioned into a smile. "It's a real pleasure — a surprise, but a pleasure. Olga, I don't think I'd made the connection that you and our fine congressman were related!"

Olga winked at her brother from her perch on the exam table. Puta. He knew this favor was for him, but he fucking hated the way she always managed to get her way. Prieto shook the doctor's hand.

"Well, Marilyn, you know, I don't like to go around bragging, but believe me, I'm very proud of my brother!"

Dr. Gallagher now paused. Prieto could tell she was a smart woman, beyond just the medical books. "So," she began, "and don't get me wrong, I'm a political junkie, so it's a delight to meet you, but it's . . . uncommon to have a brother accompany his sister to her gynecologist."

Olga replied before he could think of an explanation.

"Well, Marilyn, as I mentioned in my email . . . some stuff has come up recently that made me think it would be good to do a full HIV/STD screen."

He found himself relieved, but irked, that Olga always had an answer for everything.

"Okay," Dr. Gallagher answered, slowly, knowing there was more.

"It's just that it's not me that needs the screening —"

There was a pause. Prieto looked down at his shoes and the vinyl beige marbled tiles.

"It's me," Prieto said, raising his hand up. "I, um, engaged in some risky behavior with someone I now know contracted an STD and I just want to, *confidentially,* get myself checked out. I don't really have a personal physician that I trust."

"What kind of STD? Do you know?" Marilyn asked.

He swallowed. "HIV."

"You know, Congressman, they have home tests that you can send in the mail, completely confidential. Totally anonymous."

"Marilyn?" Olga now interjected. "Would you let your brother take a correspondence course AIDS test?"

Marilyn shook her head no. There was a silence; Prieto wondered if her sense of rules and regulations was as gray as his sister's.

"November sixth. Seven P.M. The Bowery Hotel. Be there."

"Excuse me?" Prieto asked.

"My husband and I are cochairing a gala for a charter school network we support. We need a high-wattage keynote."

Damn, Prieto thought, everyone really does have a price. Three attempts to get blood later, Dr. Gallagher finally found the vein.

"Now, Olga, the lab will reach out by phone in a few days —"

"Wait!" Prieto interrupted. "I, uh, I'd read about these rapid HIV tests. You know, where they tell you right away. I was kind of hoping we could do one of those?"

"Congressman," Dr. Gallagher offered, "I'm sorry to disappoint you, but my office isn't equipped to do the rapid test. That might be an oversight on our part; it's just that HIV testing . . . my patient demographic is mainly concerned about weight loss and fertility specialists. I'll have to send the results out to the lab."

Prieto sighed and the doctor continued.

"Olga, don't ignore random calls, because they won't leave a message and they don't send me the results. It's truly confidential."

He was seated on a chair, keeping his focus on the tiles, one hand on his head, the other putting pressure on the site where blood was drawn, trying not to hyperventilate.

"Congressman," the doctor said as she squatted down so that they were eye level. Like Lourdes's pediatrician would do. "Probably, you're worrying more than you need to. But I just want to remind you, there are a lot of resources out there now and people with HIV live very long, robust lives. Especially, if you don't mind me being so frank, people with some access and connections. Don't spend too much time sulking, okay?"

He wanted to tell her that he wouldn't, that he appreciated her favor, even if he was fundamentally opposed to charter schools, but he found his throat too tight to speak past. She patted his shoulder and just as he thought he might actually break down, his phone began to ring. It was the governor.

■ ■ ■ ■

It didn't take a crisis management expert to understand that the federal government had chosen to put their heads in the sand when it came to preparing for Maria's arrival. Excuses abounded: FEMA was too overwhelmed with recovery from Irma and Harvey to preemptively assist P.R. The Navy was worried about the comfort ships weathering the storm in the Port of San Juan. But for Prieto, the ultimate tell that this was a case of willful neglect was the failure to fully deploy the National Guard in advance of the storm. Always the first line of defense in a disaster, out of eight thousand guardsmen, they called in five hundred. On an island already suffering a blackout. It was clear that Puerto Rico was being left to dangle in the wind. This was a familiar place for the United States to leave the island, but somehow, it felt more ominous this time. Prieto was unable to shake his recollection of the Selby brothers' recent interest in the goings-on down there.

Prieto had been on the ground for disasters before — September 11, Superstorm Sandy — but he was unprepared for the destruction and disorder that met them in

San Juan. They had divided the governor's envoy into three small groups, each being helicoptered to a different area of the island to survey and deliver critical drinking water and supplies: formula, insulin, battery-operated respirators. Prieto found himself in Maunabo, a town that, after years of corporate chemical dumping, the EPA had named a Superfund site. On a good day their water was at risk of contamination. The people there spoke of Maria like a monster, barely fighting back tears while they waited for jugs of water. With the power out and the cell towers destroyed, their anxiety had only heightened from being cut off from the outside world. His entourage had been the first officials anyone in the town had seen and they felt relief at being "found." Feeling the heat and his own thirst, Prieto assessed their supplies.

"Is this all the water we have?" he asked one of the congressional aides in his group.

"They are saying FEMA should make it out in a day or so?"

"These people need water now. Give out everything we have here; we'll go back for more. We can't have people dying of thirst. It's still fucking America."

"Honestly? If this was a foreign country, we'd likely be doing more," the aide replied.

In the distance, Prieto heard a commotion. On the outskirts of their long distribution line, people were chattering and, family by family, peeling off, heading in the opposite direction. He followed. Down a side street sat a pickup truck. Two men stood on the flatbed with AK-47s in their hands. Two others were distributing gallon jugs of water to the growing crowd. All four of their faces were covered by black bandanas. One of the gunmen noticed him and called for the others' attention. Prieto stopped, and gave a head nod in their direction. They raised their rifles, and even as Prieto turned, slowly, to walk away, he could feel their aim on his back.

The envoy was only meant to stay for a few hours before heading back to New York, but when their tour was over, Prieto felt unable to leave. It was hard to imagine going back, sleeping in the comfort of his home, with AC and drinkable water, refrigerated food, access to phone service and internet, knowing that a short flight away, there were Americans who looked just like him, with none of those things. Unlike when Sandy took out power in New York, or when Houston was flooded after Harvey, or when fires burned the houses of Sonoma to the ground, these people had no one to go to. They had no real voice as far as the government was concerned. They paid taxes, served in U.S. wars, yet there was no one with actual power whose job was to fight for them. No one to represent them and demand action. On a good day, Prieto didn't trust this administration not to fuck anyone who wasn't a part of their "base." He could only imagine the cruel neglect they would subject upon an entire island of disenfranchised Brown and Black people. It was playing out before his very eyes. He wanted to stay to help, yes, but also so that no one could deny what he saw. No one could "spin" it and say the footage was worse than the situation. He needed to bear witness.

For the next two days Prieto embedded himself with a U.S.-based news crew who'd been sent down to cover the storm. Prieto trusted them over the government to give him unfiltered access to what was really happening. The first day, Saturday — three days after the storm — they made their way over to Toa Baja, where search and rescue for people trapped in flooded houses was still going on. Sam, the reporter, and his cameraman, Jeff, documented the people stranded on roofs, the homes subsumed with water. Prieto waded through flooded streets helping to put the sick and elderly on floatation devices, wading them to barely functioning hospitals. He was struck that, rather than express fear, those whom they rescued met them with gratitude. Gratitude that they survived. Gratitude that it had not been worse. Gratitude that their brethren had not forsaken them.

The irony, Prieto realized, was that for Borinquen, surviving the storm was just the beginning. Each hour seemed to bring new reverberations of Maria's impact. Landslides in the mountains were taking down what remained of homes that had survived. Even if you could get your car around the blocked and collapsed roads, there was a gas shortage. Even if you could find gas, because of the power loss, the only way to buy it was if you had cash. On Saturday afternoon, back in San Juan, they'd spotted a line that snaked around a block and discovered it led to an ATM being powered by one of the island's few working generators. Sam and his cameraman were talking to the waiting people being desiccated by the sun. Prieto's eye was drawn to a man sitting on the curb. He was skinny and his long gray hair was offset by his dark complexion. His head was resting in his hands. Prieto could see his shoulders shaking with sobs. He walked and sat down next to him.

"Sir," Prieto said, touching his shoulder as he introduced himself. When the man realized he was with an elected official, he moved to smooth his hair and placed his POW*MIA cap back on his head.

"¿Estuviste en Vietnam?" Prieto asked.

"Ya, eso es verdad. Two tours for my country."

"My dad, too."

The man looked at him and blinked. "My granddaughter is pregnant. We ran out of water. I'm out of cash. I just . . . I just . . ."

The man buried his head in his hands.

Prieto took out his billfold and gave him $60. The man took it and crossed himself, giving Prieto a bendición, and rose to go and find the next line to wait in.

That night, huddled around a few solar-powered lanterns in the Telemundo parking lot, Prieto sat with Sam and some other journalists, trying to make sense of all that they'd seen. They passed around a bottle of rum.

"You know what I can't get over?" Prieto said. "That no one is expecting any help to come."

A local journalist named Mercedes replied, "What evidence did we have that it would be anything but? That was clear before this storm happened."

"Do you ever feel bad?" Prieto asked.

"About what?" Jeff replied.

"You're able to get all over the island, but all you're doing is holding your camera. Do you ever feel bad you're not physically helping?"

"That's hilarious, dude," Sam said, with attitude.

"I didn't mean any offense," Prieto said. He hadn't. He really was wondering what it felt like to document and not intervene. For his part, Prieto felt, weirdly, better than he had in months, if only because he knew he was really, directly helping people.

"No offense, Prieto," Jeff said, "but if we weren't here, do you think anyone would be thinking of these people and this place?"

There was a moment of silence. Even the coquís had gone quiet, just the hum of the local AM radio station reporting check-ins from the various municipalities. Satellite phones had been set up in some of the island's larger urban centers, but cell service was still out. Radio was their only source of any inkling of news from other parts of the island. So they all listened. Intently.

"Wait," Prieto said, "what did they just

say?" His Spanish was good, but the newscaster spoke fast.

"Fuck," Sam offered. "They're saying that there's been a prison break in Guaynabo?"

"No," Mercedes offered, "they are saying it was a breakout — a group came and liberated the prisoners."

"Shit," Sam said. "If it's bad out here, can you imagine how fucked people in jail here are?"

Prieto thought back to the thirty days he'd spent locked up in MDC for protesting the military occupation of Vieques. Yes. He could begin to imagine about how fucked those inmates were.

"The thing is," Mercedes said, "I'm from around there. That's not really a jail. It's like, for kids, you know? What do they call them in English?"

"Juvie hall," Sam offered.

"Some group comes in and frees up all the persecuted bad children?" Jeff offered. "No real mystery. Pañuelos Negros."

"Hold up," Prieto cut in, "do you mean the dudes in the black bandanas? Is this, like, a thing? I heard about them in La Perla and I saw them Friday when we were up in Maunabo giving out water."

"Well," Mercedes said, "it's all more lore than fact but . . ." And she proceeded to tell him about this group of rebels who some say were descendants of the Macheteros of the generation prior, under new leadership. There were rumors that they intended to be the Zapatistas of Puerto Rico, to go to war with the government, create a state within a state, but it was all speculation. All accounts placed them in the mountains, on a self-sustaining farm rumored to have its own supply of power, food, and young recruits from all over the island.

Prieto slept on a cot in the Telemundo newsroom that night, thinking of Los Pañuelos Negros. As soon as Mercedes began to talk about it, Prieto knew his mother was involved. The timing, the objective, it all lined up with what he'd seen in her FBI file. He needed proof and, above all, he needed to find her. Giving out water was one thing; doing so with rifles was another. Liberating prisons — juvenile or otherwise — landed yet somewhere else on the spectrum. When finally he drifted off to sleep, he dreamt of worms. He woke up dripping in sweat.

Prieto contemplated skipping his flight home. He felt, for the second time in his life, that fate had put him in the right place at the right time to create positive change.

That part of his destiny was tied to protecting this island — his island — from exploitation. He just didn't know exactly what shape that would take. In the end, however, what drew Prieto away from San Juan was a middle school talent show. When he remembered it, his first thought was, But I'm doing important stuff here! Then he thought of his mother. How many things she'd deemed more important than her role as a parent. How secondary he'd always known he and his sister were to whatever the cause at hand was. Many things in Prieto's life were, especially lately, out of his control. However, the kind of father that he chose to be to Lourdes, that was not one of them. He made his way to the airport.

As he rode home from JFK he ruminated on his existence the past few years; he felt as if he'd lost the beat to a song that he'd written. The larger his public life had gotten, the more abstracted his personal existence had become. The higher the stakes, the more the positive returns of his career diminished. He'd felt himself a matryoshka doll, the real him buried and obfuscated underneath levels of commitments and compromises. Only with his daughter did he feel his core self engaged. Until these past few days. A sense of utility had blossomed while in Puerto Rico that had evaded him for years. He understood that on the island, that ravaged strip of land, was the map back to the person he had lost sight of.

It was Monday afternoon, September 25, 2017, when his car pulled up in front of his house. He saw his sister sitting out on the stoop, her face awash in worry. He knew immediately that he had tested positive.

Good Morning, Later

It crossed Olga's mind that perhaps she was having a nervous breakdown. The past few weeks had worn her to raw nerve as she endured a torrent of facts, eroding her armor and unlodging carefully confined emotions. She could tell by the way that the nurse on the phone confirmed her patient number that Prieto's results were positive. The woman began walking her through options for follow-up resources, but Olga just hung up on her. She wasn't retaining any information. Her brother had been out of touch, without phone service, since he left for P.R. on Friday, but she had seen some clips of him on the news — knee high in mud, passing out water in the sun — reminding her of why she'd put her brother on his pedestal so long ago.

There wasn't a good way to tell him. As soon as he saw her face he would know. So, rather than shock him, she figured she would sit outside, so he could see her first and decide how he wanted to react. She wanted to give him that moment. Anticipating the worst, she asked Lourdes's mother to keep her for an extra night so they could have some space. Despite knowing that this was a completely treatable, livable illness, the well-worn sense of disquietude she'd experienced when her father got sick materialized again now. She knew her brother would bear these old angsts as well.

When his car pulled up, Prieto sat in it for a minute. Then he got out and put his hands up — like he was under arrest — and just kept saying, "It's okay, it's okay. I'm okay, I'm okay." Which just made Olga lose it. Which she realized was the opposite of the point.

Once they were inside, they sat in the kitchen, at the same table they'd sat at their whole lives. She remembered him lanky and lean, when he took up so much less space in the world. Now he made the table look miniature. So solid, he looked. So healthy.

"Mira," her brother said once they were inside, "had I gotten this news before I went down to Puerto Rico, I'm not gonna lie, I think I would have been a fucking mess. And don't get me wrong, I'm fucking scared. I'm so fucking scared. . . ." He began to cry. "It's hard to not think about Papi, you know?"

They'd had dinner with their father countless times at this same table. This table where he'd played his records and charmed their whole family. Where he would teach them his history lessons. Where they'd sat together and cried after he died.

"I know," she said, her eyes brimming.

"I couldn't bring myself to go see him, Olga. When he was dying. I was just so ashamed." Now he was sobbing. "Do you think this is his revenge?"

"Papi's revenge?" she asked. Her brother nodded.

The question was so out of character for her brother, and her father, that Olga started to laugh.

"Wait? You think Papi, who literally let insects out of the house instead of killing them, has become a dark and vengeful ghost? Blighting his own son — whom he worshiped — with disease? Now, maybe that's some shit our mother would do, but Papi? Come on! That don't even sound like him, Prieto!"

She couldn't stop laughing and once she said it aloud, her brother found the humor in it, too, and soon enough both were giggling.

"I was thinking of how sad Papi's end made me. Mami told me to walk away from it, to try to forget the person he'd become —"

"Yeah," Olga said, "she told me that shit, too."

"And I tried, but you can't forget, right? You shouldn't forget — it was part of his life. Anyway, I was thinking about Lourdes and how if this shit did kill me, I wanted to go out strong. So her memory of me would be as good if not better than the father she's had up till now.

"This trip made me realize how much I have to do with myself. For my daughter, for our family. But also, right now, for our people, Olga. I decided when I was down there that no matter how the test came back, I was gonna buck up and keep going. Better than before. I'm fired up. They are going to let Puerto Rico wither away, unless we fight."

His words watered a seed of worry already planted in Olga's mind.

"Prieto, we've got to talk. About Mami. Karen reached out while you were away. Mami is in P.R. She's safe, but she's there."

Prieto did not even look surprised. "I know."

"You do?"

"Well, I should say, I didn't know, I suspected. There's a group down on the island I'd heard some rumors about. Liberation radicals. Sort of had her written all over it."

There was a pause before he asked, a little desperately, "Did she say anything about me? Karen, I mean."

"No," Olga lied again, this seeming easier than involving him in the truth. "It was a very quick conversation."

They stayed up for hours, drinking together, remembering their father, talking about Prieto's next steps for his medical health, his trip to Puerto Rico. Finally, when they were both a little drunk, Olga confronted the elephant in the room.

"When are you gonna tell Lourdes?" This was, essentially, the same as asking when he was going to go public, because they couldn't ask Lourdes to not tell her mother and, Olga knew, once this was out beyond the two of them, and maybe Titi Lola, it was just a matter of time before it came out.

"I, uh, haven't decided yet."

"I've thought a lot about this and if you want a chance at keeping your seat, you have to come clean about everything, right away. You will garner a lot of sympathy, and then you'll have till the mid-term to be able to establish yourself as more than the guy who'd been in the closet with HIV."

Her brother was quiet for a moment.

"But what if it doesn't go that way?" he asked. "What if it becomes a controversy and I need to step down? I can't leave my seat. Not right now. Not with this president and not with what I saw down in P.R. I've got to get back down there. I can't have this as a distraction."

Her brother's diagnosis shook her core. The rational part of her knew he'd live a long, wonderful life. But she was feeling far from rational and she couldn't stop imagining the worst. A life without her brother felt unbearable. Rootless. Recognizing this, though, only made Olga more aware of how rudderless her existence already was. Her brother, who even now, in the face of this illness, was directed by a larger purpose: his fight for others. It provided him a beacon, a way to redirect himself. Olga felt she had been paddling for years in no discernable direction except away from her fear of not being enough.

As a child, when people found out that Olga had been "left," she could see how quickly she was recast as a victim in their eyes. She felt their pity and it made her feel broken. Damaged. Her grandmother astutely observed that any foible or stumble at school would be attributed, with an air of inevitability, as the ramifications of her being "parentless." Any success Olga found would be attributed, with an air of disbelief, to her "resilience." Very early on, Olga and her grandmother calculated that, if given the choice between the two, Olga's easiest path was to be a success.

This strategy worked well initially: do well in school, excel at a talent, look pretty, make people laugh, solve problems for yourself, don't trouble anyone, when possible be helpful. Success, then, looked as simple as escape: from the chaos her parents had left in their wake, towards "opportunity." After high school, though, with her grandmother ill-equipped to guide her through the new terrain of the Ivy League, the goal began to be less clear, her toolbox less adequate. As a result, Olga fumbled in the dark, trying to adhere to a path that led to a fuzzy destination known simply as "success." In college, she became convinced that meant affirmation by institutional powers. After college, celebrity and its proximity were what she thought she should be striving for. Only in adulthood did she ascertain that no, it was money that would inoculate her from feeling less than.

Her parents, of course, had always viewed success as a White Man's construction. Her mother used her letters to continually remind Olga of this, to emphasize the futility of her pursuits. Her mother, though, didn't know what it was to be deemed the thing less important. Less important than drugs, less important than a cause. Her mother didn't understand what it required to shake that label — "less" — to prove it wrong to the world. A world that, despite how her parents liked to see things, valued the way you looked, the kinds of clothes you wore, the places you went to school, the people you could access and influence. Even her brother, rooted as he was in his place of good, understood all of this. Olga formed her ambitions in reaction to her mother's absence, but she surely calcified them in rebellion to the very values that led her mother to abandon them in the first place. Grounding her identity in the realm of the material seemed to her the perfect revenge.

Until one day it didn't.

After *Spice It Up* and the Great Recession, Olga began to notice that her clients were growing steadily richer while the people doing the work were getting compensated in exactly the same way. Even the rich people appeared less content than before. Simply existing seemed an immense burden to them. Their wealth bought them homes that were "exhausting" to deal with, vacations that were "overwhelming" to plan for. What was required to please them, to make them feel joy on their most joyful day, became increasingly impossible to achieve. Olga raised her prices, inflated her bills, increased her markups. But the money didn't make any of it feel better. She began, gradually at first, to find not only her actual day-to-day work tedious and stupid, but also the entire project of her life. Around this time Olga noticed that her mother's notes no longer filled her, even for a moment, with smug satisfaction.

She began to wonder if the only person she was enacting revenge on was herself.

Sometimes, like now, a feeling of unease would come over her and last for days, a strange kind of melancholy with no starting point or definitive end. A therapist she was forced to see at the fancy college told her this feeling was likely a longing for her mother, a suggestion Olga had rebuffed by storming out of the room. But over the years, Olga revisited this conceit, quietly wondering what her life would be like had her mother deemed her worthy of her time and affections. What would she, Olga, have done with all the energy she'd spent convincing anyone and everyone else that despite this lack, she wasn't broken? So, although Olga very well knew that her mother's affections were fickle, when Reggie said that she needed her, Olga could hardly stop herself from wondering, what if the therapist was right? What would happen if she could alleviate that longing? What sense of peace and purpose might she find for herself if given the chance to earn her mother's admiration?

Given her state, Olga knew better than to say yes to the producer from *Good Morning, Later* suggesting she come in to do a live segment. She'd been waiting for the lab to contact her with her brother's test results when they called. She hadn't recognized the number and had reflexively picked up.

"The news has been so depressing lately," the producer said, "we were thinking it would be great to do a nice, happy wedding segment. Weddings make people feel good. And, *Good Morning* is about the news, but at *Good Morning, Later,* we're about making our viewers feel good, you know?"

"Right," Olga said. "What's the angle?" There was always an angle with these things

— beat the heat, holiday weddings, June brides, do's and don'ts.

"Well, Tammy's recently engaged, so we were thinking we could do a 'kickstart your planning' thing with her. Sound good?"

It did not sound good. But it was easier to acquiesce than to explain why, so she just said yes.

"Okay, great. Someone on my team will get back to you with a call time and to run through your demo items, but we're looking forward to seeing you on Wednesday morning."

"The idea of going into a TV studio to get my hair pressed out and a mask of makeup happiness applied to my face feels beyond unappealing right now," Olga called out to Matteo, who was finishing dinner in the kitchen while she stared at the ceiling in his music room. It was Tuesday night. *Good Morning, Later* shot in just a few hours.

Matteo had made pasta and he brought a bowl to her now.

"Why didn't you ask ME-Gahn to do it for you?"

"Oh my God, I wish I could. I wish I could just give her the whole fucking business and never look back."

"So, why don't you?" he asked.

"Because," Olga started, not sure of where to go with it. "Because I guess I don't know how I would support myself? I don't know what else I am even qualified to do."

"You?" Matteo asked, genuinely incredulous. "You, girl, could do anything. You could easily go back to P.R."

"Pero, Matteo, I wanna live in America!" she joked. "No, seriously, if I'm not going to do this, I'd like to do something meaningful."

"Well," Matteo said, "if your brother decides to run for reelection, you could run his campaign?" Olga had told Matteo about her brother. She knew she'd broken the circle, but she trusted him. She really did. And besides, after watching her cry for so many days, she was worried he was going to 5150 her if she didn't at least attempt to explain herself.

"Matteo" — she threw a throw pillow at him — "I said I wanted to do something meaningful!"

They both laughed.

"It's funny, when I was going away to college and my mother was all up in arms about losing me to the bourgeoisie, I couldn't see any downside then, because I'd touched the holy grail. The Ivy League."

"Society's finish line!" Matteo chimed in.

"That's the rub! It felt like a finish line *to me,* because I knew what it took to get there and survive it. But to everybody else? The kids whose parents and grandparents had gone there before them? This was just their starting line. To something bigger. Something I couldn't even imagine. I feel like I've spent all of this time since then trying to figure out where I was supposed to be headed. What thing could I achieve that would make me feel . . . enough?"

Matteo put his bowl down and looked at her with all his attention.

"Olga," Matteo said, "if you did nothing for the rest of your life of any note, you'd be more than enough."

She felt unsure of how to receive such kindness, and unsure if she actually believed it to be true.

"Did I ever tell you that I was named after Olga Garriga? Brooklyn native, Puerto Rican nationalist, and political prisoner arrested for protesting Ley fifty-three."

"Is that right?" Matteo asked.

"Yeah, my dad picked it. Wanted to make me 'ambitious.' But my mother worried that I would take after the Olga from *Puerto Rican Obituary.* That Olga was ashamed of her identity and died dreaming of money and being anything other than herself."

Matteo raised his eyebrows. "Piñero?"

"Close. Pedro Pietri."

Matteo got up and went to a section of his record collection. "Damn. I gotta admit I'm light on spoken word."

"It's okay. I mean, I know it by heart."

"So," Matteo said, cuddling her now, "recite it for me."

And so she did. In its entirety. And Matteo gave her a standing ovation.

"Brava!"

Olga curtsied.

"But, ma, you realize the solution to Olga's dilemma is in the poem?"

"Wait," Olga asked, "how do you mean?"

"I mean, it's a tale for you to learn from. It's about not chasing an external ideal, not trying to fit someone else's vision for you and instead building with the community of people who simply accept you as you are."

"Somehow, I don't think that's what my mother got out of it."

Olga was in the greenroom waiting to be called in for her segment, hoping it would be over quickly. Monitors silently played the broadcast from the studio just down the hall. Olga could see that the anchors of *Good Morning,* two slightly more serious versions of the hosts of *Good Morning, Later,* were just wrapping up. The camera was focused on Nina, the perfectly coiffed female cohost.

Olga read the closed captioning. *We leave you this morning with some of the absolutely heartbreaking images out of Puerto Rico, where exactly one week ago today, Hurricane Maria made landfall and completely decimated the island.*

On the screen was a slideshow of anguish. Aerial shots of flattened homes, people wading through filthy water to gas stations, snaking lines of people waiting for food, shipping containers languishing in a port, doctors evacuating sick babies onto a helicopter, nurses working in hospital wards dark without power. The final image: children lapping up brown rainwater that they had collected in a pool.

Just devastating, Nina. The camera had cut now to John, her cohost, looking solemn. *If you want to know how you can help the people of Puerto Rico, please visit goodmorning.com/maria.* He paused for a split second, just long enough to replace his serious expression with a wide grin. *And now, let's toss it over to America's favorite loony ladies of the morning!*

The camera cut to Tammy and Toni, already cutting it up.

Thank you, John! Tammy said with a broad smile, the words on the screen slightly trailing the movement of her lips. *Well, I don't know about you, Toni, but boy am I excited for our show today!*

Without sound, Olga thought, this show was a grotesque pantomime.

You're just excited because we are talking EVERYTHING WEDDING today! I hope we don't have a Bridezilla on our hands!

Me? Tammy reacted with exaggeration. *Never!*

It was almost over. Olga had already walked the highly enthusiastic Tammy through a Getting Going Checklist to help begin her wedding planning journey ("Because it is a journey, Tammy," Olga had ad-libbed. "You and Glenn will get to know one another in completely new ways!") They had talked through the importance of a budget ("That's never been your favorite word, Tammy," Toni had quipped) and how to make your guest list ("I'm just worried about hurting people's feelings," Tammy lamented). Then, they got to the last topic, questions to ask when looking at possible venues.

"Well, you want to be sure you understand their capacity. You'd be surprised how many people book a venue they fall in love with and don't realize they simply won't fit."

"Oh my goodness! Can you imagine? What a nightmare!" Toni offered.

"I know," Olga continued. "And, of course, if there's an outdoor component, you should inquire about your contingency plan in the event of inclement weather."

"Oh yes." Tammy nodded. "Especially these days! All of these horrible storms!"

"Just terrible, Tammy," Toni agreed. "These poor people down in Puerto Rico! Can you imagine?"

Olga nodded, a tight smile of concern crossing her face — concern that they would try and tie this segment about nothing to a humanitarian crisis. Only Tammy, Olga thought, could get this segment back on the fluffy track where it belonged.

"Oh my!" Tammy suddenly exclaimed. She paused. "Olga, I just remembered. You are of Puerto Rican heritage, aren't you?"

"Yes," Olga said with a solemn nod. Internally, she screamed, Fuck. Fuck! Tammy!

"And is your family over there okay?" Tammy asked, gently resting her hand on Olga's shoulder. "The images look just awful."

"Well, Tammy," Olga began, and as soon

as she opened her mouth she knew that she was not going to give them the *Good Morning, Later* version of this conversation that they wanted. She wasn't even going to give them the *Good Morning* version of this conversation, "the images look awful, because it *is* awful. This morning, right before I came on, I saw pictures of American children lapping up rainwater because their water supply has been contaminated by the dumping of toxic waste by U.S. corporations all over the island —"

"Yes, Olga," Toni tried to cut in, "it really is hard to —"

"No, Toni, Tammy asked me how my family is, so I want to tell her. My cousin can't locate her sick grandmother because they have no cell service and in the unlikely event that she got to a hospital, she's still probably dead because the hospitals don't have enough fuel to operate the generators. But she won't be the only one. When this is over, mark my words, thousands will be dead, because this is just the beginning, and I want to be really clear here —"

Tammy tried to cut in, but Olga swatted her away before a word could get out of her mouth. She could see that the red light of the camera was still on. The producers were going to let her keep going. Fuck it, she thought.

"These deaths will be blood on this president's hands, this administration's hands. They can try and blame the Puerto Rican debt; they can blame their lackey — the governor down there — but he's just a figurehead. At the end of the day, this was not an earthquake, it was a hurricane. A hurricane that the government knew was coming for a whole week and did nothing to prepare for. What we are witnessing is the systemic destruction of the Puerto Rican people at the hands of the government, to benefit the ultra-rich and private corporate interests."

Toni awkwardly laughed. "Oh my, Olga, that sounds a bit conspiratorial, no?"

"If it does, Toni, it's just because you aren't informed. It's not your fault. Our schools whitewash history. So, let me explain. Puerto Ricans are Americans, but they have no elected representation in Congress or the Senate, and because they also aren't a state, their governor has no authority to do things other governors can do, like call in the National Guard. Only the president can do that. Only the president can call in FEMA. Fifty percent of the island didn't have power *before* Maria, but somehow the government didn't think to call in the USS *Comfort* until this weekend? They knew before the storm that the island's infrastructure was fragile, that they would lose communications, yet they only sent two Black Hawk helicopters? My brother — a U.S. congressman — traveled with the governor of New York to Puerto Rico two days — *two days* — after Maria hit. And the federal government just sent someone on Monday?

"Listen, private interest has been trying to gain control of Puerto Rico — the land, the agencies — for ages. The government has always been their coconspirators. As I speak, this administration still hasn't lifted the Jones Act! People are suffering — starving for food — but still being penalized with taxes on produce and other goods just for living on an island the U.S. government stole from them in the first place! That's criminal! It shouldn't be law. They are going to starve the Puerto Rican people of resources and support and, because there is a cap to what people can take — no power, no clean water, no schools, no jobs — they will effectively smoke people off the island, and then, that's when the vultures will sweep in. They are already circling."

Olga stopped and noticed that Tammy was rapidly rotating through variations of a smile: a mask of sympathy, puzzlement, and possibly even a grimace of fear flitting across her face as she attempted to find the proper expression in the lexicon of morning TV responses. Toni had her hand to her earpiece.

"Well, Olga," Toni said, "it's very clear how passionate you are about Maria recovery. We are going to need to cut to break, but before we go, any final words for the president? He is an avid news watcher!"

Olga was a little surprised they would let her speak again.

"Yes. Yes, I do." She paused to think of exactly what she wanted to do with this opportunity. "Mr. President, I hope that the ghosts of every Puerto Rican who died at your hands in this catastrophe haunt your dreams each night, dancing an all-night salsa party in your twisted mind."

She had just hailed a cab home when Matteo reached her.

"Now that's what I call going full Kanye!" Matteo said.

"On a positive," Olga said, "I don't need to figure out how to get out of the wedding business."

"It was so hot."

She laughed. "It was semi-psychotic. You

just think it's hot because you like me."

"Because I love you."

And she knew then that she loved him, too.

The Gang's All Here

Despite the fact that the ten Eikenborn & Sons retail locations on Puerto Rico had suffered millions of dollars in damages, Dick found himself with a full and happy heart as his plane began its descent onto a private airstrip near San Juan. He glanced at his daughter, Victoria, who sat across from him, craning her neck to take in the aerial view.

"Holy shit," she said, "it's like a giant came and just stomped it all to pieces."

Dick now looked out the window as well. She was right. The stores had opened two days before and many workers hadn't made it to their shifts. He now had a sense of why. The once green island now a patchwork quilt of electric blue. FEMA tarps where roofs once were.

"Worried about the damage, Dad?"

Dick didn't mean to smile, but he did. This was the first modicum of interest or concern that Victoria had shown in him since he and her mother had separated. She'd been working at an NGO focused on women's health and when she heard, through her brothers, that her father would be coming down, she asked to tag along. It's not every day we get to see third-world conditions in a first-world country, she had said.

"Hmm," Dick replied now. "A bit. More on an operations level. Insurance will take care of the rest. I'm a little worried about you, though. Those volunteer tents won't have AC, I hope you realize that."

She rolled her eyes at him.

"I work in humanitarian relief, Daddy. I can live without creature comforts for a few days."

"Well, that makes one of us!" he said. "If Nick hadn't assured me his house is fully up and running, there's no way I'd be staying the whole weekend."

"How?" Victoria asked.

"He's got his own solar grid. Apparently, the property sustained some damage, but generally speaking, it's all cosmetic. He says he's barely missed a beat."

Once they landed, Dick arranged for Victoria to be safely dropped at the FEMA headquarters to shadow some workers, while he boarded a helicopter to tour his facilities. With most of the local employees unable to make their way to work, due to lack of gas, blocked roads, or their own tragedies, Dick's head of retail had begun flying in managers and assistant managers from across the mainland as soon as the airports reopened. Several locations had sustained significant flood damage, rendering much of the equipment and lumber in questionable condition for sale. There had been a thought to simply give the "irregular" supplies away, but their general counsel determined that too much of a liability, so they were restocking these locations. Of course, in order to collect insurance on the damaged goods they would need to be destroyed, but the communications team decided that had to wait, for fear of bad press. No matter. This had hardly been the first storm weathered by Eikenborn & Sons.

In fact, this season had been so bad they had set up an emergency command center in Austin to service the Gulf Coast, and Dick's inclination was, given the trajectory of the climate, they should make it permanent. If there was one thing Dick knew, storms like this one hurt his bottom line in the short run but were money in the bank long-term. His New Orleans stores were never more profitable as in the years immediately following Katrina. Already, gross receipts from their Texas locations after Harvey were higher than ever. So, this was bad now, but ultimately, it was a logistical hassle that they would push through. Indeed, at the stores that were fully operational, already long lines of people were seeking generators, solar-powered lights, batteries. They would build bigger and better. If the local market could sustain it, this could be an opportunity for Eikenborn Green Solutions. A massive opportunity. At least this was what Nick Selby had said.

Nick had been planning this retreat for a few weeks now, describing it as a "casual beachfront gathering of various parties with vested interest in the future and possibility of Puerto Rico." It was first delayed by Irma and of course, with Maria as catastrophic as it was, no one imagined that it was still happening. Dick was certainly surprised when he got a text from Nick saying it was indeed still on. The house was great, the beach was not, but this gathering was more important now than ever. Also, Nick wondered, could Dick bring down some steaks from Peter Luger's if he managed to get them to Teterboro before Dick went wheels up?

And so, after touring his eponymous stores, ten days after Maria made landfall, Dick Eikenborn's helicopter landed on the lawn of Nick Selby's Puerto Rican estate, with his weekend bag and a cooler full of porterhouses on dry ice. Trees were knocked down and the shrubbery bare, but he was startled by how much less affected this piece of paradise seemed from what he'd seen on the rest of the island.

"Dick!" Nick cried out over the chopper propellers, "I see we've got you *and* the steaks. Good man!" He slapped his back. A guy from the staff grabbed the cooler and the bag from Dick and they all made their way into the house.

Outside it had been humid and overcast, but inside it was cool and dry. The Rolling Stones played on the sound system. Dick marveled at how intact it all seemed.

"Shatter-resistant glass," Nick offered, seeming to read Dick's mind. "That and the solar grid. Best investments. Scotch? Rum?"

"Rum!" Dick said. He hadn't been drinking much lately. Training for a tri. But he figured he'd take the weekend off.

"How've you been?" Nick asked. "I haven't seen you since your spicy little girlfriend was organizing the busboys at the Blumenthal party."

Dick didn't mean to get a pouty look on his face, but it was reflexive.

"We broke up, actually."

"It's for the best, Richard."

"Why do you say that?" Dick asked sincerely. Because he was very much wanting to get back together. He'd made a few overtures — had Charmaine send flowers to her office, sent a book of love poems — but received no response. He got the sense it was better to not press. She would come back in her own due time, Charmaine had assured him.

"Well," Nick now offered, "let's just say she doesn't necessarily come from the best . . . stock."

Dick rolled his eyes. "I'm very aware of who her brother is. I haven't been able to put my TV on anywhere but Fox without seeing his face this past week."

Nick laughed. "Dick, her brother's a team player, I assure you. But, all will be revealed soon enough."

A couple of hours and a few rums later, Dick found himself finishing up dinner with an intriguing lineup of, as Nick called them, "stakeholders in the New Puerto Rico."

There was an undersecretary of energy who asked to be called only by the name Manny; there were two members of the PROMESA board; an executive named Linda from one of the major airlines — which one was never established; a man named Pedro from PREPA, the failed power company; a woman named Carmen from the water company; and then the straight money people: Dieter, representing cryptocurrency miners; Dennis representing the financial interests buying up and getting repaid for the bonds on debt the government had sold them; a man named Kirk who said he represented a global Ayn Rand society, whatever that meant; and of course Nick's older brother, Arthur.

"Okay, gentlemen and ladies," Nick offered, "this is a time of gravity. But also, for us free-market enthusiasts, a time of great opportunity. I've asked you here this weekend because this island has long been a passion of mine, and I know Dieter's as well. So, first, I want to make a toast to Act Twenty and, for me personally, for Act Twenty-two, which has made me a bona fide puertorriqueño! Who wouldn't want to claim an identity that allows them to pay zero taxes on capital gains, interests, or dividends? Puerto Rico represents a chance to live the American dream as it was intended: the freedom to reach our full potential without having to support a welfare state. This island is an opportunity in microcosm, to live out an idea that we'd previously thought fantasy: a chance to create a stateless society where we can step out from the thumb of rule by statute and allow free markets and contracts to create social order.

"So, what I see here right now, in the aftermath of this tragedy, is boundless opportunity. My brother and I have a plan for this island — a plan that will make all of you, and the constituencies you represent, very rich. Or, I should say, *richer*! Well, maybe except for you, Manny! This will make you and the governor rich, but not the actual people who voted for you!" He paused. Manny laughed. "You're a sport, Manny!

"To the uninitiated, it could seem like we have competitive interests, but I assure you, if we focus on the larger goals, long term, all of us here will benefit. Further, I want to be clear, our plans have the full, absolute support of the current U.S. administration. Puerto Rico is effectively our playground as long as we don't contest them awarding the contract for PREPA to rebuild the power grid. That's apparently a nonnegotiable. It's been promised to the nephew of a major donor, but it's literally just a shell corp, Pedro, so I doubt you'll have to even deal with them much."

"Hold on for a second, Nick," Dick chimed in. "No offense, Pedro, but PREPA barely seemed to be doing the job before Maria. Why would we let them oversee their own rebuild and with a shell firm at that? To me, this seems like the perfect time for privately owned solar energy."

"Richard, you are wise beyond words!" Nick said as he slugged from his wineglass. "Yes, no offense, but Pedro, you and Manny have done just absolutely abysmal work here. The whole place is in the dark with no hope of fixing it anytime soon. But Richard, the truth is *their* customers are not *your* customers. I am your future customer. Kirk, Dieter, and Linda are your future customers, and, if my plan plays out, within five years, this island will be flooded with people like us. The hotels, the private estates, all of it, could be yours, Dick, to supply with solar power. Possibly working with PREPA. Right, Manny?"

Manny nodded over his half-masticated Luger's steak.

"But Nick," Dick offered, "shouldn't the

people here have an option other than PREPA? I'm seeing a big play to be made here to market solar to the population at large. I have the factories; I have the teams. It's environmentally sound."

"Richard, Manny and his friends are prepared to work with you to make it worth your while to limit your work to private estates such as mine. Isn't that right, Manny?"

Manny again nodded. Richard noticed how little he'd actually heard Manny's voice during the dinner or afterwards.

"Solar could be a major win for Puerto Rico, Nick. Could get them out from under a lot of this muck, it seems like."

"Dick, what I think you maybe haven't had a chance to absorb is that for Manny, this is a short-term play, but for you this is a long game. You see, everyone, FEMA? Reconstruction? Well, it's going to be a long haul, if you know what I mean. Those who can't stick it out will leave. Quickly. And there will be more Puerto Rico for the rest of us."

This, seemingly, made Linda from the airline uncomfortable. "It's not our fault that we're the only people who run direct to Atlanta and New York! I fought for those routes for these people! I wasn't trying to destroy anyone!"

"Linda," Arthur cut in, "Linda, calm down. You aren't doing anything wrong. It's not your fault people are leaving. You're just a bystander here to keep tabs on what's happening. You've already put in the work, okay?"

Linda anxiously sipped her wine.

"What I was trying to express," Nick continued, "was that there will be people with family on the mainland. Who knows when schools here will reopen? When grocery stores will get restocked? We didn't get these steaks locally, let me say that. I mean, if you had another option, wouldn't you go? Lots of land will be freed up. By my estimation, given the demographics of the island, lots of coastal land will be freed up. And people with less options will stay and people like us will find a very grateful labor force. And so —"

Arthur interjected, "By doing very little we can do very much to advance our interests."

Dick laughed out loud. "Gentlemen, I'm sure you have friends at the highest level of this administration —"

"Richard, I'm loath to call those people friends, they're more like thugs, but we do have an understanding."

Everyone chortled.

"But," Dick continued, "my point is that all of this is subject to congressional oversight. Of FEMA, of PROMESA. This stuff doesn't live in a vacuum. And I know for a fact that there are certain members of Congress —"

"One whose sister you used to fuck," Nick offered.

"Oh Nicholas! How crude!" Arthur exclaimed.

Dick rolled his eyes. "The point is, Acevedo isn't going to roll over and allow anything to be slow walked without bringing fifty news crews along while he investigates and calls a session and does whatever stunts he's known for. This is *his* signature issue."

"Richard," Arthur replied, "we have a few bits of leverage over Congressman Acevedo that we think will prove to be persuasive."

"I hope," said one of the PROMESA officials, "it's something more than him being gay, because a few local reporters spent some time with him and said it's more or less an open secret."

Arthur looked to Nick with concern, which Nick relished with a smile.

"Everyone, I assure you, Acevedo is no issue."

"Well," Dick countered, "I want to go on the record as saying that I'm not yet convinced."

"Richard." Nick sighed. "Nearly everyone of consequence is on payroll and our leverage over Congressman Acevedo is far more personal than his sexuality. Elisa, will you please show our guest in? I suspect he will convince Richard here to get on board." Nick gestured to one of the housekeepers.

A well-dressed gentleman walked in, a large manila file under his arm.

"Agent Bonilla," Nick offered, "can I get you a rum? Everyone, Agent Bonilla has some very interesting information to share with you all about Congressman Acevedo's roots. Very intriguing information, indeed."

Put It in the Bag

In just a matter of hours, a business that Olga had built for nearly twelve years collapsed in the wake of what some on social media had called an "Epic AM Meltdown." It was, aside from meeting Matteo, the best thing that had happened to Olga in years.

The *Good Morning, Later* clip had gone viral, something she'd imagined possible the second the producers allowed her rant to continue. Going "off script" was only permissible if, of course, it would lead to clicks. In the immediate aftermath, as she walked off set and made her way home, she felt buzzed and a bit nauseous, like she'd quickly drunk a bottle of champagne. But, after an hour or so, she felt remarkably good. Like she'd come to the end of a *Scooby-Doo* episode and pulled off her own mask, revealing that all this time she'd been playing the part of Happy-Go-Lucky Party Planner when in reality she was the terrifying Educated Woman of Color. Her clients were polite enough to wait until the afternoon to begin their awkward calls to say that they didn't want to fire *the business,* per se, but that they were worried that Olga might "call too much attention to herself" at their affair, or that her presence might "upset" some of their more conservative guests. One former mother of the bride went so far as to compose a lengthy email saying how "betrayed" she felt by Olga's "little speech," that Olga had "bitten the hand that fed her" by "villainizing the rich" when they were "just living the American dream," which she was "sorry Puerto Ricans have not tried to take more advantage of." Olga wrote back to say that she always knew she was one of the 53 percent of white ladies who had put this moron in the White House, so she hoped the ghosts of dead Puerto Ricans danced in her head at night, too. But, other than that one incident, Olga had taken a very conciliatory tack.

Meegan was at first distraught, then unnerved, and then, ultimately, excited by how this moment could be her windfall.

"Here's what I'm offering," Olga said, in an effort to calm Meegan's hysteria at the upset calls that had been coming into the office. "For all our clients already under contract, you take them over and you'll get the rest of the money they owe us. My business name is mud, so start your own LLC. You can keep all the photos for your portfolio and any leads that might still come in. It's time for you to hang your own shingle anyway."

"What will it cost me?" Meegan said, with skepticism.

Truthfully Olga wanted to just walk away from the whole thing and not think of it again. The ability to shed this entire persona felt, in the moment, priceless. But she couldn't be stupid. Her monthly expenses were high, her savings pathetic. She needed to buy time to figure herself out.

"Let's call it twenty percent off of anything you book for the next year."

"Wow!" Meegan said cheerfully. "You know, Olga, you've been such an amazing mentor to me. I've learned so much. Often, before I make decisions, I ask myself, 'How would Olga handle this?' "

"That's sweet."

"And true. Even now I'm asking myself that and thinking, wow! If someone with pretty dubious bookkeeping practices and a stockroom full of possibly stolen liquor, caviar, and linen napkins asked Olga for twenty percent off the top of her receipts for a year, what would Olga say? She would probably tell them to fuck off and then call Page Six. That's definitely what Olga would do. Am I right?"

Olga laughed. She'd underestimated Meegan. She almost felt she owed her protégé an apology. Almost.

She sighed into the phone. "I've taught you well, then, Grasshopper. Okay. How about this? Take over the office lease, pay my health insurance for a year, and we'll just call it a wash? In fact, I'll thank you for taking this off my hands and not totally pissing these families off."

"That," Meegan said, the joy of conquest in her voice, "sounds reasonable."

"Then it's a deal. I'll call my lawyer to make sure it's all aboveboard."

"Wait!" Meegan said just as Olga was about to hang up, "what about Laurel?"

Laurel Blumenthal had just requested a contract two days prior, but as Olga now informed Meegan, she had been the very first call Olga had received to inform her that she was sorry, but "it just wasn't going to work out." Olga had been surprised, given what a champion of liberal causes Laurel had claimed to be.

"Olga, I want you to know that I am fully with you *in spirit,*" Laurel had said over the phone, "but *in practice* you just are a little left of center for Carl's taste and, at the end of the day . . ."

Olga told her not to worry, she completely understood. Laurel assured her that, to prove how much she was with her *in spirit,* she and Carl were stocking Bethenny Frankel's plane with supplies to bring down. Olga thanked her for her generosity. She meant it.

Happy as she was, Olga still had some highly practical problems on her plate, mainly, her lack of income. There was, of course, a simple solution available: give up the lease on her Fort Greene apartment and move back to Fifty-third Street, where she could live off her paltry savings, rent free, while she figured it out. But she had promised Christian, had gone to the mat with Prieto about it, had gotten Matteo to help her paint, and replaced the cabinets in the kitchen for him and everything. Her word should mean something, no?

Besides, no one in her family knew that her business had dissolved; her role was to be there for solutions, not to show up with problems. With the exception of her Tío Richie — who felt that she, and the rest of the Libs, needed to be more respectful of the president — her family thought that her outburst, and its virality, had been by turns "dope," "fierce," and, as her brother said, "absolutely necessary to cut through the noise of disaster platitudes." Her cousins, aunts, and uncles saw the clip appear on *The Shade Room,* tweeted by Don Lemon, discussed on *The Breakfast Club,* and replayed with subtitles on *¡Despierta América!* and couldn't see a downside. They didn't see that there was a separate, shadow media universe where she'd been positioned as a villain, a traitor, a radical. She knew, with the exception of her brother, that none of them could ever conceive that truth telling could have negative consequences. They also didn't understand how precarious her financial ecosystem was, how her personality and personal views only had room to exist so long as they were in service of her clients' ideas and ideals.

The only one who did seem to understand the fiscal implications of the incident, despite being mildly amused as it played out in real time, was Matteo, whose occupation also involved the whims and desires of others.

"You're the main story on Fox News!" he said that night at Olga's place.

"Get out of here!" she said, walking to get

closer to the TV.

And there it was: the host of one of the opinion shows playing her clip. Talking about how unhinged she was. How irresponsible it was of *Good Morning, Later* to air her crazy conspiracy theories. How, upon basic research, they discovered she'd made her living working with exactly the kinds of families she was now implicating in some kind of "plot" to destroy an island of people who had driven up their own debt, had proven unable to govern themselves, and were fully at the mercy of our American benevolence to rebuild their island. Then, he said that if Olga didn't like the way they did things in America she should go back to Puerto Rico.

"Puerto Rico is America, you fucking dummies! And I'm from fucking Brooklyn! Jesus!" she screamed at the TV.

Matteo shut it off and turned towards her. "Well, no looking back now. You're officially a part of the radical left!" He laughed. "In seriousness, though, Olga, you good with money?"

"Why moneybags," she joked, "you gonna float me?"

"I mean, I would if you need it. Even if it's just some breathing room."

Olga was unsure why Matteo felt so

confident about either his own finances or her ability to regroup. She had a bit of cash she could live off. For a bit of time. She'd gone her entire adult life without relying on anyone for fiscal help, let alone a man, and this was one of the few things she was personally proud of. She would land on her feet.

"You don't even know how much I appreciate you," she said, crawling next to him on the sofa, "but, no thank you. I'm gonna be good."

Two weeks later she found herself in a small restaurant in Brighton Beach underneath the elevated B train having borscht with Igor.

"It's better with the cream," Igor said, gesturing towards a small bowl of sour cream that had been laid out on the plastic tablecloth. Above his head a small television screen played RU. The restaurant was completely tiled, with silver-backed chairs. A casual, family-style establishment.

Olga complied and put a dollop into her bright red soup.

"So, what do they need exactly?" Olga asked. They had been making chitchat for the past fifteen minutes and while she liked Igor, she wanted to get the show on the road. Recognizing herself unsuited for a nine-to-five job, she weighed her options and, with much trepidation, picked up the phone to let Igor know that she'd finally "come around." She'd love to help their friends with their problems.

"They need you to make them a little party, for the daughter's first birthday. Somewhere nice, like the Plaza or something. You know, Eloise."

"Okay, and?"

"You make it look like it cost, let's say, half a million."

Olga laughed. "For a kid's party?"

Igor rolled his eyes at her.

"Make it look that way on paper," he said flatly. "And nice enough that if someone saw the pictures, they might believe it."

Olga nodded. "And how much am I really supposed to be spending?"

"Let's say our friends would like to get about four hundred thousand back."

"And if they don't? What happens to me?"

Igor laughed. "Olga? Are we not friends? Why do you worry so much? We've never had problems with you delivering your end of the bargain before."

"We," Olga said, "meaning, you and I, are friends. But I don't know who these other people are, and they don't know me —"

Igor interrupted her. "Of course, you would get your normal fee for this kind of thing, in cash. Plus, you know, a bonus."

He pulled a gym bag from the empty seat next to his and handed it to her. She pulled it up on her lap and unzipped it just enough to peek inside. There was cash and a velvet box.

"It's fifteen thousand and a nice necklace that I figured you could keep . . . or sell. Your choice, but the boss thought it would look nice on you." He smiled. "You know, if you go back on TV."

Olga eyed him cautiously. "You saw that, too?"

Igor laughed. "But of course! I have the Twitter!"

Olga giggled slightly.

"You know, Olga, my people really like your president. He is, what we call, a useful idiot. So, on that, we'll agree to disagree."

May 2016

May 20, 2016

Prieto,

Borikén, the original name of the island from which you and I descend, means Land of the Noble Lord. This name was given by the Taíno, the native people. For centuries, the Taíno lived in small, organized communities, until 1508, when a man named Ponce de León arrived. In short order, he robbed and cheated the Taíno of their soil and freedom, leaving them subjects and slaves to the Spanish. After the Spanish pillaged the island of its metals and ores, they claimed land that previously belonged to no one and stole African bodies to work it. In time, these acts of horror led to the birth of the Puerto Rican people as we know them today — a mix of Taíno, Spanish, and African blood. Our nation born, some might say, from the pain of colonialism. I, however, choose to see our people as birthed from the Land of the Noble Lord.

I believe this because for nearly as long as Puerto Rico has existed as a place oppressed, we have fought to break free. The year 1527 saw our first slave rebellion. In 1848, our first outright revolt. And of course, in 1868, el Grito de Lares. Each rebellion undermined the same way. Puerto Rican traitors. Weak-minded individuals, full of self-loathing. Who didn't believe in the power of their Taíno blood, the strength of their African ancestors. Individuals who could only hear the voice of the colonizer, whispering to them that without a white master nation, we, Borikén, would fail.

In 1898, after four hundred years of Spanish dominion, Puerto Rico had its first free election as an independent nation. We did not know that as we took this step towards self-determination, one of our own — a true lombriz named Dr. Julio Henna — was meeting with U.S. senators, convincing them of the treasure to be had if they annexed Puerto Rico. Their nation — America — was restless after the collapse of slavery. White supremacists were desperate for new Brown bodies to dominate; the capitalists salivated for new lands to exploit. And so began their destruction of Puerto Rico.

The next year, 1899, nature assisted. A great hurricane came to the island, killing thousands, leaving a quarter of the population homeless and wiping out all the coffee crops the jíbaros had been growing. With our people bankrupt and hungry, the gringos came and stole whatever was left. The Americans took farmland, they taxed crop exports, and, in the greatest blow, they took over our schools and our language. They forced on us a second-class citizenship, one where we could be drafted into their wars, segregated by their racism, but not allowed a voice in our own governance.

But we never stopped rebelling. Some refused to become citizens, refused to fill out their census forms, refused to identify as one race when we were always made of many. We insisted on our language, insisted on flying our old flag. We rebelled in ways big and small. Boricuas like Pedro Albizu Campos began to organize our people. We began to rise up, but just as quickly, traitorous snakes would sell us out, telling the police of our plans and actions, getting Nationalists assassinated in the streets.

Elected officials are the favorite henchmen of this puppet American democracy. In 1937, months after ordering the massacre of Independendistas in Ponce, a Boricua governor legalized the sterilization of our women. If they couldn't kill us off in the streets, they would stop our growth in the womb. In 1948, lombriz officials passed la Ley de la Mordaza: on the world stage America bragged about freedom of speech, while in Puerto Rico, we "citizens" were imprisoned for flying our flags, singing patriotic songs, speaking aloud the belief that we, the children of Borikén, could exist independent of an American master. Governors like Luis Muñoz Marín, or Pedro Rosselló, or this current pendejo, García Padilla. They distract us with rhetoric, pocketing money with one hand and tightening our chains with the other.

Prieto, this boot has been pressing down on Puerto Rico's neck for far too long, held in place by politicians of our own kind. I had taken pride in the fact that you, my son, were different. That you were trying to lift the boot off. That you were "our champion" on the mainland. Now, I no longer feel so sure.

For months, I've been writing to make what should seem the obvious case as to why you cannot support PROMESA. Yet, I see nothing in public from you but silence. You've yet to indicate how you will vote. No op-eds, no official statements against this garbage legislation. Is this indecision? Or is it treachery?

This will be my final plea. This bill you will vote on, PROMESA? It's not a promise, but a death sentence for our people. The last bit of pressure that will finally break our necks. It's designed to worsen our people's lives while stuffing the bankers' coffers. It forces puertorriqueños to foot a bill run up by gringos and our complicit compatriots. Anything this American government feels we owe them was paid for, in full, by the land and crops and lives that their imperialism has already stolen from us.

And so, I will wait. To see if you will be my son of the Noble Land or just a son of a bitch.

Pa'lante, Mami

you were trying to lift the hood [illegible] that
you were "our Cheryl" [illegible] the
land. Now, I [illegible] so sore.
For months, I [illegible]
what should seem [illegible]
why you cannot [illegible] PROMESA
You'll see nothing [illegible]
silence. [illegible]

[illegible]

■ ■ ■ ■

October 2017

■ ■ ■ ■

In the Mountains

Though blindfolded by a band of fabric gone damp with his own sweat, Prieto could tell from the pitch of the road that they were heading into the mountains; the weight of his own body pushed against the back of the hot car seat. The drive was slow. They stopped frequently to, by the sound of it, clear blockages from the roads. Periodically one of the Pañuelos Negros would cock their pistol, pressing it to the back of Prieto or Mercedes's heads, reminding them not to touch their blindfolds. The first time this happened, Mercedes grabbed the fingers of Prieto's hand and he squeezed them in return. By the third time, they kept their hands bound to each other for comfort.

Prieto hadn't planned on returning to Puerto Rico quite so soon, but when Mercedes reached out to say she was pursuing a news story of concern to him, he booked himself on the first flight his schedule would allow. He'd been surprised to hear from her. They had struck up a friendship, but given the difficulty making calls from the island — even with the solar-powered cellular balloons Google had deployed — he knew it must be of import.

They arranged to meet for a beer at a bar in Condado, and as Prieto made his way to the café, he took in the surreal state of the capital. This was his third trip since the storm hit nearly five weeks prior and the chaos of recovery had developed a rhythm of its own. He left his hotel air-conditioning — now powered via industrial-sized generators — and walked through the sun-baked streets where, unaided by FEMA or anyone else, residents had taken up the arduous task of cleaning the streets: removing stagnant water, gathering rubble, chopping wooden debris. Traffic lights still didn't function, but a self-regulated system had developed that somehow kept order. There were still lines — for food, for water, for a patch of sky where your phone might get service — but an air of determination had somehow wedged its way into the despair. He passed a park, where a small crowd gathered around a group of pleneros, and smirked as he absorbed the lyrics of the song they were singing:

> With his red hair he came to mock us,
> go back to the White House, leave us in
> peace.

The café itself was crowded. People sipped cocktails, a salsa band played, and operations were in full swing, while at the building next to them, a work crew was making repairs to a roof. Across the street a group of men — civilians, not PREPA employees — aimed to repair a fractured utility pole while news crews filmed coverage in the foreground.

"Isn't it crazy," Mercedes offered, when she arrived, "how fast people can move when money is on the line?"

Prieto raised an eyebrow at her.

"The pace of recovery here is like nowhere else on the island, completely driven by the real estate developers repackaging this area. Haven't you noticed how many gringos are here?"

Prieto had in fact noticed. The area was marked by several high-rises that looked as luxurious as anything he'd seen built in New Brooklyn and had suspected they were interrelated.

"The Puertopians. They've been coming

for the tax breaks. Certainly no one wants to keep them waiting too long for their air-conditioning," she said with a sarcastic laugh.

They ordered drinks and Prieto marveled at how together Mercedes seemed, despite the stress of documenting a disaster that she herself had been experiencing.

"Does this ever get you down?"

"Of course, but living here was Kafkaesque before Maria, so?" She shrugged her shoulders and raised her glass. "So, we have to keep laughing, drinking, dancing when we can, right?"

Prieto toasted her, and she continued: "Besides, here in San Juan, me and my family are fortunate. En el campo . . . people are washing their clothes in streams, rationing water. I talked to one woman living completely without a roof; every time it rains, she wades through water. It's surreal. More than anything they are fleeing, but you know that."

Prieto did indeed know that; an exodus of over two hundred thousand had already relocated to Florida, New York, Massachusetts. Who could blame them? Especially the college students, the people with school-age children. The lights were out, the schools were closed, and there was no way to know when they would open again.

"So, now," Mercedes said as she leaned in, "why you're here. I was really intrigued by what you saw that day in Maunabo —"

"About the Pan —"

"Yes," she cut in, and he understood what should and shouldn't be said. "As I've been traveling around the island reporting, I've been making some inquiries, in a more serious way. From what I've come to understand, this compound that they've built —"

"Wait, it's real? Last time we spoke you said it was lore."

"The last time we spoke, I hadn't spent as much time in the mountains. I hadn't seen the graffiti."

Mercedes took out her phone and scrolled through some photos before handing it to him. Prieto lost his breath. The image was a black spray-painted stencil of a woman's face, a beret on her head, her face concealed by a large bandana, but it took him just a second to recognize the eyes, even as rendered in a crude stencil. He had just seen them the day before he left, on Olga. His sister, who'd inherited them from their mother.

"What is this?" Prieto asked.

"Well, it's their mark. They have been leaving it in all the rural towns where they've delivered supplies. Mainly water, but also rice, beans, dry goods that, with the water, the people can use to sustain themselves. They've managed to get to many places FEMA seems to have struggled to reach."

"But who is this?" he said with more insistence than he'd intended, gesturing to the woman's face on the stencil.

"I don't know exactly, but I've made contact with one member who says she is their leader. Which, I must say, is pretty fucking badass in a machista culture like ours." Mercedes paused to sip her drink. "So, about a week after I managed to convince this . . . member to speak with me, I get a letter at the paper's office, no return address, and it didn't come by post, offering to bring me to their compound to hear what they are about and bring word to the people down the mountain."

"Really now?" Prieto said, trying to mask the nervous energy that had begun to bubble up in him.

"There were a number of conditions laid out. I would have to agree to be blindfolded, to have my phone confiscated for the journey, to only use one of their devices should I feel the need to record, and, most unusually, to bring you."

"Me? Specifically?"

"Most specifically." She now pulled the letter from her purse and read, " 'And, of course, we hope you will arrange to bring your friend, the Honorable Pedro Acevedo, known once as the people's champion on the mainland.' " She showed it to him. He knew the handwriting immediately; the word "once" triple underlined. His mother. So subtle.

"Hmm," Prieto offered.

"So, will you do it?"

His mother, the enigma of his life, was luring him in, but he was unsure if it was a trap or something else. His nervous energy, he realized now, was not that of excitement, but that of dread.

"Yes. Of course. When do we go?"

Two days later they found themselves in the parking lot of Mercedes's office a few hours before dawn, a challenging feat given the curfew still in effect. Indeed, it was a police detail that initially approached them in the empty carpark. They had worked out a story should this sort of thing happen, but as the vehicle drew near, they saw that both of the passengers' faces were shielded by black bandanas, guns drawn in their direction. The story was unnecessary. They raised their hands in surrender.

■ ■ ■ ■

By the time they reached their destination and were told they could remove their blindfolds, the sun was high in the sky. From the police car, they'd been transferred to a helicopter. After the helicopter, an SUV. He had no clue how long the journey had taken. Mercedes, as his proxy, had agreed to all of the Pañuelos' conditions for the meeting while offering only one of their own — that they would be back in the parking lot no more than twenty-three hours after their departure. They had only the Pañuelos' word that they would adhere to that concession, and Prieto was now starkly aware of how insecure their footing was.

It was only after they were instructed to get out of the truck that worry gave way to wonder. There, not even a hundred yards ahead of them, surrounded by bare ceiba trees and bald shrubbery, was a large, two-story structure, painted jungle green, with big, open windows through which they could see oversized ceiling fans, blades twirling. Electricity. In the midst of the forest. For a moment, Prieto assumed it was a generator, until he noticed the solar panels on the roof and, in the distance, a large wind turbine, all of which somehow survived the storm.

A young man named Tirso approached the vehicle. He wore a Brooks Brothers shirt with the sleeves rolled up and no bandana. As he greeted them by name, he offered what he assured them was fresh filtered water and cool wet towels. Their welcome rivaled an arrival to Fantasy Island, minus the three armed Pañuelos standing behind them. Tirso informed them that he would be taking them on a brief tour of the compound before taking them to meet, as he phrased it, "Leadership."

"She doesn't like that term, as we are intended to be a decentralized organization, but, for practical purposes, labels can be helpful, no?" he asked. They nodded before being frisked one more time and the guns, finally, put away.

The building they had seen on their first approach was, on their tour, merely a pass-through. Beyond it lay the courtyard of a much larger compound, all formed in a clearing of the now storm-ravaged forest. The edifices of the series of small buildings were each emblazoned with murals: Pedro Albizu Campos, Che, Zapata, Ojeda Ríos, and, to his disbelief, his own mother. Everywhere people were at work: some repairing damaged roofs, others carting water.

"In the main building," Tirso explained, "we have our classroom — for the children of our membership as well as for cultural studies and, as needed, learning opportunities for members who've been previously disenfranchised from their right to a proper education, either by economic or systemic discriminatory practices."

"Like being locked up in a juvenile detention facility?" Prieto offered.

"Some, yes," Tirso offered with a smile; the smile never faltered. He continued: "The main building also holds our administrative offices and some dormitory space. Across the courtyard is our medical building, which currently is being used to package supplies for distribution around the island — insulin, birth control, asthma inhalers, and other basic medical needs suddenly in short supply due to Maria. To the right is our commissary and dry goods storage — again, it is servicing the compound, but it's also being put to use as a staging area to distribute rice, beans, and other foods to more remote villages rendered isolated by the storm. Our greenhouse — which you can see to the right — sustained significant damage, as did the outdoor gardens just beyond it, but we managed to salvage and preserve what we could quickly, and we're already beginning to replant. Most significantly, just past the medical building is our water collection and purification system. We have been water and energy independent on the compound for the past five years. Our water reserves are so plentiful, they've enabled us to bottle and distribute our own supply of water to many of the neighboring towns —"

"That FEMA hasn't reached," Mercedes interjected.

"That FEMA has not tried to reach," Tirso corrected, smile still beaming. "But the people see that we, fellow puertorriqueños, are reaching them, with water from our island, filtered by a system designed by engineers educated on our island. They see that most of our problems can be resolved with the cooperation of the people of Puerto Rico, without the help of the United States."

"And the problems you can't solve here?" Mercedes asked.

"Well, that's just a matter of time," Tirso offered.

Tirso had a polish about him that felt familiar to Prieto, but out of place for a radical militant compound. It stunk of spin rooms and lobbyists.

"And how long," Prieto asked, "have you been here?"

"Me?" Tirso laughed. "A little less than a year. Your m— Leadership had been in touch with me for quite some time, inviting me down, but honestly, it wasn't until after the election that I realized I could no longer use my talents to support a system that had no regard for me or anyone like me."

"Can I ask what you were doing before?"

"Running Spanish media crisis communications for Facebook."

A young kid ran up to them from the compound's main building, handing Tirso a note.

"Leadership is ready to see you now, Mercedes."

Prieto's stomach and heart fell, and he was startled by his conflicted emotions. Mercedes locked eyes with him. He could sense her surprise as well.

"And me?" he offered, attempting to seem nonchalant.

"They've asked just for her, right now. But I was told you can explore. We are proud of what we've done here; nothing to hide, really."

And with that, they walked away.

Prieto wandered the expansive courtyard of his mother's compound, finding himself both impressed and disturbed at the scale of it. There were easily forty to fifty people that he could see, all busy at work, and God only knows how many he couldn't see.

This couldn't have all been here during the Ojeda Ríos days. The FBI would have shut it down. Burned it down. No, his mother had built this. All of this, hiding in plain sight. But from where had the money come? Who was funding all of this? He wandered into the medical building — a simple concrete structure maybe big enough to hold half a dozen sickbeds and a couple of exam rooms, but now filled with folding tables where a dozen Pañuelos had formed assembly lines, boxing up packages of medicines for distribution. At work, in the privacy of their compound, they wore the black of the Pañuelos, but their bandanas were down. They were mainly kids — teens, college students — boys and girls, both. Bad Bunny was blasting, and they rapped along: *"Tú no metes cabra, saramambiche."* You ain't shit, son of a bitch. They barely acknowledged his presence in the room.

Prieto gave them a head nod as he made his way towards one of the tables piled high with boxes of insulin, all marked with the same giant S logo. He pulled out a vial stamped *Sanareis.* Where did he know that name from? He wandered back outside, curious to check out the water filtration system. His mother was clever, tapping into the youth. The University of Puerto Rico had long produced some of the country's best engineers, only to lose them to the mainland. Somehow, with this manic dream of hers, she'd figured out how to lure some of them up here.

The flora around the compound had been severely damaged, but he could see how, in normal circumstances, the jungle would have obscured much of the infrastructure that had been created around the compound. But nothing, he thought, would have ever masked the massive wind turbine he found himself approaching now; he was dwarfed by it. The base had a small staircase leading up to a portal door, for maintenance, he imagined. Above the door, a manufacturer's label of sorts. He climbed the stairs to read it: *Podremos.* Fucking Reggie King. This was the company he was a partner in. The fucking insulin, too. That's why it had seemed familiar. He saw a small garage in the distance, painted the same dark green as the main house; he'd have missed it were the trees not stripped bare. As he made his way over, he thought of the op-ed. Replayed Reggie's interrogation from his Hamptons fundraiser. How much had his mother been a part of all that show? How the fuck did they link up in the first place? When Reggie had been dating Olga, their mother had sent Prieto countless letters attempting to enlist him in the cause of breaking them up; now he seemed to be, at least in part, financing her commune? Or was it a cult?

He pulled at the garage door, which rolled up easily, the bright sun illuminating a small arsenal. But before Prieto could take in the full scope of weaponry it contained, he heard what had suddenly become the familiar sound of a Glock cocking. He put his hands up before he could turn around.

A few minutes later he was back at the big house, his armed escort right behind him, smiling Tirso waiting to greet him, another bottle of water in hand.

"Yo, man," Prieto called out as he walked towards him, "I thought you said you had no secrets here?"

"We don't! All those weapons were legally purchased. We're U.S. citizens. We are protected by the Second Amendment. But, obviously, we keep it guarded as we do have minors on property. That's only being responsible, isn't it, Congressman?"

Prieto decided that he hated Tirso.

"So, um, when do I get to meet with 'Leadership'?" he asked.

"Actually, now." And so, Prieto followed Tirso into the main building, down a corridor and to a closed wooden door, goose bumps forming on his arms, despite the oppressive heat.

The Call

For nearly two weeks, Olga had been trying to give Chef José Andrés $9,999 to help with the makeshift kitchens he had set up to feed Puerto Rico in Maria's aftermath. If videos of the hurricane's devastation had been her tragedy porn, their antidote were the clips of the dynamic chef making meals for thousands under impossible conditions. She searched social media for them, each one eliciting cathartic tears. The issue with the gift was, of course, that it was in the form of a duffel bag of cash, adding a layer of logistical difficulty to her philanthropic inclination. She tried to send it down with her brother on his last trip, but when he realized that she didn't want him to pass along a check, but actual cash, he balked.

"Why do you have this much cash?" he asked.

"My client's in a cash-based business and pays me accordingly."

"¡Loca! Just deposit it and make an online donation like everybody else!"

She didn't bother making an excuse, instead resorting to guilt. "Why do you have to make everything so difficult? I do so much for you; why can't you do this for me?"

"I don't even think this is legal! He won't be able to accept this."

"I purposefully made it under ten K to keep it aboveboard. If you get it to him, he'll figure out how to put it to use. He's a hospitality person; we figure shit out."

Still, he refused. She had thought about going down herself but felt paralyzed to book a ticket. Though she knew it was important work, helpful work, something about swooping in and handing out supplies like she had seen all the white relief workers do on TV made her grimace. Not the labor of it — she was not a person afraid of hard work — but the feeling of it. It made her feel American in the worst possible way: dropping in and out of your own comfort, doing work of limited skill, then patting yourself on the back for it. Or worse, feeling pity for a people to whom she was connected. Furthermore, she had not heard from her mother, directly or otherwise, since the encounter with Reggie, and Olga felt somehow that the island was her mother's place. She should not go without an invitation.

For related reasons, Olga had been steering clear of Reggie King. However, she recognized now that he could easily resolve her charitable dilemma. Since the storm, Reggie had been going back and forth on his own plane — with supplies, with the media, with musical artists — and, as she suspected, he listened to her objective with little question or concern, saying only that he would send Clyde to get the bag. This disappointed Olga only in that she was sorry to hear Clyde had not yet gone back to school. So, when she heard the knock on her door, she quickly ran through her planned script to gently scold him.

But it was not Clyde. It was her aunt Karen, flanked by two escorts, their faces covered by black bandanas. The sight pulled the breath from Olga's mouth. Before she could say a word, they had pushed past her and were, as Karen explained, doing a sweep for "bugs." Her brother had told her wild things about her mother that Reggie only amplified and colored in, yet these stories failed to prepare her for the terrifying and surreal sensation of the Pañuelos Negros invading her apartment. Of seeing that it was all true. Of knowing that if they were here it was only because her mother had sent them.

"Okay," Aunt Karen declared when the place was deemed secure, "if we are all clear, you can wait downstairs now, okay?"

Karen had spent most of her life in front of a classroom, and her professorial delivery reared its head even in moments such as now. Her casual demeanor made Olga herself relax, take her aunt in. Olga had not seen her in nearly a decade, since shortly after her grandmother died. Karen had aged, but not nearly as much as Olga would have thought. She had always found her aunt beautiful, and she was still so now. Olga imagined that Karen and her mother must have been quite the pair when they were young.

"Olga," her aunt offered with warmth, "you are glowing. Are you in love?"

Olga's mother had never believed in witchcraft, but her grandmother had, and she had always felt — with some degree of fear and reservation — that La Karen, as she called her, had a bruja's touch. Olga felt herself blushing but unable to speak.

"You reveal yourself, girl!" Karen sighed with a smile as she made her way to the sofa. Olga felt her eyeing the apartment.

Judging. Taking in the accoutrements of bourgeoisie that Olga had, at one point, been so proud of having accrued, and now felt embarrassed of. Olga and Prieto had grown up with Karen in their lives, but the relationship belonged, first and foremost, to their mother, who had, according to their grandmother, worshiped at Karen's altar when they were in high school. Karen: the first person their mother had ever connected with utterly independent of her siblings or her family or her neighborhood. Theirs had been a closeness that nothing rivaled — not their mother's relationship with her children, and certainly not with their father. Olga's mother had once said that in her life only Karen had never disappointed her; only Karen lived a life as big as she was. To Olga, this was as close to having her mother near as she might ever get.

"So, sit your butt down," Karen commanded. How did she feel so comfortable bossing Olga around in her own house? Karen pulled a flip phone out of her tote bag. "Your mama's gonna call us" — she checked her watch — "soon."

Olga's heart began racing, at a pace that scared her. Karen pulled her down to the sofa and patted her hand.

"I know," she said, "it's been a while, but

it's still just your mama. Time means nothing when it comes to our mothers."

But Olga couldn't breathe. The tears welled but wouldn't come. She couldn't remember her mother's voice. She couldn't even imagine it. And then, she didn't need to. The phone rang and Karen answered.

"We are here," Karen said. "Both of us." She put it on speaker.

"¿Querida? ¿Querida, mi Olga? Are you there?" her mother said.

"¿Mami?" Olga asked, the word quivering in her mouth. She was thirteen, or younger, again, her mother's voice rewinding time, and pain, and hurt, and bitterness. "¡Mami! It's you!"

"Sí, Olga. It's me! Mija, someone showed me the clip of you on the news! I was so proud. Finally, you've found your voice."

The tears had come now, but Olga smiled through them. Pride was a feeling her mother had always reserved for Prieto; she bathed in it now.

"Something just came over me, Mami," she said.

"What came over you was the truth. There comes for each of us a moment when we can't turn our backs to abuses of power, and this was your moment. It's still your moment, Olga. Here in Puerto Rico we are on the cusp of the liberation that has evaded our people for over a hundred years, and I believe that you, mija, can help deliver us the key to unlock this door."

"Me?" Olga said with disbelief.

"Claro, mija. Olga, you see the news; how the government has had us on our knees — before Maria, even — begging for power, like citizens of a third-world country? We have long known our need to get out from under the thumb of this corrupt government and PREPA. Slowly, we have been accumulating solar and wind energy sources, but we can no longer afford to move slowly."

"Mami, this makes sense, but why not talk to Prieto —"

"Ay, Olga," her mother said, not even attempting to conceal her disgust. "If I wanted the help of a bureaucratic lombriz, I'd sit around waiting for Ricky to do something."

Olga was taken aback. Wounded on her brother's behalf. Prieto had said their mother was angry, had told her about the box of worms, yet the vitriol with which their mother spoke of her son still shocked her.

"Mami, I know you're upset about the PROMESA stuff, but —"

"Olguita, we can't waste time on Prieto,"

her mother said, impatience in her voice. "If it was just his PROMESA vote, I'd think him weak willed, but no, it's much, much worse. He's been lining his pockets voting against his own people! The worst kind of traitor —"

"Mami," Olga pleaded, "there's got to have been a mis—"

"Nena, please," she offered firmly. "Enough. We don't need Prieto. We really just need you."

Olga was quiet for a moment, straining to absorb this deluge of emotions and information. Her mother continued.

"Olguita," she said, the coo back in her voice, "what I need now is the kind of intervention that can only come from the private sector. Where they can move outside the confines of government. What I need now is someone to commit to selling us — the people of Puerto Rico — large numbers of solar panels, and to commit to getting them to us quickly. I'm not looking for a handout now, mind you. We have money — we have some very generous patrons to our cause — but, for the volume of panels that we are looking for, we need someone willing to . . . bargain. And, of course, not ask too many questions."

"And you think I know someone like

this?" Olga asked, dumbfounded.

"Por supuesto. I think you know them well. I saw a picture of you two together in the Style Section, mija, at one of those fancy Hamptons parties you are always going to."

A chill ran down Olga's spine before she intellectually understood why.

"Did you know your novio, Richard, is one of the largest producers and distributors of solar panels in the United States?"

Anxiety flooded Olga; she was unsure how to disrupt her mother's plans with the inconvenient realities of her love life.

"I, um, didn't know that, Mami. I didn't ask too much about his work. Pero, Mami, I cut things off with Dick —"

"¿Y? So?" her mother interjected. "People reconcile, no?"

"I . . . I . . ." Olga felt, instinctively, that she should not mention Matteo; that to do so would only expose him — their relationship — to her mother's verbal assault. She knew that, in service of the revolution, her personal happiness — anyone's, really — was of little concern. She didn't need her mother to confirm that. Her mother, seeming to sense her hesitation, pounced.

"Your whole life, Olga, you've been able to charm your way in and out of anything you've wanted. Wrap people around your finger! I've always admired that about you. I have no doubts you can do it again now with this Richard. It's a chance to put your talents and connections in the service of something important for a change. Wouldn't you like the chance to do that? For your Mami? For your gente?"

Her pulse quickened. In Olga's heart there was a pin-sized hole of infinite depth that made every day slightly more painful than it needed to be. She thought of it, this hole, as a birth defect. The space where, in a normal heart, a mother's love was meant to be. Olga felt before her a chance to finally heal this aching wound. Tears welled again in her eyes and she sniffled in the silence before she finally spoke.

"I . . . I can try."

"Bueno." Her mother concluded: "Señor Reyes will reach out with details. Pa'lante, mija."

And with that she hung up, though her energy hovered in the room for much longer.

Karen's gaze felt warm against the chill the call had left her with. Neither woman spoke for a long time.

"I take it this Richard is not the person

giving you the glow?" Karen eventually asked.

Olga shook her head no.

"You don't have to help her, you know. At the end of the day, this is your life."

Olga was surprised that Karen, her mother's ride-or-die, was saying this.

"But she's my mother. How do you turn down your mother?" Olga asked, not quite rhetorically.

"Olga, I love your mother as much, if not more, than my actual sibling, but there's a reason that I never had kids. Mothering and birthing a child are not the same. Children don't ask to be born. They don't owe anybody anything. This is one area your mother and I never saw eye to eye on, frankly. I'm down for her cause — no American can be truly free while we still have colonies. If your rights are less because you're born in one place, not another, how meaningful are those rights in the first place? But, and this is a big but, that's why you should talk to this Richard dude, not because you owe your mother anything. If you've got a good thing going on and this business opens a whole can of worms . . . Well, all I'm saying is, it's okay to choose yourself. This is, I assure you, what I'd do.

And it's certainly what your mother would do."

Olga thought about Matteo. How for the first time, really ever, she had been consciously imagining a future with someone. How good it had felt to begin to really let someone in. How she felt the constriction in her chest that she'd held for years begin to release. How different the whole thing had been from whatever it was she'd had with Dick, which she'd let drag on for far too long. Dick. She sighed. The world felt so heavy again.

"Did you hear her say that she was proud of me?" Olga asked.

"I did. It was a bold thing you did. Radical, as we used to say in the old days."

It had felt good, that approval, something she'd previously thought only her brother could earn.

"Karen?" Olga asked. "My brother. I think she's —"

Karen sucked her teeth. "Olga, your brother is a sorry-ass sellout. Hell, I'm . . . 'furious' is not the word. And PROMESA is just the tip of the damn iceberg. When he canceled the hearing this summer, well, that raised some eyebrows with your mother and some of her . . . supporters. They did some digging; he's been on the take from the

Selby brothers for years."

"What?" Olga asked, incredulous. "What do you mean? For money?"

"What else could it be? They have a big stake in the debt down in P.R., have been buying up land. But it goes back longer than that. They looked at his votes from when he was on the City Council. Every fucked-up thing that's happened to this city over the past fifteen, twenty years — the luxury developments displacing normal, working people, the retail and grocery stores only the 1 percent can afford to patronize, all of it — if the Selbys had a hand in it, which they almost always did, your brother voted to pave the way for them."

Olga did not want to believe it, but her aunt's words sparked a recollection. How upset her brother had been when Olga had mentioned Nick Selby. How vigorously he protested the notion that he and the Selbys were friends. A wave of nausea overtook her.

She looked out her windows at her beloved Fort Greene, the landscape now spiked with luxury high-rises, many of which the Selbys built after the City Council had voted to rezone the area for the stadium. She thought about Bush Terminal, the bars creeping up Fifth Avenue. She thought about the small businesses lost after the recession, after

Sandy, their retail corpses replaced by hotels and big box stores. The creep of wealth and whiteness that had slowly, steadily been frog boiling her hometown, pushing out and scattering families like her own.

"The most painful wounds," Papi used to say, "are those inflicted by our own kind." He was, she realized now, absolutely right.

By the time Olga met Matteo for dinner that evening she was quite drunk. After her aunt had gone, Olga poured herself a large glass of vodka and did not stop drinking until she could stop her body from shaking. She could not bring herself to tell him about the visit, she could not imagine articulating her mother's request. He could see that she was upset and tried to comfort her, to dig into whatever ill was plaguing her. His niceness and kindness enraged her. She bit into him every chance she could, gnawing on anything and everything that came out of his mouth as viciously as possible. When he walked her home and said perhaps they should spend the night apart, she was pleased. She was alone. As she deserved to be.

Todopoderosa

He hadn't thought that he would cry, but as soon as he saw her, the tears blinded him. Thick, wet, large drops. He could hardly step closer; words choked in his throat. It was just that he couldn't believe how small she was. No more than five-foot-one or -two, thin as a wisp. When he'd seen her last, he'd been just shy of seventeen. He was scrawny and knock-kneed, just starting his last big growth spurt. He remembered hugging her goodbye before the trip from which she never returned. He had just passed her in height, and when he'd wrapped his skinny arms around her slight shoulders, she'd commented on how tall he was getting. Over the years, she had grown to a presence bigger than any physical body, looming large over the choices he made with his life each step of the way. Now, he stood before her, forty-five and broad-shouldered, easily half a foot taller than the last time he saw her, and he was shocked by the power of such a tiny wight.

The room was clearly her office. There was a desk, but she had been sitting on an armchair in a corner of the room. The shutters to the room were drawn. Slats of light came through and the ceiling fan cut them into shadows. Blanca gave him a moment to collect himself, her face oddly expressionless. When enough time passed, she broke into a smile.

"Okay, mijo, it's okay," she said calmly. "Come. Sit with your mother."

His ears took in her words, but his body was unable to process them, his legs laden down by the weight of the years that had passed since he'd seen her last. Sound faded, everything replaced by the pulsing of his heart pumping blood, rapid and hot, through his body. His heartbeat echoed into his brain, his head, his eyes, throbbed from it. A brain, a head, eyes, blood, a body. All of it sprung from this stranger before him. That a short cord connected them once, that her body once nourished his, felt a shocking notion.

"Prieto. Siéntate," she now commanded.

He registered the impatience in her voice and felt a familiar, childish fear. He somehow willed himself to move. Slowly he crossed the room, his eyes transfixed by her countenance. Just the finest of lines drawn around her mouth and eyes betrayed her age. Up close, his fear melted away by the familiarity of her face; he saw a resemblance to Lourdes he'd never been able to see before and couldn't contain his emotions.

"¡Dios mío, Mami! I had never realized how much Lourdes has of you in her face! Damn! Wait until you see her; I have pictures from Mabel's wedding and she's so tall right —"

He moved to take out his phone, forgetting that the Pañuelos had confiscated it hours earlier.

"Prieto," his mother said, gesturing for him to stop, "we have other things we need to discuss. Things more important than genetic inheritance."

"Don't you want to see your granddaughter?" he asked, but as soon as he said it, he knew that she didn't.

"I want you to know," his mother said, "that in the end, you did us a favor with your PROMESA vote. The media rarely talks about it, but this austerity has caused an outrage. Students have been taking to the streets. I've recruited more brilliant puertorriqueños to our movement this year than in any other single year. PROMESA highlighted the neocolonialism that this pendejo governor and his father before him have tried to gloss over while they line their pockets with the Yanquis' money."

It was hard to comprehend that, after almost thirty years apart, she wanted to talk about PROMESA, and yet Prieto didn't know what else he had expected her to say.

"Did you really try to assassinate the governor?" he blurted out, hoping he could at least use this time with her to parse fact from fiction about these missing years.

"Many years ago, yes," she answered flatly, "and I would try it again now if I didn't think the timing was wrong."

"Is that what the guns are for?"

"I'm sure Tirso gave you a much more political answer, but in short, yes. The guns are for the day that we are truly ready for liberation."

"And when will that be?"

"When half the island — and most importantly, the jíbaros — are running like we are, independent of the government for power and clean water."

"And this is what you need me for? To help with this . . . sustainable energy project?"

She laughed, but her eyes, he saw, were

cold. "No, Prieto, no. Your sister is helping with that —"

"Olga?" he asked with concern. He could not imagine how she could possibly help. "Does this involve Reggie?"

"Ay, bendito, now you care? After you stabbed me in the heart by being the worst of our kind —"

"What are you talking about?" He was angry now, frustrated by the singular lens of her worldview. "I just don't want my sister doing something crazy —"

"Is this what you think of what's happening here? We are saving our people: giving them water, food, medication. We are liberating them from one hundred and nineteen years of oppression. We are the revolution. But this, this here is what you think is crazy?"

She sighed before she continued: "I'm giving your sister a chance to finally put some purpose to an otherwise wasted life. I thought you would understand that. But, then again, I never thought you'd sell out your own community just to get your hands on some developer money."

She was standing now, hovering over him. He looked her in the eyes.

"Mami, I never took a dime from the Selbys. That, I want you to know. But they did blackmail me; I did make votes — many votes — that advanced their interests, all to the harm of Sunset Park, to the harm of Brooklyn. But no one asked me to vote a particular way on PROMESA. That was the best choice on the table. The Selbys are interested in Puerto Rico, they like PROMESA, for obvious reasons . . . but more importantly —"

"So you admit it."

"Don't you even care what they were blackmailing me about?"

"Please tell me it's about something more interesting than you fucking boys."

Prieto stared at her, dumbstruck.

"It's no secret, Prieto. I've known since you were six years old. A mother always knows."

His entire body tensed itself as if bracing for a blow, but it had already landed. His pulse quickened and he could feel his hurt morphing into rage. Not towards her, but with himself. For having kept himself, and his life, in a box that he thought she would find pleasing for so long. He wanted to see what could puncture her. What, if anything, could elicit an emotion.

"I have HIV, Mami."

"Weak, like your father," she said, shaking her head. "I had always worried that you got this from him. . . .”

“Got what? Being gay? Disease? What the fuck are you talking about?”

She looked impatient with him. “No, Prieto, your weakness of character. Your inability to sublimate your personal satisfactions in order to live your full potential.”

He was consumed with a desire to shake her. To rattle her until something resembling a mother came out.

“ ‘Your full potential’! Spare me the hypocrisy, Mami. Me. My sister. Fuck, even Tirso out there. The only ‘potential’ you care about is that which potentially benefits your agenda. You and Nick Selby are cut from the same fucking cloth. Everything you’ve built you’ve done by exploiting the needs of those around you.” He found himself so frustrated, he got the courage to ask what he never thought he could. “All these years away from us. You don’t even care about us as people. Why did you even have us?”

This question stopped Blanca in her tracks. Her posture slackened and she sat back down and looked him in the eye.

“Because your father wanted a family so badly, and at the time, I was very in love.”

“And then?”

“And then I realized love, that kind of

love, would not change the world."

Her words cut through his anger. He sighed and with his breath he released something he hadn't realized he'd been holding in: a fantasy. Some mythic, emotional reunion with a version of his mother that had lived, tucked deep in his imagination.

"I knew no one would understand," she continued. "But to be honest, no one's ever really understood. My whole life I felt my skin was too small for what I knew was possible for me. I spent years fighting my way off of this narrow path laid out for me — as a woman, as a Boricua. And yet, despite all my efforts, there I was. In exactly the life I'd been so desperate to avoid. I felt I was choking in Brooklyn, choking trying to compress myself into that life. I knew what everyone would think. What kind of woman leaves her family? But to me, what I did *was* an act of love. For what I believed I could do here, in Puerto Rico, but also for myself."

She was softer now, her voice gone quiet. A quiet covered them for a moment.

"Why did you want to see me?" he asked.

"To tell you to leave us alone; this island isn't yours, we don't need your help."

"Who are you to say this isn't mine? This is as much my homeland as it is yours."

"Ay, but it isn't. It's barely my island, but what I didn't give to you and your sister, I've given to mi orgullo. To this place. What we're doing here? We're creating a model for what will ultimately liberate Puerto Rico."

"Communism," Prieto stated.

"Hardly," she scoffed. "I greatly admired Ojeda Ríos, but I quickly saw that he didn't have enough strategy. In Cuba, for all my idealization of Castro as a younger woman, I found too much ego. Too much hierarchy. No, it was when I traveled to the Zapatistas that I found our answer: a society led by community need. Unbeholden or dependent upon government, completely without hierarchy —"

"But they still have a leader. You are still a leader."

"I provide creative direction. But *this* is what will finally liberate Puerto Rico."

"Anarchy."

"Agency." With that she raised her voice and shouted. "¡Oye! Entren!" And two Pañuelos armed with AK-47s walked into the room and stood at the entrance.

"Prieto, this is why you need to leave us alone. Only Puerto Ricans can unshackle themselves. Just as PROMESA helped our cause, so will Maria. Don't fight for aid for us; stop bringing the cameras down with you. Stop being a hero. . . ."

"But without public pressure, the government won't act, and people will die."

"¡Coño! Don't you know that they're already dead? Let the people see what the government really thinks of them. Let them be reminded that they were considered worthless. And they will see that it was their own people who saved them. Their own people who created power, who grew food, even provided water. And you" — and now she looked at him — "you should worry about your own backyard. Because it looks like a hell of a mess from where I'm standing."

He stared at her.

"Mercedes is already on her way back to San Juan. These men are going to take you directly to the airport."

"Wait. So, you're telling me to go home?"

"Yes, mijo. And do not come back. That's a command and not a request. That is the best thing for you, personally, and for Puerto Rico. ¿Entiendes?"

As she moved in to embrace him, he recoiled. It occurred to him that she'd not even tried to hug him when he first arrived. After all those years.

"Don't touch me," he said as he pushed her away and walked out the door.

Control

Although Charmaine had assured him repeatedly that Olga would come around, Dick was still surprised — and delighted — when she texted saying she had a business proposition for him and wondered if he might want to discuss it over dinner. She'd suggested that they meet at a restaurant downtown, but he wanted to make himself clear; he had missed her, he appreciated this second chance. So, he insisted that she come to his apartment where he would, personally, make her dinner. She didn't reply immediately, which made him feel, for a moment, insecure regarding her intentions. But just as he had talked himself around it — what business proposition could she possibly have for him? — she wrote back saying that sounded sweet, but certainly too much trouble. To which he replied that she was worth it.

Dick had been ruminating on Olga, the

individual, not just as his preferred physical companion, more than ever. First, of course, because of her television rant, which Nick and the boys from Exeter were all too excited to share on their group chat. But also because of all he'd learned from Agent Bonilla. While he was sure Olga didn't know most of it, just the broad strokes — being raised and then abandoned by a radical lunatic, losing her father to such a terrifying disease — it obviously had to have impacted her. Yet she had thrived. Had climbed into the same rooms with men such as himself who had been born with what some might think of as a bit of a leg up. It shone on her a new light of admiration. Indeed, he even gave her odious brother a moment of reconsideration. Such a remarkable rise. It made him feel oddly patriotic; the American dream, still possible.

He decided that, given this new information, if he had another chance with her, he would make it a point to look past foibles that led to incidents like the one at the party; it was akin to blaming a cat for having claws. The same could be said of her outburst on that morning show. At first, he'd been offended. Olga had made plenty of money off his family; her late fees alone were just short of highway robbery. Capitalism and the "elite" had serviced her well as far as Dick could tell. But he recast the episode after reviewing Bonilla's file. Given the tree she'd fallen from, he was frankly happy she wasn't more extreme. Besides, they had been in love; Dick of all people knew that while Olga might harbor feelings of resentment for the wealthy on an intellectual level, she did still see, and appreciate, people as individuals.

Dick made a beef Bolognese; it was his favorite thing to cook, having worked on this recipe since his college days. He made a playlist for the occasion, which now streamed through his Sonos. He'd given the housekeeper the night off. In his mind, he hoped they might do the dishes together. He wanted Olga to see that he was relatable.

She arrived exactly at 7 P.M. and brought a bottle of wine, which he found a sweet gesture, as she of all people knew that he had more than enough wine to get them through a hundred dinners. He was a bit surprised at her appearance. Normally when they got together, she was clad in high heels and some sort of dress, but today she arrived in jeans, sneakers, and a V-neck sweater that only hinted at her ample cleavage. She wore just the faintest touch of makeup on her face.

"No work today?" he asked.

She let out a bit of a laugh. "You could say that I had the day off, yes."

She was simply very pretty, he realized, as he took her in, kissing her cheek. He decided it was a good sign that she was so casual, it meant she still felt comfortable with him.

They made small talk through dinner — which she complimented heartily — and though it was slightly awkward in moments, he found her warm towards him. They both drank more wine than usual, he noticed, and wondered if she was as nervous as he was. After dinner, as he had hoped, they went back to the kitchen and she laughed at him doing the dishes.

"Better be careful, Dick. Don't want anyone mistaking you for the help," she quipped. She was leaning on the counter of the island next to him and he took her joke about their fight as an opening, wrapping his soapy hands around her waist.

"I'd work as a busboy if it meant I could spend every day with you," he said as he leaned down to kiss her neck. But she pulled away from him.

"We should talk, don't you think?" she said. He shut off the water. She was right.

They should clear the air.

"Of course, Cherry. I've been thinking that, too. I . . . I want to apologize for my behavior at the party that day. I drank too much and was far too harsh, and —"

"It's fine, Richard," she said. "I think in some strange way it was good for me to hear that. It's motivated me to do some soul searching about what I'm doing with myself . . . professionally."

"Really, Cherry!?" he said with a bit of excitement. He hadn't been expecting gratitude: a bonus. "Do I get rewarded for my inadvertent good deed?"

She laughed. "Let's not get ahead of ourselves. As I mentioned, I come with a business proposition."

His heart dropped a bit — just a bit — considering for a second that perhaps this was legitimate and that she didn't come here to get back together. Then he realized this was likely just her way of breaking the ice.

"Do you want to embark on a new career with Eikenborn and Sons?" he asked, with a smile.

"Well, no, not exactly, but it does involve your business."

"Really, now? This is intriguing." He leaned in towards her, his hands resting on the counter, framing her body between his arms.

"There is a party in Puerto Rico, a group, really, interested in purchasing about two million dollars' worth of solar panels."

"Okay," he said, "I'm listening. For private estates?"

"No," she said. "I'm not at liberty to discuss the plans, but the condition of the purchase is that they need the panels ASAP."

"Are they trying to resell these?" he asked, stroking her hair. "Because I'm not about to consider supplying a competitor. I could stand to make a killing with solar down there."

"No, that's definitely not the intention," she said. He noticed the smile had fallen slightly from her face.

"Who is this buyer, Cherry?" he asked. He had taken one hand and placed it on her waist. She had not pulled it away.

"A philanthropist who would like to remain anonymous."

He nuzzled her neck now, and felt her stiffen slightly. "Ah, a do-gooder! That's nice. We need more do-gooders in the world." He moved his hand towards her waist and undid the button of her jeans. She grabbed his wrist.

"So," she said, "will you do it? Because if

so, I can introduce you to their representative."

"Can you now, Cherry?" he said, with a bit of a laugh as he bit her ear. He was mildly curious who this philanthropist was. If they had this kind of capital to expend on a charitable act, surely he'd have met them before. Unless they were foreign? An interesting possibility. Either way, this was pennies compared to what he could stand to make with Nick Selby by *not* providing solar panels to Puerto Rico, something he did not think he should share with Olga. He was fairly confident this would ruin his seduction. And besides, he hadn't given Nick his commitment yet anyway.

She suddenly pulled away from him, but had not let go of his wrist.

"Richard," she said, "I'm being serious. These are real potential buyers."

"Ah, plural," he said as he attempted to re-catch her in his arms.

She pulled away again.

"Dick," she said quietly. She took a breath. "Richard, I'm seeing someone."

"What?" Barely two months had passed since they stopped seeing each other. He decided that she must be trying some sort of joke. He laughed. She didn't.

"It's serious, I think," Olga said now. She

was not joking.

Heat rose in his neck; he was unsure if it was anger or humiliation.

"Then what the fuck are you doing here?" he asked.

"I . . . I shouldn't have suggested dinner, I realize . . . I'm sorry if you —"

"You aren't fucking sorry, Olga," he said. It was anger. He could feel it. "You're a manipulative cunt and you knew what I would think you wanted when you reached out to me."

He saw the words hit her like a slap and he liked it. He had forgotten how tricky she was. How many times had she done this to him? He had lost count. She always twisted his actions and desires into a version that best suited her, until finally he would forget what he had wanted in the first place. She had done this when he left his wife. She had done this to him in the Hamptons. He could see it very clearly now. Somehow always pulling each situation out of his hands and assuming control of it all.

"How long have you been fucking this other guy?" he asked. He was very close to her now, but she didn't move away. "Have you been fucking this other guy the whole time?"

She was leaning away from him now and

he could see a touch of fear in her eyes.

"Richard," she said flatly, "does it really matter?"

Of course it fucking mattered. He leered at her in silence. Everything had a different cast: the casual attire, the lack of makeup. She wasn't comfortable with him, she was indifferent. He was filled with such rage when he realized he had slapped her. He had not hit a woman in years. She stepped back from him in shock, but only backed herself against the counter.

"Richard, you're right. I knew what you might think when I texted you. And I even thought I might be able to go through the motions —"

"Go through the fucking motions?"

"I just meant, I didn't intend to come across as a tease. But when I got here —"

"When you got here, what? I disgusted you? You changed your mind?"

"No!" she said, and he could see now that she was scared. She realized she had lost control of the situation and this gave him a strange pleasure.

"So, what? You were going to come here and 'go through the motions' with me, like some kind of whore, and then what? You thought I'd just sell your friend whatever they wanted because of you and your magic pussy? And then what? You were going to go back to fuck this other guy?"

He was screaming now, he realized. He wanted to lower his voice, but he couldn't.

"I don't know!" she said. "I'm sorry! I'll go! I'll just go!"

She was always making him chase her. Always.

He grabbed her and spun her around, pinning her face down against the counter. Now, she would see what it felt like to be the one without control.

Later, after she had gone, he still found himself boiling. He picked up his phone.

"Nick? Dick Eikenborn here. I've thought about it. Count me in on the Puerto Rico deal. . . . I'll stay out of the market until you give me the green light. At the terms discussed, of course. . . . But, and this could be nothing, there's someone trying to bulk purchase solar for down there. . . . I don't know who. But I heard about it through the Acevedo girl. . . . Yes. Of course, that one. Anyway, do with that information what you will. I don't fucking care."

Truth and a Slice

After seeing his mother, Prieto was left to grapple with the reality of who she was and not the versions that had lived in his mind for the past twenty-seven years. She was not a hero nor an impotent kook. She was some sort of mad genius — for that compound had surely required genius. And she had felt herself meant for a different life. Stuck in too-small skin. So she freed herself. Shed her old life. For Prieto, this truth blew through him like a bullet. Fast and clear. Not a fatal wound, but the kind that forces a reappraisal of life. He, too, knew the sensation of too-small skin. Knew what it felt like to experience thousands of tiny deaths, year in and out, as he watched the life he wanted escape him while feeling trapped in the life he had. But instead of empathy or sympathy for his mother, he felt regret. And rage. And despair. Despair that a large part of what had kept him here —

inside his own too-small skin — was to please the woman who had left him behind in order to shed her own. Yes, it hurt to know his mother had never wanted to be a mother at all, but an equal weight of his sadness came from the deprivation of life he'd inflicted upon himself in this futile quest for her love.

On the plane home, as he watched his island disappear into the distance, the tears came easily. He ran through all of the compromises of both his values and desires he'd made over the years. All of these shameful actions and choices, he now had to acknowledge, were made to present to the world a person, a life, that his mother would be proud of. Whom his mother would love. Somewhere, deep down though, he had always known she had no such capacity. He and his sister had been pining for a mother who'd never wanted to be a parent to begin with. But Prieto had. His daughter was a gift in his life his younger self never thought he'd be able to have. She gave him purpose and filled him with love.

When his plane landed, his intention had been to go directly to Olga's. To tell her everything. About the visit, about the Selbys, all of it. When she didn't answer his calls, he didn't want the courage he'd mustered to go to waste and decided that that day was as good as any to finally talk to Lourdes.

She didn't like getting picked up from school anymore. She was big now and wanted to walk home with her friends, but he figured if he tried to lure her in with a slice from L & B, she might look past him "embarrassing her" by showing up. The drive there was uneventful, mainly peppered with recaps of the latest season of *The Voice.*

"So, Lourdes, what's up at school?" he asked once they were seated. "Are people, like, crushing on other people yet? Or are y'all too young for that?"

"I mean, I don't like anybody, if that's what you're asking."

He felt relieved but also guilty that he couldn't find a more creative way into this topic without giving her the third degree. Where was his sister? She'd have known how to do this.

"Nah, nah. I mean, you're young. There's time. I'm just curious. . . . You know when I was your age, everybody made a big fuss over what girl liked what boy and vice versa and if you didn't like anybody after, I don't know, seventh, eighth grade, everybody called you gay, you know?"

"So?"

"So, what? What do you mean so?"

"So, they'd call you gay. So what? Tomás is into boys. He told us last year."

"Sonya's kid? That little boy told you last year — when he was ten years old — that he was gay?"

"Queer, Papi. But, yeah, he told us he likes boys."

"And he's the only one?"

"I mean, probably not, but like, it's not a big deal. People like who they like."

"That's true," Prieto said.

"I feel bad for them, though."

"Who? Tomás?"

"No. The little kids when you were young. That were gay. That they would get made fun of. It's stupid."

This was his window. He knew. He took a sip of his Coke.

"You know, Lourdes, when I was little I wasn't as cool as you. My sister, she was more like you. Didn't care what anybody thought about nothing. Lots of confidence. Me? I was worried about getting picked on. Always wanted to fit in. Make people like me. It's probably not my best trait."

"I mean, we all have our flaws. That's what Mami always says."

"True. But my point is, I was too afraid of getting made fun of to let people know who

I really was, if you know what I mean." He paused here. This was not the time to punk out. "Or, more clearly, I wanted to tell you that I'm gay."

Her eyes got a little wide.

"Does Mami know?"

"No. I wanted to tell you first. But, I'll tell her. She might be a little angry. Because the truth is, I knew I was gay when we got married, but I really wanted . . . well, you."

"You know guys can get married now, right?" she asked.

"Yes, mija. I was a city councilman when that law passed here. But you probably don't remember."

"So, is that it?" she asked, as if he hadn't just done the hardest thing in his life.

"Well, the truth is, not really. Recently, I found out that I am HIV-positive. But I promise you, I am totally healthy."

"Like Oliver on *How to Get Away with Murder*?"

"Excuse me? Why are you watching that show?"

"I watched it with Tía Lola one night and now it's on Netflix. Anyway, he has HIV and he's fine."

She took a bite of her pizza as he wondered why he felt so stupid.

"Do you have a boyfriend?" she asked.

"Oliver does."

"No. I don't. Would you mind if I did?"

"No. As long as they were cool. Like, Matteo is cool."

"Matteo is cool. I'll make sure if I get a boyfriend, they're cool like that. Do you have other questions? Because I'm happy to answer them."

"Are you going to tell the people on New York 1?"

"At some point, I'm going to tell everybody."

One of the primary perks of being a congressman was that you could get a meeting with pretty much anyone you wanted. Yet Reggie — who really had always been a prick, Prieto now thought to himself — would not even return his calls. He had been trying to reach him since his trip to the compound, both to get some answers and to tell him to keep his sister out of this shit. This took on a new degree of urgency for Prieto as the days went by and his sister failed to return his text messages or phone calls, until finally she sent a message telling him to fuck off and leave her alone. He knew Reggie was somehow in the mix and he was determined to talk to him.

After the second week of being dodged

and ignored via text, through assistants, DMs, and tweets, Prieto felt forced to play hardball. He called his buddy Bonilla with the FBI and asked him to pay a visit with his partner to Reggie's office; Prieto thought he might have some information on the juvenile detention center break after Maria.

"Really now? What gives you that idea?" Bonilla asked.

"Did you see that article I sent you?"

"The Independistas distributing water in the mountain towns?"

"Yeah well, there's a lot of chatter down in P.R. that they were behind that prison break and King's name keeps coming up."

"Interesting."

This information, Prieto knew, carried the risk of leading the FBI directly to his mother, a step that Prieto had seriously considered since his trip. He'd left not only stripped of his ideal mother, but somehow also stripped of his motherland. When Blanca told him he had no place there, he'd felt ashamed. But why? He felt Puerto Rico in his veins, and yet a part of him heard what she said as true. How was him, even being of Puerto Rican descent, telling the islanders how to govern themselves any different from any other mainland American butting in? Benevolent colonialism is still colonialism. Still, he refused to let her take this place — his cultural inheritance — away from him. His first trip to the island, back when he was in college, had been life affirming. Just as he felt his world — his family — was washing away, he found a place that made him feel rooted. Anchored. He was a part of a larger something. A part of a people. He would go back. He would not let people forget. He would not let the people suffer from government neglect.

Despite all that he knew, he found it hard to believe that she would harm her own son.

Yet even as he thought this, he was unsure. Her threat to him was barely veiled. And so, he considered telling Bonilla everything.

But, remembering the fate of Ojeda Ríos gave him pause. He could not, in a serious way, compromise his mother without talking to Olga first. Ultimately, for now, it was strictly a ploy to get to Reggie. Prieto knew he'd play dumb; Reggie was far too street smart to get spooked by a visit from a cop. But it would be a nuisance. One that Prieto would offer to make go away on the condition he and Reggie have a face-to-face.

It irked Prieto, as he sat in the reception area of Reggie's lavish office suite in Tribeca, that Reggie King had more personal security than he, an elected official, did. A massive bodyguard stood outside the closed office door of Reggie's tenth-floor private office suite, meanwhile Prieto, who walked the streets like a regular Joe, was getting death threats to his Twitter account right as he sat there, all for just doing his job. But, no matter. There was nothing Reggie could dish out that Prieto couldn't take, and he wasn't leaving until he gave Reggie a piece of his own damn mind. He felt strong. Invincible. Somehow the meeting with his mother had unleashed a burden from him, one he had not even known was strapped to his back. There was nothing for him to be ashamed of anymore. No more secrets for him to keep.

Prieto was struck by how, despite having long since expanded his empire beyond music, Reggie's office still retained the air of an early aughts record label. His assistants — there were three of them — looked like the girls from Danity Kane, but old. Prieto suspected they'd been with Reggie for a while.

"Mr. Acevedo?" the one who looked like Aubrey O'Day said.

"Congressman," he corrected. Why did he fucking care?

"Excuse me?" she asked, confused. "Mr.

Reyes will see you now."

Reyes now, Prieto thought to himself. She led him into Reggie's office and shut the door behind her. Reggie was on a call. Of course.

"All right, son. It all sounds good, but I gotta bounce, some bitch just walked into my office that I've got to deal with."

"Go fuck yourself," Prieto muttered under his breath.

Reggie hung up the call.

"You've got to admit, calling the fucking Feds is a pretty bitch move, even for you."

"You left me no choice. What the fuck did you say to my sister?"

"Me?" Reggie leaned back in his chair. Prieto realized it was made out of ostrich skin. What a prick. "I've said a lot of things to your sister. But I feel like you've got something specific you want to know."

"She's not talking to me, and I need to speak to her, so I want to know what the fuck you and my mother said to her about me."

"Look, I don't like to get into the family business — because that's what this is — but I will tell you this: she spoke to your mother, and from what I understand, so have you. So, connect the dots."

Fuck, he thought to himself. He needed

to get to her. He needed to explain himself. He needed to tell her about their mother. Tell her to let it go; that they would never be or do enough. Tell her that she had to listen to him, and she had to try and understand why he did what he did. Because in the end, they were all each other had. Their mother was a figment of their imagination.

"When was the last time you spoke to Olga?" he asked Reggie.

Reggie leaned forward now. "Two weeks ago. She was given a mission and she failed."

"What kind of 'mission'? I swear to God if you asked Olga to do anything illegal —"

"Man, I didn't ask her for shit; I was just a middleman. The request came directly from Leadership and, as missions go, this was tame."

"Do you fucking hear yourself? You sound as batshit as my mother —"

"Your mother is a revolutionary. If her plans sound crazy to you, it's only because —"

"My mind is still colonized?" Prieto offered. He noted the surprise Reggie registered upon him saying this. "Yeah, son, I don't know how long my mom's been whispering in your ear, but I've been hearing this shit my whole life, so . . . I don't think you're about to 'drop any knowledge' on me, you know?"

Reggie cleared his throat. "I need to know that you're gonna call your friend at the FBI off. Please tell me you aren't such a sellout you'd sacrifice the good work that we're doing for our people just because you don't feel loved by your mommy."

"Oh, fuck you." Prieto sighed. "My mommy is a fugitive who attempted to assassinate an elected official. And she said herself to me that she'd think nothing of trying again. She's a fugitive who has somehow amassed a giant cache of weapons on a compound littered with evidence of your entanglements in her efforts."

Reggie raised his eyebrows. Clearly something Prieto said caught him by surprise.

"Man," Prieto continued, "I've got to ask, what are you doing here? You have so much going on. Legit shit. Have you really thought this through? What happens on the day revolution actually comes? Because my mom is out for blood and I'm not sure you're that kind of dude. Not really. You just play him on TV. You're hitching your wagon to my mother, and my mother does not give a fuck about you or all you stand to lose."

Reggie started to say something, but Prieto cut him off.

"Save it for a friend. All I'm saying is, you say you're all about making an impact. Ask yourself what you'll be able to do if you end up dead or in jail."

He stood up and started to walk out the door.

"I'll tell Bonilla to back off, but you better stay the fuck away from my sister."

"Necesitas una Limpia"

Olga wasn't sure why it surprised her when Matteo came by her place. Did she really think she could just disappear and he wouldn't notice? She wasn't really thinking, she supposed. She was drinking to stop from thinking. Not just a little, not just at night. As soon she opened her eyes, she poured vodka into her coffee cup — the big one with the mascot that now, she decided, served only as a reminder of her deficiencies — without even the premise of orange juice. She would drink until she could sleep and then wake up and drink until she slept again. The liquor store delivered. She rarely ate, and if she did, she got that delivered, too.

She wanted to stay in her apartment until she died. Or until she felt the waves of humiliation pass her. She felt confident that death would come first.

Her intention was not to hurt Matteo.

Anything but. She knew it hurt him when she didn't pick up his calls, did not reply to his texts. She had promised to not do this again. Knew it could be perceived as cruel, after all these weeks — no, months, she realized — to go completely dark. But she loved him too much to lie and she could not bear to tell him the truth, and for once, she could not pretend nothing was wrong.

She hadn't, she kept thinking — in those moments when she couldn't stop herself from thinking — ever really said the word "no." Had she?

Dick had been right. She knew what he was expecting when she reached out to him. She didn't correct his assumption because she wanted something from him. When he invited her to his house instead of the restaurant, she knew he assumed they were going to sleep together. She went there almost convinced she could will herself to sleep with him if that was what it took. She had just changed her mind. But the intent was there, wasn't it? The intent to betray Matteo's trust. To fuck up the first real thing she'd had a chance at in ages, to poison the first joyful feeling she'd felt in years. She disgusted herself.

She cataloged all the times she had fucked Dick in that exact same location, in the exact same position, as well as their variants — different homes, bathrooms instead of kitchen, bent over, belly up. She recollected all the occasions she had been mentally absent during the act, her acquiescence driven less by physical desire than desire to shut him up, to get to sleep, to get back to work. She remembered all the times Dick had pulled her ponytail or slapped her ass or spoken about her cunt, and how she had enjoyed it then. Why had this instance hollowed her out in such a gutting way? What variant made this instance feel like poison in her mind and body? Humiliation. Humiliation wielded violently.

The first time Matteo came by the apartment he was angry. In a way that surprised and also scared her, though everything was scaring her just then. He was banging on the door and screaming her name. He said he knew she was in there. That the doorman told him she hadn't left the house in days. That she had promised she wasn't going to do this to him again. Her neighbors came out to tell him to keep it down and he told them to fuck off. Then, later, she could hear him knock on their doors to apologize. The second time he came (she'd begun to lose track of how many days she'd been in the apartment by this time) he rang the bell and simply left flowers with a note apologizing for whatever thing he didn't realize he'd done. Telling her that whatever was wrong, they could work through it.

The third time he came, he had just called out her name and started to play her songs. "A House Is Not a Home." "I'm Not in Love." "Sometimes It Snows in April." The sounds of the recordings coming through the door. She cried and cried and she was pretty sure that he could hear her. When she could hear him crying, too, she could barely take it and scribbled him a note and slipped it under the door.

I'm sorry, it said. *I told you I'm a terrible person.*

"Olga," he called through the door. "Nothing can be this terrible."

She didn't know how long he sat out there after that.

He wasn't the only person she was ignoring, of course. Her brother. Mabel. Her aunt. Igor. Fucking Igor. She missed an appointment with him and he got pissed and she was terrified. She begged forgiveness and from then on he was the only person whose calls she returned. She wanted to die but not, she realized, get killed.

She didn't hear a peep from Reggie, or Karen, or her mother. She had fucked up. Had been given a chance to do something important and hadn't come through. Still, it stung to be deemed so immediately useless. To feel so disposable. To know that the love she had hoped would fill the hole in her heart was conditional. To know her birth defect would remain unrepaired.

After, immediately after — in the car ride home, in fact — she texted Reggie to say it hadn't worked out. He replied right away that he'd let Leadership know. She couldn't bring herself to actually say what happened, but she wrote more: *Things got ugly, he was very angry, I can never see him again.* Reggie never wrote back. If she was being honest, she had hoped he might ask or guess. Had hoped her mother would want to be sure she was all right.

She had been so stupid. She thought she was so clever, but she had been truly stupid.

This wasn't the first time something like this had happened to her. She was old. These things happened. The first time she was younger. In college. She'd fallen asleep at a party and woke up with some guy humping her. He came on her leg. For some reason it gave her night terrors and her roommate complained to their resident counselor and the resident counselor confronted her, and that was how she ended up in the school psychiatrist's office. When they told her she was likely grappling with abandonment issues.

She had come home for a long weekend or maybe it was spring break, she couldn't remember. Her grandmother had taken one look at her and said, "Necesitas una limpia," then took her to some bruja she knew who lived on the other side of the park. The woman had wrapped her naked body in a white bedsheet and lit velas all around her. She prayed over Olga's body and made her lie there until all the candles burned out, and then she cut Olga's shroud open with scissors and bathed her in Agua de Florida and rose water while she swatted her back with eucalyptus leaves. When it was over, Olga had never felt cleaner or more loved or more at peace. The night terrors stopped.

That woman must be dead by now, she thought.

One day she was still in bed when she heard the key turn in the lock. For a second — a split second — she wondered if it were her mother coming to check in on her. Then she realized her mother didn't have a key.

"Hello?" Olga called out from her bedroom. She felt scared, but also desperate to be rescued.

"Olga, honey?" It was her Tía Lola. "Olga, Matteo came by the house today; he's worried about you. We, um, we're worried, too. No one has heard from you and you missed Richie's birthday dinner."

"Oh," she said. "I'm sorry."

She could hear Mabel's voice whispering to their aunt.

"Mabel?" she called out. "Mabel, come lay down with me?"

Mabel came and climbed onto the bed and started to comb Olga's hair with her fingers. When they were girls, in junior high, they would fall asleep like this sometimes, lying in bed, listening to music, Mabel combing Olga's hair with her hands. They lay there quiet for many minutes. Olga couldn't remember another occasion when Mabel had gone so long without speaking.

She could hear her aunt cry out to Dios when she entered her kitchen. Olga could only imagine how it looked. She heard her cleaning up, bottles being taken to recycling, glasses into dishwasher. Laundry started. Water into pot. Chopping. Chopping. Her aunt began to hum to herself and broke the silence of the apartment.

"Olga," Mabel said very gently, "whatever Matteo did, you should give him another chance. He's a good guy."

"I know," Olga said, staring up at her ceiling. "He didn't do anything."

Mabel didn't say anything.

"I fucked up."

"Ay." Mabel sucked her teeth. "You fucked somebody?"

Olga nodded, and felt the tears begin to flow again.

"Okay, okay," Mabel said. "Pero, why so sad? He obviously doesn't know yet. So, you fucked up. You either tell him and ask him to forgive you, or put it past you, keep the secret, and try again. Why throw the whole thing away?"

"You don't understand," Olga said.

"You're right, I don't," Mabel said. "Why do you always have to make your life harder? I've watched you do this before, you know."

Olga knew she was talking about Reggie.

"Mabel, this is different."

"I know this is different. You're happier this time. You're a vieja now; you take twenty more years to find another dude, and no one will want your dried-up ass. I can't let you fuck up again. I won't be able to forgive you. Or myself. So, tell me what's really fucking going on here so we can figure out how you fix this."

Mabel had minored in psychology in college and Olga wished now that she had followed that pursuit. If there were more shrinks like Mabel maybe she would have tried going to one. Olga thought of the years she had been single after Reggie — not lonely, per se, but not exactly happy. She thought about the calm Matteo brought her, how joyful their time together was, how at ease with her own self he made her feel. She covered her face with her hands.

"Mabel, what if I don't deserve to be happy?"

"Olga," Mabel whispered in her ear, "unless you kicked a puppy or have a body buried someplace that I don't know about, you deserve to be fucking happy. Okay?"

She couldn't talk about this and actually look at anyone — not Mabel or anyone — so she kept her face covered and told her what happened with Dick. Mabel never stopped stroking her hair.

"I'm sorry. I'm sorry." She paused. "You didn't do anything wrong, you know. You can't punish yourself, mujer."

"But what do I do?" Olga asked.

"You tell him what happened to you. You let him listen. You let him tell you he still loves you, because he will."

Olga took a very long shower. She washed her hair and, to her own surprise, put on mascara and lip gloss, just to bring some life back to her face. She felt lighter for having told Mabel. It wasn't Mabel's words that made the difference as much as it was, she realized, that speaking what happened aloud had begun, ever so slightly, to deflate the balloon of humiliation that had been taking up so much space inside her. When she came out of the bathroom, she could smell her aunt's cooking and felt an appetite, a desire, return to her again. She felt excited to eat and a smile broke out on her face for the first time in many, many days. But, on entering the kitchen, she was surprised to see Lola and Mabel sitting at her kitchen counter with such serious expressions on their faces. In front of them, a pile of her mother's letters.

Basta Ya

It had been Tía Lola's idea to gather the letters from her mother, in chronological order, and read them, all together, out loud.

She had found them on Olga's desk; Olga had taken them out and reread some of them while she had grappled with her fateful decision to visit Dick and, well, she'd not given them another thought. Mabel had been disturbed by what she described as "psychological abuse." Lola latched onto the notes about Reggie.

"I always knew your mother talked you into breaking up with him; my mother wouldn't say, but I knew it was her."

Olga just shrugged. She felt exposed knowing other people could hear the voice that had been whispering in her ear for so very long.

"This is wack, Olga," Mabel exclaimed. "Wack. You realize that, don't you?"

Again, Olga just shrugged. "I never

thought of it as good or bad; it's just always been."

"When was the last time you heard from her?" her aunt asked. "Is this the last time?" She held up the last letter.

Olga felt like a child in that moment, too overwhelmed to worry about what she should or shouldn't say. She told them about the visit from Karen, about the phone call. This led to more questions. Why did she call now? What did she want? Which led to more disclosures: Reggie, the Pañuelos Negros, the solar panels. She watched the shock form on their faces.

"So," Mabel asked, "if I'm following this, you went to see your ex on behalf of your mother?"

"Yes, but she didn't know we were broken up." She didn't realize it was a lie until it was already out of her mouth. "And she didn't know about Matteo —"

"Good! Because she would have probably told you to break up with him and go with this other motherfucker, because God forbid you have any joy . . ."

"You don't know that, Mabel!" Olga pleaded, even though she, herself, knew that's exactly what would have happened. That this was why she didn't tell her mother about Matteo in the first place.

"Why do you defend her!? ¡Coño! She left you! She never called until she needed something — and then that something is fucking batshit crazy. You made a whole life without her and she's literally been telling you that you aren't shit for years, but you defend her!"

"Ay, Mabel," Lola interjected, "calm down. You're frustrated, I get it. But there's no reason to take it out on Olga."

"¡No, Tía! This is too much. This woman hasn't done dick for them, and my cousins twist themselves into knots to please her?"

"Do you know if she's been writing to your brother, too?" Lola asked.

When Olga didn't immediately answer, her tía just pulled out her phone and called Prieto directly. She went into the other room, and when she came back, she announced her plan.

"Your brother is coming back from D.C. on the first flight tomorrow; we're gonna put all these letters together and air this shit out. Enough with the secrets!"

"I don't want to see him," Olga replied. "He's a fucking piece of shit."

"Why do you say that?" Mabel said, cutting her off. "Because of something your mother told you? Or one of her brainwashed friends?"

Fact stymied Olga from answering; it *was* her mother's brainwashed friends who told her about her brother. That didn't change the truth of what they had said; the heartbreak of it. From the day she went into Manhattan to begin high school she'd been navigating worlds that felt foreign to her: her language, her values, her way of seeing people and the world always requiring explanation and context. Only in Brooklyn did she feel at home. Yet year after year she watched this place — as she knew it, as it had been for generations — erode away. Corroded by the very people who, just years before, turned their noses at crossing the bridge. How could she explain to Mabel that each new development, each elegant restaurant and pop-up shop made Olga feel that she herself was disappearing? That she had counted on her brother to be their defender — of Brooklyn, of their culture, of their family — and that he had sold them all out . . . for cash?

"He's been taking bribes for votes," Olga said. "Money from developers. The ones who did Bush Terminal."

Mabel and Lola seemed taken aback by this, and Olga wondered if it was the money or who the money was from that they were more disturbed by. Certainly, for Olga, it was the money. She'd always envied Prieto's disinterest in the material, a virtue that cast his character as superior to her own — one that concurrently loved and loathed money and the things it could buy. But, at the end of the day, Matteo was right, and Prieto was just like every other politician.

"Well then," Lola said, after a pause, "we're gonna ask about that shit, too! ¡Basta ya!"

In the end, Tía Lola decided against inviting their entire family for this exercise, out of concern that people clam up and figuring that if she included Mabel, all the salient details would make the rounds to everyone else within a week anyway. So, Prieto, Lola, Olga, and Mabel gathered around the dining room table at Fifty-third Street with all of the letters their mother had ever sent. Not just to Prieto and Olga, but the ones she'd sent to Papi and Abuelita, too. Letters Olga had never before considered, but whose existence seemed so obvious when her tía laid the small stack of them on the table, and Mabel placed them all in chronological order.

It was a brutal exercise, wrestling with objective reality. To see how their mother had manipulated their lives and their feelings. To see how she attempted to subtly poison the way they saw their aunts and uncles, their cousins, their father, and even, in some instances, their grandmother. All the people who had loved them in her absence. All the people, Olga thought, who loved them without condition. But most of all, to see how their mother tried, year after year, to sow discord and resentments between them.

The letter that hurt the most, though, was one neither of them had seen before. The one their mother had written to their father when she left, the one in which she lamented the lead weight he had become. The one that accused him of having tricked her into thinking their life would be extraordinary only to turn them into *"a stereotype of a Puerto Rican family that the younger you would have despised."* Their father had loved them so much, their father who was dope sick and a crackhead, yes, but who still had feelings. Whom she still had no trouble kicking, even when he was down. Their father, who was the reason they existed.

They cried for Papi that night, the two siblings.

When Olga first heard that Prieto had seen their mother in the flesh, had touched her, jealousy consumed her. Another occasion on which he felt the warmth of her sun. But, by the end of the night, depleted but clear headed, she vowed to never think of it again. Their grandmother had been right: she never had the mothering gene.

"The best thing we can do," Olga said, "is to bury her, like we should have long ago, and move on."

Presser

"I want to start by thanking you all for coming out here today — to my 'hood. To one of our city's most beautiful parks, Sunset Park. And, most importantly, I want to thank my family — many of whom took the day off from work, which, y'all know, means I've got something important to talk about."

"I am here today primarily as a representative of the people of the United States, of New York, and, most specifically and most proudly, of Sunset Park, Brooklyn. The spot in Brooklyn where you can catch the best view of the city for a quarter of the rent. But I am also here as a man — a Latino man —" Prieto paused here for a breath.

Olga felt Tía Lola pinch her and she realized that she'd been whispering Prieto's remarks under her breath; she had worked on this introduction with him for so long that she had it memorized. Despite hours of practice and his tremendous anxiety, she was amazed at how the words emanated from his mouth so naturally. It was fine, she thought, that he steady himself here now.

"— and as an HIV-positive gay man." The reporters, many of whom had known and covered her brother for years, audibly reacted.

"I, uh, know I'm supposed to use the new vernacular, and all." Here he ad-libbed a bit. "My daughter told me I'm supposed to say 'queer,' but I hope the kids will cut me some slack since I'm forty-five and, let's just say, this was hard." The crowd, and their family, twenty deep, assembled on the top of a hill in the park, chuckled. "For many years I kept my sexual orientation a secret, out of fear. Fear of disappointing my family, fear of falling short of expectations of my culture, fear of rejection from my constituents.

"The keeping of this secret prevented me from having closer ties with my daughter, my sister, my community. It kept me from earnestly pursuing love. So, when I was recently diagnosed with HIV, I realized I could not keep my orientation or my status secret any longer. There was too much at risk.

"Now, I know I've been on the scene here in New York since before y'all had websites, but here is something that very few people know: in 1994 we lost my father, Johnny Acevedo, to AIDS. He was an IV drug user and he was one of forty-one thousand people who died in America that year of HIV/AIDS, more than half of whom were Black or, as my daughter also tells me I should say, Latinx. Today, although the number of people who perish from this disease is thankfully low, Black and Latinx people — especially men like me — account for nearly seventy percent of the HIV-positive population in the United States, and that number is on the rise. I didn't think that I could properly address this issue from my place in the closet.

"Nor did I want a secret such as this looming over me as we head into this absolutely critical twenty-eighteen mid-term election, a year when I will be running again, and, with the support of party leadership, helping to flip some seats!"

At this, as practiced, Olga and the family cheered and a number of the reporters started to ask questions: about his health, if he thought this might affect his chances at reelection, but he kept going. This concluded the portion that Olga had written with him, the rest was platform and policy, which, though she had a vague notion of what he'd planned to say, she'd left to him. She could see that now, with the worst of it over, he was relaxing into his element.

"I promise I'll answer your questions in a moment, but I just need to let you all know why I'm finna to keep this seat! When we won the popular vote but lost the election in twenty-sixteen, more than three million American voices were silenced, but none more so than those of the poor and working class in our cities, and especially people of color. Families who, like my own, help to make their urban centers run, only to find their efforts to get by crushed by gentrification. We see it here in New York, here in Sunset Park, but this is afflicting people across this country. San Francisco, Chicago, all around Hawaii, and, of course, in Puerto Rico. In my next term I plan to roll out legislation that will, at the federal level, combat rising housing costs, hyper-development, and real estate tax breaks that allow people to buy into our cities while giving nothing to our schools, hospitals, or transportation."

At this, the crowd cheered. The subways were abysmal, though since her brother always drove, he had no idea.

"I want to close lending loopholes that allow landlords to benefit from empty storefronts, which incentivize high rent and de-incentivize small and mid-sized business. And, of course, I will continue to push back on the cronyism that is hobbling recovery in Puerto Rico. The island is in darkness while the president's friends and family reap billions in contracts. So, this is, you can say, my official reelection kickoff announcement. And now I'm happy to take your questions, of which I suspect you'll have many!"

Was he dating anyone? (No, but he had a crush on someone. Which was news to Olga.) Had he been on PrEP? (No, and while he had no sound excuse, given the blessing of his congressional health insurance, everyone should recognize the cost barrier often presented to low-income people when it came to drugs like PrEP.) How was his health? (Fantastic! He wanted to fight for everyone to have healthcare as good as he got.) Was it hard to tell his family? (Yes, but as you could see, they were fully supportive, most especially his daughter and his sister.) Did he have any thoughts about Reggie Reyes's announcement that he was opening a solar panel production facility in P.R. in the coming year? (Sounds like jobs and green energy. What's not to like?) What were his views on the recent scandal involving several of his congressional colleagues receiving kickbacks from the Selby brothers? (He would let his colleagues speak for themselves, but the Selby scandal is just indicative of the unruly power and influence that private and corporate wealth have wielded in our government since Citizens United.)

After Prieto had told Lourdes and his ex-wife and the family, he was chomping at the bit to do this presser. He'd been nervous, of course, but excited to be done with this chapter of his life. Olga, however, knew it wasn't quite that simple. After so many years with Prieto in their back pocket, she didn't think the Selbys would let him go that easily.

"I've got nothing to hide anymore, hermana! ¡Nada!" he said with joy.

Pendejo, she thought to herself. She was surprised he hadn't been blackmailed by more people.

"Really, Prieto? Because the last time I checked your mother was a fugitive plotting the rebellion of an American colony, and the only reason that hasn't derailed your career thus far is because our electoral system is so wack, you've been uncontested in every election you've run in."

"You always gotta be a wet rag."

"I'm trying to be pragmatic. Gay. AIDS. Drug-using dad. Fine. News gets out that your mom is a nutjob anarchist, it starts to feel like too much. Who else knows about Mami?"

"My man Bonilla at the FBI is the one who showed me her file. If he knew about the Pañuelos, he'd have told me. Besides, he's a friend. He's one of us."

"Alejandro García Padilla is one of us, too. Doesn't mean he didn't sell us out. We should assume the Selbys know everything that Bonilla knows." He looked dejected, but Olga pressed on. "Remember when you were on City Council? How everyone was on their payroll?"

"Of course."

"Do you think it's the same way in Congress?"

And so it was that question that Olga brought to a journalist she was friendly with at *New York* magazine over a delightful lunch at DUMBO House. Olga's treat, of course. The young woman, Olga knew, was bored with churning out Lifestyle content and eager to cut her teeth on something more relevant. The City Council story broke in a matter of days; the paper trail tying

Selby money to the councilmembers had been hidden in plain sight since 9/11. Almost immediately the New York AG opened an investigation into both Nick and Arthur Selby, as well as several current and former city councilmen and women. (The national story — the one that would eventually entangle nearly twenty congressmen on both sides of the aisle from New York, New Jersey, Georgia, California, and Florida — was slower to percolate, with new bits coming up week by week.) And while Olga and her brother knew the Selbys' influence was hardly crushed, the so-called Selby scandal seemed enough of a distraction to get Prieto out of their crosshairs. At least for now.

When the presser was over, after her brother had answered all the questions, shaken all the hands of any constituents who had shown up, and seen all their family off to start their days, it was Olga and her brother left at the top of the hill in Sunset Park, on a brisk and clear November day. He was beaming.

"Papi'd be proud," she said as they made their way over to a park bench.

"Remember when we were real little and he'd take us here? We'd come to the pool and then he'd make us just sit here, quiet, and look at the water?"

"Of course. He told us to tell the Statue of Liberty our dreams."

"Yeah. I know we were supposed to be dreaming of, you know, world liberation and shit, but you know what I used to think about? Finding somebody to love as much as Papi and Mami loved each other then."

"You know what's funny?" Olga asked. "Me, too."

"ADESTE, FIDELES"

When it was dark and Olga saw a light go on in Matteo's window, she crossed the street and pulled his spare key out from under his neighbor's doormat. When he first revealed this hiding place to her — the night of Mabel's wedding, when he was too drunk to figure out which key was his — she could tell he'd thought himself quite clever, and remembering his self-satisfaction made her laugh. She had not seen his face in nearly a month and the prospect both unnerved and excited her.

She had known Mabel was right. This was too important to throw away. She had to push past her fear and tell him what happened. But the full truth wasn't immediately ready. It was Mabel who convinced her to at least send him a message. To at least let him know that it wasn't him. To stop, in the active sense, torturing him. ("Pero, every day you don't follow up, that's mad hurtful.

You know that, right?" And she did. Of course she did.) Still, it took her time to reach out. To push past the part of her who felt, on some level, that deprivation of love was something she deserved.

I know I broke my promise and I hate not keeping my word, but something kind of bad happened to me . . . , she had eventually written. She couldn't deal with him asking her if she was all right. It was simply too much kindness. So, she added. *I'm physically fine, but . . . well, "I'm sorry" isn't good enough to account for me disappearing like that. This is not how you deserve to be treated.*

He started and stopped typing a number of times before he eventually sent his reply.

I know. I don't. But. I've been too worried about you to be pissed, frankly.

A pause.

You are right, though. Sorry isn't enough.

It was the truth, she knew, but it still stung to see it written as fact.

Tell me what you need and I'll do it, she had replied.

For ten or fifteen minutes, for much of which Olga held her breath, Matteo was silent.

I'm willing to talk. Are you? he finally wrote.

She thought of his eyes and the Coca-Cola brown color of them and she felt very sad all over again. She knew, intellectually, that what happened with Dick was not cheating. That factually, she had been raped, though she despised that word because that meant that she was a victim of something else now. She felt, though, a sense of shame that paralyzed and terrified her. She could barely breathe from the space it occupied in her. She was scared. Not only by the scale of it, but by the revelation that this feeling did not start with the rape, it had been there long before. The rape had merely laid it bare, rendering her unable to mask it with a substitute emotion. If Matteo heard the truth, if he discovered the depth of her defects for himself, then it would really be over. At least now, in the in-between, she had a spark of hope.

Can I have more time? she asked.

If he gave her more time, she decided, she wouldn't try to gild or varnish herself. She wouldn't try to charm her way out of his ire.

Por supuesto, mami.

It took her two more weeks. When she finally got up the courage, this day, a rush of adrenaline hit her so hard that she headed straight to his house. But as she approached, she grew paranoid that he'd had a change of heart and wouldn't let her in, which she knew was irrational. Still, she staked out his house and decided to use the spare key. At the last minute, as the key was in the door, she worried that he might think she was an intruder and wondered if he had a gun. She doubted it, but still wasn't sure. If he shot me, she thought, he might not ever forgive himself. So, she rang the bell and turned the key and bellowed his name all at once.

"Matteo?" she called out.

"Olga?" She could hear him upstairs, scrambling to his feet. He leaned over the banister and smiled, faintly. Her heart stopped for a moment and she felt nervous but . . . happy? "How did you . . ."

"The spare key," she said. "Sorry about the racket . . . I didn't want you to think I was a burglar and shoot me."

He laughed. "I don't have a gun and there hasn't been a burglary on this block since Giuliani was mayor."

"What are you doing up there?"

"I'm in the Christmas room."

It was mid-November, Olga realized, nearly Thanksgiving. "It's almost appropriate."

"Yeah, I've been spending a lot of time up here lately."

"Can I come up?"

"That would be nice," he said bashfully.

They were lying in silence on the floor of the Christmas room, the tree lights twinkling, listening to Nat King Cole. Next to each other, but not touching, when Olga blurted out, "I've been working for the Russian mob. I've been laundering money for them since the TV show, when all the business dried up."

The night that they went through the letters, the night that every secret anyone had ever harbored came out — including how, as they had suspected, Mabel had been paying all of Julio's bills for years now — Olga promised her family that if and when she tried to make things work with Matteo she would do so under the premise of total transparency. In her large cache of secrets, talking about the Russian mob seemed, to her, an ice breaker.

"Wait. What?" Matteo asked. "Olga, did they threaten you? Is that what's been going on?"

Igor could be testy, and she knew she couldn't — shouldn't — keep working with them, but what they were capable of seemed to pale in comparison to what she'd been going through.

"No, but I am trying something new —

with you, my family. Everybody. I am not keeping anyone's secrets anymore. So hear me out and you can decide if you want to give me another chance. So that you'll understand why I vanished like I did."

Olga wanted Matteo to say that he would give her another chance regardless of what she said. But he didn't say that. He just said, "Okay." Which was terrifying, because it implied that what she was going to say mattered. That he could hear it all and tell her to fuck off. But it also meant that he could hear her out, and if he still loved her, she could trust it. Olga wanted to trust it.

So, she told him everything, including stuff she thought she'd forgotten and tried to forget. She told him about *Spice It Up.* She told him how she had been fleecing her clients for years. She told him about her past relationship with Reggie. She told him about her abortion. She told him about her mother's letters, about the Pañuelos Negros and the compound, about her brother's trip to Puerto Rico and their mother rejecting him, her disinterest in Lourdes. She told him about the Selby brothers and how they had been blackmailing Prieto, about the visit from Aunt Karen, about talking to her mother on the phone.

She told him how they had put all their letters in order, how hearing them out loud, in front of other people, in front of each other, had made them feel: like dolls in a rich kid's toy chest — occasionally played with, largely neglected, sometimes abused. How impossible their mother had made it to tell her who they really were and how she had made it impossible because she found their inner selves insignificant. How much that hurt. How much, she and her brother realized, they had internalized this, becoming these people who needed to be seen in order to exist. How, particularly since Abuelita had died, Olga had been full of rage and haunted by this sense of lack so strong, it blinded her to all the love she still had around her; how it had made it very hard to love herself.

Finally, long after all the Christmas records on the stack had played and they had been listening to the turn of the table for longer than either of them noticed, Olga told him about Dick. All of it. And then she told him about the incident in college. And the very bad online date. And the drunk groomsman who trapped her in a stairwell at work that one time.

And she felt the balloon in her chest — the one that had been taking up so much space, pressing everything out of its proper place, pinching lungs so they could not get enough breath, pushing on her heart so that it altered its natural beating rhythm — deflate. Not completely, but nearly. Each story, each sentence she put out into the world allowed her insides to resume their proper place, reclaiming the space as its own. And when she was done, for a moment, she lay there, appreciating the freedom to fully breathe and relearning the beat of her own heart.

Matteo took her hand and after a long minute finally spoke.

"I don't know really what the right thing to say is."

"I don't know that there is one right thing to say," she replied.

"Then, I guess I'm afraid to say the one wrong thing. Except, I guess, to say that it's okay. Not what happened to you, but — fuck, see? So easy to say wrong things. . . . I guess, thank you. For telling me. For . . . trusting me."

Olga let his words wash over her and they felt good. Warm. Yet still not enough. Not obvious enough for her to know she was safe. Not enough to know she was still loved. She was frightened to ask for what she needed now, but felt no other choice.

"And me? Do you still like me? After all of this?"

He rolled towards her now. "What? Girl, are you crazy?" He went to put his arm around her and stopped himself. "Actually. Wait. Is this okay?"

"Coño." She laughed. "Don't be that guy. Don't make me that girl."

"What girl?" he asked, confused.

"The girl who is going to break." She pulled his arm over her. "I'm still me; you just know a lot more now. And you are cool with it," she said, more to herself than him.

"Well," he said, "most of it." Before her heart could fully sink, he quickly began again. "Olga, I want to do this with you. For real. But I told you what I needed, and that was for you to not disappear. I trusted you and you broke that trust, and I know it wasn't intentional. It's your very fucked-up coping mechanism. But I think for this to work, we can't accept that as a way to deal with things. You need a new coping mechanism. And to go to therapy."

"Matteo, no. I don't believe in —"

"— hold up, let me talk for a second. We" — he made a point of saying — "need therapy not because you are broken, or because I'm broken, but because it's a lot to manage. I need to learn to live without . . . all of this stuff, and you need to learn how to not shut me out when you're going through shit. Because that hurts, girl. Both of us. Bad."

She put her face close to his. "I'm really sorry."

"I know you are." And he kissed her softly. "But, there's another thing. Olga, you can't be washing money for these Russian cats. It's all blinis and vodka shots until you end up dead in Little Odessa, and I love you too much to risk that happening. If you need money until you figure out what you want to do next, please let me help you."

Olga laughed a bit. "Matteo, listen, I absolutely will stop, I promise, but I think when you offer to help you're misunderstanding how much money I'm making off this right now."

Matteo sat up and took her hands and took a deep breath.

"Okay. Listen. Now I guess I have to tell you something. It's, uh, not a secret or anything, I just never had a reason to tell you . . . but, I'm, like . . . rich? Not, you know, Selby brothers rich, I'm not there, but, I, uh, I own a lot of properties."

"What?" Olga asked, sitting up now.

"When I left the banking job, and sold the

loft, I had a lot of cash. And when my mom passed, I was so sad and lost and all I had, I felt like, was here — this place. The neighborhood, the borough, the people I'd gotten to know. So, you know the bodega on the corner? Well, the owner of the building wanted to sell, and Sammy — who owns the bodega — was sure if they sold, they'd kick him out and knock the building down for one of those shitty new constructions like you live in. And, well, I just didn't want to lose the spot. I like getting my coffee there, seeing Sammy, seeing the boom-box dude, shooting the shit. So, I offered the owner all cash, and . . ."

"Sylvia's!" Olga exclaimed. A light dawning on her now.

"Yes . . . and, well, frankly, a lot of spots. Lots of old spots. Here, Williamsburg, your 'hood. I mean, that's why I was in Noir that night in the first place. This Irish pub I dig over on the other side of the park . . . a bunch of spots, and they all have apartments upstairs and I just kept everybody's rent the same and, frankly, it's a lot of fucking money. Every month. And I get to keep going to these places I love, and they get to keep their stores and their apartments. Ninety percent of my real estate work is filling up my own apartments, though, honestly, most of my tenants don't leave. And, Olga, it's so much money I frankly don't get these other cats. How much money does one person need? But I guess that's the quintessential American question, right?"

But Olga was too busy beaming at him to engage in a philosophical debate about capitalism. She felt something that she remembered was desire begin to tingle in her.

"Matteo Jones, why didn't you tell me that you were a superhero?"

"Because of the money?" he asked. "I'm happy to —"

"No! Not the money. Are you kidding?" she asked genuinely. "Because you're saving me — all of us — from being washed away. You've put down little anchors, even if it's just a few. Even if we're just little dinghies floating in this big sea. I didn't think I could love you more."

"Oh yeah?" Matteo asked with a smile.

"Or, frankly, find you hotter."

"Oh yeah?"

"Have you ever fucked in the Christmas room?"

"Girl," he said as he crawled closer, "what we're doing is making love."

■ ■ ■ ■

September 23, 2025

■ ■ ■ ■

Sol Libre

Olga had just walked out of the bodega and onto Fourth Avenue when she heard her phone ring. She'd lingered, drinking her coffee and gossiping with Sammy for longer than she intended and was now running late, so when she saw that it was her brother, she hit ignore.

She was genuinely delighted when he had met Marcus, truly happy when they fell in love, and ecstatic when they got engaged, but if she had to talk to him one more time about his fucking wedding plans, she was going to shoot herself. She was happy to put on her old hat and lend a hand, but he was worse than the worst of her brides, or grooms for that matter, fixating all of his attention — and calls — on micromanaging the music selections. He and Marcus had picked a song with "meaning" for everything: the usuals, like walking down the aisle and first dance, but also the ridiculous, such as pairing songs with food courses like one would do with a wine. Each time Prieto would send another request to the DJ, he would call his sister so that she could assure him that yes, that was a good selection and yes, she would stay on top of the DJ. Which she had zero intention of doing because at the end of the day, he'd be having too good a time to remember what song was playing in the background when he was served his braised short ribs.

Milagros had a cold and the pre-K teacher told Mabel she had to keep her home, but since the gallery was usually pretty quiet on weekdays and on Mabel's way to work, Olga offered to watch her so Mabel wouldn't have to miss a day of work.

"If only Julio wasn't a piece of shit," Mabel lamented, "then I wouldn't have to bother you."

It wasn't a bother, and frankly, Olga was happier to babysit than to have Mabel involve Julio too much in Milagros's day-to-day life. They weren't married for more than three years before Mabel realized he was spending money faster than she could make it, but never managed to keep a job for long enough to actually bring anything in. Then Mabel got pregnant, right as the corona-virus pandemic began. Stuck in a house with Julio for nearly a year, she quickly discovered that she didn't have the energy for two babies and, just before Milagros was born, she moved out of the apartment in Bay Shore and back to Fifty-third Street. Christian had, as Olga suspected, missed Manhattan living and, having gotten on his feet, used this opportunity to find a place uptown in one of Matteo's newer buildings. Olga had encouraged him to start investing in other vanishing neighborhoods and he'd found a music store and a Chino-Latino restaurant that he wanted to be sure "we can take our kid to if we want."

He had said that when they were still trying, of course. Before Olga decided that the process — the nightly injections in alternating ass cheeks, the daily "monitoring" visits requiring early morning schleps uptown, the constant false hope — was too exhausting. She felt, she told her therapist, that she had only recently become content with her life and herself and didn't want to become fixated on chasing another imagined love. For Matteo's part, he assured her, he was relieved. Not that he didn't love kids, but he was happy not to have to share her with a baby. To Olga, that felt very honest, and put her mind at ease knowing that she hadn't disappointed him. Slowly, they had been getting rid of furniture, replaced all the old TVs with one flat-screen (Olga liked to watch the news in bed), and had recently sold his collection of *Vibe* magazines to a twenty-four-year-old cryptocurrency miner who was obsessed with golden-era hip-hop. Olga decided that she didn't mind if the thing he still wanted to hoard was her time.

The gallery was in Gowanus, in a corner building of Matteo's that used to house a tire shop but was vacated when the owner died. Olga had been inspired by Matteo's Brooklyn salvation project. She remembered her earliest days in Fort Greene, filled with these fabulous Black and Latino artists, and wondered where they had gone. Then she remembered why she herself had abandoned her art and had the idea to start a nonprofit gallery. The proceeds from each sale split between the artist and a foundation that helped artists of color with emergency expenses. She had gotten the gallery a fair amount of publicity and, on the weekends and at their annual benefit, many of her former clients and other New Brooklyn residents came. Olga enjoyed using her old skills to steer them towards the pricier works. She had named it Comunidad.

As she approached the gallery now, she saw that her brother was once again calling.

"Prieto, I can't with the wedding right now," she started into the phone.

"No, Olga." His voice sounded urgent and a nervous sensation fluttered in her chest. "I got a call this morning . . . I mean, at this point, it's on the news."

"I was running out to help Mabel with Milagros. Is everything okay?"

"She did it."

"Who?" she said. But then she knew. "Fuck." She was fumbling with her key in the lock. She ran over to her computer to check out the news for herself.

"Early this morning a bomb went off in La Fortaleza; it didn't do too much damage, so I think they were trying to keep it quiet but . . . well, fuck, just look."

They had not heard from their mother since just after Maria. They had, after much torment and a commitment to therapy, come to the familial decision to mourn her like the dead, so speaking of her now was like being grabbed by a ghost. Of course, she had lingered in the back of their minds. Her brother had served two more terms before deciding to run for governor of New York, and though he did plenty for the people of Puerto Rico, he never did go back.

They had both, of course, seen the headlines: after Maria, as their mother predicted, the awakening among the people that had begun after PROMESA only became louder, more organized and intense. Estimates on Maria's death toll ranged in the thousands; one team of scientists put the count at 4,645. Outraged and grief-stricken, people stopped looking to the central government and strengthened the organization of their smaller municipalities. Just as they had been organized in the beginning, when the land was Borikén.

Then, two funny things happened.

The first seemed innocuous enough, though not to Olga. Two years after Maria, in the summer of 2019, a mysterious hack unearthed a trove of private messages between the governor and his cabinet. Journalists had been steadily unraveling the web of corruption that had lined these politicians' pockets — both before and after Maria — but these texts were different. They revealed the disdain, disregard, and disrespect that the governor, and by turn his government, had for the people. They mocked their own citizens while patting each other on their backs and laughing en route to the bank with their FEMA money. People demanded Ricky's resignation. In his obstinance, he ignored their calls until the people — millions of people — flooded the streets, day after day. He was eventually forced from office, and though he was merely one piece of a vastly corrupt puzzle, his ouster signaled a shift. The people saw and remembered their power.

Olga watched the protests in Puerto Rico that summer, her heart swollen with pride. On the news, on the covers of all the papers, on social media, Olga saw them, Los Pañuelos Negros, mixed among the people, getting tear-gassed, getting goaded by the police. She knew her brother had seen it, too. After their mother met with Mercedes, the Pañuelos, their demands for Puerto Rico, and their vision of liberation did receive periodic press coverage. Unlike her predecessors, however, their mother insisted on complete anonymity. Still, rumors swirled. The Pañuelos and their mark had begun to generate a folklore of its own. That they had been behind the hack; that they had amassed hundreds of thousands of followers around the island. That they were backed by wealthy Boricuas from the diaspora.

The second thing that occurred happened so quietly, when Olga saw it in passing, she almost missed it. For more than two years much of the island sat in darkness as PREPA and the government failed to rebuild the power grid and contracts were issued to inept consultants and shell companies owned by the U.S. president and other administration officials. Residents and municipalities, tired of waiting for PREPA to come and charge them extortionary amounts of money for an unreliable utility, slowly began to pool their money for their own solar panels. Building, in effect, their own solar grids. Two years after Maria, the island was ravaged by earthquakes and within seconds, the entire island was again in darkness. The people, realizing that their infrastructure was still as fragile as their citizenship, were exhausted of being held hostage to this ineptitude. The public recognized what Olga's mother had seen several years before and began, en masse, to organize themselves towards solar. The climate was ripe: Reggie Reyes had successfully opened a mid-sized solar production facility, which in turn led Dick to make a push with Eikenborn Green Solutions. Solar suddenly became accessible. PREPA, seeing their client base take matters into their own hands, began to panic and, with the cooperation of the Puerto Rican legislature and private industry, passed a Solar Tax, ensuring they made money even on power that nature provided. A municipality, aided by a mainland-born lawyer of Puerto Rican descent, filed a lawsuit protesting the tax, which slowly wound its way to the Supreme Court. In the ensuing years Sol Libre became a rallying cry as the issue of taxing the utilization of a resource God had provided to everyone seemed to touch a raw nerve. Songs — trap, bomba, salsa — were written about Sol Libre. Logos were created. Chants were uttered. Adding to the fury was that the Puertopians had installed their solar grids years before. They had been living with power. They would be exempt from the tax.

An injunction was placed on the tax while the Supreme Court decided if and when to take up the case and, motivated by a window of opportunity and a gesture of political defiance, solar energy was adopted by large swaths of the island. Families on the mainland were pooling together money for their relatives — their houses, their buildings, their towns — to obtain solar panels. Puertorriqueños across the diaspora were crowdsourcing to fund solar energy for the villages and cities they had descended from. Quite recently, the *Washington Post* had reported that the campaigns had gotten nearly 50 percent of the island's households operating completely on solar. Olga had texted the story to Prieto, but they never discussed it.

Online, Olga could not believe her eyes. The streets were flooded in a sea of black, the masses flowing through the streets like a slick of oil, the only color emanating from their flags. They carried the black banderas of the austerity protest, yes, but also the flag of Puerto Rico before 1898. And, here and there, the flag Olga now knew to be the mark of the Pañuelos. Her face, but older.

"Are you there?" Prieto asked.

"Yes."

"Did you get the news alert?"

"If I'm on the phone with you, how could I see the alert?"

"Why do you have to be such a fucking smart-ass? Oye . . . they bombed the airport."

She gasped and hit refresh on her browser. And she saw it now. Chaos.

"Luis Muñoz Marín . . . ," she said.

"The traitor." Parroting the way their parents would talk about the Yanqui lapdog.

"Oh my God," Olga gasped. "So many people . . ."

"Yeah . . . ," Prieto said.

But then Mabel was at the door, struggling with the stroller, and Milagros was fussing and Olga needed to go.

"I've gotta help Mabel. I'll call you later."

"Wait, Olga. Do we just let her do this?"

There was a pause and she had to let go of the phone. In truth, she didn't know.

For the rest of the day, bombs and unrest in Puerto Rico took over her newsfeed. In the streets of San Juan, the people had taken over government buildings, removing the U.S. flags from any and every flagpole they could reach, while the Pañuelos systemically bombed the airports, military outposts, and ports, cutting the island off, at least for a moment. Pigs' heads were mounted on stakes outside the Fortaleza, police cars set on fire. This, Olga could tell, was it. This was what revolution looked like. What she'd sacrificed so many parts of herself for.

She'd been hearing about it her whole life and now, finally, she was seeing it with her own eyes. Her mother had told her that when this day came, Olga would be proud. This was true, but the pride that welled was not related to her mother. This, she could see, was bigger than one woman. Her mother had anticipated the cause and the effect, but it was not her mother who had ushered in this metamorphosis, this force. No, this was a sea change, an awakening to over a century of abused power, the last drop of water in the glass. This would continue tomorrow, and the day after tomorrow, and the day after that, regardless of what or where her mother was. This was by, of, and for the people.

After Mabel picked up Milagros, Olga walked from the gallery over to the Fulton Mall. She stopped at the ATM, picked up a nice bottle of wine, and then made her way into one of the last gold fronts/collectible sneaker/unlocked cell phone spots that still existed in Brooklyn. She liked bringing Matteo little gifts, so she bought him a money clip, paid cash for a phone, and stopped to sit at a café table at one of the new ped malls they had put up. She looked up Bonilla's number on her own phone and dialed it on the new one.

"Hello?" she said. "Yes, I'd like to report an anonymous tip. . . . It's regarding the bombings of the airports in Puerto Rico. . . . Yes, I can hold. . . ."

But as she waited, a voice whispered in her head. It took Olga a second to recognize it as her own.

What do you think happens next? She goes quietly? Nah. It'll be guns blazing and she'll be a hero and for the rest of your life you'll have to see her fucking face on murals and T-shirts and have people talk about what a martyr this puta was, and do you really need that shit?

No, she decided. She did not.

She hung up, dropped the new phone into the nearest gutter, and got on the R train so she wouldn't be late for dinner. It was a glorious fall day. Matteo was going to grill.

ACKNOWLEDGMENTS

Thanks begin with my two most devoted readers: Mayra Castillo, my mother-sister-friend, and Yelena Gitlin Nesbit, whom I met in a Brooklyn public library when we were eleven years old and to whom I first confessed, while picking through the racks of Neiman Marcus Last Call, that I would, at forty, like to try writing. She told me that this was what I was meant to do.

My prayers were answered for the perfect team: Mollie Glick, who had a vision for my writing career before one existed, and Megan Lynch, whose love and care for this book — and for big, weird novels — moved me so. Thank you for being such champions of both Olga and me. Thanks to Dana Spector, my savvy lodestar, and to André Des Rochers, who reminded me to always bet on me. And to the passionate Flatiron team that so lovingly cared for this book: Kukuwa Ashun, Malati Chavali, Nancy Trypuc,

Katherine Turro, Marlena Bittner, Claire McLaughlin, Keith Hayes, Erin Gordon, Nadxieli Nieto, Dominique Jenkins, and Lauren Peters-Collaer.

I am in creative debt to the art of Alynda Segarra and the critical journalism of Naomi Klein. This novel crystallized during a morning Q train commute as I read *The Battle for Paradise* while listening to Hurray for the Riff Raff's *Navigator.* "Rican Beach" came on, and suddenly I was near tears and it all clicked and Olga was born.

To the people of Borikén, whose resilience is the root of this novel, thank you. Thank you to Centro, the Center for Puerto Rican Studies at Hunter College, for being an invaluable resource not only for this book, but for the entire diaspora. And to Iris Morales, whose film, *¡Pa'lante, Siempre Pa'Lante!,* and book *Through the Eyes of Rebel Women* were invaluable resources.

This is in no small part a love letter to Brooklyn, my hometown, and its people. Shout-out to my teachers at P.S. 48, P.S. 105, I.S. 227, and the late Gail Katz and Saul Bruckner. To John Faciano, Georgia Scurletis, Sheila Hanley, Scott Martin, and the inspiring teachers at Edward R. Murrow High School: You made me a better reader, writer, and thinker. And my Murrow crew, who've always had my back: Alex Rosado, Tascha Van Auken, Jace Van Auken, and the entire Joyce family, especially Rebecca and Josh.

To my Brooklyn fam: the incomparable and beloved Marcy Blum, Aja Baxter, "Cousin Danny" Lubrano, Indira Goris, Destin Coleman, Yohance Bowden, Brandon and Iman Nelson, De'Ara Balenger, Pao Ramos, Walt Brown, Nya Parker Brown. And to Ian Niles, Kendra Ellis, and my heart, soul, third-line, and no-nonsense hype woman, Sharon Ingram: Be you in D.C., L.A., or anywhere in this world, your time in Brooklyn touched my life, and I love you.

I started this book in Fort Greene Park but finished it in Iowa City. Thanks to Lan Samantha Chang, the faculty at the Writers' Workshop, and the University of Iowa for the life-changing financial support that allowed me the time and space to complete this novel. Thank you to Disquiet International, *Ninth Letter,* and *Joyland* magazine for supporting my writing.

Eternal gratitude to the 2019 IWW Novel Workshop: Jeff Boyd, Belinda Tang, Ife-Oluwa Nihinlola, Aaron Huang, Elliot Duncan, Elaine Ray, David McDevitt, Marilyn Manalokas, and Jing "JJ" Jian. And to

Alonzo Vereen and Abigail Carney, who talked me off many a revision ledge.

Alfonso Gomez-Rejon, the best film teacher a girl could ask for: Our work together brought so much depth and clarity to this project. Thank you for loving Olga so much.

The Bread Loaf Writers' Conference is a special place from which emerged my invaluable writing circle: Cleyvis Natera and T. J. Wells. On the mountain I found magic: Lizz Huerta and Mai Schwartz. Amazing readers, writers, and even better friends.

Many strong women have supported this midlife journey: Sofija Stefanovic, a writer of unbelievable generosity; Karen Rinaldi, an inspiration; Jennifer J. Raab and my colleagues at Hunter College, who encouraged this pivot; Melissa Martínez-Raga, whose perspective as a writer and an island-born Boricua made this book infinitely better; Jackie Furst, who put Humpty Dumpty back together again; and my magnificent aunt Linda (and my uncle Frank), who fueled my love of books and writers and writing — I love you.

Christina H. Paxson, Celeste Perri, Caryn Ganz, Margo Gallagher, Elyse Fox, Pam Brier, Heather Ortiz, Steven Colon, Carmen Vargas, Suyin So, Sarita Gonzalez,

Kirsten Johnson, Michaela RedCherries, Marisa Tirado, Ruben Reyes, Natalee Dawson, Indya Finch, Maggie Mitchell, Vix Gutierrez, Hannah Friedland, Emily Upton-Davis, Jordan Helman, Tony Tompson, Camille DePasquale, Roxanne Fequire, Payton Turner, Abby Adesanya, Alex Norcia, Quinn Murphy, and my godbabies, Rocco Van Auken and Vivi Baxter, who've all lent support and inspiration in ways big and small.

My grandparents, Alberto, Assunta, and Raquel, and all my ancestors, for holding me up.

And thanks, above all, to God.

Pop. We did it.

ABOUT THE AUTHOR

Xochitl Gonzalez received her M.F.A. from the Iowa Writers' Workshop, where she was an Iowa Arts Fellow. Prior to writing, Xochitl wore many hats, including entrepreneur, wedding planner, fundraiser, and tarot card reader. She is a proud alumna of the New York City Public Schools system and holds a B.A. in art history and visual art from Brown University. She lives in her hometown of Brooklyn with her dog, Hectah Lavoe.

The employees of Thorndike Press hope you have enjoyed this Large Print book. All our Thorndike, Wheeler, and Kennebec Large Print titles are designed for easy reading, and all our books are made to last. Other Thorndike Press Large Print books are available at your library, through selected bookstores, or directly from us.

For information about titles, please call:
(800) 223-1244

or visit our website at:
gale.com/thorndike

To share your comments, please write:
Publisher
Thorndike Press
10 Water St., Suite 310
Waterville, ME 04901